Rachel
LeMoyne

Other Forge Books by Eileen Charbonneau

Waltzing in Ragtime
The Randolph Legacy

Eileen Charbonneau

Rachel Le Moyne

A Tom Doherty Associates Book
New York

RACHEL LeMOYNE

This book is printed on acid-free paper.

A Forge Book
Published by Tom Doherty Associates, Inc.
175 Fifth Avenue
New York, NY 10010

Forge® is a registered trademark of Tom Doherty Associates, Inc.

Library of Congress Cataloging-in-Publication Data

Charbonneau, Eileen.
    Rachel LeMoyne / Eileen Charbonneau.—1st ed.
        p.   cm.
    "A Tom Doherty Associates book."
    ISBN 0-312-86448-5
    1. Choctaw Indians—Fiction.   I. Title.
PS3553.H318R33   1998
813'.54—dc21   98-5556
                                                 CIP

        2 3 3 3 3

First Edition: June 1998

Printed in the United States of America

0 9 8 7 6 5 4 3 2 1

For Maria Falasca—
who helped me to give birth and to sing out
and who got herself to Oregon

acknowledgments

Many thanks to Natalia Aponte and all the good folks at Forge, for presenting me with this opportunity and seeing it through to the end.

I'm grateful to Diane Crawford, Turtle Woman, my first reader and little big sister, who keeps me on track always, and Charlie Rinehimer, who first got me thinking, like Rachel, in the rhythm of the waves.

Father Paul Healy was invaluable in sharing his passion for the Irish people, his knowledge of *An Gorta Mor,* and providing research books not available in this country. Does that make you a smuggler on top of all your other sins, Father? I think some of your humor slipped into Dare, too.

Thanks to Marv Ross, for writing the rousing musical *Voices from the Oregon Trail,* companion when my own traveling was hard to bear. And thanks to the troop that performed it: Lex Browning, Mick Doherty, Ron Nagy, Gayle Neumann, Phil Neumann, Skip Parente, Rindy Ross, Cal Scott, Dan Stueber, Don Alder, Bryson Liberty, Mary Marsh, and Scott Parker.

Thanks once again to fellow Blue Ridge Writers Jim Green, Jean Gold, Florence Kay, Barbara Ward Lazarsky, Robin O'Brien, Dolores Oiler, Margie Rhoadhouse, Patricia Rodgers, Susan Shackelford, Laurie Maxwell Tenney, and Alice Thuermer. I treasure our camaraderie and friendship, even now, across the miles. And thanks to my new writing friends, the Hudson Valley RWA women, who provided much help and encouragement: Terri Hall, Kathy Attalla, Renee Simons, Karen Drogin, Claire Ruane, Bette LaGow, Blair Lavey, Liz Matis, Jeannie Miraglia, Janet Walters, Paula Keller, Elaine Lindenblatt, Grace Bizzarro, Georgia Carey, Nancy Hajeski, Karen Larsen, Helen Grishman, Jennifer Probst, Mildred Lubke, Sunny Hogg.

I also received great bolstering from my fellow Loop Women: Deborah Barnhart, Kathy Caskie, Cindy Haack, Mary Jo Putney, and my dear Celtic sister Susan King. All had their own projects going, but had time to listen to my latest dilemma or disaster and offer words of love and encouragement, and, from Susan: plotting!

Thanks as always to Scott Meyer and his wonderful family and staff at Merritt Books.

Finally, thanks to Juilene Osborne McKnight, anam cara and Native American Celt, who taught me by way of her twin passions that a novel of contrasting cultures would turn out to be one of astonishing similarities because *mitakuye oyasin*—we are all related.

Nanih Waiya, Mississippi

The Choctau Nation

October, 1832

prologue

Nanih Waiya, Mississippi
October, 1832

Rachel's mother wrapped tiny Sleeps Sound close against her heart. She took Rachel's hand and walked, tall and beautiful, to the white elm tree nearest their cabin door. Rachel's parents had planted the elm when Atoka was born. It was now finely made, like her brother Atoka, lifting its branches like a fountain from the ground, its leaves reaching for the warm October sky. Atoka's afterbirth had been its first nourishment, as Rachel's was for the oak planted five years later.

Rachel's tree was in the shadow of her grandmother's white oak, and was the oak's child. The counselor oak told the Choctaw the place to build their homes. Its roots went deep in rich soil. Its wood was both strong and beautiful. Someday Rachel's small tree would be wise. She would advise the time to plant corn—when her new pink and silver leaves are the size of the mouse's ear. But who would hear the wisdom?

Another of the grandmother tree's children now grew from Sleeps Sound's birth gift. Rachel worried about her new sister's seedling. Once they set off on their journey, the Americans would take over the lands and cabins of the Choctaw. Rachel knew enough of Americans to be afraid for Sleeps Sound's tree. She wanted to cry for it, and to cry for her sister, who would not remember the ancestral home of the people except in her deep dreaming.

Rachel was named LeMoyne from her father's French ancestor, Rachel by way of the missionary teachers who baptized her a Christian. But she'd also earned her first Choctaw name, *Yalabusha*—Tadpole—for her swimming prowess. Some had begun to call her Gathers Stories, too, for the way she listened to the old ones. She would tell her sister of this day, of their mother leading the women in this new ceremony, born of their circumstances. She must heed every detail, every sound and smell. What was the bird called, who flew down the branches of Atoka's elm? A shy, tufted titmouse, offering a lament. The song stopped suddenly. Then all was silent, even the season-change cold wind.

Her mother stroked the leaves of Atoka's elm against her face. Jagged dancing leaf, spiraling out, in an off-center swagger, like her brother's stride after slipping off his horse. The leaf was rough to her mother's touch, and still dark-blue green. Green, like Atoka in his ten summers of life. Her mother moved on to the oaks. She took their sunset-colored leaves between her hands, to her cheek—both the bright, touched-by-sun sides, and the pale underbellies. She bent a branch of the grandmother tree down to Rachel.

Rachel took a red leaf between her fingers. Thank you for the shade, and the welcome into your limbs, and the seed pockets that Atoka and I made into whirl toys and nose ornaments. Rachel let the thoughts flow through her fingertips to the oak's understanding. In return she felt the tree's strength, and sorrow at parting. Felt its blood singing another lament.

Her mother took her hand, led on. The women followed Elizabeth LeMoyne, honoring their trees in farewell, proceeding to the next homestead, and the next, stroking the leaves. Some wept silently. None of the children, who ranged in age from eleven years to Turtle Woman's six-day child, were afraid of their mothers' wet cheeks, Rachel thought.

Finally, down the road from Makes Sweet Cider's cabin, the federal soldiers waited, their blue uniforms striking against the gray sky. This journey would not become the horror that last year's group faced, their leader, Captain Armstrong, promised. Peter LeMoyne's clear voice translated the captain's English into Choctaw. Atoka sat tall on his mount Likes Water, beside their father on Two Hearts. Her brother's eyes were angry and cold until they found hers. They lit with a gruff tenderness then—for her, their mother, the baby. We honor you, they said. Carry the seeds in your pouches. We will bring you to the new land. We will live again.

Surely the vicious snowstorms and cold of last year were unusual, unpredictable. This year's band was departing earlier. The steamships would be waiting at Natchez to carry them up the Mississippi and its tributaries. From Little Rock they would walk to their new land. Last year hundreds had starved when heavy rains washed out roads and trails, slowing them to fifteen miles a day. Not this year, Captain Armstrong proclaimed. This year President Jackson had put the army in charge.

Worry strained Rachel's father's clear, beautiful voice. He was a Mixed Blood, trusted like the ones who'd gone to Washington. Peter LeMoyne had not gone, had not signed his name to the agreement, but looked after his family and all the ones left behind. He'd met Andrew Jackson once, though, on Choctaw land. He had seen the American leader lose control of his temper. Old Hickory disliked asking for anything, her father had said. He preferred to threaten. There were only two choices, Andrew Jackson said, for the people standing in the way of progress: emigration or extinction. And now this man who had turned on his wartime allies, the Creek, was President of the United States. It was time to think about the new country, even Peter LeMoyne advised.

Still, when the men returned from Washington and told him of the agreement, he had walked out to their woodpile alone.

Rachel followed. It was the only time she had seen her father weep. Now his eyes scanned small wagons loaded with provisions for six thousand. How many blankets, how much food, would it be enough? Rachel almost heard his thoughts.

The other leaders and their horses were dressed in their finery, gifts of the Americans. As if this were festival time, or a celebration, not an exile. Peter LeMoyne wore his red wedding-day shirt and buckskin trousers. No decorations, only that symbol of his love for their mother. And his worry.

Rachel wanted to climb on Two Hearts with him, and mold his face free of troubles. She wanted to be a peacemaker, trusted speaker among the missionaries and the soldiers, like him, there in the new land. And she wanted to do the dances and ceremonies, like her mother.

At the school, the missionaries said she could not do both, that she must choose. They had shown Rachel a globe of the world, and the place from where the English language had come. It was a small place, surrounded by blue. An island. But those who spoke the language of these islanders had power over all the world, and over the greatest parts of its wisdom and knowledge. The missionaries said the only way for the Choctaw people to become happy and respected was through this people's language, its ways, its great God who said that men should do women's work in the fields and women stay inside a house the day long. When she'd asked her father about these things, he'd smiled and said, "Know them, Tadpole, but swim as you're guided by your own heart."

He would teach her how to find the things that made the Choctaw kin to the white people who also dwelled in her blood—not only her Frenchman grandfather, the one who drew wonderful likenesses of the Old Ones, but the English speakers too, the Americans. The Americans did not visit or trap only. They did not become Choctaw, as her French ancestor had. They wanted to live, not beside them but instead of them. They called Choctaw land the Southern Frontier and came with their black men slaves. They wished to work the land for cotton instead of the Three Sisters—corn and beans and squash. And for tobacco.

Cotton was for clothing, tobacco for ceremonies. What would they eat, these new, foolish people, Rachel wondered, without the Three Sisters?

Rachel turned toward the horse soldiers. Some had eyes that reflected the sky, like Atoka's gift from their Frenchman grandfather. Nothing else about the soldiers was like her brother. They were not a dark and shining people, but whey-faced light and hairy. One, with yellow hair that sprouted all the way to his chin, pointed rudely at her mother. Why? Was he laughing at her ceremony, her grief? His eyes were greedy. Rachel didn't understand what he wanted, but she knew it was something bad. The soldier beside him pushed his shoulder. Rachel knew English almost as well as Choctaw, she was her father's "quick study." But these soldiers spoke the language in a different accent. They were from another English place, far from Mississippi, perhaps. A hard place, she decided, for they ground their R's like corn through a mill. Rachel could not understand all their words.

Suddenly, from out of the small grove of pine by Makes Sweet Cider's cabin, an old man stumbled. His clothes were ragged, his eyes hollow with grief. He spread his hands wide as he chanted.

My voice is weak.
It is not the shout of a warrior
but the wail of an infant.
I have lost it in mourning
over the misfortunes of my people.
These are their graves,
and in those aged pines
you hear the ghosts of the departed.
Their ashes are here,
and we have been left to protect them.
Shall we give you their bones
for the wolves?

Chief Cobb. Rachel barely recognized him. Atoka slipped down from his saddle and approached their elder. Her father spoke to the soldiers in English. Yellow Hair did not listen. He shouted at her brother, barking orders in too-fast English. Atoka ignored his threats and calmly took the old man's arm, leading him into the woods where three women rushed toward their kin.

They were in the soldier's path. His horse bore down on Chief Cobb, the women, and her brother, at a gallop.

Rachel hissed "stay" followed by a sharp whistle. The horse stopped so abruptly the whey-faced officer almost catapulted over his saddle. He regained his seat, but not his lost face . . . how do the white people say it? His dignity.

Atoka put Chief Cobb on the arm of his eldest daughter. The women guided him back into the woods.

Peter LeMoyne watched, the reins of Atoka's mount in his hands. The pride in his children had banished even the worry from his eyes, Rachel thought. She basked in the pride, smiling. Then she took her mother's hand for the long journey ahead.

Oklahoma

Harvest, 1847

one

Oklahoma Territory
Harvest, 1847

"This great god, is he a Choctaw god, Miss Rachel?"

Rachel sighed. She was much better teaching arithmetic or sewing than religion, a point Miss Wakefield made constantly. But neither Miss Wakefield nor her reverend brother were at school today, so she would have to make do.

"Well, we—that is, our Choctaw Old Ones—have no great god, Thomas. So perhaps we can add the Christian god to our spirits of the forest, water, and sky."

That wasn't right. The missionaries did not graft one religion to another. Even when there was opportunity, like now, to do so. What did Reverend Wakefield have her commit to memory on the subject? "A diluted Gospel or any emulsion of Gospel mixture with other cults will be vapid and powerless." But the children were nodding, smiling. And she so loved to see them smile.

"And this great god, he lives in this other home, this heaven, the place from where Miss Wakefield says none will ever drive us?" Thomas, again. Bright Thomas, who still wore his hair braided, whose parents were, like most of Rachel's people, unconverted.

"Yes. The great Christian god lives in heaven."

"And this is a good place?"

"Oh very good, full of plenty and happiness."

Thomas made a face. "Is the white man there?"

"Yes."

"Huh." He folded his arms. "It is not for me, then. If it is as you say, the white man would soon come along, and, if he saw I had a good place, he would want it for himself."

The children nodded, acknowledging the sense of Thomas's theology. Rachel winced. Where were the right words? The ones Miss Wakefield said were Rachel's duty to the mission—to teach, not stand by callously while more and more of her people fell unbaptized through the gate of death and into hell with each passing year?

A little girl touched her shoulder. "There. Thomas has had his say. We have only our spelling words left, Miss Rachel. May we walk to the creek to recite them?"

They'd put Katy McCombas up to the request because of her perfect command of English and those large, dark eyes. Rachel tried to hide her smile. Miss Wakefield wouldn't approve of taking the class outside either. But the missionaries were guests at the council meeting. And Rachel LeMoyne was a translator's daughter. She knew how the council liked to deliberate, sometimes into the night. "You have all been diligent scholars," she agreed. "And the day is a very fine one for a walk. Carrying our slates and Webster spelling books, of course."

The creek bank was high, reminding Rachel of its level when she and Atoka had first seen it, on that cold spring day fifteen years before. They'd worn the ashes and dress of mourning then. Rachel remembered the icy water as Miss Wakefield scrubbed off the ashes. She remembered her brother's angry protests from downstream, where large-boned Reverend Wakefield did the same for him. Atoka's insults were all in ringing, indignant Choctaw. She'd endured her scrubbing in stunned silence. The feathers she'd carefully woven into her bark skirt rushed downstream. The missionaries sighed. "The wilder the woman, the better the bead and fancy work she makes," they'd complimented her mother, who was now dead beside Sleeps Sound and their father. Where? She couldn't remember the name of the place along the trail, just that it had red, muddy ground. The graves were dug by people weakened by the sickness. Not deep enough. She was still haunted by dreams of wild dogs eating the flesh of her parents and sister. Better the bone pickers of the Choctaw old religion had used their long fingernails to make her family part of the land again. Better the bone pickers, who the missionaries denounced, than the dogs. Sometimes the hungry dogs came for her in her dreams. Why had she and Atoka survived that terrible time, Rachel wondered, even now.

"Might we take our shoes off, Miss Rachel?"

Rachel raised her head, put herself in the world again, where she was responsible for these little ones. "No, children. Stay firm on the banks, and avoid the temptation to slip toes into the water." No resistance, even from the boys. Was she becoming as stern as Miss Wakefield? Davis, the youngest of her twelve students, pulled on her skirt. "You would save me, if'n I fell in too deep. Mama says your name was once *Yalabusha,* Tadpole!"

Rachel touched the spiraling crown of the boy's hair. "That was long ago, before I wore many petticoats."

"You didn't forget. Uncle says we might come to the missionary school because you didn't forget, and still know who you are. That you allow us to speak of singing water spirits and that you still know our crops are gifts of the Three Sisters."

"Who were all created by . . . ?" Rachel asked, nervously looking over her shoulder.

"The new god, Creator."

"Not new. Always here, remember? 'I am who am.' "

Katy giggled. "Yes, the Christian god, who would fail his English grammar!"

Rachel shook her head, but thought Katy's joke so quick-witted that perhaps even the Christian god was laughing.

"My uncle speaks up for you at council," Katy said more seriously, "because he says Rachel LeMoyne does not forget the Old Ones, and tells Choctaw children good stories of this new god I Am, remember the one where he makes himself a bush that burns without ash?"

"*Ma!*" several children answered, as their elders did at council, with the hearty Choctaw affirmation. Rachel wondered how they'd gone so far afield again.

"Your uncle honors me," she said quietly.

Davis's older brother stepped forward. "We all honor you, teacher, and thank you for this good time under the sky."

Rachel smiled. "Under the sky and singing out your spelling words, if you please."

But they had barely distributed the books before Rachel caught sight of her brother on his painted horse, High Head. They roared over the banks, splashing onto all of her squealing, delighted scholars. Atoka slid to the ground with the ease of the finest Choctaw lighthorseman. But he fit in among the company of the native police force about as well as she taught Christianity.

He grinned in that broad way he used to when they were very young, and their parents still alive. What was the occasion? Perhaps Helen Grant had accepted his marriage proposal? "School's out, by order of the council," he declared.

"The meeting is ended already?" Rachel asked.

"Yes. They have agreed on how much of the corn surplus to send across the Atlantic. And the relief money collected? More than seven hundred dollars."

"Atoka! How wonderful!"

"Tonight, the peace chiefs have declared a feast and dance to celebrate."

Rachel fought the urge to squeal with as much abandonment as her students. But she was likely already in trouble for leaving the academy's confines, if the Reverend and his sister were back home, and knew. The children gathered around her handsome brother in a joyous cacophony until he held up his hands. "No more questions. Go home while I tell my sister how she herself is the cause of the celebration."

The scholars looked to Rachel for her permission. Atoka crossed his arms, behind them. "Ruled by women," he muttered. Rachel sighed. "Class is dismissed. My disruptive brother will help me put our poor creekside schoolroom to right."

Atoka watched the children disappear over the banks. "You are doing well by them," he said quietly.

"Why, thank you, Atoka."

"One or two of your scholars could be your own children by now. With boys to teach the hunt, my life would have more purpose. And you would be warm at night, and enjoy their father's company, and not frown so much."

Tricked with a compliment into an old argument between them, Rachel realized. She tried to relieve her face of its displeasure, but spoke firmly. "Your life's purpose is your pursuit, not mine, brother."

"Have the missionaries instructed you to forget our common blood?"

"No." She knew where this was going, but did not have the power to stop it.

"Have they made our men ugly in your eyes, then?"

"Atoka!"

"So you have an obligation to me. This is how I see it."

"You are five years my elder. And have not married, helping to repopulate another woman's clan," she challenged.

"Not from lack of courting."

Success with his latest woman was not the cause of the pride she'd seen in face, then, Rachel realized. "Oh, Atoka. Has Helen Grant's family refused your suit?"

"Yes."

"I am very sorry."

He shrugged. "Missionaries," he complained.

"Now what have they done?"

"Made many of the people value working all the time. Getting things, always things. Not to make us all rich, but to horde like misers with no kin obligations. Helen Grant's father ignored my presents! He counted my horses, looked at their teeth. And the woman I sought to make my wife? She counted the too many steps from my house to the spring. They found me wanting. He called me poor, this man who has no time to talk, to play in ball games. He only attends missionary ceremonies, not our own! I wonder if Helen Grant only counts things. I wonder if she dreams? Am I better off alone, if she does not dream, little sister?"

"Perhaps she is not for you," Rachel agreed softly, in traditional, circumspect language, her heart aching for her brother's disappointment and wounded pride.

He smiled ruefully. "She is the fourth to refuse me. My flute playing will be very fine when I'm done with courting and finally catch a wife. But perhaps by then my ancient bride will be deaf to the music?"

Rachel shook her head at her brother's ability to heal himself with his humor. She wondered again why Atoka's courting choices had been town women of progressive families, not traditionalists like himself. All were too tame a match for his wildness, she thought. Why did he set his sights on them? He was a woman's man, not meant to be alone, like her.

Atoka's eyes brightened as the creek hollow rang with the distant sound of the children's happy laughter.

"Their shoes will be off, laces tied together and over their shoulders before any reaches home."

"I know," Rachel agreed, pushing him toward the spellers piled on the flat rock's surface.

"And I am a man of five and twenty years, not your fetch-and-carry boy, little sister," he intoned, eyeing them.

Rachel cocked her head. "You disrupted my lesson. There are consequences."

"Spoken like a Christian woman."

"I am a Christian woman, Atoka."

"And an eagle clan woman besides. A diminished clan, in need of new blood. But you give us no children, sister."

"I teach all the children."

"Yes, and tell us of the wide world, and now wish us to feed these people whose crops have failed, these Irish. You make me dizzy with your purpose! Surely you can let one good man make you a wife, too? The clan and our nation are proud of your blood, and our mother's before you. How else do you have this high privilege of a feast in your honor?"

"The feast is not in my honor! You should not have put it that way. The children think too much of me as it is. I only read the accounts to the council, of the need across the Atlantic. Our feast is called to celebrate last year's harvest. And the bounty it provides to help the great hunger in Ireland."

"And the one called to deliver it."

"The one—?"

"There. Rendered speechless at last. My magpie of a sister. You are that one, our new peace chief. The only one both the Wakefields and the council trust with the corn shipment."

"They wish to send me to Ireland?"

"They wish to send a representative of the nation. You were the only one all factions could agree on—the Wakefields, because they think you are at their bidding; the Choctaw, because we know you are not."

Rachel felt a deep need to sit. Her brother took her arm, lowered her to the flat surface of the rock. "Tadpole Who Gathers Stories," he summoned her by her childhood names, "this calling, it did not surprise me as it does you."

"Why?" she whispered.

"Because I have dreamed of a ship with great white wings and a fire in its hold, sending you across the water. To this place, this Ireland of terrible suffering, of skeletons. You fed the geese our corn in my dream. And one filled your belly in return, and protected you within folded, broken wings. This dream kept me quiet, when they said your name, though I fear for you on this journey, so far from me."

Rachel touched the blue glass bead he'd woven into one of his hair plaits.

"You will go?" he whispered, with a tinge of the same abandonment he'd hidden so well when their sister and parents left them with only each other for warmth on their desperate journey to Oklahoma Territory.

"If you have dreamed it," she said softly, "then I will go. Your dreams are sacred things, brother."

He growled softly. But she sensed pride and contentment with her decision living beside his worry. "The lighthorsemen will travel with you to the port of New Orleans. I can go no farther. Only you, with the missionaries. To watch over them, to watch over the corn, to make sure all is done in the right way. This leaving grieves me." He reached for his skinning knife and slashed his beaded braid in one deft stroke. He hadn't cut his hair since that day in the cold creek when the missionaries robbed him of it and his mourning. Now he placed the braid and its gleaming indigo glass in her hand. "Come home. Do not become one of those skeletons," he urged.

"You are our own, our very own dusky angel, Rachel!" Miss Sarah Wakefield said again. "And your kind heart our inspiration! The home office is so pleased. This Atlantic voyage, this new mission, is exactly what my brother needs to regain his health and to secure his position as a great shepherd of heathen souls!"

Rachel did not feel any part angel, of any color. She only wanted to help feed the starving she'd read about, to help the ones who reminded her of her own people. She didn't want to leave the Choctaw. She didn't seek to spread a religion whose precepts she still needed guidance on herself. But that was what Sarah Wakefield and her sickly brother talked about most. At least he'd already gone below to rest in his berth, so Rachel didn't have to listen to them both as she searched the dockside.

Rachel only wanted to ease distress, not bound over the Atlantic to the island beside that one where all the English started. That small place that could swallow up nations, why wasn't it feeding its own sister island, she wondered. Why did the Irish need the Choctaw? Why was she standing beside this stern, black-clad woman who towered a head over her own height and was as sure of her station in life as Rachel was conflicted?

Atoka had dreamed her where she was now, aboard an American steam and sail ship about to head into the Gulf of Mexico and across the great Atlantic. She should be content, not full of doubt.

Rachel breathed in the sea air. Was that the salt of the Gulf that cut though the tar and sweat of the sailors? It was tart and fresh. She liked the scent. Rachel searched the dock again for the last sight of her brother. He'd scowled and walked off from Miss Wakefield's offer of money for the work he and his lighthorsemen comrades accomplished. Where did they go? Rachel only recognized three of the city Choctaw, ones like those she'd recognized on the streets of New Orleans, the ones who had shocked her, dressed in filthy blankets, trading what little they had, even their bodies, to remain drunk all day. Miss Wakefield had pulled her away from the beggars, reminding her that she could have easily become one of them, and her brother and his friends yet might, if she did not work harder toward their salvation.

How could the headmistress say that? The lighthorsemen of the new nation were different, were proud and brave and purposed. How could she speak of them in that way when they'd hauled sacks of corn on and off riverboats from the Arkansas to the Mississippi to New Orleans? Rachel searched harder. She didn't want to remember Atoka's face enraged at being treated like a paid laborer. She had understood both the intention of the missionaries and the insult to her brother, of course. She had her father's gift of understanding, without his genius for pulling warring parties onto common ground. She now understood why Peter LeMoyne had often looked so tired and sad.

She knew her brother's temper. Rachel admired the forbearance it took to stalk away from the handful of silver. Perhaps he was gone already, finding a place to run off his frustration. No. There he was, carefully balancing himself on the rim of a rain barrel, above the dock's crowd, where she could see his full form, and even the piercing blue sky of his eyes. Their father's red shirt graced his shoulders. The river wind picked up his fine black hair and sent it skimming off his shoulders. Except for the braid he'd cut away, that Rachel had pinned close to her heart. He was singing. Loud. Beautiful. In Choctaw.

> You will be running to the four corners of the Universe:
> To where the land meets the big water;
> To where the sky meets the land;
> To where the home of winter is;
> To the home of rain.
> Run, sister!
> Be strong!
> For you are the mother of a people.

He sang it four times, and Rachel's heart swelled with each singing. He was giving her a new woman ceremony, years late, years after she'd followed the advice of the missionaries and declined it. Taking communion replaced it, the Wakefields said. Running with the other newly menstruating women would be a sin against Jesus. But Jesus was a kind man who loved children, who loved her brother and his wildness, Rachel felt sure. She asked Jesus to look after Atoka while she was gone.

She felt Sarah Wakefield's hand on her shoulder. "What is he saying, child?"

"A prayer."

"Blasphemy."

"No, Miss Wakefield."

"I do not have Reverend Wakefield's command of the language, but I know all the Christian prayers in Choctaw, Rachel. That is not one of them."

"It is not a Christian prayer."

"That brazen boy. We must counter his wickedness with a prayer of our own," she determined, her jaw clenching as she leafed through a book in her hand. "Here we are. 'Our efforts will continue until the waters of life shall have rolled their healing floods over every part of the earth, washing the bloody temples of Paganism, quenching the fires on horrid altars, and refreshing thirsty, dying men from the debasement of the brute to the dignity of the sons of God.' "

Miss Wakefield's book closed with a thud. "You must pray harder for your brother's salvation," she urged. "There is always hope."

What Rachel hoped was that Miss Wakefield would not talk about Atoka's salvation in the last moments she saw her brother's straight, proud form, his hand raised in silent farewell. To his sister, a new woman.

Ireland

1847

two

Rachel lifted the delicate lace curtain from the window. Sligo was not a city like New Orleans, bright and brimming with life and movement. It was a gray, colorless place, bulging with beggars from the starving countryside. Their desperation scented the air along with the smoky peat fires of the hearths. It was not always this way, her hosts said. The hunger had cast this great pall over the town.

Miss Wakefield fit into this place with her iron hair and gray eyes, and even her suspicion. She'd complained that their hosts were not real Christians at all, and called them "foot-washers." John and Memory Allen were American Quakers from the state of Indiana. To Rachel they seemed deeply devoted to the people they'd come to assist. Perhaps her teacher was too occupied with the care of her sick brother to see this.

The Irish themselves saw it. Rachel enjoyed helping the Allens serve the once-a-day meal to the growing ranks of the city's poor.

She marveled at how a little food could restore some of the luster in the people's eyes, the lilt to their speech. She was even getting used to the way the Irish spoke their English, and laughed, along with their children, at her efforts to try a few Irish words. They were a resilient people, like the Choctaw. She longed to get the Choctaw corn to the countryside, where the need for it was the greatest.

"Rachel! Come join us!" Memory Allen called her to the simple tea and marmalade cake laid out on the table.

She turned to see the American Captain Lawes of the *Hammersmith* offering his arm. The *Hammersmith* had been Atoka's vision—a great winged creature when all its sails were filled with wind. Life at sea had enhanced Rachel's senses in a way she'd never expected. She found the Atlantic bracing, the ship full of wonders. Even here in Sligo, she was still sleeping soundly each night, still dreaming in the rhythm of the waves. The glowing confidence that was the sea's gift had carried over here, where Rachel would normally be shy, sipping tea at a table of white strangers, their English accented all different ways.

"Miss LeMoyne, would you have had me deliver your precious Indian corn even if the English import embargo was back in place?"

Rachel considered Captain Lawes's question.

"Well, after our talks on board the *Hammersmith,* you seemed so fond of the people of Ireland, sir. And we are very determined to get this food to them."

His dark brows descended in a way that was becoming familiar to her. "You call yourselves Christians? Expecting me to break the law?"

"Oh, no sir," Rachel tried to assure him. "Only to leave us to do it!"

Memory and James Allen laughed heartily, surprising Rachel. She didn't understand how she was the source of their amusement, but she so liked to see them smile, just as she did her little scholars. It was both simpleminded and a great fault in her, Miss Wakefield said.

But Rachel felt fortunate to be caught in the circle of these generous Quakers. Prompted by their mirth, even the sad-eyed English artist Mr. Combs managed a smile.

Captain Lawes raised the teacup that looked very small in his hand and offered a toast with it. "Miss LeMoyne would have gotten her corn to Ireland, if I'd have had to haul each sack off myself. I think her story quite extraordinary. A reverse Pilgrim feast of Thanksgiving, if you will. You understand my meaning, do you not, Miss LeMoyne?"

"If it is that the Indians of Plymouth helped the colonists in their homeland to survive, and now the Choctaw people bring their excess corn to ease the famine in this country."

"Exactly."

"But captain, only the place is reversed. The constant is that Europeans still seem unable to feed themselves."

He laughed like a singing bellows, like Uncle Bridges on his cabin porch in Mississippi, this man that Rachel was beginning to see as her great bearded brown bear, her protector.

Not all eyes were amused this time. Mr. Combs, the *London Times* sketch artist, raised his head, looking as if her words wounded him. He seldom spoke, though their hosts often tried to engage him in conversation.

Rachel thought English newspapers must pay their artists well. Indifferent, even slovenly about his appearance, Mr. Combs neither shaved his face nor dressed his hair with any regularity. But his clothing showed wonderful attention to details, from his elegant braided trousers to his rich crimson vest and gold watch fob.

"You are new in Ireland, Miss LeMoyne," he said quietly. "But if you keep your keen child-of-the-forest eyes focused, you will notice that quite to the contrary of your supposition, this city of Sligo is an export center."

"Export, sir? I was given to understand that the wool and other exports left Ireland's east coast."

"Not wool, Miss LeMoyne. Food."

"Food?" the word made her mouth dry. "Ireland exports food while her people are starving?"

"Exactly so."

From the Allens, no denial. Rachel looked to the *Hammer-smith*'s captain. His merry eyes sobered. She turned back to Mr. Combs, forgetting his handsome attire. She listened.

"The Irish have long fed England," their cheerless teatime companion explained. "Thanks to your New World potato, they found a crop they could survive on while they grow oats and wheat and barley for their masters. The landlords sell these grains to England—to feed the city workmen who run the machinery of English industries. The Irish are forbidden, on pain of death, to eat what they grow for the landlords."

"Is this possible?" Rachel asked her hosts.

Memory Allen touched her hand. "I'm afraid so. Mr. Combs has been able to trace the worst of the consequences of the system on his excursions here in the west. The folk of the countryside know him quite well. Some even trust him."

"But, if this land is not barren, is still producing food, can the Irish people not grow it on their own plots?"

"The plots allowed them are meager gardens. Still they've been extraordinary husbandmen—coaxing a quarter acre's potatoes to feed a large family. Before the blight. But this is not the vast American wilderness where your people were driven, Miss LeMoyne. The Irish are on their native soil, but they own no land. The Celts are tenants on land the English dominate."

"Was this always so?"

"Oh, no. Some of the poor wretches still hold deeds to vast holdings, passed on through families, now stashed in their hovels. Mighty chieftains, kings, in greatly reduced circumstances. Starving beggars at the feast."

The artist's eyes scanned the room's edges—where walls met ceiling, encompassing picture frames, the outline of the room's clock. He looked at people that way too, around the edges. How could he make good likenesses, if he saw that way, Rachel wondered. Perhaps that's why he'd shown them none of his sketches, because they were vague, shadowy ghosts? Then the thought struck her. If he had seen terrible suffering, perhaps this was mourning behavior.

"Where is it the worst, Mr. Combs?" she asked him quietly. "I will bring the corn there."

"When your superiors recover their health, I doubt they will allow the journey to where I have been."

"The Wakefields are not my superiors. I represent the Choctaw. We are like the Allens, our hosts. We are in service. I remember the suffering of my people's recent past. The missionaries helped us then. We wish to help here, because we understand."

The artist looked suspiciously at Memory and John.

"Are you sure she is not a relation of yours?" he asked.

Memory shook her head, smiling. "I would gladly welcome Rachel into our family for restoring that fighting spark in your voice, Mr. Combs."

"Americans," he muttered, reaching behind his chair for the portfolio that was never far from his side. What did he mean, Rachel wondered. Did he think that she was an American?

"Allow me to transport you inland as best as my skills will allow. And explain why your trip will be much more dangerous than you can imagine."

Rachel felt her hostess's hand at her shoulder. "At last," Memory Allen whispered. "I knew you could do it, Rachel."

Rachel looked up into eyes flashing with approval. What had she done? "Let me clear guests and crockery to suit your purpose, Mr. Combs," Memory offered.

Once the room was emptied of all but the artist and Rachel, he arranged his watercolor sketches on the dark mahogany of the dining room table. Sketches signed only "Combs," which matched their starkness. They did not picture shadows, as she'd feared, but well-wrought likenesses. They were not like other newspaper sketches of the Irish, which made them look like monkey-faced buffoons, their small eyes glaring with hate even as they bowed and scraped to their English masters. Mr. Combs's work reminded her of the pictures the American artist George Catlin had painted when he visited the Choctaw Nation during ball playing season. In the first few, sturdy cabins reminded

Rachel of her people's own in Mississippi and Oklahoma, only constructed of stone instead of wood, and covered by thatched roofs. Then the pictures showed those roofs caved in, or burned, as devastation visited the small structures. The people standing outside them disappeared with each progressive sketch, too . . . parents, grandparents, kin, until a lone child or two foraged in the blighted gardens, reduced to rags.

Such old eyes peering out at her. She had seen these eyes before. Rachel knew this story. Weren't those two, that brother and sister scrounging, weren't they the children Rachel and Atoka, wild with grief, searching for roots under Oklahoma soil?

The Americans had gone to war twice against these English, but had acted like them in the ancestral home of the Choctaw, the Cherokee, the Seminole, the Creek. Taking. Always taking. And the artist had called her one of them?

She raised her head. "In my ignorance I made light of these people's suffering, Mr. Combs. I ask your forgiveness. And guidance on my journey."

His eyes found her at last, perhaps for the first time since they'd met. They traced the contours of her face, looking deeply into her eyes. His own went sadder. "Why, you're quite young," he said.

"I have twenty years," she protested.

The amusement at her indignation lasted only a moment. "If you go into the west it will age you twenty more," he promised.

Rachel placed her upturned hands over the gallery of suffering, and offered a silent prayer for guidance. "Tell me of this place?" she asked the artist quietly.

"There is only one mill to grind your raw American corn, in Manor Hamilton. And it is in disrepair."

"Surely someone can fix it?"

"The millwright can. He and his grandfather built it." He brought forth a sketch of a dark-haired man, his face turned from view, his long, lithe-boned form dancing with a small, heart-faced woman, their bare feet in midair. High, graceful, moving. They were bathed in a wash of crimson and blue tones. Rachel's hand hovered over the strokes and colors, so brimming with life.

"What is he called?" Rachel asked.

"Ronan the Millwright."

"And his given name?"

"Darragh. Darragh Ronan."

The way Mr. Combs pronounced the man's name—"Dare"— it did not sound strange to Rachel, the way some of the Irish names did. It sounded like her brother's name, the name of a man who was not afraid of challenges.

"Darragh Ronan is one of the dark Celts," the artist continued. "Quick-witted, with a good command of English. Went to a national school for a short time, I believe. Came home to become the bridge between his people and their English landlords— the translator. That position cost him dearly."

"What do you mean, sir?"

Mr. Combs voice turned softer. "I mean the very reason it is not safe for you to go to Manor Hamilton is because of what happened after the last Indian corn shipment there."

"The last shipment, sir? Of corn?"

"Yes. A government scheme. Underground Indian corn was shipped in, to get the hungry fed and back on their feet again. The Manor Hamilton mill was built for oats, barley, and rye. Cash crops. For export, protected by the government's support of private enterprise. It was not for Indian corn, Lord Hamilton told his tenants. Darragh Ronan knew better. He said that the wheels could be adjusted for a harder grain like your corn. He could do it, good as he was with machinery.

"But there was no need of that, Lord Hamilton insisted. A memorandum proclaimed the government's relief supply of unground Indian corn could be boiled whole and eaten, thus milling was not required. The millwright, with his fine command of English, translated the words into Irish."

"But, that's not true," Rachel whispered, horrified. "Corn must be ground several times before it is good for eating."

"The millwright's own starving kin proved you correct, Miss LeMoyne."

"How?" she whispered, afraid of his answer.

"Upon his landlord's instructions, Darragh Ronan gave a small supply of the unground corn to his widowed sister and her children. She cooked it as instructed, fed it to them. The unground corn pierced their intestines. The children died in agony, followed by their mother. Of grief, perhaps."

Rachel pressed her hand to her mouth, but the artist's story continued in the same even tone. "The millwright's sanity went with their screams, they say, the ones who would still talk with me. Others claim he held on to some semblance of coherence until after he'd lost his own wife and children to fever.

"The mill is abandoned now. It frightens away all with its screaming gears, they say. But the Irish love to weave their stories, Miss LeMoyne. It may be Lord Hamilton merely finds it preferable to ship his profit grains well guarded and not yet ground to Sligo these days, all things considered."

"And the millwright?"

"Taken to the mountains above the town, where Irish renegades have hidden out for centuries. A wild man, quite mad. I found no trace of him this last time, only stories and shadowy reminders of his family's gracious hospitality to me over the years. He's dead up there by now, most likely. That might be his way to take his leave, for he was a proud man and has none left of his own to bury him."

"I hope he lives. And can still run a mill."

"Miss LeMoyne, you can hardly expect you or your gift to be welcomed, after what these people have suffered."

"I expect to deliver corn, sir. And to see it ground thrice," Rachel said, gaining power from the quiet confidence she heard in her own voice. "Our gift is a life-giver, when people are not ignorant of its preparation. Those who are of a mind to accept it and turn it into food might get through the coming winter. I will teach them this, if they allow it. Then I'd like to go home."

"Here." Mr. Combs handed Rachel the watercolor of the dancing millwright and his wife, then another of the heart-faced woman flanked by a small boy and a bright-eyed girl. In her lap, another tiny face peered out from her shawl's depths. His wife, three children. And his sister and her five. Darragh Ronan had lost them all.

"Take the sketches with you," Mr. Combs instructed. "If he's alive, you may need something more than your Yankee persistence to get him out of those hills."

three

To keep his mind off the hunger, Darragh Ronan thought about the ancient circle of mammoth stones on the ground above his earthen cave. The stones had been shelters of time, of space, of the religion of the Old Ones, people said. That's why he and Bevin had dared each other to spend the spring and fall equinox nights in the middle of the fallen circle, back when they were children.

What had knocked down the thirteen stones, long ago? Did the great oak that grew up in their midst absorb their power, along with their position, aligned to the constellation Pleiades? Is that why he was disoriented here, in the earth chamber beneath the oak's roots?

The disorientation drew him to this place. That was the truth of it. He loved the feeling of being lost to self under the damp roots. He deserved this time. Because he'd become useful again. He'd found a job. He was always good at finding jobs. People had brought him things to fix since he was a child working beside his grandfather. Now the dead sought him out, calling from the shallow graves, some dug up by the wild animals. Not right, not proper, their bones gnawed on, then scattered about the hills. But he, the once mighty fixer did not have the strength to dig them safe from the animals. So he'd gathered, brought them here, the dead who would not lie quiet. Like the ancestors of his mother's people, Darragh Ronan mounted their bones and skulls on dug-out shelves in the chamber beneath the ancient oak. His new, last, home. He'd made the oak a Celtic skull tree as he waited, praying to his Christian God for his own death, careful to end each prayer with "not my will, but Thine," just as the Savior did in the Garden of Gethsemene.

The oak rewarded him for his work. With visions.

Sometimes he would see Bevin asleep in the corner, wrapped in her mother's shawl, as she was on those equinox nights of their childhood. Sometimes she would appear as she was at their wedding, shy and trembling under his touch, as if he were a stranger, and they'd not grown up in the shadow of each other's cottages. He could see her bright eyes, feel the lines of freckles he traced that night to make her laugh, to make her remember that they were friends; that, as clumsy and young as he was, he would never hurt her.

But after the pleasure they took in each other's bodies, the children they had planted hurt her. He'd endured Bevin's screams as they came into his mother's hands, him outside the cottage door, weeping. Until Sheea, who'd slipped as a sleek new seal into his own workman's hands the day his mother was at market. That child taught him the other side of birth, and why women endure it. Sheea, her father's heart, so impatient to see what little was left of the world. She'd outlasted her brother and sister. Because of the milk, he supposed, though Bevin had put all three back on the breast, so desperate she was to save them.

At least Bevin had the milk to give them. He could only feed them stories of *Tír na nóg,* of the girl with the magic apple branch with crystal flowers who would soon invite them to the endless feast. "And will you come, Da, with your dancing?" they'd asked.

After her ranting about the potatoes, ranting enough to make him mad, Bevin had promised, smiling, clear-eyed, before her last breath, to send the girl for him next. Had she forgotten? Why was he still here?

He leaned back, feeling the sharp bones of his back as he lay on the hard ground beneath the oak. Guarding his skulls and bones, listening to the rain starting to fall above, soaking into the soil, intensifying the rotting odor of blighted potatoes. He close his eyes and the years began to jumble again. He saw the birth, not of his children, but of his sheltering oak's ancestor. When the kingdom of Connacht was forested, before the English came into the west and stole the trees for their ship masts, for their bloody great halls. The oak's mighty roots displaced the great standing stones of the Old Ones. Some broke, their fractured power gathered by the learned monks to build the garden walls of Tartan Abbey nearby. Was it all connected then—the stones, the trees, the animals and people—the way his mother always said it was? Centuries. Was he seeing the birth of Ireland's Golden Age of saints and scholars? Was this a gift from God? Or was it the hunger's last sickness coming on? Darragh Ronan felt something he thought he no longer had the strength for: fear.

There. Light. Light in his dark, damp shelter for the bones. Bevin hadn't forgotten him. She's sent this glistening girl standing, her rush torch high, holding out her hand. Her clothes were miraculous, shimmering silver, without a rent or tear. She was raven-dark beautiful, lit from within with purpose, like a saint. Needing him to come. Of course. He saw that in her eyes. He sat up slowly, found his voice. He greeted her politely, asking if she were human or of the spirit. But she didn't answer. He tried again, the traditional greeting.

She asked him to speak English.

English? Darragh Ronan did not know the wisdom of the world around, but he knew that no one from the land of *Tír na nóg* spoke a word of bloody English! This girl was mortal, then, not sent by his wife, not a spirit? She said something about the gristmill at Manor Hamilton. He couldn't understand all her words. Her teeth were chattering from the cold rain falling on the ground above them.

The English avoided skull trees, even as they accused his people of still being wild, pagan barbarians. But their marksmen were certain to be waiting just outside, to kill him. He was not the millwright any longer, but a wanted man, who could be hanged three times over for his crimes. Who was this woman the cowards had sent to ferret him out? He was curious enough to want to know that, before they killed him.

He stood. "Speak slowly," he advised, in English.

"My name is Rachel LeMoyne," she said.

"Not English. French, then, are you?"

"No. Choctaw."

"Chock—?"

"Choctaw."

"What is that, Choctaw?"

"America. I'm from America. I've brought corn. Maize. Indian corn."

He heard his sister's children screaming there, inside his head. "To torture us before you kill us, Choctaw?"

"No! Mr. Ronan, my people have been growing, eating corn for centuries. I know how to prepare it, the way the others, who came before, did not. That is what killed the children, that ignorance. Feeding it to them unground. If we grind my corn, at the mill, if you'll come, help me—"

She raised her rush torch higher, illuminating the skulls and bones behind him on their shelves. The sight of them stopped her mouth at last. Good.

He let loose an onslaught of Irish curses as preamble. Then, in English he told the woman that she was an agent of the landlord, sent to lure him to the mill with her story of saving children. Lord Hamilton meant to kill him, not to save children. Then he showered her with his curses in English translation, so she would run away. Because he wanted to throttle her soundly, and he had promised his mother never to raise a hand to a woman, even when one tried him sorely.

She stood firm. Her white teeth bared as she widened her stance. "Do not seek to frighten me with your incantations, Darragh Ronan!" she shouted. "I come from the people of the bone pickers. There is no horror for me here. I am not interested in this dead place. It's the living I serve. Will you use your skill to help those left, or will there be no one left to tell what happened here?"

He blinked in the soft, choking smoke of her rush light. She was not afraid of the skulls, of the eons of time that dwelt beneath the tree's roots with him. She had courage, then.

Her torch illuminated something else: the standing stones. Burrowing down. Crashing in. Invading this small space beneath the oak. Returning, out of time. Returning, to entomb them. Did she not see them? No. There was still only that fire of purpose in her eyes. This woman from the country that had beat back the British, where liberty was lord. She should not be buried here, this American, with him. That would be a sin. His thefts, his work for Young Ireland, his raids on the fields of three landlords around, his grave robbing, all the things they would kill him for—they were not sins. But this would be.

"Get out," he entreated her now, wanting only the peace the stones would bring.

"Not without you."

So his death was not to be here. Would not be quiet, already buried in the chamber beneath the oak? Was it waiting outside, at the hands of English? Or, worse, hired Irish marksmen? Was that to be the price of taking his leave of the world? Did he have the courage for that? Not my will, but Thine.

He took her outstretched hand. Strong. Like his wife's in childbirth. Yes. He'd forgotten how strong a desperate woman's grip could be.

Rachel led the man who seemed to be made of straw more than flesh and bone out into the clearing dawn mist. He released her hand. His sunken eyes surveyed a tight circle, then a wider one. He did not move from her side.

"Where are they?" Even his voice was cracked, dry, strawlike.

"Who?"

"The marksmen."

"There are no marksmen," Rachel said, perplexed. "I came here alone. No one followed."

Gaunt face, but those eyes still held life. "I will not hurt you. I will not take you hostage, or use you as a shield. Just tell me where they are, so I have a chance."

"And I tell you no one tracked me here."

He didn't believe her. His eyes kept up their wild, hunted search of the settling mist, the shrubs, the heather banks on the surrounding hills.

"Many warned me not to come," Rachel said, trying to anchor those frantic eyes.

"Why did you come, then?"

"My people's gift is of no use without the mill."

"Why do American Red Indians bring corn to Manor Hamilton?"

"Because we are no strangers to suffering. And because we are all children of God."

"God, is it? Your God?" He took her arm in his bony grasp. Startled, Rachel forced herself to face him. He had the age-obliterating look of all the starving people she'd seen, even the children. He was tall, taller than Atoka. She wondered what a madman's eyes looked like.

"What religion are you?" he demanded suddenly, his voice gaining timbre. "Church of England?"

"No."

"What church?"

"I—I'm Presbyterian."

"Bloody Scots Protestant," he muttered with only a little less disgust. He pulled her in against his chest. There was strength in him still. "The pledge. You would have us take the pledge, then?"

"The pledge?"

"To your church, woman! Your Protestant church. Before we might have this gift of your Indian corn must we renounce our religion?"

"No. Of course not."

He released her abruptly. "I have heard such things."

"Not about us. Not about the Choctaw people."

"I have your word on this?"

"You do."

He searched the hills again, before his fierce eyes, eyes that re-flected the mist, the gray dawn sky, grew wistful. That, and his slanting brows changed the look of him completely.

"So. Let us repair the mill and grind your corn, Rachel LeMoyne, Queen of the Choctaw."

Rachel frowned. "We have no queens, except in silly Euro-pean stories. And it is now your corn, sir. And your neighbors'."

"Oh, aye," he said indifferently. Though his raw-boned frame and quickly hooded eyes could not hide his weakness, his hunger, his own body's desperate need, Rachel still felt her people's gift was a bother to him personally. "Give me that useless piece of finery before you catch a chill," he chided, compounding the im-pression. She held out her wet shawl. He replaced it with his cut-away coat, its style from the last century. Although in tatters, it was warm and armed with life, his life, still in it.

"Better?"

"Yes, thank you."

"If there are Hamilton marksmen about, they'll take aim on the coat, you understand?"

Rachel looked up at his changeling eyes and saw a remnant of something he might have once had in abundance. Humor. She smiled.

"It's good for me as well as yourself that I speak the truth then."

"Aye," he agreed as they began their journey together.

four

Darragh Ronan spoke patiently in the ear of the draft horse, convincing the animal to pull the heavy millstone into place. It was almost ready to take on its new task-grinding American corn. As the pot heated on the outdoor fire, Rachel watched the man and beast at their dance. It reminded her of the same movements from Atoka and his horses. She would make a story of this day they ground Choctaw corn for the people of Manor Hamilton. The story would be a returning gift to her brother.

She longed for the scent of ground corn to replace the terrible smell of the blighted potato crop, the sickness, the decaying bodies, not buried deep enough by mourners who lacked the strength to do so. Starvation was a long, lingering way to end, a hard path to death.

Rachel drew her stringed pouch from where it was tied to her skirt's waistband. She tested the iron pot with a sprinkle of water. It sizzled, evaporated. She smiled.

"Just right."

"What is right, little one?" The woman asked, stepping forward with the sure footing of the long sightless. Blind Maeve stooped beside Rachel at her work. "What do ye need my iron so red hot to accomplish?"

"Listen, grandmother," Rachel urged in a low tone, as she saw the children watching from the shadows. Blind Maeve sensed them too, she knew. Did she also know how Rachel longed for her own little scholars at the academy, their laughter and trust? She wasn't sure she could draw forth these beings with ancient eyes set in small faces. But with the black-draped woman's help, she would try.

Rachel removed a kernel from her stringed bag and dropped it in the bottom of the pot. Waited. She felt Maeve's hand grip her shoulder.

"Brigid and Padrig! Something's cooking," she whispered.

"Yes."

The kernel burst, flowering in tender whiteness. Rachel picked it out of the pot gingerly, and placed it in the old woman's hand. "This is corn, too," she explained. "A special variety called *Zea mays everta*—popcorn."

"It feels like nothing at all."

"It's a treat. For the children. I'll put more in the pot. Would you like to taste it?"

"I might! I might just taste this gift from America! Do you think I should, children?" she proclaimed. Then, under her breath, "Are they any nearer, little one?"

"They approach. I believe you've granted me safe passage, grandmother," Rachel confided, placing the lid on the iron kettle just as the kernels of *Zea mays everta* began to explode.

A group of six children burst forth, wailing in their own language, surrounding Rachel, pulling at her skirts. They were louder than the exploding corn, and were soon joined by a cadre of others. Blind Maeve chucked. "Well, passage maybe. But not safe, I'm thinking, little one," she said.

Suddenly, Darragh Ronan left his work and swooped down among them like a dark angel. The children backed away. Out of respect, not fear of him, Rachel thought.

"Just in time, Mr. Ronan," she said as if he'd joined her for afternoon tea. "I will need help pulling the pot off the fire before my bounty burns."

"Bounty?"

"Onto the ground. Just so. Thank you."

He stared at the still popping kettle as it sat cooling on the ground. "Your Indian corn needs grinding! You said—"

"Not these kernels. Look." She lifted the lid. One of the last kernels popped, hitting his cheek, before it jumped back into the pot. His jaw set in a grim line before he grabbed three of the light puffs, swallowed them quickly, waited. For what? Signs of the painful death that had claimed his sister's children? All his neighbors watched, holding breath. When neither death nor pain visited, Dare Ronan said something in his own language, something he did not have the grace to translate. But the people nodded, took handfuls of her bounty for themselves and their children, then ate slowly. Rachel delighted in the many manifestations of wonder as the puffed corn melted on their tongues.

The people of Manor Hamilton trusted Darragh Ronan, mad or not, Rachel realized as all but the children set off about their duties again. He was the center of the story she was weaving in her heart to take home to her brother.

They worked in secret there at the mill. They were used to secrets, these painfully ragged, fair-skinned, copper-haired people of the rolling beautiful green hills. Scouts among them watched for strangers. A few emaciated children made the youngest ones more popcorn as they waited for the adjusted millstones to grind the corn to more substantial food.

Blind Maeve had a quick mind, full of stories. Before she'd granted Rachel the use of her big iron pot, she had granted her several. One was about an Irish saint, Brendan, a seafarer who visited her own ancestors, the Woodland Indians of North America, in the long-ago time. There was no one left this old and wise among the Choctaw, so Rachel had felt privileged from the moment she stood before the Irish wisdom-keeper.

"*Comhar na gComharsan,*" Maeve said now. "A much used phrase, a much practiced art."

"What do your words mean?" Rachel asked.

"Neighbors who help each other."

"My people do that too."

"Do more. Help us. Under the English noses, you come quietly, with your food. You must take the dark one away from here, Rachel."

"The dark one? Mr. Ronan?"

"His family once numbered among them the kings of Connacht. He is the last. Apart from us now, the selkie's child, and ready to return to the sea."

Rachel smiled, remembering the old woman's shape-shifter stories about selkies, seal people who swam the shores of Ireland's coasts and its deep, cold lochs. They sometimes took on human form and made their descendants mighty swimmers. One of those stories explained why Darragh was not copper-haired, but one of the Irish "dark ones," though he would have been considered very pale among the Choctaw.

"I've seen him leaving. I've seen it in a dream," Blind Maeve pronounced.

Miss Wakefield would not approve of this woman, or her divination. But Rachel kept that small war inside her, and quiet. "What did you dream, grandmother?" she entreated.

"That you turned the selkie's child into a goose, and carried him over the two hanging post place, across the water. And there . . . oh, little one." The lids closed over her sightless eyes, and she began to chant. "Deep peace of the running wave, the quiet earth, the shining stars, and the Son of Peace to you in your trials." She crossed herself then kissed her fingers. A superstitious, papist gesture, Miss Wakefield once told her, when Rachel had seen a French trader do the same. It did not seem so to her then or now, Rachel thought.

"I saw more," Maeve continued. "You walked across a sea of grass. Dust holes cradle what our Padrig banished from this land—serpents. Did they all go to America?"

"We have many snakes," Rachel said. "My people think they are the keepers of the lightening and thunder medicine."

"Oh, aye. That would be the proper place of beings so fearsome quick. Deadly. You must be quicker, with your knowledge of them, for Darragh Ronan has none. I saw mountains, too, little one. Not like ours. Mountains so high the snow never melts from them. You and himself and your *meitheal,* you were bringing trees, bringing your life to a land at the corner of the world."

"Grandmother. Maeve. What is—"

She raised a gnarled finger, closed her lids over her whitened eyes again. "If you don't take him away from here, he and his kind will end. He has lost his *meitheal,* all of his family, this one from the clan of the best swimmers, the selkie people. He is *Oisin indiaidh na Feinne,* Oisin after the Fianna, his comrades, were all dead. He cannot return to us, just as the hero Oisin could not. Rachel, listen well to me now. Here the British will hang him, and cover his form in black tar so none can bury him. The birds will not even feast on his eyes. That is what they did to my good man in the uprising of '98, the year of the French. That is what they'll do to yours, mark me, if he does not go over the ocean to America. I have dreamed this."

Suddenly, silence. Rachel felt a ringing in her ears. Everything went on as it had before. The millstone grinding, Darragh's gentle prodding of the mare, the men oiling gears and hauling sacks of corn. And the scent of death on the wind.

"I don't understand," Rachel whispered to the wise woman.

"Aye, you do. You're only afraid of the journey, I'm thinking. You have brought us great stores, and have greater inside you. He does too, do not let the look of him and his black grieving deceive you. This is his wake, his American wake, this celebration, this moment of hope you bring. He must go. For the English sniff out these moments, and ride on the heels of them, killing the very air of possibility. They will start with him, this time, with their killing."

In the next moment Darragh Ronan slipped on a mossy patch of the old stone wall, landed in the mill pond. There was a cleft below his right knee when he rose, dripping and sputtering Irish curses. His blood stained the water and the stones of shore. Blind Maeve called out to him.

"Your voice is a touch lower toned than when I helped your mam knock yourself into the world, Darragh Ronan!"

"Go 'way with ye, wicca woman," he groused in between streams of Irish, "and take that young one as well!"

Maeve smiled. "Ach, then. She interests you enough to curse, does she, our Rachel?"

Inside Blind Maeve's almost roofless cabin, Rachel cast a quick prayer to the spider spirits before she pressed the webbing against the Irishman's cleaned cut. No. To God. Her Christian god. To please work through the spider spirits of course, she amended the request, before she caught Darragh Ronan staring at her battle with herself. "You should keep your leg raised," she told him.

He shrugged.

Rachel shoved the three-legged milking stool under his foot. His gaunt form smelled of the sluggish mill pond, making him even more the old woman's mossy sea creature. Rachel straightened his drying clothes by the small turf fire and sat. He looked as if he wished to be anywhere but beside her, under a threadbare gray blanket. To keep herself calm, Rachel breathed in the scent of fresh-ground corn, the mill's first batch, so familiar in this strange place. She brought out the chipped crockery bowl and set it on the dirt floor.

"You do not have a care for your own health, do you, Mr. Ronan?" she asked, intent on her cake-making.

"Does it appear that way to you, miss?"

"Yes. As it appears you avoid a direct answer to the simplest of questions."

"Oh? English lends itself to the art, maybe?"

"Shall I have to learn Irish, if I'm to get any real conversation?"

"That may be, American Miss."

"*Choctaw siah!*" burst forth.

"Beg pardon?"

A deep breath. "This is difficult for me. English is not my first language either."

"I had not thought of that," he admitted.

Rachel rolled back her sleeves and began to add the water to the cornmeal. The look of her *tafula*-in-the-making soothed her. Another piece of home.

"Did your missionaries not try to drum your language out of you, then?" Darragh asked, surprising her. His cynicism was edged curious.

Outsiders often berated the missionaries. They usually wanted something bad to come of it, like the traders selling whiskey, offering another god for the people to worship. Rachel kept her voice calm, like her father's would be, to honor him. And because this outsider, for all his anger, was listening. She kneaded the corn dough against the side of the crockery bowl as she spoke.

"The first missionaries learned our language. They defended us at treaty times, they came west to the new nation with us. My schoolbooks were in both languages. They are mostly in English now, though."

"And why is that, if you Choctaw have your own nation within the great United States of America?"

Rachel threw the dough against the bowl's side. "Perhaps because there are so few of us left, and we are surrounded by English speakers. Reverend Wakefield says it is because our own words are too few," she said softly, without meeting the Irishman's fathomless eyes. "He . . . he says our language has a great wanting of expression to convey religious truths."

Darragh Ronan made a cynical sound. "Their truths. Is that any wonder to me?"

Rachel smiled, looking up from the third cake she'd placed on the griddle. "You sound like my brother."

"Do I? And what is his name?"

"Atoka."

"Atoka," he repeated her inflection exactly. "That is not a name like yours, is it now? A name the missionaries gave him?"

"They tried to change it," Rachel admitted. "He wouldn't

say its English meaning. 'It's too deep for you to understand,' he told them, 'you have too few words.' "

She saw that rare thing, his smile. "I would like Atoka, I'm thinking."

Again, he'd honored her brother with an exact pronunciation of his name, this listener. "And he would cherish your ways with horses," Rachel told him. "Atoka has four. They are like his children."

"Your brother owns horses?"

"Yes."

"They allow him this?"

"Who?"

"The ones who lord over you. Your missionaries. The government."

"No one lords over us! I told you, we invited the missionaries." Rachel drew in another calming breath. "No one can prevent Atoka from owning his horses. Only his foolish tendency to gamble sometimes loses him one or two." The eyes were no longer challenging her, she realized. They were full of longing. "Mr. Ronan, can you not own horses here?"

"That we cannot, if we are Catholic. Not a horse worth more than five pounds, that is, which is all, of course, isn't it?"

"Why?"

"Now, you'd have to be asking the politicians that, miss."

Rachel turned each of her five cakes on the fire. Darragh Ronan stole glances at her in her silence. Is that what he was doing on the wall before he fell into the mill pond? The next sentence out of his mouth was not a question.

"Tell me what you assaulted my ears with."

"Assaulted?"

"What you spat at me, when I called you American miss."

Rachel felt herself color in her shame. "*Choctaw siah*. It means 'I am Choctaw.' It is our battle cry."

"You do not make it sound like a battle cry now. Now it sounds like music out of you."

"I am no longer angry."

"And if you were? Would my life and limb be in danger? Do Choctaw women fight in battle?"

"Some."

"So did ours. The Celts, I mean."

"Truly?"

"Oh, aye." A small, pained sound came on the heels of the word, starting her.

"Does your knee hurt, Mr. Ronan?"

"That was not my knee, but my hollow insides, responding to the scent of your food. With my insides I must again test your good will toward my neighbors, Miss LeMoyne."

"How?"

"By seeing if you'll offer me one of your cakes, though I'll not pledge myself to your religion."

There it was again. A spark of humor.

She took a cake from the fire, and held out the steaming plate. "Don't let it burn your tongue," she advised.

five

Once the corn was ground three times, Rachel suggested they cut and refashion the hundredweight sacks into smaller bags. That way the weakened heads of households would be able to carry them into storage in caves in the nearby hills. It was a good plan, except for it putting the hobbled Darragh Ronan amidst the women sewing the sacks closed, and under Blind Maeve's iron hand.

"Too wide apart, and crooked besides," she informed him of his work.

"And how do you know—"

"I have ears. Do you have eyes?"

He bristled, then pulled out the stitches, muttering, "I am no fine-baste seamstress."

"Ach, is there one talent that shuns you, then, fixer?"

He gripped the long needle, fisting it at the old woman as she passed, listening to the sewing of others. Rachel touched his back.

"Kindly use that instrument for its intended purpose, or find another crew to plague."

Maeve turned sharply. "What is he doing?" she demanded.

"He is only—that is to say . . ."

Darragh Ronan's grip eased. "Ah, surely any charge of wrongful intent against me is conjecture, Miss LeMoyne, and would not hold as evidence in an American court of law, where all are equal."

Instruct, Rachel, she heard Miss Wakefield's voice demand there inside her head. Use this attention of the Irish for proclaiming the glory of God, shining through the laws that men had made. "You have heard principles, Mr. Ronan," she stated evenly. "Have you also learned that some American principles were taken from ways of the people you call Red Indians?"

"Now, that I had not," he admitted, his eyes firing. "And do your high-minded Red Indians also own African slaves, like their white neighbors?"

"Some do. Because the United States is founded on ideals not yet in widespread practice."

"Ah, I see."

Rachel smiled. "I hope you will, Mr. Ronan. Then you might stop this teasing."

"Teasing, is it?"

"I believe so. Though Atoka says the missionaries have it drummed out of me, I believe I can still recognize the tone of it."

She saw the brief shine of his white teeth. Had her words caused this precious thing, a flash of laughter?

Suddenly, a sharp whistle sounded over the mill's gears. From one of the scouts. Darragh Ronan broke his sack's cord with his teeth. He tied it closed and handed it to the nearest woman. He called more of his neighbors to him, then spoke in the swift, strange sounds of the Irish language. They gathered their children, left their cakes and took the sacks on their backs. Below, Rachel saw the mill emptying of its workers even as its wheel kept turning. It was all happening so fast. A second whistle, higher. And then, in the distance, the muffled thunder of hoofbeats over dirt road. Darragh Ronan swung her around, held her arms between his callused hands.

"Rachel," he summoned. "Hold them off as long as you can. Will you do that, in the name of our common God?"

"Yes," she promised, understanding only the desperate need in his eyes.

Then, she was alone.

The horses belonged to a dozen English soldiers, led by three men, perhaps Irish men, but in unpatched clothes and with full stomachs. And there, behind them in an open carriage, sat a large, dark-clad man with shining silver hair. Miss Wakefield sat beside him. Instinctively, Rachel wound her shawl about herself more tightly as she stood in the ghostly smoke of the abandoned fires.

Sarah Wakefield got to her feet. There was something wrong with her eyes. The man took her arm to steady her. "Rachel!" she called out, "are you well?"

"Very well, Miss Wakefield," she said slowly, calmly. "And you?"

"I am . . . better."

"I thank the Heavenly Father for it. These corn cakes are burning. Perhaps the gentlemen could help me retrieve them? It would be a sin, in this country, to lay food to waste."

The horsemen looked to each other, then to their leader, a man in uniform of red and gold. He looked to the black-clad man, whose mouth tightened.

Sarah Wakefield descended. Her voice rang in its fury. "Foolish girl! What have you done?"

Rachel breathed in deeply. "What I was bade do by the Choctaw council, Miss Wakefield. I brought the corn surplus here to this place of great need. People came to this mill, to grind it. We distributed the meal among the hungry."

Her teacher was beyond words, but not beyond those terrible eyes Rachel remembered from her childhood. She felt herself turning back into that small child so far below her benefactor's iron grip. Ungrateful child, not saved enough. Rachel began to say whatever came into her head, in another voice—the high, pleading voice of that child. "I made corn cakes, Miss Wakefield, see? The women were most patient with my instruction. This is not food they usually eat, did you know that?"

"You have no idea what you were about here!"

"But I have just told you—"

"Keep still!" she almost screamed, before swallowing hard, "while I attempt to smooth things between you and Lord Hamilton."

Silver Mane's head rose from his talk with the army officer. Silver Mane was Lord Hamilton, then? His look was cold, distant, even a little afraid. Rachel recognized it. It was the look of the soldiers who brought the Choctaw west. They knew that for all their mighty weapons, they were both vastly outnumbered and surrounded by the Western wilderness. So were Lord Hamilton, the English soldiers, and their full-bellied Irish scouts. That look helped Rachel find both her courage and her calm, deeper voice again.

"This gentleman has some smoothing of his own to do. With his tenants, I think," she said quietly.

Her teacher's face went whiter, but her shaking voice was as quiet as Rachel's own. "Simpleton. Foolish, obstinate girl. These Irish misbelievers have brought you back to your own heathen ways."

"Surely not, dear lady." Silver Mane stepped forward, bowed to Miss Wakefield. He made a deeper bow to Rachel.

"You were most brave in your captivity, Miss LeMoyne," he announced, so the troops could hear.

"I was not a captive, Lord Hamilton."

"Miss LeMoyne," his twitch-mouthed captain assured her, "you would have been the first sacrificed if those cowardly devils had decided to take a stand against us."

Rachel faced his shining uniform. "Surely you can find more formidable devils than starving women and children, sir."

"Starving women and children did not start the wheel turning on this mill again, young woman."

"Oh, but they did, along with the help of their men."

Lord Hamilton stepped between them. "And with the help of

my renegade millwright, who is a very dangerous man, Miss LeMoyne."

"I did not find him so, sir."

Silver eyebrow raised. "There!" he called to his tin soldier accomplice. "We have it from our little Red Indian saint herself. He lives. Worn down by this time, I wouldn't wonder, for all his poaching on my land. A party of five into the hills should do the job, Captain."

"Yes, m'lord," the soldier agreed, before barking out names to join his search. The selected men seemed only too glad to jump to their horses again.

The corn cakes burned on the fires. Rachel felt a sickening ache at her bones, thinking of Darragh, weakened by his leg's wound, being run down by five soldiers. Because of her. Because she'd let them know a wanted man was alive, and had been here. She reached out to Lord Hamilton. His eyes went even colder, telling her he had no more need of her services. But the eyes still had interest, an interest she did not like. Still, she took his sleeve.

"Mr. Ronan only worked at my bidding. If you could see what I have seen, sir! I am sorry, so sorry if I acted improperly, but I am what my teacher calls me, a simple woman, and a stranger here, and the people are so hungry."

He patted her hand, then smiled in a way that made her feel soiled.

"Darragh Ronan is no stranger to us, Miss LeMoyne. Rest assured his crimes are of sufficient consequence to have hanged him long before now. Think no more of him. But come, return as a guest to my home. I would know of the many savage practices from which Miss Wakefield has saved you."

"Rachel, drink your tea."

"I will not eat or drink until I know what has happened."

They sat in the parlor of the stone-cold house, a world away from the mill and Blind Maeve's cabin. Rachel was supposed to have come here first. She did not, because there was no need here. And now she was prisoner in this place of crystal chandeliers, oil paintings, majestic trees, and a trout-filled river in which the poor might be killed for fishing.

"You are being blinded by these people, you foolish girl!" Miss Wakefield summoned her away from her contemplation of the white marble fireplace. "The authorities at Sligo, and now Lord Hamilton himself, have warned me this might happen. And those dreadful Quakers putting their schemes into your weak mind!"

"Miss Wakefield, the Allens did not—"

"It is criminal, taking advantage of your sheltered life at the mission, and your defective bloodlines to mold you to their purpose. But it will all be set to right. Salvage. We must salvage what is left, for the glory of God, in the name of the Mission Society."

"Miss Wakefield—"

"Listen! Listen only, you ignorant girl!"

Rachel realized suddenly that Miss Wakefield was right. It was a good idea, listening. The best idea. She sat still, folded her hands in her lap. Watched the mantle clock. Listened.

"There. That's better. Now. What we have left to build upon is as follows: Lord Hamilton is delighted the mill is running again. It had been sabotaged you see, by his tenants themselves, not by any landlord's cruelty! And now he says it can be used to relieve these people's suffering. Is that not of good consequence?"

"Yes, Miss Wakefield." If it were true. And Rachel felt in her bones it was not.

"The distribution of the remaining food will be supervised by myself and Lord Hamilton. How much maize remains?"

"None."

"What?"

"We worked hard. We ground it all. It's gone."

"Gone where?" her elder demanded.

No. She would not be trapped again. "I don't know." That was true. She did not know where in the barren hills they were headed. Didn't Darragh Ronan speak in the Irish language to keep her from knowing? "They all left so suddenly when the soldiers came," Rachel said, staring at her hands, wishing they'd brought her with them, up into the hills, for she now felt she was in the splendidly appointed camp of her enemy.

"And why would they do that? Run away?" Miss Wakefield demanded. "I don't understand the Irish at all. The soldiers and Lord Hamilton's hired men were only sent to help the poor creatures."

"The creatures were doing well helping themselves."

"Exactly. Helping themselves to Manor Hamilton's gristmill, equipment. For the which their gracious lord has forgiven them. Well, now he has purchased a new supply of Indian corn for them. In your honor, he says. Could there be a better gesture of his good will?"

Rachel strongly suspected it was not her good will the lord of Manor Hamilton wanted. She knew that look in white men's eyes for Indian women. She'd seen it first long ago in the eyes of a soldier. For her mother, even with a baby at her breast. Should she be so suspicious of Lord Hamilton? He'd bought more food. Mr. Combs said that the farmers' eviction would mean death. Rachel wished the artist was here to guide her now. Could she convince Lord Hamilton not to evict his remaining tenants? She made herself look at Sarah Wakefield. "Who will distribute this ground corn?"

"Us, Rachel. What do you think of that? Lady Hamilton is even drawing up our pledge papers in her own hand."

"Pledge papers?"

"To have their runaway tenants ally themselves to our good Protestant faith! The lord and his lady have agreed to allow us to seek our converts among their tenants in thanks for your assistance in getting the mill started. And in acknowledgment of our part in bringing the needs of his people to his attention. Is that not most generous of him? Is this not a wonderful opportunity to bring these unfortunates out of both their hunger and their darkness?"

Rachel felt the cold seeping into her bones, along with Darragh Ronan's hatred. He had heard of such things. "They are already Christian people," she whispered.

"Oh, Rachel. Papists are as the unsaved Choctaw. I don't expect you to understand this, in your blighted state. Only to rely, as you always have, on my superior comprehension. Now, perhaps you would like to help us draw up the pledges? You have such a lovely handwriting yourself. I would enjoy the lord and lady of this place to see your fine hand, to see how far you've come out of your own darkness. It will erase their first impression of you, I feel sure."

"No."

"I beg your pardon, child?"

"I am not your child. I am the child of Peter and Elizabeth LeMoyne. And I wish to go home."

"Home? With only half our mission complete?"

"All of my mission is complete. I have no ambition to offer these people the choice of my religion or starvation. That . . . that is against American principles. Religious freedom, written by Thomas Jefferson, first for his Commonwealth of Virginia, then adopted by the new United States of America. Separation of church and state."

"Rachel LeMoyne, do not lecture *me* on American principles! Or that Deist Jefferson! What do I care for laws that men have made? I serve a higher purpose. I thought you did too. God has put us here in this terrible time to use this famine terror He's sent! He requires us to bring these people around to the path of their true salvation."

"This terror was not sent by my God but by greed, I think."

"Careful. Your thoughts have been bent dangerous by the Quakers and these people, these thieves."

"I think I know who the thieves are. Of flourishing land that grows all but one crop. I know thieves of souls, too. And I will have nothing more to do with either. I wish to go home."

"I see. Well, perhaps you'd like to make restitution to Lord Hamilton for your own trespass and use of his mill?"

The cold fear, again. Of this stone house. Of this man with

greedy eyes for her. Restitution. What restitution would he demand, alone? In the dark? In the night? "I have already apologized for not seeking his permission before I—"

"And now you could join the party looking for those renegades who escaped into the hills, couldn't you?"

"Escaped? These are their hills, their country!"

"This is Lord Hamilton's land. Do you think the people who helped you were any of his good, loyal tenants? No. These lazy arrogant people who started the mill turning again were the evicted, with no right to remain here. And the millwright is worse. He is a traitor—a terrible criminal who needs to be tried and punished. You know where he is. You found him, when the authorities have been searching for months. It is your obligation to deliver him."

"I do not see it that way."

"As I thought! You are infatuated!"

"I do not see it that way," Rachel repeated. She tried to be her father's daughter, and keep her voice calm. "Miss Wakefield, perhaps you should give me my return passage ticket. I can return to New Orleans on my own."

"On your own? How far do you think you'd get without me?"

"I think I could find my way home. If you'd—"

"My brother's death will not be in vain! I will carry home the news of pledges to the mission. Of souls to add to the roster!"

"Reverend Wakefield is dead?"

"Yes, dead! You selfish, ignorant girl! Did you never once wonder why he did not accompany me to Manor Hamilton?"

"I assumed he was recovering in the Allens' care."

"Foot-washers? Do you think I would have left him with those foot-washers? No, he is dead, and I had to bury him in the soil of this putrid-smelling country!"

"I . . . I'm very sorry for your loss." There. Rachel saw the raw grief overcome the emptiness in her teacher's eyes, and knew how she would feel if she lost Atoka. At last. Sarah Wakefield became a human being again to her. She took her teacher's arm.

"I'm so tired, Rachel," her elder whispered. "Don't fight me anymore."

"Please, Miss Wakefield. Let me bring you home."

"Yes, home," she whispered. "What was I thinking? No triumph. How can there even be a hint of triumph? You and your love of these filthy people have killed my dear brother and polluted everything. There is no hope here. Only your cleansing remains."

six

"They've got your millwright locked up," John Allen informed her without taking his eyes from the horse he guided gently through the streets of Sligo.

Rachel felt a pain between her eyes. "Where?"

"We will be passing in just a moment. Yes, there it is, directly ahead of us."

Rachel gripped the open carriage's side as a large building with two permanent gallows erected out front came into view. The Allens were good people, Rachel reminded herself, who gave food to the starving without conversion to their religion as condition. They had shown her nothing but kindness. To whom else could she give her trust? Still, they were strangers. And she had been so foolish already. John Allen kept talking in his familiar, animated tone. "The jailer is an amiable fellow, and fond of his drink. He's worried that if Darragh Ronan gets any weaker he won't be able to stand in the accused box, never mind last to the hanging. That would reflect badly on Friend Jailer, of course."

"We must get him out of there," Rachel whispered.

"Pardon?"

"The *Hammersmith* sails tomorrow. Captain Lawes is a compassionate man. We've got to get Mr. Ronan out of that place, and on board," she told her hands, fisted together there in her lap.

"Why, that was just my Memory's line of thinking," John Allen said, grinning, when she finally looked up at him. "Perhaps you *are* distantly related to my wife, Rachel. And she believes we can enlist Mr. Combs in our efforts. Don't tell me you've thought of that, too?"

"I've thought of nothing until just before I gave it speech," Rachel whispered, shaking her head.

"Ah, well. Some of the most wondrous ideas come about that way. Spontaneous, through the heart."

Rachel's elation was short-lived as she thought of a new complication.

"Friend Allen?"

"Yes?"

"I'm not sure Darragh Ronan wishes to be rescued."

"Ah." He paused just long enough to give his horse gentle encouragement. "Then we'll have to convince him."

That night Rachel stood between the two men, willing herself to look more like Darragh, and so be taken for his sister. She prayed to the spirit of his real sister, the one dead beside her little ones, to help her deliver the one who would remember them. Beside her, Mr. Combs weaved. He dropped his sketch pad.

"Are you—?"

"Practicing," he assured her. "I would like to appear so inebriated that it would be possible for a fierce but decidedly small Choctaw woman and a pious Quaker man to bring me down."

His voice was muffled with spirits-soaked scarves draping his fashionable clothes. His was the greatest risk. Mr. Combs would be the one spending the night in a cold cell if they were successful, and he'd be running the risk of time of his own in prison if

his story of becoming a forced accomplice was not believed. All
for the hospitality that Darragh Ronan's family had shown the
sad-eyed artist over his years of visiting.

Money and a bottle of whiskey changed hands between John
Allen and the jailer. Rachel couldn't tell how much money. But
she could never hope to repay the gentle Quakers except in a life
well lived. The gruff jailer bent down to Rachel's height and
peered inside the hood of Memory Allen's beautiful Quaker cape.
"Don't you be afeared of me, little sister," he said. With kindness,
Rachel thought—a miracle in this dark place.

Inside one door, then another. Twin doors to the inner keep,
like the twin gallows outside. Rachel thought of Blind Maeve's
prediction. She was charged by the wisdom-keeper's dream to be
here now, Rachel reminded herself.

Darragh was lying on a pallet of straw. Unmoving, but not
chained by the cold iron lengths attached to the wall. His jailer
shoved his side. "Visitors," he said gruffly. "Your friends have
not forsaken you all together, millwright. Look, they've brought
your wee sister." He shuffled out of the cell.

Rachel leaned over Darragh Ronan. His eyes opened, trying
to blink back the darkness. Gray eyes, like the walls around.
"Water?" he whispered.

John Allen was ready. He handed her the cup. Rachel lifted
his head, held it to Darragh's lips, trying to avoid the festered cut.
He had not gone gently into his captivity, then? Though grieved
for his already ravaged body, Rachel felt heartened by this sign
of his spirit. Did she have a right to the trust in his eyes as she fed
him the laudanum John Allen had slipped into the cup? "I want
you to come with us," she said, once Darragh had swallowed.

"Into the west?" he asked.

"Yes."

"All right, then," he agreed. His eyes closed.

"There," John Allen touched her shoulder. "He appears willing, even before the drug does its work."

"The west and death are the same to the Irish," Mr. Combs
said behind them.

"I'll teach him to separate them," Rachel maintained, thinking, if God, his and mine, grants him life.

The men exchanged the millwright's ragged clothes with Mr. Combs's finery. To her surprise, Darragh Ronan's homespun tailcoat fit Mr. Combs. Had they once been the same size, before the hunger had reduced the Irishman who'd once graciously fed the Englishman? The artist's hands shook as he doused himself with more whiskey. "I hope this keeps the vermin at bay until morning's light," he said, smiling grimly as he leaned over the still form lost in his fashionable frock coat with its flared skirts and matching long trousers. "Darragh!" he called out, as if he were hailing the millwright's cottage, "Darragh Ronan!"

Gray eyes opened again, glassy with the laudanum now. They stared hard at the man who'd called.

"Mr. Combs, is it?"

"None other."

"How have you been keeping yourself, sir?"

"Tolerably well, thank you."

"My daughter has been painting wondrous great likenesses of the pigs since your last visit, did you know?" Was the laudanum wreaking this havoc with is memory, Rachel wondered.

Mr. Combs seemed undisturbed as 'ie answered. "Has she?"

"Oh, aye. It was a great present you left her, the paints. A passion she has for making likenesses, Mr. Combs. Akin to yours even, in time. Plucked the swine of their hair for her brushes before she takes to immortalizing them on the stones by the water's edge! Do painters ever take on apprentices of the female persuasion, sir? Or have they schools that my daughter might someday—" He blinked, staring harder at the artist. "Mr. Combs?"

"Yes?"

"What would you be wanting with my coat, sir?"

"I told my friends of your family's celebrated hospitality. They were doubting Thomases. Had to see to believe you'd give me the clothes off your back. So I've . . . ah, taken the liberty."

"A joke, then? Some manner of English joke, is it?"

"Yes. Exactly."

Darragh's eyes looked over Mr. Combs's shoulder, found Rachel. "I know this woman, sir. She . . . she brings something— I don't remember."

"You don't have to. Just remember her a good woman, and go with her now."

Darragh Ronan grabbed the artist's sleeve. The sight of Rachel was breaking his voice of the lilting artifice he'd used with the Englishman. A dark, raw-edged desperation took its place. "Where is this, Mr. Combs? Where is my family?"

"Rest from your questions," he urged. "Trust us."

"To—to send your likenesses of us as word to the queen?" Darragh groped now, "To show her how her subjects are starving, as you said last time?"

"Yes, exactly."

"Good of you."

"Not at all." The artist's voice was finally gruff with unshed tears, Rachel suspected.

Darragh turned his face to the wall. "Bloody English," he muttered. "How can we trust any? After the Battle at the Boyne? After the year of the French?"

"What? What do you say to me, Darragh Ronan?"

The millwright remained still.

"I believe the truth has finally won over thy friend's famous hospitality, Friend Combs," John Allen rendered an opinion.

"Get him out of here, before I change my mind," the artist charged, hauling Darragh Ronan to his feet. "And hit me hard, you damned Quaker, so I don't spend the rest of my life in here."

Miss Wakefield would not be favoring the idea of smuggling Darragh Ronan out of Ireland. Of that Rachel was sure. But Captain Lawes of the *Hammersmith* was a kind man. And they would be well at sea by morning. Perhaps he'd understand, and would help her to repatriate the millwright to America.

She leaned over the bunk, grateful for the cabin's darkness. Perhaps all will be well, until morning, she dared to hope.

Darragh Ronan slept so soundly. Due to the drug, she reminded herself. Still she checked his breathing, like she once did
with Atoka, crammed with her aboard the steamship on the
way west. Suddenly, out of the darkness, a flash of movement.
She felt the Irishman take her wrist. In a hold, not a grip. One
that was gentle, but strong enough to steal her breath. And so
cold . . .

Now, here was a switch: Bevin standing over him. How was
he tucked in bed before her, Darragh wondered. Perhaps she had
gotten up to check the children? He felt the rapid pulse at her
wrist before taking her small hand in his. He called her name,
then urged her to get into bed beside him. She did not answer.
And it was so damp, cold outside the bed.

"Bevin, is something wrong?" he asked.

A little murmur. Was she angry? Had he forgotten the bless-
ing, and climbed into their bed without its recitation? He thought
of a short one, for his mind was fogged with sleep and darkness.
He sang it softly in his best Irish.

> *Bless Thou, O God, the dwelling,*
> *And each who rests herein this night;*
> *Bless Thou, O God, my dear ones*
> *In every place wherein they sleep,*
> *Both bab and begetter,*
> *Both wife and children,*
> *Both young and mature,*
> *Both maiden and youth.*
> *Michael, bright warrior*
> *Brigid, fair and tender*
> *And Columba kindly*
> *Giving benediction*
> *On those within.*

There. Did he have everyone under their roof covered? Her
hand was warming. Still, she did not come into the bed. He
pulled himself to his elbows.

"Shall I build up the fire then, love?"

She pushed him back and quickly climbed in at last. What was this game? He liked it, even her strange silence. The whole cabin was silent with every mother's son and daughter deep in dreams. Bevin smelled like she never had before, like a forest at midnight. Perhaps he was not so tired . . .

Rachel tried to stop the frightened catches in her breathing. Mr. Combs said laudanum had unpredictable results. But by morning Darragh Ronan would be himself again. Please, God, just keep him still until morning, until they were well out at sea. The Allens said Rachel should go to the captain with the request for his asylum then. They didn't tell her what she should do now, with Miss Wakefield expecting her for evening prayers, while she was lying in a man's arms. Send him back to sleep, please, God, so she might slip away. But he was speaking at her ear now, in a language she didn't understand. He was asking for something as he reached down, drew her shift up her leg. Of course. How stupid of her . . .

He smelled her tears. "Bevin. You're crying. What is it, love?"

She shook her head.

"What has you worried?"

No answer.

"Is it the raid at the newspaper?"

She curled away from him.

"Don't you be fearing for me. I only ran the press for Young Ireland. I don't have the head for rhetoric those more formal educated boys do. It's they, the bright lads, and know where to hide until cooler heads prevail. And they won't call on me again until they want me to get the press up and running. And I stay clear of the Whiteboys, do I not, then? It's them the bloody English will be seeking out first."

Rachel felt his hand slip around her middle. He asked her something. Just one word, this time, not related to that speech that sounded like an apology. A question, she was sure of it. Rachel searched her mind for a word of his language, some phrase that might make sense to him. Perhaps, if she answered, he would go back to sleep. There, that strange Irish word again, more insistent.

"Warm?" he asked his wife.

Rachel nodded slowly. She felt his lips beside her ear. Along with a longer sentence.

"And would it please you to be warmer still, my sweet, silent wife?"

He kissed her throat.

"Rachel!" Miss Wakefield shouted from the doorway. Light flooded into their cabin. Into Darragh Ronan's eyes. "Rachel?" he repeated, squinting into the light, then yanking his hand back from the small waist as if it were on fire. *"An Mhaighdean Mhuire,"* he whispered, *"briongloid?"*

"Speak English, you filthy heathen!" a grim woman in full black fury demanded.

"Not— Not a dream," he translated, putting his too heavy head in his palm.

"You'll have to do better than that, if you want to avoid a hanging at sea."

"Sea?"

The woman sneered at him. "I thought he was clever. They all spoke of him as clever." The look on her. Saint Michael, what had he ever done to this woman? "Perhaps you'll be more lively company for the captain, in his irons."

"Miss Wakefield," Bevin, who was not Bevin, but was Rachel LeMoyne, called out. Darragh saw a flash of her leg before the nightgown covered it in her flight from the bunk. He shivered without her warmth. She caught the woman's arm. "You must not go to the captain yet! Not until we're well out, please! You must—"

The woman turned, freezing back any other protest with her eyes. "No 'musts' from you, backsliding into your own heathen ways! They warned me. They all warned me. You are like the rest, possessing only the faintest spark of moral conscience, pathetically insufficient to enlighten your dark nature, or to prevent you from wallowing in all kinds of sin." She gave Darragh the hard stare again. "You now have two choices regarding this man, now that you are his whore. Watch him hang, or marry him. I am done with you."

* * *

Rachel couldn't bear to look behind her in the ringing aftermath of the woman's departure. She fought back the tears that threatened. Without success. Finally, she felt a gentle swipe at her elbow. "You didn't have to indulge me in an ocean voyage to convince me to marry you, Rachel LeMoyne," his voice, light, teasing came out of the darkness like spring.

Laughter joined her tears as she turned to her scarecrow. "English! You're speaking English! And you know me!"

"I was on my way to that, maybe."

"Mr. Ronan!"

"Miss LeMoyne, as you are the one subjecting me to drugs, jailbreak, abduction at sea, and one more thing I'll have the delicacy not to mention, I hardly think you ought be taking that tone on yourself."

"You know me," she said again, unable to stop her relieved weeping. "Oh, Darragh, we were so worried about you."

"We? Who? Not that battle-ax just left us, surely!"

"No, not her." She wiped her nose on her sleeve.

"Will you stop this forsaken caterwauling, and tell me what you're up to this time?"

She bowed her head, bit her lip. "Marriage, I think."

"Bloody hell! You cannot be obligated by that woman's preposterous . . . Rachel?" He scanned her loose-weave shift and reddened. "You wouldn't tell them that . . . I— I did not, did I?"

"No. But I think you'd best let me marry you, just the same."

He cocked his head. "Why?"

"Because you are a dead man in Ireland. In America, you have a chance. And I can make you an American."

"American? I thought you were queen of the bleeding Choctaw Nation!"

She fisted her hands at her hips. She'd taken enough from this man tonight, despite his desperate circumstances, and in or out of his dreams. "*Oke,* I am a peace chief from the Choctaw, who were thriving in my country before your great seafaring Brendan the Navigator was a thought in the mind of his grandfather!" she informed him. "If that country is now America, then I am American."

He ran his hand through his lifeless black hair. Rachel watched him struggle to clear himself of the drug. Rachel's own mind tried to catch up with what her mouth had proposed, almost without its knowledge. To go back to his own country meant death. He did not have a place, except for the one she'd made for him, here on the *Hammersmith*. He did not have a family, except in his dreaming. She'd passed for his sister, there in the dark of that hanging place. They were not so different. Would that help? Or would Atoka be furious, Rachel wondered, by her sudden, strange choice in husband?

SEVEN

Captain Lawes was kind and solemn and respectful. So respectful Rachel almost changed her mind, until she saw his compassionate interest lighten the occasion of her shipboard wedding. He was her great protective bear. She longed to fold herself in his soft fur, and not have to marry this flinty man who smelled of death beside her.

She had not thought of being married in years, except when Atoka badgered her about it. She had chosen another path, an honorable path. Had the missionaries chosen it for her? Is that what she'd had to travel across the Atlantic to find out? The first mate lit a candle that burned with little smoke and smelled of beeswax. Her Uncle Bridges kept bees, isn't that what Atoka had told her once? Was this a sign then, of her family's approval?

It was not a true marriage. It was being done to save a life, this promise. Did that make it less a lie? Who would counsel her? Not Miss Wakefield, a tight-lipped, gloating witness to the lie, to Rachel's fall from grace. That caused her satisfaction, perhaps? The possibility made Rachel's hands tremble. It was not a good thing to have such a person standing beside her at the ceremony.

Rachel had never loved Miss Wakefield or her brother, nor any of the missionaries, not with the fierce love she gave Atoka, her parents, sister, her people. The missionaries didn't seem to want love, for all their devotion to the life and afterlife of the Choctaw. But she had respected them, and tried so hard to follow, to be a good Christian and a good Choctaw. Was that so impossible? Her throat was dry. Would she be able to speak, to declare herself for Darragh Ronan?

These people—the missionary and the ship's captain—were binding her in this Christian marriage, to a man who still slept with his dead wife. "Death do us part?" The words shocked her. They were not part of Choctaw marriage. This was her first time attending a Christian marriage ceremony, even after all her years at the mission. When she faltered, she received comfort from the place she least expected it. Darragh Ronan took her hand. She looked up. Yes, comfort in his calm eyes, helping her to repeat the strange words.

She leaned against his side and closed her eyes, feeling spent, like when Atoka told her that her parents had joined Sleeps Sound in death.

"My wife could use the benefits of the salt sea air, I'm thinking, gentlemen," she heard this man, her husband, say as he anchored his long fingers at her waist.

They departed the captain's quarters with congratulations, with the slammed door of the cabin she'd shared with Miss Wakefield, the key turning in the lock.

Rachel wore the hooded cloak that Memory Allen had given her as they reached the open deck, and carried the document that still waited for their signatures. If she loosed her grip, the paper might sail off in the breeze and into the depths of the Atlantic, never signed, never legal. Perhaps that's why the captain, her protector bear, left them alone here, left the inkwell and pen. Waiting for a final decision.

But they'd said the spell of marriage, and words had power.

Rachel felt married. Was marriage to Darragh Ronan a punishment for all Rachel's betrayals of her Christian faith? For enjoying the brief feel of a man's hands along her spine, and his gentle, persuasive kiss? Rachel felt dizzy with questions that ate themselves, like the tail of a snake.

"Breathe deeply, little one," her husband counseled.

She nodded, following his instruction, and felt better.

Darragh Ronan released his hold on her, then leaned on the rail to brace his healing leg, watching the stars come out.

"If I jump overboard, you'd be rid of me," he suggested.

She stepped forward. "In no time. I know you, in the water. How you sink like a stone."

He winced. "Aye. Yet I can't go that way unless you push. I'm no coward, mind you. But my religion forbids suicide."

"I see."

"That's why I waited, there, in my own country. For death to come to me. Instead you came with your corn. Perhaps this is a dream within a dream. I don't understand it at all."

"Does your religion require understanding of all things?"

"Oh, no. It is full of mysteries."

"Mine, too."

"Ah. Common ground, then, Mrs. Ronan."

"Swimmer."

He turned, facing her. The moon cast a silver halo around all his darkness. "Swimmer?"

"Yes. Our name is Swimmer. Mr. Combs thought it best, to change it. To protect—"

"Combs? The English artist?"

"You don't remember? He took your place in the jail."

His mouth twisted in its displeasure. "No Englishman took my place."

"And no Irish had ever shown him such hospitality, he said of you and yours."

She watched him work the sense of what she said through his still-fogged mind. "Well, he can be a comb if he wishes, but I'll not be turning myself into a fish. My name is Ronan."

The pressure of her grip crushed the document in her hand,

but she willed her voice calm. "Ronan means 'swimmer,' Blind Maeve told me. That and many wonderful stories. So when it came time to choose, I thought it might be a respectful name, if it was a translation. I am a translator's daughter. I was trying to ease your journey to my country. I was trying to keep you safe."

He frowned deeply. "The name mocks me as it honors you."

"Not once I teach you to swim, and so honor your ancestor."

"My ancestor? What are you about now? Ah . . ." She saw understanding brighten those intelligent eyes, even as they struggled out of the vestiges of the drug. "One of that bane's stories, is it then? Of the seal woman?"

"Selkie. That's what Blind Maeve called your long-ago grandmother. Daughter of a seal man and mortal. She says this grandmother is why you have dark hair."

His mouth twitched again, but suppressing a smile this time. "She or a Norman usurper, or a wrecked Spanish sailor. Let me see the paper, then, before you destroy it in your great strength." Rachel loosened her grip, and placed it into his hands. He sniffed, scanning the document. "*Crois na Slanaightheoir.* That's not my given name either!"

"It's not? I-I have never seen it spelled out, so I wrote it out the way it sounds to me."

"Darragh," he insisted. "D-a-double r-a-g-h."

"But—"

"Irish! I'm Irish, woman!"

His eyes were sparked by the moon's light and his anger. She could see the whites of them curving under the deep gray of the balls. She had offended him in her ignorance. Nothing she'd done was right. Rachel felt her lower lip trembling, but she kept a steady gaze on those sunken eyes of his.

"I know only the spellings of American English, which is simpler than your language, or the language of England, I think. D-a-r-e. A word that means brave. I thought—"

"Bloody English," he muttered, walking away from her.

Rachel followed, wishing he'd loosen his hold on the certificate and let it float out to sea, instead of crushing it between those fingers that had stroked her back with such tenderness.

Then she was ashamed of the thought, and of wanting to be free of him and his ghosts. "I will change it. The ink is here, see? Tell me the proper way again. I'm sorry."

He turned, looked down at the marriage paper, at her hands offering the inkwell and pen. "Dare Swimmer," he said, his voice so weary it made her want to weep. "Rachel LeMoyne Swimmer." He grabbed the inkwell from her hands and slammed it on the first flat surface he found, a signal flag box. He leaned over, signed the paper with a burst of his own language. Were they curses, those strange sounds? Would she have to burn sage against their power? He realized her puzzlement and gave her a short, courtly bow. "Pardon me, wife. I said, 'Christ and his saints help us.' "

"Yes," Rachel agreed, breathing easier. No sage, then, except perhaps in thanks, that her new husband was not cursing her already.

He took up her hand. She felt his long suffering, his hunger through the bones. Perhaps these were the last things still feeding him, these short bursts of anger. She could bear them, if so.

"Rachel," he said her name gently. "I respect our circumstances, and your brave generosity, though I feel it was wasted on me. This thing we have accomplished. This shipboard marriage. My religion requires more than the paper your captain has given us. It requires vows before a priest, and consummation. I will look after you as best I am able for as long as you can stand my company. This I promise you before God. But I will neither priest-wed nor touch you as a husband. Please do not you be afraid of me."

"I'm not afraid." It did not occur to her to be afraid of him, not since the first time she'd seen him under the great oak with his bones and skulls. But the strangeness of that fact only now struck her. She did not even think of Darragh Ronan, Dare Swimmer, as a white man: rapacious, always taking, the kind from whom she'd been warned since she was a child. Why was that? What did it mean? This man clouded her mind with questions. Now he looked relieved. Too relieved. She tilted her head, annoyed with him. "Does your religion allow divorce?" she asked.

"No."

"Mine does. It is very simple. I put your belongings outside our dwelling, we divide our blankets. We are divorced."

She saw the shadow of a pout crease his unshaven chin. "And does washday count?"

She swiped the handsome fitted shoulder of Mr. Combs's fine coat. "No."

"A smile is it I see out of you, Mrs. Swimmer? If you can smile this day you've been saddled with me, there's hope for us, I'm thinking. At least until your mighty brother kills me."

She frowned. He loved courting death, this man, this very white, glowing-like-the-moon's-face Irish man. She didn't like having such a husband. It reflected badly on her. "Now why would Atoka harm you, when he's been badgering me to marry for years?"

"Has he? Why?"

She couldn't tell him about the children they would never have, because he was not her true husband, and slept only with his dead wife. She was furious with that dancing woman and her children, suddenly, for not staying in those beautiful hills. Why should they follow her husband, Dare Swimmer, to the territory that belonged to the Choctaw, begging comparison?

His curious, intelligent eyes were searching her face for an answer to his question. She turned away, leaned over the rail. The moon led a shining trail through the water to itself.

"Rachel?" her husband called again, softly, beguiling her, if such a thing was possible. "Tell me why your brother badgers you?"

"I—I like it when you're not all questions. That was a good marriage gift. And now you have spoiled it."

"I'm sorry. Please don't cry."

"I'm not crying. It's cold. I'm cold and tired, and Miss Wakefield has locked us out of the cabin."

"Might I hold you then, making myself useful?"

She nodded, sniffing, feeling ridiculous, like a child. And he held her like one, though he was as rough and brittle as a diseased tree that the next storm might bring down for tinder. He spoke softly into her hair. To her. Not to a child.

"Ach, Rachel. Were I to die this night, it would be the one thing that grieves me, bidding you good-bye. Why is that do you think, wife? When all you've done is—what is this good word of your brother's? *Badger* me?"

"You've deserved it."

"Aye," he agreed, and she felt the warmth of his deep sigh in her hair. "But, no more weeping out of you. First let me make myself worthy of your tears, Queen of the Choctaw."

The cabin boy gathered up the inkwell and tapped his shoulder. "Mr. Swimmer?"

He was answered with a whirling turn and a stream of Irish invective.

The boy stepped back, startled. He looked to Rachel. "Mrs. Swimmer?" he tried.

"Yes?"

"Captain Lawes has made a gift of his cabin. It is now ready for you both as his guests over the voyage to New Orleans. I'm to say there's fresh linens on the bed and a hot tea awaiting."

Her bear had heard Miss Wakefield's key in the lock, too. Astonished, Rachel smiled. "That is very kind of him."

"Oh, aye. He's kinder than most, ain't he, ma'am?"

"Isn't. Isn't he," Rachel corrected, out of schoolteacher habit.

"Isn't. Beg pardon, ma'am, sir."

Rachel pressed her fingers to her mouth willing her voice to work, to not frighten the child with her tears.

"The kindest man on board, we're thinking," her Irish husband said softly.

The boy straightened his stance further, even as he peered into their faces. "Captain Lawes, he says you require his space because you are royal company he's wed together this night. Are you really an Indian princess like Pocahontas, ma'am?"

Rachel loved the way the boy looked at her differences with

wonder, because of the story her great bear captain had planted in his head. She went to one knee beside him, her skirts billowing in the night air, awing him further.

"Well, my new husband has notched me up. He's made me a queen now, as he's the king of Ireland."

Dare grunted. "Just of Connacht. Not the High King. Just a king."

"Wait until I write to my mother on this! Imagine!"

Dare touched the boy's head. "Aye, lad," he directed. "Imagine."

The child was about the size of his son in Mr. Combs's last drawings, Rachel realized. Dare watched the lively form of the cabin boy until it disappeared in the night mist. But he tried mightily not to, Rachel surmised, just as she'd tried not to hear her sister in every baby's cry.

"Tea's waiting," she said softly, touching his arm.

Once the cabin boy had removed the tray the new Dare Swimmer sunk deeper into the captain's chair. He unbuttoned Mr. Combs's colorful embroidered vest and rubbed his middle.

Rachel touched his sleeve. "Are you unwell?"

"I may not swim a stroke, but I don't get seasick. I've taken on the highest swells of Loch Allen in a storm without a twinge. Damned laudanum," he murmured.

"May I—"

"No. Leave me alone."

These were their quarters. She couldn't leave him alone. Perhaps he didn't mean for her to go, she decided as he looked away from her, moving nothing but his thin fingers along his middle. He'd drunk the strong tea, but only finished half the rich cakes of their wedding tea. Eating seemed to pain him. Perhaps it did, after he'd lived on so little for so long.

Captain Lawes's cabin, under the soft glow of the whale oil lamp, mahogany woods, maps, and a library of a dozen books, beckoned with its warm comforts. Rachel removed her traveling

suit, then placed her dressing gown over her shift before she un-
pinned her braids. She sat at the edge of the bed to brush them
out, then rebraided her hair in a single loose plait, the tradition
among Choctaw married women. Her husband's face had lost its
surliness when she dared look upon it again.

"Feeling better?" she asked softly.

"Aye. I beg your pardon for my bad temper, Mrs. Swimmer."

She sighed at him slumped there in the spindle-backed chair.
"Dare, come to bed."

His tired eyes brightened. "Might I?"

"Of course. Look. It's big enough for both of us."

"Aye. Thank you, Mrs. Swimmer."

"*Yalabusha.*"

"What is this word?"

"It is one of my Choctaw names. It means tadpole, good
swimmer."

A little dance there, in the corner of his eye. A pocket of him
where his humor slipped out.

"So, wife," he summoned her, "it's your own name you've
given me?"

"Yes," she realized.

"Or is it that we always had the same name, and were searching for a common language, translator's daughter?"

"I like that better still. Dare?"

"Aye?"

She stood. "Get into the bed first. I favor the outside."

He grinned. "Done, *madame.*"

He pulled off boots that were too big for him, making Rachel
wonder if his feet had shrunk in his hunger. No. They were Mr.
Combs's boots. He removed the artist's expensive gentleman's
clothes like a Choctaw, without any hint of modesty, until he
was down to the pearly cotton and linen shirt. She had seen her
own people in starving times, and how thin their bodies became.
His was worse than any, and his paleness made him seem even
more fragile. The shadows of purple bruises showing through the
shirt's light weave spoke of captive punishments beyond those
that caused his cracked lip. He caught her staring. Men were

proud creatures. God, let him not think I feel pity, Rachel prayed as he spoke.

"Changed your mind?" he asked her pointedly.

"No. But you're in sore need of fattening, husband."

"And I never asked if you can cook."

"Well enough."

"Anything besides those yellow flat cakes that burned my tongue?"

"A few things."

"Good. I have an appetite, I recall."

He climbed into a bed that hardly sagged under his weight. She followed. He was warm and alive, this bone picker, picked clean himself. "Do recall it," she urged.

He sighed against her hair. "Sweet dreams, wife," he said, as if he were amused at her taking his real wife's place, or as if he were a brother, indulging her in a marriage game. And of course, that's what it was. He kissed her temple before he turned his back to her and his face to the wall.

Rachel stared at the stars though the porthole. She touched her throat, remembering his kiss there, the delicate sweetness of it, even though it had not been for her. She had spent much of her life in the companionship of sleeping partners. Her brother. Other girls at the mission school. Why did this one's bony back discomfort her so? He was not her true husband. Perhaps he would never be. She realized the cause of her disturbance suddenly, sitting up. Her new husband had distracted her from her nightly ritual, praying over Atoka's braid to keep him safe until morning. She pulled it from the pouch she'd sewn into her shift. Her breath caught in her throat. The fraying cornsilk tie had broken. The braid was unraveling. Its woven-through bead slipped between her fingers. She uttered a small cry. Dare turned.

"Rachel? What is it?"

"My brother. Something's happened."

"What?"

She began describing what she saw, somewhere back behind her eyes. "He's breaking things. Furniture. Oh, Dare."

"Tell him to stop. Tell him you're coming. You're almost home."

"But look. The tie from his braid is gone! And I've lost the bead!"

"All right, then. Be still. Talk with Atoka. I'll find it. Work the braid tight again, will you do that?"

"*Oke.* A-all right," she stammered, feeling like a fool, though he wasn't treating her like one, wasn't angry with her for disturbing his sleep. He crawled around the captain's fine, wine-dark carpet until his fingers retrieved something, held it between her eyes and the moonlit porthole.

"Is this the bead, then?"

"Yes!"

"Work the braid, work the braid," he reminded her, "I'll keep a grip on this fine piece of midnight until you're ready to weave it in."

"I'm ready."

He climbed back into the bed, handing her the shimmering glass. "Aye, and a fine job of it you've done, Mrs. Swimmer," he soothed. "Now, shall we put a bit of Mr. Combs's shirt to better use than shrouding your near useless bag-of-bones husband?"

"Oh, Dare—"

"Weave, and hold that heathen talisman fast," he warned, ripping the hem of the long shirt until he had two thin strips rolled between deft fingers. "Now, then, one end at a time, lift for me, there's a good lass. Now, if you'll place your smallest finger here?"

Rachel watched the spiraling crown of his lank, depleted black hair as he concentrated on the task of securing Atoka's braid at each end. He did it without losing a strand in the process, as if this was a task he was used to. Was he? Did he secure his wife's, his young daughter's hair? Had he braided his mother's as she lay dying? Rachel realized she was seeing these things, in the same place, back behind her eyes.

"Did I not do it up proper?" he asked softly, alarmed by her tears.

She touched the high, sharp cheekbone of his ravaged face.

What right had she to add to this man's torment? She felt suddenly unworthy of his concern. "You've made it better than it has ever been. Dare. Look." She held it higher. "Your hair is almost the same color as my brother's."

"Is it? Do you think selkie people travel up your mighty Mississippi, then, Mrs. Swimmer? Or might Atoka make me a relation by way of St. Brendan the Navigator and his amorous crew?"

"He won't need to. We are all of us related."

He turned his face into the curve of her hand, and rested it there. His stubbled beard was soft, surprising her. "He's well, now," his voice soothed. "You'll see him soon. You'll set everything right between you."

She nodded, not trusting herself to speak until he took her into his arms, and bolstered them both snug against the pillows. "I am not sorry. For anything," she whispered against his brittle collarbone.

"Nor am I," he admitted. "May God, His Mother, and all the saints forgive us both then, Rachel LeMoyne. I fear we are some kind of married."

eight

Rachel expected no help in getting her husband safely on American soil from Miss Wakefield. Her teacher was furious that this punishment she'd devised—marriage to a heathen Irishman— was not proving a punishment at all. Instead of being shunned in disgrace, the newlywed couple were, beginning with the awe-struck cabin boy, doted on. Officers, passengers, and crew alike claimed they were the cause of everything from the unseasonably balmy breezes that ferried them across the Atlantic to the company of laughing dolphins off the bow.

Dare had more than endured Miss Wakefield's shunning. He'd never failed to greet her without a tipped hat and shower of pleasantries. He'd grown up bowing to the Manor Hamilton gentry every day and seldom being acknowledged by them. He was used to Miss Wakefield's icy countenance, he'd assured Rachel.

Though her Irishman walked slowly and bore the ravages of his hunger, Rachel sometimes felt very plain and shy beside him, he dressed in Mr. Combs's finery, with his affable manner among all the ship's passengers. Other times she was less shy, like when she held his coat and vest as he crawled close to ask his questions and sigh with wonder at the workings of Captain Lawes's fire-bellied bird.

"Sweet dreams," he repeated every night. Turning away each time. But he would turn back again in his sleeping, dreaming of his life with his Irish wife perhaps, or of soothing one of his children. Rachel didn't mind, and sometimes dreamed herself—that Atoka was holding her on the trail after the others had died, the earth scent of their graves still under his fingernails. Every morning she and Dare awoke to find themselves spooned in each other's arms. At first Rachel saw the hot blush rise up his neck and color his face as he apologized. But this morning he'd kissed her forehead and bade her good morning, without an expression of regret.

When three mastmen broke bones during the only storm on the crossing, Rachel and Dare helped the ship's surgeon tending them. The captain proclaimed their efforts publicly at the main dining table that night. Rachel slipped her hand in the crook of Dare's arm then, and he patted it fondly, as if they'd been married years instead of days. Tender gestures were part of his game, like their marriage itself, of course. But Rachel liked the game.

The cabin boy sent children in small flocks of three or four to view the royal couple as they took walks around the forecastle. Dare's eyes would get that haunted look at the sight of them, making Rachel wonder if he would ever visit her classroom. If she had a classroom, or was a teacher any longer. The missionaries ran her school, not the Choctaw.

He listened intently to the stories she told of her people, from the days of the Choctaw's first spirit guided journey eastward, to the time of the Mound Builders, to their exile in Oklahoma. He asked open, simple questions, not his teasing ones. He was like a child seeking knowledge at those times, and not like any white man she had ever met.

His interest in her people gave her courage to ask him why

they would hang him in his own country. He enumerated his crimes, from running a printing press for an outlawed political movement that sought more rights for Catholics, to helping desperate neighbors in need with food and shelter. For these things he would be admired by the Choctaw, she'd assured him. He'd put his head in his hand and stared off toward the place over the water where the sun had risen.

The dark circles under his eyes looked like bruises to her then. He missed his country. Of course, she must allow him that. And what had she to offer to replace it? She would lose her place at the mission school, surely. Atoka would have to take her in, and Dare as well. To the council, Miss Wakefield would paint their time in Ireland a failure, and Rachel a disgraced menace. Would the council agree? Would Dare be safe from Miss Wakefield and her fury? Would they have to leave? What could Rachel offer him then? A hiding place in the hills, where the American and Spanish, French and Mexican renegades sought refuge? No. Atoka would help her find a better path than that one. Rachel tried to calm herself with that thought, as she clung tenaciously to the notion that she had done something right in freeing Dare from the Sligo prison, that even a hard life in his new country would be an improvement.

As they entered the port of New Orleans, Rachel's Irish husband gathered up their small bag of belongings. If she'd married a Choctaw man, that would be her job. Atoka wouldn't know this was her husband if he saw them together in this way, she thought. She longed to see her brother. She eased her longing with a touch of his braid, now secure again thanks to her clever husband who was once rich in his own braided women, but was now *Oisin indiaidh na Feinne,* Oisin after the Fianna—a man out of his time, his family and friends all dead. Or was he reborn? That would be for him to decide.

Captain Lawes had been right—the fresh-minted Dare Swimmer escaped a rigorous customs examination in light of their first-class passenger status and her great bear's intervention. But she must be vigilant. Once on shore Dare's sanctuary would end.

Rachel caught sight of Miss Wakefield lifting her umbrella to use as a wedge in the crowd. She was working her way toward a uniformed man on the dock. Captain Lawes saw too. He sent forth his cabin boy. The boy served as the captain's wedge. He managed to trip Miss Wakefield, then sat on her umbrella until she pulled him off by his hair. "Go," the captain whispered, before squeezing Rachel's hand. He interceded between the boy and woman, holding the missionary secure in his iron grip. Rachel fought back the fear freezing her mind as she grabbed her husband's hand and bolted.

Dare must not go back, not before he'd had a chance in America. They would hang him in Ireland. There was only one direction from here. Away. From the commotion on board the *Hammersmith*. From the high-pitched orders from the anchored woman who Rachel had once thought her friend.

When they reached the street, Rachel ran into a red woven shirt, and the sage-scented man it contained.

His gruff embrace felt warm with love and relief. Atoka, as if he'd been waiting at the dockside since he'd chanted her into her new womanhood. She took his hand, linking herself to both her brother and husband for the first time. The air charged with possibility.

"Atoka! How—?"

"That woman wailing there sent word of your return. I came, watching the ships since that letter."

"We must get this man away."

Atoka's brow arched as he surveyed Dare. "Without her?"

"Yes," she whispered, "I . . . I have done with her." Rachel felt her new husband's short, winded breathing, his fingers trusting hers. He struggled, as she did, for balance on newly landed legs. "Please, Atoka. Help us."

Interest sparked her brother's face. "Can you ride a horse?" he asked Dare.

"Better than I can walk, at present."

Atoka nodded toward the three horses standing in the shade near the crowded dock. They'd advanced only halfway to them when another shout to halt was followed by a shrill whistle. "Don't turn," Atoka warned. Rachel needed the warning, but the man who could barely keep pace with her brother's strides did not. He was more used to running.

They mounted. Atoka made a polite request in French, and the crowd behind them filled the gap and slowed the movements of their pursuers.

Dare leaned over his mount, speaking softly at the horse's ear. His ways went far to ease Raven Mocker into his task over the streets of New Orleans. Her sharp-eyed brother noticed it too, even as he led them through a maze of cobblestones, then out onto an open course of countryside.

They rode hard for an hour until they approached another Mississippi dockside, piled high with chopped wood. A few men were watching downriver. None noticed them. Atoka sidelined them among some moss-laden trees before he slid off Sassafras's back. Rachel and Dare dismounted, still shipboard, with less ease.

"Who is after this man?" Atoka asked.

"Immigration authorities. The magistrate. Miss Wakefield."

Her brother grinned. "Powerful enemies." He turned to his saddlebags and pulled out a bundle of clothes. "Here." He shoved them at Rachel. "Out of those skirts. We must save fare money."

"Fare money?"

"Change. Remake yourself. This next journey we take together, as we rode away from your missionary school together some nights long ago, remember, little sister? In the time before you became one of them?"

"*Oke.*" She nodded and began to pull on the trousers under her skirts. Dare stared until Atoka shoved his shoulder, making him face forward to give her a privacy shield for her transformation. Rachel stepped out of her skits and hoop, then yanked her corset higher, so that her breasts were within its confine. She loosened the strings until her waist was no longer pinched. She donned Atoka's blue gingham shirt then, hoping the shirt's tucks and generous fit would further render her breasts obscure. As she pulled out her combs and pins, freeing her thick braid, she grinned, feeling twelve again, about to sneak out of the mission to ride with her brother, to swim with him under a full summer moon. Finally she called to the broad-backed men: "Done."

"She doesn't look like a boy," Dare protested.

"It's not your eyes we need to fool."

Atoka stood back and looked doubtful himself. "Put your braid inside here," he advised, throwing her a boatman's cap. Rachel did as he asked, stealing a look at her husband, who was frowning. Her brother then went to his knees and rolled up the too-long trouser legs. Next Atoka scooped some dirt off the ground and smeared her cheek. "There. You were too clean, that's all, Tadpole."

He turned to Dare. "This way, we can all travel topside, third deck. And we two can look out for our little brother."

"That makes sense," Dare agreed reluctantly.

"Who—"

A shrill whistle sounded from the river.

Atoka shook his head. "Come," he commanded. He led them down to the dockside. Rachel and Dare held the horses, which helped keep them steady. The man supervising the woodpile surveyed them quickly, removed his hat. Rachel smiled politely, forgetting his cordiality was not for her. He addressed only Dare. "Fine-looking horses, sir!"

"Thank you."

"Do you all seek passage on the *Carolina Mist,* master?"

Rachel saw her husband's slight flinch at the word. "Aye."

"Your boy, he can earn himself two dollars off the topside fare if'n he helps us haul this firewood aboard to feed those mighty boilers. Captain might take a dollar off the small one's fee as well, if he can manage a half load. We could use the help, sir. Time's money, on the river."

Rachel watched her husband and brother exchange quick glances. When Dare spoke with the man again, his accent changed. There was no singing in its new tones. "We need our Tad to look after the horses. But Atoka and I will haul wood, gladly." He was imitating the language of his enemies, the English, Rachel realized. He sounded like Mr. Combs.

The man raised his eyebrows. "You? Times as hard as that, sir?"

Dare nodded, smiling. "Fully as hard."

"Well. Pleased to have your company, then." The whistle of the steamship *Carolina Mist* blew again. The vessel came in sight around the river's bend. Rachel stared at its massive form. It was not like the deep-keeled ocean ship, or the river steamboats that had helped to bring them to the new nation. The *Carolina Mist* was grand, full of fancy carved woodwork and two tall black smokestacks powering its stern wheel. Rachel felt Dare's excitement as he watched its approach, too. A new vessel for him to learn, she thought. He handed his fine coat to her, just as he had done before inspecting the engine room of the *Hammersmith*.

"They think us your servants," Rachel whispered as their fingers made contact.

"Why?"

"Your clothes. Your whiteness, compared to us."

He sighed. "Aye, then. And shall we let them think as they wish?" he asked both herself and her brother.

Atoka glared, but nodded curtly, handing the reins to Dare. "Go up the gangplank first, with the horse. Keep her calm."

Rachel felt her husband's hand at her elbow. "He meant the horse, Dare," she told him with a wan smile.

"Did he now, little brother?" His smile disappeared. "Take longer strides," he advised. "And stay close by the horses, until we come for you."

"I will. Don't worry."

He gave her arm a small squeeze, then turned to join her brother.

On a boat again. On the Mississippi. Where were they going? Did her brother know? She'd needed the calming touch Dare gave to her and the horses, Rachel realized as she watched him join Atoka and the other men. Together they loaded firewood that would enable the ship to steam up the river at astonishing speeds. Rachel worried that her husband would be humiliated by the others for not carrying the full loads that her brother was. But it seemed that most discomfort stemmed from his fellow workers, at having a man clad in gentleman's clothing working beside them.

Suddenly, a rough-looking man who smelled of pork fat grabbed her arm, startling her. "What are you doing here? Where's your ticket?" he demanded. Her throat went dry. "My brothers—" was all she could manage before she heard Atoka give a soft war yelp. He appeared, looking ready to break the man's neck. Dare reached him first. "Tad's waiting for us," he said calmly, "holding the horses, like a good lad, before we purchase our tickets." Pork Fat backed away. "Oh, is that the way of it? Beg pardon, sir," he muttered at Dare's choice boots.

"Come on then, little brother," Dare half-soothed and half-demanded in his new English tones. His fingers twitched. She nodded quickly, tying the horses secure, then following her husband and brother up the stairs.

Once on top of the ship, they all scanned the dockside and the road beside it. No one was coming, searching for them. Jumping in the muddy waters of the Mississippi would be the only escape route if the authorities found them now. And Dare Swimmer would sink as fast as Darragh Ronan would. Was the fear in his eyes caused by that prospect? There. He did love his life enough to be afraid, Rachel decided, and deemed it good. The whistle sounded again. The great tiered steamship pulled away from the dock.

Atoka led them to a deserted corner of the deck to stake their claim for space.

"How long will we be on board?" Rachel asked. "Where are we going? How did you know to bring clothes for me to—"

He frowned. "No more questions out of you. I will ask the questions now. Who is this man?"

"My husband."

Dare winced. *"Dia Dhuit,* Atoka LeMoyne. Patrick and Brigid keep you well all your days," he said, offering his hand.

Her brother stared. Long. Hard. He knew a challenge when he heard one. He put his brown hand into the blue-veined one of the Irishman, pressed hard, closing his eyes. In the space of seconds, they shot open, fierce.

"You!" he claimed, startling Rachel with his chanting voice. "I have seen you!"

"Have you?" Dare asked evenly.

"You are a chopped oak, scarred with hatchet marks, like your country. A woman of the Choctaw people walks in your soul. You must remake yourself, or she will cast you aside."

Dare smiled. "Aye. I've heard as much from your sister."

"Look down there," Atoka commanded, a flash of annoyance in his voice. "Do you see my horses?"

Dare's eyes scanned the decks below, squinting, though the sun was not strong. Again Rachel wondered if his hunger had damaged his sight. "I see them," he finally said.

Atoka sighed out, almost snorting. "They are Coosa, Raven Mocker, and Sassafras. I saddled Raven Mocker for a missionary woman who now has daggers in her eyes for my sister, worse than the ones she's always had for me. And that missionary woman cannot sit a horse with any grace. You are an improvement over her in that, at least."

"Thank you."

"Go down to them, your rich man's clothes will give you passage. Greet my horses by their names while I ask my sister if I should welcome you or cut your heart out."

Dare turned, hesitated, and turned back to them. "You were supposed to add a saint," he told her brother quietly.

"What?"

"I greeted you with the blessings of Patrick and Brigid. You were supposed to respond in kind, adding another saint. That's the proper way of it where I come from, you see?" He grinned suddenly, with that flash of white teeth. "But I take pleasure in your horses' names salutation all the same, brother."

Rachel watched her husband's comfortable, seafaring gait launch him down toward Atoka's skittish horses. But there was no evading her brother's eyes boring into her soul.

"Is Red Clay still in your stable?" she asked quietly.

"No. Can this husband of yours race horses?"

"You've lost her again." Rachel clucked her tongue at his gambling, making her feel at home in this loud vessel full of white people's smells—steam, machinery, pork, whiskey. There, her husband emerged below. Dare greeted Atoka's skittish horses. Another man touched his back, began a conversation, a man in a high hat, with boots like Dare's. Rachel held her breath in fear until the man offered him a brush to use on Sassafras's whithers. She leaned into her brother's side, relieved. He pushed her away gently.

"Be a man," he admonished with a frown of amusement.

Rachel suddenly did not like that men and boys did not touch each other except to fight.

"From what tribe are your 'breeds, son?"

Dare turned, smiled affably, out of habit with the English. "Tribe, sir?"

"Cheyenne? They're said to be splendid horsemen."

"They are Choctaw," he said, hoping the man would go away. He handed Dare a grooming brush instead.

"Ah, you've got yourself a couple of civilized ones. Very wise."

"Civilized?"

"You know, missionary-tamed. They say some of them can even read. Yours?"

Dare stopped brushing midstroke. "They are not mine," he maintained in the careful, precise English of his blasted teachers at the national school. Sometimes he cursed his own gift for mimicry. "And my brothers and I are all literate, yes."

Expecting to enjoy the man's shock, he received a slow nod of understanding. "It's that way, is it? Been put out with only those splendid horses and the family bastards to look after you? What are you recovering from, then?"

Dare resisted saying "hunger," but didn't know what would make the man loose interest in him.

"Nothing catching, of course?"

"No, sir."

He looked relieved. There. Would that make him go away?

"Well, your servants, they're in better health by half. Your Red Indian brothers are not doing so well by you at present."

Dare was growing more perplexed by the minute, but knew enough to keep listening.

"Allow me to guess," the man speculated further. "You're a third son? Fourth? What did you do to displease them so? Did they give you a trade over there, or on the plantation? Pushed you out of the nest and into the world with some training, at least?"

Mildly amused eyes. Dare had seen those eyes on so many of the damned gentry, looking at him like a monkey who could do tricks that gave him the semblance of humanity. Not here. Not in this new country that was called the cradle of liberty, by God.

"May I ask to whom I make my answer, sir?" he asked.

"Oh, I beg your pardon! I am Albert Chambers, Mr.—?"

"Swimmer, Dare Swimmer. And I am set out into the world with some training, as you say, Mr. Chambers, yes. In fact, I believe if you had the parts of this fine vessel dismantled, put in a box and shaken well, I could get her on the water and running again in the space of a day."

To Dare's continued astonishment, Chambers threw back his head and laughed, before offering him a cigar.

What did a person in this strange country have to do to insult Americans?

Rachel watched. Her husband wore his false face, the one he'd always greeted Miss Wakefield with aboard the *Hammersmith*, as he stroked the fear from Atoka's horses. The laughing man beside him unsettled her. She looked away from them, and out over the trees, the green islands and houses on the Mississippi's shore. All of them were drifting past as though they were the things moving. The marvel of it. Everyone on board, regardless of fare, shared these beautiful, continually changing vistas. But there would be no kiss, no "sweet dreams" out of her husband this night, she thought sadly, when they slept among all these rough men. Atoka brought her out of her thoughts quickly.

"Does this stray dog in winter of yours have a name?"

"Dare Swimmer," she said, facing her brother. "He thinks you very rich, even with three and not four horses. He's forbidden to own them in his own country."

"Forbidden? Why didn't he leave sooner?"

"Atoka—"

"He is very white," her brother interrupted, claiming control of the conversation's pull. It was his right, as her elder.

Rachel bowed her head. "Yes."

"And not in good health."

"No. Because of the great hunger."

"I choose my horses better."

"Your horses choose you," she claimed. Quietly. With her head down, still.

"Will he darken in the sun?"

"I don't think so. On the ship, his skin burned red, then he turned white again."

Her brother considered her words. "I have met this kind of white man," he said. "He is like Lieutenant Connor, at the horse soldier's fort. Dare Swimmer will need a hat. Not like yours, little brother. One with a wide brim. I will buy him one, a marriage gift."

"Oh, Atoka." She pressed her hand to her mouth.

"Are you full of tears?" He looked down at the waist of her rope-tied pantaloons and lowered his voice. "Is there a child coming already?"

"No."

"Then where is your brash tongue?"

"Quieted by your acceptance of this man."

"Not beaten out by him? He is good to you?"

"Yes."

Atoka's eyes found her husband below. The man in the tall hat was finally gone from Dare's side. His stance relaxed as he put the brush away and rubbed Atoka's horses behind their ears.

His lips moved, but she could not hear his words. Rachel thought of his language, full of bursts and gutturals, not soft like Choctaw. Did he speak to them in Irish, or his new, clipped and precise English? Whatever language he used, the horses listened.

"He is tall. Taller than I am," Atoka commented begrudgingly now. "When he gets meat on those bones he will be strong. That will keep me stronger, of course. But *Yalabusha,* it is a hard thing to be uncle to a white man's children. They think they own them, like they seek to own the ground. You have not chosen an easy way for me. But you have chosen, at last."

"You see too much. I married him in haste, to save his life. He sleeps as a brother beside me. He dwells still in the black, in that scarred place you saw when you took his hand."

"Well. I will make a ceremony to help get him out of this place."

"Thank you." Rachel smiled, grateful for the straightforward way her brother saw the world. It was good to be in his company again.

"You look tired. Sit," he commanded, making a place for her between the saddlebags. She sank down gratefully.

He pulled off her hat. "Make two braids of your hair, until you are a true wife. Do not presume on our customs. And try to muddy up some," he advised.

"Atoka, don't you want to know why Miss Wakefield sent the police after us? Why my husband is a criminal in his own country?"

He shrugged, slouching down beside her. "Later. Braid. And rest. We made a good run, in the right direction, I know that."

"Reverend Wakefield is dead."

"I know. Word of it reached us. That is how I knew to come. I do not mourn him. He had only duty. He followed a strange path. Is his death the cause of his sister's madness?"

He watched her fingers do their work on her hair, and waited for her to find the words. Patiently, her headstrong brother. That was a wonder to her. "That may be true, the cause of Miss Wakefield's madness. But, Atoka, I caused her great grief. I gave our corn to the hungry, without question, without insisting they become the Presbyterian kind of Christian. Then I married Dare, on the ship. She has disowned me for these things."

Atoka snorted like his horses. "The council would have put you in disgrace if you had not done the task required, without foolish conditions. You left the Irish their honor, and their own god. And you may marry whom you please." Rachel wound her new braids around her head, and replaced the cap. Atoka came closer, his eyes angry. "What is this? Tears?" he whispered furiously. "That woman never owned you, how can she disown you?"

"Atoka, they raised us."

"Our parents raised us in the ways that mattered. The missionaries did not love us for who we were, but for what they might make of us, fearful people full of dreams of burning. I do not grieve the loss of them. I will not waste my time on people not worthy of your beauty."

"I must carry my disgrace alone, then?"

"You should carry it not at all. You have other burdens now. And will someday have another, if that man of yours can make Choctaw children."

"Atoka, you must not talk with him on this!"

He smiled at her burning cheeks. "Only to you?"

"Yes, to me if you must. But you must welcome him without condition."

"Now, what negotiator does that?"

"One who loves his sister, and respects her mind on this."

"Mind or heart?"

"Do we come in pieces then, like the white people?"

He held up his hands. "When will I learn not to argue with you?"

She sighed, her burdens lightened by her brother. "Atoka, please. Do we have an agreement on this?"

"*Oke,*" he muttered.

"Good. Now. Tell me where we are going?"

"Upriver. North to St. Louis. In the spring, west." He grinned wide. "We jump off."

nine

"St. Louis?"

"Gateway to the West."

"I know what the city is called, brother. I have not been away that long. What I want to know is why."

"That needs a story."

"I am listening."

He looked about the deck, where a few of the black roustabouts had set up, away from the flat boatmen. Atoka had chosen a quiet square over the ladies' cabin for their territory. Perhaps too quiet. She felt herself getting drowsy. She moved closer to her brother's warmth.

He shoved her from his side, the way he never would have his sister, but might a brother, growling.

"I'm sorry," she whispered.

"Do not do things so . . . softly," he finally decided on the word.

"I will remember," Rachel promised.

He grunted.

"The story, Atoka?" she asked, as if he were about to tell her Alligator and the Hunter or How Poison Came into the World.

He looked ahead, vigilant, as he spoke. "It begins with me, visiting the mission every day to look for mail from you. With the Wakefields gone and Slips in Cider collecting mail—"

"Mary Ross, Atoka, not Slips in Cider! Must that poor woman live in the story of her early bad housekeeping her whole life?"

"She slipped again when I saw a letter addressed to us both, in care of the Reverend and his sister. A letter from the Oregon Territory. I was glad for her bad housekeeping then."

"Letter? From—?"

"Our Uncle Bridges."

Rachel felt all the breath push out of her lungs. "Atoka, is this possible?"

"More than possible. When Slips . . . when Mary Ross saw my face as I read his name and words, she gave the letter up. She braved the missionaries' wrath to do this."

"Why?"

"I did not seduce her. Her husband is my friend, and I have enough trouble with single women who are good house-keepers."

She smiled at her charming, wayward brother, glad that his charm was wedded to his honor. "Does our uncle live, then?"

"He wishes to know the same about us. If we live. If we want nothing to do with him, as our silence and the missionaries' letters have claimed."

"Our silence? How could we write when we never heard from him since he went away?"

He bowed his head between his arms as he spoke. "Do you remember that day in Nanih Waiya, little sister?"

"I do, though I clung to our mother's leg, not yet reaching her hip."

"For many months he'd asked Daddy and Mama to come before they took our lands and desecrated the mounds of our ancestors."

"To walk to the country not owned by Americans. To come to the big salt water," Rachel remembered.

"Yes! To this corner of the world, where the land is rich as our homeland, where the French, Spanish, Russian and English and Flathead and Nez Percé people trade and farm and marry each other in peace."

"You remember more than I do."

"You were only three. I was eight."

"But I remember our uncle's cabin porch, and wide smile," Rachel claimed.

"He has a porch now, Tadpole, and a big house and rich river bottom land in the Willamette Valley. He has a Nez Percé wife. They have no children but us, who have been so cruel to them."

"Cruel? But Atoka—"

"There were many letters! And maps. And books on the overland passage. All pressed with—what are they called? Provisionals—glued on, words saying that the postage was already paid, so the missionaries couldn't refuse their delivery. Someone kept them hidden away from our eyes, Rachel. Kept them from us for years, tied in corn silk cord by that woman you grieve for. The one who has shunned you."

"Why did Miss Wakefield do this?"

"To keep you tied to her, I think. When I broke up the missionary rooms, their chairs and stools and crockery ware, it was as if I could break up the world, I was so angry, until . . ."

"Until?" Rachel prompted, her heartbeats sounding in her ears.

"Until I felt you stroking my head, like on that night, that bad night on the trail—remember?"

"I remember. And what did I tell you, in your vision?"

"To stop this destruction of things. You told me that you were coming home, I was not alone. Rachel, you know this part of the story," he whispered.

She smiled, wishing she could touch him. She reached into her shirt and pulled out his hair token from its place pinned to her camisole. "Your destruction reached me on the great Atlantic. I cried and prattled in my confusion until my husband found your hair's blue bead, and wove it back into your mourning braid."

Atoka looked up at the circle of a gliding hawk before he continued. "The Christian Choctaw denounced me. Until I allowed them to see the letters, see what this woman and her brother have kept from us these years."

He leaned his head on his arm. Rachel wanted to hold him, comfort him, left to go through this trial without her. Almost without her, for they'd had each other through his braid, and her patient, hair-weaving husband. She tried to send Atoka the message of her soothing through the hawk.

"I have the letters here." Atoka reached into his pack, then dropped an oilcloth packet in her lap. "You must read them, Rachel. See if you think it was best to keep us from knowing the heart of this man, our uncle."

Rachel opened the oilcloth, then stroked the corn silk tie pinning the stack of correspondence. Miss Wakefield might have destroyed these links to their uncle. As it was, she must have thought the letters not worthy of a piece of her lace or ribbon or scrap of cloth. Rachel was glad she had chosen the corn silk. Her brother smiled, though it was a womanly act, her stroking. It didn't matter. No one was paying attention to them in a corner of the top deck of the *Carolina Mist*.

Atoka's voice softened. "I think the reverend did not always agree that this was a good path. Perhaps he kept his sister from burning all this. But you were his sister's prize, before you went across the water with our corn. You taught the young ones the way the Wakefields cannot, with love, and stories. That's the only way to hearts."

Her brother began answering questions her overwhelmed mind could not even form. "Once I'd read the letters, I sold Red Clay, the horse you think I gambled away. We traveled to New Orleans, the other horses and I, determined to wait, watching each ocean-faring ship for the one that brought you home. To capture you a little while, as I used to steal you away from the mission when we were children. I needed to tell you these things the way I saw them, to show you these letters. To seek your counsel on them, away from the missionaries. Your new husband has done that part for me, gotten you away from them. For that I will thank him, so he knows he has not married into a savage race.

"Enough," he decided, looking deeply into her eyes. "Sleep now, sister." His brow arched. "Your eyes are very heavy with burdens. You are sure your husband did not once turn to you during the night?"

"I'm sure!"

He held up his hands at her shout, showing his palms, an apology. "Rest," he urged again, gently amused this time, "we have a long journey ahead."

"To St. Louis."

"Yes. It will take three days. Do you think we can keep the horses healthy and your husband out of trouble for three days?"

"It is not work beyond us, brother."

"Good. Then, come spring, to Oregon."

He kissed her forehead the way he used to each night for the year of mourning after their sister's and parents' deaths. Even if he were beat for coming to her window at the orphanage, he came. And now he was going to welcome her husband into their family. How could she not walk to Oregon, if he asked her?

Rachel dreamed about the misting, rolling hills that she'd left in the east. Of her mother's ceremony, of saying good-bye to the oaks and elm. When she woke, she smelled the fine tooled leather of her brother's saddlebags under her head. And the birds' songs. It was almost dawn. The *Carolina Mist* was slowing beside another riverside landing. She stretched, realizing that Dare's black coat was serving as her blanket. Both it and Atoka sleeping beside her were wound in ceremony scent. Rachel slipped the coat over her shoulders and went to the rail. Below, she saw her husband with a fine wide-rimmed felt hat on his head. Its grosgrain ribbon band had faded to purple and danced along the rim as he helped black men load bales of cotton onto the dock. The strongest of the men had partnered with him. Rachel felt like weeping at the sight of them, her pale, scrawny husband and his opposite in coloring and strength, who'd taken pity on him, grateful for his help, but protective of his limited abilities.

She felt Atoka's presence beside her. He touched her back lightly as he took in what was capturing her attention.

"He has lived only as long as I have, your man."

"He told you that? He has only twenty-five years?"

"Yes. It's the look of death that carves him so deep. He lost a wife and children in his country. When were you going to tell me that?"

"Atoka—"

"I burned sage, but his grief for them lies like a stone in his heart. Will it make him cruel to you, this grief?"

"It has not. And I have been entirely myself with him," she added, giving her brother a sideward glance, "which you know can prove trying to some men."

He smiled. "This is good. A good beginning. And he can make children, if he has fathered these lost three already. If he can heal himself, he will make some for you. For our clan. Good choice, sister!"

She frowned. "You have few requirements."

"The rest I can read on your face. You like him. You have the beauty that comes with pride in your mate."

Rachel felt herself blushing. It was a pleasant, new sensation. She would never be able to hide from her brother. "My husband wears a new hat."

"Not so new. It used to belong to a French trapper, who bought it from a Hungarian miner. Its top is varnished. It's a good hat. The Frenchman said your husband can use it to wash, drink, or carry ore samples, besides protecting his tender skin from the cold and sun."

"He wears your gift with pride. He likes you, Atoka."

"He doesn't yet know our ways. That I have bought his children with that hat. And that he still needs to purchase you yet as befits your station as a peace chief among the People."

That day she and Atoka took turns reading the letters to her husband. When they finished, Dare Swimmer sat back and ran his thumbs along the rim of his wedding gift.

"Like letters from America they sound. A person in the village would get one, then we'd all gather to hear it read. Letters that spoke of impossible wages, strange and wondrous sights, and freedoms."

"Atoka wishes to go to this place Oregon in the spring," Rachel said quietly.

"To leave your homeland?"

"The Oklahoma Indian Territory is not our homeland," her brother explained. "It is a place the soldiers have put us. It is surrounded by the United States, who are warring with the Mexicans, and might some day be at war with each other over the blacks who are slaves. The Americans have wasted our people with war and disease since before their Revolution. We have gained nothing from it but our exile, where we have to make new peace with the Comanche and Kiowa, Caddo and Osage and Wichita—people who lived in that place before us."

Rachel touched her husband's arm. "My brother and the lighthorsemen police cannot even bring to justice the criminals who take their refuge in Indian Territory. They have made our new land their haven from the United States law."

Dare shook his head. "And after this long walk, will Oregon Territory be any different?" he asked.

Rachel remembered her uncle's letters, and her geography. "It is in the corner of the continent, against another water, not the Gulf of Mexico or the Atlantic, but the Pacific."

"Who owns it?"

Questions. This man was so full of questions. "It . . . it has been claimed by many nations."

His sharp eyes bore into her. "Who owns it, Rachel LeMoyne?"

"The British said they did. Along with the Americans, but—"

He let out a stream of his own language that made Atoka raise his eyebrows.

"But they do not settle there, husband! The endless people, the people from the United States go there, to make farms, as my uncle has. It will belong to this new country, the one not ruled by kings. Soon. That's what the council, no, the *congress* in Washington is deciding. It takes them a long time to decide anything, because there are so many states. They are like us in that, my father used to say, with many leaders, all needing to talk. Oregon. It is waiting in Oregon, Dare. A farm. In a cool land, like your own country."

"You invite me? You and your brother invite me on this journey?"

She looked to Atoka, who only narrowed his eyes a little before he nodded. "Yes. You will have the winter in St. Louis to think on it. Will you think on it?"

Dare watched the snakelike turns of the muddy Mississippi ahead before he answered. "I will, aye." The same words he'd used when Captain Lawes had asked if he'd have Rachel LeMoyne as his wife.

"Thank you."

He took them both into that hollow-eyed gaze. "It will be your time too. To decide. It may be you will not wish me along, after the winter."

"That I doubt." Rachel smiled. "If you'll eat. I would like to see your true form."

"You're a brazen thing, wife," he teased. His face's shadows could not hide the creases of mirth. Even Atoka smiled.

"Folks?"

The roustabout who'd been working with Dare stood before them.

"You and yours look like you could use some nourishments," he offered a linen-wrapped bundle quietly.

That night her men slept sitting up against their belongings, with Rachel between them. She must have followed her shipboard habit of nuzzling under the crook of Dare's arm, for when the long, cold shadows fell over them, she heard her husband's heartbeat accelerate.

"Mr. Swimmer?"

Rachel instinctively wrapped her arms around his middle and held tight. Too tight, making him cough before he gave out a small, confused laugh. "Easy, Tadpole." She released him, letting her fingers glide over his ribs. Atoka's hand anchored at her shoulder.

Rachel stared hard at the men, recognizing High Hat and his mean-looking walking stick. The smaller man in the blue coat and whiskers looked friendlier. But the remaining two blue coats were out of sorts. She recognized the three as the captain and two pilots. Their steamboat was quiet and stock-still, unlike the night before, when it chugged along, slow and sure. The captain spoke first.

"Mr. Swimmer, we have run aground on a sandbar, and our rudder has become deranged, and rendered unserviceable."

High Hat interceded now. "I took the liberty of making your astonishing claim of engineering ability known to Captain Harris and the ship's pilots, Mr. Swimmer. They would like to hire a man of such prodigious talents to repair it."

Rachel didn't realize she had hold of Dare's shirt until he tried to rise. He laughed again, more easily this time. "Let go of me, you little pest!" he chided in that voice without music, one that went with his false face.

"I can swim," Rachel offered, thinking only that he could not. "I can help, too!"

The captain gave her a smile for a child. "Your indulgent brother is lucky to have such a willing apprentice." One of the pilots crossed his arms in front of his chest, but the other said, "The rudder is much lighter in the water, sir."

"And I swim too," Atoka claimed, rising. "Let's go."

The water was cold, dark, and muddy. Rachel was glad to have Atoka's help with untangling the roots from the ship's rudder. Too glad even to argue that he was the horseman, she the better swimmer. She was glad for the clouds before the moon too, casting her drenched form and corset stays in shadows as she climbed back aboard the vessel. Dare growled low, dropping his coat over her shoulders.

"All right," he told them both sternly, "my work starts now. Go."

Atoka glared at him. Rachel took her brother's arm. "I'm cold," she said.

The captain smiled. You two might find some warmth around the fire in the galley while your master helps us here, how would that be?"

Rachel squeezed her brother's arm. "That'd be good, wouldn't it, Atoka?"

He grunted, but she would not let go of him as she tried to talk as a servant might. "Could I fetch a little something for Mr. Dare, sir? Keep his strength up? He's been poorly for a time now."

"Of course, little one."

Suddenly, without warning, the captain pulled off her soaked cap. Her braids descended. He stepped back, startled. He blinked twice, then laughed, directing his remarks to Atoka. "Good this wee one keeps those braids inside that cap. You can look after yourself and your wild mane, boy, but your brother here is as pretty as a girl. A flat boatman would love to pin those braids to a tree trunk, good targets for his knife throwing."

Rachel looked to Atoka.

The man with the high hat laughed at her shock. "How old are you, boy?"

"Seventeen, sir," Rachel tried, in the deepest voice she could muster.

He frowned. "Nonsense. Didn't the missionaries drum that heathen lying out of you? No trace of a beard. Maybe fourteen. Your little brother's memory is faulty, isn't it?" he asked Atoka.

"Yes, sir," he bit out, his arms tense. Her brother had little of Dare's cunning.

Rachel began to shiver.

"Stevenson, give me your cap," the Captain demanded suddenly.

"But, Captain—"

"This boy has done us a service, and you have two others. Give it here."

He took the black wool watch cap from the pilot's hand and placed it on Rachel's head, tucking her braids in its confines. "There. Warmer?"

"Yes, sir. Thank you."

"Now, you little scoundrel," his tone became stern. "The truth for this kind gentleman. How far was your memory off?"

Rachel raised her eyes to High Hat's eyes. "Three years, sir."

"There. Just as I said, eh? Good boy. You people can tell the truth when you want to!"

The captain took her shoulder. "Now. Have your master charm a few hairpins from the ladies downstairs from your quarters if you want to keep wild locks like your brother's. They work wonders, hairpins."

Rachel shot Dare a quick glance, and, despite their peculiar predicament, enjoyed the roll of his eyes.

Dare rifled though the toolbox, wishing the man Chambers would leave him to his work as the captain and pilots had. What did Chambers want with him? Rich men always wanted something. Or to make a joke. Perhaps that's all Dare was to him. A source of amusement. That made his insides gnaw a little softer.

"You are too good to them both, you know."

"Sir?"

"The little one is devoted to you. But that blue-eyed devil, I'd watch your back around him, son."

"Why is that, sir?" Dare asked, not looking up from his task.

"There have been terrible murders, even among blood-tied servants and their masters."

"I see."

"No, I don't believe you do. Dare, were you very pampered before being kicked out of the nest?"

What did the man take him for? "Is it that obvious, sir?" he tried to question it out of him.

"It is, quite!" Chambers trumpeted, pleased with himself. "Now, whatever you've done, is there no possibility to go home and ask your family's forgiveness?"

"Why would I want to do that, sir?"

"Why?" He laughed. "Why, indeed! When you're of such comfortable means to sleep among niggers on the top deck alongside your own red servants? Dare, I'm trying to befriend you. Is it a gambling debt that's put you so out of favor with your family? A duel? A woman? Are those the effects of a beating by one of these riverboat thugs on your face? Who have you angered? Might I intercede in some way? Confound it, man!"

Chambers had taken him for gentry. Anglo gentry, maybe. Transplanted to America. Was that it?

"I'm trying to help, and you're being as slippery as a damned Celt!" Chambers exploded now.

Dare cocked his head, grinned. "Do you think so, sir?"

Albert Chambers hid his twitching mouth by sighing hard. His thick silver hair had some of the moon's light in it. "All right then. I'll speak no more of your family troubles. But tell me. Where are you going, with your Choctaw and those splendid horses, all of which are eating better than you are?"

"St. Louis, sir."

"And what are you after, son?"

He went on with his work, resorting to the truth now, the man had confused him so. "A job. Usefulness is what I'm after, sir. I appreciate your help in getting my brothers and myself this position."

"Can the *Carolina Mist* be running again by morning?"

"That will depend on this sandbar and the river, Mr. Chambers. But the rudder is fixed."

"It . . . it is?"

"Yes, sir. So I believe my kin need to be called from their repast for another dunking. This time I will hold Tad's new hat for him."

"As you wish. But then you will leave those two with their Indian gruel and come with me, for a decent meal. And we'll talk about your future in St. Louis."

*   *   *

When Dare returned from his time below with High Hat, Atoka left the ship's upper tier to check on his horses. Rachel heard jangling music and rough amusements on the below decks. She was glad for Atoka's time with his horses, for the disgruntled man who'd slumped beside her was challenge enough.

"Our fares are forgiven, for services rendered. I've got your brother's money returned to me."

"That's wonderful, Dare."

"And I accepted a job in this city, St. Louis."

"A job?"

"Aye. At a newspaper Mr. Chambers owns."

"I—I don't like that man," she whispered.

"Neither do I. Chambers would hate me if he knew who I am. But these damned clothes have made me into a relative of the damned Englishman who first they were made for, it seems. So I have a job."

"It does not honor you to speak of our friend Mr. Combs in that way," she reprimanded him. "He was haunted by your country's troubles. He was doing the best he could to have them brought to light."

His look softened. "I forgot that you knew him too. He . . . he was better than most of them, I'll grant you that. And I should watch my casual blasphemies around my sensitive, missionary-raised little brother. I apologize."

She grunted.

He reached into his coat's deep inside pocket, handing her a bundle smelling of savory smoked ham and rich cheeses, different from the hard tack crackers the roustabout had procured for them. Dare reached into the other side of his coat. Were there pockets everywhere in Mr. Comb's fine clothes? A fresh apple, and some dried peaches appeared in her husband's hands from his magic pockets.

"Thank you."

He grunted. "For you, little brother."

"There's plenty, Dare. Won't you—"

"No. I ate too much, down below with that d— that . . . man Chambers. It has fogged my mind into considering your two thousand mile walk back into the hands of the British."

Rachel approached closer, as their corner of deck was empty. "You do not look over full. Only tired."

"The colors, the gilt and scarlet, the chandeliers," he groused. "So overblown, Rachel. Damned floating palace is what it is below, I'm thinking. Distracting the passengers from the fact that they can all be blown to kingdom come at any moment from those great bloody boilers, so clogged with mud that I shamed the engineer into cleaning them out."

"That was most good of you, Dare."

His hand skimmed her newly acquired watch cap. "Not nearly so good as your grace in the currents of this endless changing river, little brother."

She lent him more of her warmth as she felt his weary fingers skim her cheek. "Ach, Rachel," he breathed. "Down there, in the great dancing room—even the patterns of the ladies' dresses make me dizzy."

"Your eyes seem to pain you, sometimes," she ventured quietly.

He sighed. "No. It's not pain. I don't see into the distance as well as I once did."

Rachel touched his arm. He nodded curtly. It was the first time he'd described this thing that the hunger had done to his eyes, she surmised, and she was grateful for his trust.

"Oh, here. The ladies did redeem themselves for causing my distress with their garish finery." He fished into his vest pocket for a thin paper containing hairpins.

Rachel smiled. "You weren't distracted by their finery enough to forget to charm them out of these."

"To allow my beautiful brother to keep his hair, I'd do anything. Now pin them up, like a good girl."

"Boy," she corrected. Had he really called her beautiful?

"God in heaven, let's get off the waters. My head might then stop spinning with the different looks of you, wife, brother, woman, child, fairy spirit of *Tír na nóg* come to take me into the west."

She laughed as she glided the pins in place. But she did not replace the cap, because he was watching her. In a different way. Unguarded. Hungry, but not for food. He smelled of something else, under the cigar smoke and rich foods. Drink. Strong drink. He took her wrist and brought her hand against his cheek. It was stubbled with a beard, but he would shave in the morning. White men needed to do that every morning, to keep their faces smooth. But most of the ones Rachel had known did not. This one did. Every morning of their Atlantic crossing. Here, too, as crude as their conditions were, he'd borrowed Atoka's Bowie knife for his morning shave. Was it for her, she wondered as he kissed her palm. He was kissing her. Without being asleep and dreaming of his wife. The strong drink allowed his eyes to let go of a little of their sorrow. But she didn't think he was drunk. She knew what drunk men looked like, she'd seen too many of her own people like that. This man still knew who he was. And who she was. His wife, and not yet his wife.

"Rachel?" he called softly, sounding dense, her clever husband. Or young, maybe. Younger than he looked, so ravaged by his trials. His long fingers found, circled her waist. "Rachel LeMoyne. Might I taste your mouth?"

"I thought you were overfull?" she teased.

"Not of you. Please. I—I will not do more, I promise."

"Well," she said in her teacher voice, "all right, then."

His brows disappeared in his forelock of dark hair, hair that would someday have more substance. "Are you laughing at me, now?"

"Yes. Do I offend you in this?"

"No. Oh, no. I . . . used to laugh more, Rachel."

"I know. I can see the echoes."

"Can you?"

"Aye," she whispered, bowing her head, ashamed that she wanted them gone, those echoes, that she wanted all his dead away. He lifted her chin gently.

"Ach, the wonder of you," he breathed out before he kissed her mouth.

She did not taste the rich food he'd eaten, or the strong drink. She tasted the last of the season's wild berries Atoka had gathered on the shore that afternoon. He'd given them to Dare and to her, without eating any himself. Was there something magic in the berries, she wondered now. A charm? She wove her legs lightly across her husband's thighs, like when they slept. Was it the berries that made his heart race, that made the hardness between his legs that teased at the broad cloth of her trousers? She wished them gone from her legs. She wished this strange Irish man inside her. She soon lost herself in the texture of his tongue and the soft tingling at her breasts that their tastes of each other evoked. This is what led to making children. No wonder the taboos, the times men and women must dwell apart. There would come too many children. This was so pleasant. She could stay here forever, with his arms about her in a better way, even, than when they were sleeping.

"We should stop," he said, but did not. "If someone should see. Tad. Little brother . . . we should stop."

"Yes," she agreed, but pressed her hand inside his rich man's vest to feel the bellows of his ragged breathing.

"Rachel, I drank a glass of American whiskey. And I am not nearly so noble as I sound."

There. Longer sentences. They put space between them. Allowed him to tuck her head under his heart and breathe more easily. He held her close, his fear of doing this thing—making her a more true wife in his own religion, gone. But his tenderness remained, as a comfort.

"Have you had a man before?" he asked her gently.

She shook her head. "I have not even kissed one. Like that. Because I was raised by missionaries. To be a teacher, one who lives for many children, and has none of her own. How is it in your country?"

"Well. We marry young."

"How young were you?"

"Seventeen. My wife was not yet sixteen." He took her arms

suddenly, and made her face him. "Rachel. You are not really the fourteen years they think you?"

"Oh, no. Though I did not lie when they pressed me for the truth. I *was* lying by three years. I'm twenty."

"Oh." He held her again there, under his heart. "That's good. That's fine, my shape shifter."

"Is it?" she asked quietly. "It does not displease you that I have lived so long and not been kissed?"

He smiled. "No. I am honored. Rachel, you have not chosen a man of the world. I had no woman before—before my wife, and I was true to her."

"You are still," she sought to console the deep mourning that had crept into his voice.

"I—Rachel . . ."

He looked as if he might bolt, like Fears Thunder, the horse even Atoka could not ride in a storm. Rachel took his hand, felt the bones spread, panicked, beneath his pale white skin.

"You are safe with me, Darragh Ronan," she urged his grief forth.

"I— I need to go away from here."

"No. You need this place, this safe place I offer you," she insisted, barely having the strength to hold him, as he covered his mouth with the back of that swollen-with-work, blue-veined hand. It could only muffle the sound as his thin shoulders shook and his tortured weeping began. Rachel waited, stroking his hair, rocking them both.

"I'm sorry," he finally whispered. "It's the drink, you see . . ."

"No. I do not see it that way at all. Do not be sorry, Darragh Ronan," she spoke his old, forbidden name again. "This is a thing for me to know. That you can love so well. You are a tender man who brings joy and honor to me." She rocked again, singing softly in Choctaw, a night song. One that Atoka sang, and, before him, their mother. Her husband's shudders finally stilled with the last notes. The song was a good thing, a holy thing, Rachel decided, for it even eased her own heart and the bitterness that dwelt there, ashamed.

* * *

In the morning Rachel woke to another wondrous sight of the ever-changing Mississippi riverbank—enormous sycamores. She stood, sensing their welcome, and wished she could climb their branches. Someone shoved her shoulder.

"You're looking at the wrong side, boy!" one of the flat boatmen chided, "Come with me to see the City of the French!"

"Get away from him," Atoka warned, fingering his knife's scabbard. The man backed up. "Just bein' sociable, chief," he said, and moved on.

Her brother glared at her. "It will be worse when you're back in skirts," he groused. "Where is your husband?"

"I don't know."

"Below. With his rich friends, I think."

"Below, looking after your horses, maybe. Atoka, he has already worked back our fares."

"All three of us did that. You and I in the cold water. But these backwards people paid him. He gave me the money. He should have given it to you."

"He doesn't yet know our ways—"

"He was throwing my gift of passage back at me!"

"Atoka, no. That is not the way of it. He is a stranger. Forgive him. Give me the money now, and I will explain—"

"I lost it. At the gaming." He looked down at the deck's planks. "It is not important. It was cursed already."

"It was nothing of the sort!" she fired back at him. "Do not blame your weakness on my husband's ignorance! You shame me!"

"I have the rest of my horse's purchase price. I was angry, and used only that money the captain gave him."

Rachel returned only stony silence until she caught sight of Dare below. "Well. It is done. Oh, Atoka." She sighed. "Give my husband a chance. Your horses are. Look."

She nodded down where Dare was combing the knots from Raven Mocker's mane and soothing the horse's wild eyes with the cadence of his voice. The silk-hatted gentleman, Mr. Chambers, her husband's new boss, greeted him with a rough hand-shake.

"You look," Atoka said at her ear.

Chambers pointed across the ship's rail. He swept his greedy finger rudely, as if St. Louis belonged to him. Her husband only showed his false face to this man, couldn't Atoka see that?

St. Louis rose out of the morning river mists. The city rivaled New Orleans in its structures' diversity of form, beyond its foreground dominated by limestone warehouses. So large a place, Rachel thought, so many roofs.

People were already on the streets, vendors hawking all manner of wares, men as well dressed as Dare, hurrying. Rachel tried to soothe herself with the intermingling green of trees among the structures and, far in the distance, a fine forest of shrub oaks.

None of them had ever lived in a city. Could they do it? Rachel was haunted by the dull eyes of Choctaw beggars wandering New Orleans streets reduced to ones and twos. Is that what city life always did to her people? She looked at Atoka's flowing hair, at her child's grip on the sleeve of his red shirt.

"We'll be all right in this place. We're a family," she whispered.

He looked down, touched her cheek with the back of three fingers, even though some of the flat boatmen were watching. *"Oke,"* he agreed.

St. Louis, Missouri

1847–48

ten

Dare put the folded bills of currency into Rachel's one hand, a copy of the *St. Louis Dispatch* in the other. "You're looking at a mightily employed husband this payday, Mrs. Swimmer, with a dollar bonus for distribution advice," he said, kissing her cheek in front of their landlady, Mrs. Casey, who snorted before directing him to the place beside his wife on the parson's bench.

Rachel counted the money quickly, to distract herself from the hot blush. Fourteen dollars! The wonder of it. In her mind she added it to her modest tutoring and fine-sewing fees of the week. With the unexpected bounty she'd buy ammunition for Dare's fine cap-loading rifle, and some for his percussion revolver, the one whose five chambers lined up to shoot five balls in succession.

Atoka scoffed at both weapons, wanting only his Bowie knife and musket. But they were machines, the new firearms her husband wanted. He would make them work. Could their family's budget manage the last of the picket ropes they'd need to stake the horses at night for grazing too? It could, Rachel decided.

"Growing rich are you now? Time to raise the rent, then?" Mrs. Casey asked, looking up from her needlework.

Dare frowned at the ample woman whose dark eyes' kindness relieved the sternness around her mouth. "You'll never see heaven if you'll be cheating your own people out of their night's rest under your roof, woman," he warned her.

"My own people are you, Dare Swimmer? That's not what I hear. It's a bold mysterious Anglo lad that's taken jobs at the *Dispatch* and cheap boarding on this side of town."

He frowned deeply, calling up the ghost of that sickly, courting-death skeleton he had been when they'd first arrived at Mrs. Casey's doorstep. "What care I the things people say of me in a city that posts 'No Irish Need Apply' signs, woman? Do you not know I've become an American by way of my gracious wife, whose people have been on this soil longer than the Celts have been in Ireland?"

He flaunted that sly, toothsome smile suddenly, the one he reserved for their landlady. Mrs. Casey's stitches went erratic. "It's not your wife I'm arguing with, you silver-tongued schemer."

"I should think not, when she makes scholars out of your urchins with her fine books, and scrubs your linens, besides schooling you in her own fine needlework!"

Rachel wished their landlady would at least put her sewing away before she began her nightly sparring with Dare. She'd have to redo most of the stitches. Mrs. Casey snorted. Her hands finally rested across the lap of her handsome blue brocade dress before she spoke again. "I'm only telling you it's a dangerous thing you do, with your fine ear and mimicking voice, child."

Dare followed his countrywoman's worried glance to Rachel before he laughed. "Haven't we all learned to be—what is it in your stories, Rachel? The ones about the rabbits who wind their way around trouble instead of meeting it head-on?"

"Tricksters?" Rachel asked, remembering his lean form in the doorway quietly eating a steaming potato—he and the landlady called them *praties*—as she tutored the Casey children with the schoolbooks Atoka had brought her from the mission.

"Aye, tricksters!" Dare proclaimed. "I tell no lies, do I? And don't I know my inferior place, then? Who would I be to be telling my employer that I am any different than that man he has do deftly created in his head?"

Mrs. Casey's dark eyes ignited. "And I tell you the fine points of it will not matter when your master finds out to whom he's been doling out his generous wages. It's a dangerous dance you're doing, Dare Swimmer. And you with a family."

Dare's voice turned cold. "You got out of Ireland before the Hunger, *bantiarna*. You know nothing of my family. And you don't know what danger is."

"*Dosaire!*" she shot back. "Bite your tongue before your lady. You think you are only one with troubles? I watched my good man die after seven years standing in water to his knees building the canals of this country."

Dare's voice changed, its pitch respectful. "I seek to be as useful to this woman, Mrs. Casey, without leaving her the burdens that come with early funeral expenses."

Their landlady shook her head. "Aye, well. Ask your wife about her own long walk to Oklahoma when you're thinking yourself so superior in your suffering."

Her words left his eloquent tongue silent. He stared at Rachel. "Ladies, I ask your pardon," he finally whispered, bowing.

"Ach," the older woman proclaimed, "where would the three of you babes in the wood be without me looking after you?" She snatched the money from Rachel's hand and held each bill up to the light of the room's window. "All good. And now that the war with Mexico is done, the currency of the states triumphs too— it's as good as reales or Louis d'Or. Don't let any scurrilous merchant tell you different."

"Aye then, *bantiarna*."

"And you can leave off with your fancy lady naming me, as if you were Finn mac Cumhail himself!"

Dare grinned, his humor again flowering under their landlady's badgering. He liked such women. Perhaps he liked her a little, then, Rachel thought, for wasn't that what Atoka called her, a badgering woman? He sometimes said that was why few Choctaw men had approached him about courting her. She thought it had more to do with the missionaries' plans and his own fierce protectiveness. She'd had neither the wit to badger nor her brother beside her when she'd decided to marry this man. Had she made a mistake?

It did not seem a mistake today. It was a wonder to watch Dare's returning health. A wonder how the work that blackened his hands as a printer's devil on the *St. Louis Dispatch* had brought the life back to his step. That and their landlady's cooking. Rachel was determined to learn all of Mrs. Casey's secrets before they started on the trail, including how to make the Irishwoman's best dishes over an open fire or in a dug pit oven. Dare ate everything Mrs. Casey set before him—from roots to beans to meat boiled to what seemed tastelessness to Rachel and Atoka. Her Irish husband's thin-to-starving frame was growing strong as it filled out. Even his hair had gained substance, and now grew coal-black curls spiraling out, partless from his crown. Their landlady had pressed Dare down into one of her children's stools long enough to show Rachel how to cut his strange hair so that it tumbled gracefully over the collar of Mr. Combs's fine coat. "The height of fashion," Mrs. Casey had pronounced him. He'd allowed it, grumbling, until Rachel's fingers sifted through the soft texture, finding his scalp, that sacred part of him. He'd closed his eyes then and said, "You have a lovely touch, Rachel," honoring the moment.

Dare could fix the cranky machine that churned out the *Dispatch* as well as set its type. "It's what you did in Ireland," Rachel had guessed when he came home that first day.

"It's much less than I did in Ireland, so don't be making too much of it," he'd groused, but he could not dissemble his pride. But with it came a warning. "Rachel. Don't mention Ireland."

Rachel didn't understand the wars between Ireland and England, not the way Dare and their landlady did. They could spar with each other for hours over battles and heroes of those wars.

Would their talk start again, when there was only a little time for him to rest before he needed to be on guard as night watchman for the *Dispatch*?

Their landlady rose from her chair. "I can see I'll get no more sense into you or fine-sewing lessons from your lady. Upstairs now. Take your rest. I'll send up a tea, then be about starching the sheets. Rachel, you can commence the ironing in an hour," she glanced at Dare, "or so."

Dare stood and bowed formally even as he delivered his parting shot. "The rest of the day off would be better still, my wife is going cross-eyed with making the undergarments of the ladies of St. Louis properly steamed and laced."

"I can find some hauling work for you as well, Connacht," Mrs. Casey warned, "if a tea and short nap does not suit you between your well-paid duties." She'd known the province of Dare's birth since he'd opened his mouth on her doorstep, Rachel remembered. Now she teased him with the name before her skirts wafted by him in the doorway.

Dare approached the hearth fire, his movement reminding Rachel of a cat in a tree. Cold, he'd been cold, she realized, between his still being underweight and the coat that was handsome, but not warm enough for this St. Louis winter. Still, he'd made no complaint all the time two women sat closest to the fire. She should have given him her place, even if it was not the American way of things. His clothing warmed, gifting her with its radiant heat. Was his skin warm, there underneath it, Rachel wondered.

"Should we be about giving her what she wants before she's about the tea?" Dare asked her softly, in that teasing, intimate voice, the one that seldom failed to leave her breathless.

"What she wants?"

"A kiss between us, Mrs. Swimmer."

"Dare, Mrs. Casey is—"

"Still about," he contended. "And a busybody. Never met a rooms-letter who wasn't."

Was she truly watching? From where? How did he know it? Rachel had no sense of the woman, but perhaps he was better at tracking his own kind. She bowed her head. He approached closer, close enough for her to smell printer's ink. "You've already kissed me," she reminded him, "when you came in."

"A fonder one she wants, I'm thinking."

"*She* wants?"

"Oh, aye, and she's a desperate woman."

There was a creak at the swinging door. He was right, her clever husband. Their landlady was watching them. The pressroom's iron joined his ink scent. Did he also know her heart had been racing since he'd stepped into the room? She raised her head. Her lips parted at the look in his eyes. Summer-sky eyes, just before a shower, blue gray, full of the promise of rain. How had his eyes found their way to summer already?

"Now, will you kiss me, or be plaguing me with questions in this brief time we have, Rachel LeMoyne?"

"It's you, the king of—"

Of the questions, she wanted to finish. But his mouth was over hers and he stole what she had not yet granted him. She liked it, the stealing, though it robbed her breath and her wits, filling her instead with him. She wanted to ask him what she could do to make him feel the way she was feeling, here, in their landlady's parlor, at the close of the day. Like she could move the mountains between themselves and Oregon. But she didn't know the words to ask him these things.

"There," he proclaimed gruffly, taking her hand but keeping his distance when all Rachel wanted to do was melt into him. "That should keep the old busybody. Now come upstairs and the shepherd will see to your poor hands."

"The shepherd?"

He led their way up the narrow stairs. "Yes. The one who delivers his poetry to the doorstep of the *Dispatch*. He gave me this." He held the door open to the small attic room. She'd had to get used to him doing that, too. It was so different than how Atoka barreled past doors, expecting her to close them behind him. She liked her husband's way better.

"Sit." When she hesitated he added, "if you please," as if she'd chastised him for a direct command. Is that what his other wife would have done? Was he hearing his Bevin's voice in Rachel's silences? Once she took her place on the bed, Dare placed a small tin in her palm. "He said it would help your hands."

"The shepherd."

"Aye, the shepherd."

Rachel looked down at the tin. She couldn't imagine him telling the shepherd poet about her hands.

"Thank you. This is a fine gift."

"Twice a day. Will you do that?"

She nodded. He watched her, only removing his coat once she'd opened the tin and began smearing the substance onto her knuckles. He sat across from her in the room's only chair and began pulling off his boots.

"Good," he approved. "Your brother will not use the slippery elm I gave him for his cuts and bruises."

"He says the work will toughen him."

Dare looked up from pulling off the second boot. "Oh? Beyond the leather he is now?"

She stood, retrieved and folded his coat over her arm. "Dare. Your earnings. You must not give any to my brother."

"Why not?"

"Because his work is slowing down with the weather coming on so cold. And he sometimes gambles in winter. He is already so displeased by living in a city. I do not make excuses for him. I only wish you to understand. If we're to jump off for Oregon after the last of the snows, you must not let him have any part of your earnings."

"And are my earnings safe with you?"

"Yes. I have never given in to him. Well, not more than a few pennies."

She saw a smile play around the corner of his mouth. "Are you as hard a woman as that, wife?"

"I don't think it is hardness. I love my brother. But this is a weakness that will keep us all from that place where he dreams. He will not survive here more than a season, Dare. I know him well enough to know that."

"You are not a natural city dweller either, for all that you don't complain."

Rachel bowed her head. "There is truth in what you say," she admitted. Dare, armed with his Irish magic was getting as difficult to evade as Atoka.

The magic of his hands' knowledge, of his chameleon tongue could grant him a bigger prize, Rachel knew. Her clever husband would now grow rich at his trade, if he continued to hide this thing, his Irishness. It was easier for white people to shed their skins like snakes and become another. Rachel did not envy him his ability.

When his mourning time was over, would Dare Swimmer want a new wife, Rachel wondered. One who wasn't what some around their streets said the handsome Englishman was saddled with, a "savage," or "breed" or sometimes "dark gypsy" or "mulatto." People aboard the *Carolina Mist* were kinder when they thought her his bastard little brother.

Rachel was now vastly outnumbered by these people who judged her on sight. And she had no other kin, no clan, no nation, because of this man, and his starving country. The loneliness of it pierced her heart. A shiver of fear rose up her spine.

Dare noticed. "Rachel," he called her out of her thoughts. "Are you well?"

"Oh, aye."

He smiled. " 'Aye,' is it? And shall I be saying *oke* like a Choctaw, my queen? Is that the way into all the things you do not speak?"

He wanted to spar, to tease her. Perhaps to kiss her, after? She couldn't meet his eyes. "Dare?"

"Hmm?" he answered, pulling open his collar. He was not a hairy man, like most of the white people who traded among the Choctaw. They had hair spilling from their ears and necks and chests. She was afraid of those men, when a child. But her husband was smooth, what she could see of him lately, in his new form.

"Come," he urged gently now. "What troubles you, Rachel?"

She colored in embarrassment, but it was not as easy to see, not like when his light skin betrayed him. "What of you, Dare?" she finally whispered.

"Me?"

"Are you content here in this city, with your job and new riches? Will you stay here, come spring?"

He knelt beside the bed and took her hand. "Rachel, the money I earn is not mine. I'm working out my debt to you, to Atoka. I know I'm not what you're wanting, little one. Or what Atoka wants for you. But we have some things in common, the three of us. We're all stubborn farmers, looking for some land, some bit of green to call our own."

"This . . . this pleases me."

"Oh? Enough to stand my company on a walk to Oregon? *Oke?*" he teased, asking her in the Choctaw way, if this was so.

"Aye."

Atoka bounded into the room. "What are you two agreeing to now?" He eyed the *Dispatch*, lying on the table, with contempt. "Not anything proclaimed in that waste sheet?"

Rachel sighed, recognizing the start of a pattern of argument between her brother and her husband. "Dare's work will help send us to Uncle Bridges, Atoka," she insisted.

"While it spreads its poison ever eastward!"

"What are you saying?"

"Read for yourself! It says Americans should 'scalp every red man in the universe, for they are too bad to be endured!' "

Rachel knew the newspaper liked a colorful phrase, but she did not recall anything so harsh about Indian people printed in it before. Something must have happened. She felt a tightening around her heart.

"What are you talking about?" Dare demanded.

"Your newspaper, reporting on the Whitmans."

"The what?"

"Not what, who. You work there!"

"But my reading waits until I'm watching over the place at night."

"And after you charm your latest schemes into my sister."

Her husband's face took on a look it acquired when he was running out of patience with her brother. His voice was icy calm. "Of what schemes would you be speaking?"

"Let's start with her buying you a revolver with five shots in it, while I must settle for a musket."

"Settle? You wanted a musket. I only asked—"

"Asked? You with your white man's pay? What are we to say about what you ask for, being the two of us are only lazy Indians, both doing bone-weary work for only half your earnings."

"And I suppose I have brought those circumstances about as well?"

"You don't protest them in your fancy newspaper."

"I don't write for my fancy newspaper! Am I going to be hanged for fixing machinery here in America, too?"

"No, but you'll watch Indians hanged, maybe."

"Oh, for the love of—"

"Of what? Of who? The whores your boss sends your way as extra payment? The shanty girls who call you from dockside after my sister warms your bed?"

eleven

Rachel stood between her husband and her brother. "Stop it!" She took a breath through her nostrils before she spoke again. "Now, sit. Both of you."

Each obeyed, though they sulked and snorted like chained dogs, so that she took a firm hold on their shoulders. "Now," she said, "Atoka, why are you home before dusk?"

"I was let go." He looked at Dare. "How is it said? Relieved of my duties. Fired."

Rachel eased her grip on the red shirt's material. "Why?" she whispered.

"Ask your husband."

Dare looked baffled. She turned to her brother again. "I ask you."

"I am sent away from the horses because I am a menace, now that some of your Presbyterian missionaries are dead."

"Who is dead?"

"Whitmans. Missionaries. Killed by some people in Oregon Territory."

"Some people. You mean Indian people?"

"Yes."

"Jesus, Mary, and Joseph," Dare whispered, picking up the paper.

"For a reason they were killed," her brother contended. "There must have been a reason. Go on, read. But you won't learn the why of it there." He looked at Rachel. "All you will learn from the printed words in his newspaper is hatred for all of us. It does not matter that the Cayuse are as foreign to the Choctaw people as a Russian or Englishman is. This thing your newspaper calls a massacre has cost me my place taming the horses and mules. They cannot trust me now, the drivers say. If my kind can kill God's people, maybe I can cast spells on horses, or scalp them all."

"Someone else will give you work," Dare said quietly.

"Oh? I am not as milk-faced as an Englishman. It is not so easy for me to remake myself into my enemy. Not so easy as it is for you."

"Do you think I'm enjoying myself?"

"I think you're a coward."

Rachel watched Dare's arms tense with his desire to fight her brother. She would not have the strength to hold them from each other. "Enough!" she shouted, praying that her husband's eyes would find her soul. Did they? Is that why he took two stiff steps backward, picked up his coat and boots, and left the room? Or was he disgusted with her? She heard his footsteps on their landlady's stairs. She heard the front door close behind him.

Atoka was already regretting his words, she could see that. But she was out of patience with her brother. "Get out," she whispered.

He did not argue. His footfalls followed her husband's.

Rachel sat on the bed in the echoes of anger. As she read the *St. Louis Dispatch's* account of what was called the "Missionary Massacre" tears came. For what was said, for the way it was said, for the lives lost on both sides. For all people who stumbled in their understanding of each other.

If such things could happen there, in Uncle Bridges's blessed Oregon, and here, in her own small family, what was the hope for this new nation, America?

And what of these other things her brother's angry impetuous tongue had claimed? Is that why her husband's shirt sometimes smelled like the perfume of exotic women? Is that why he once stumbled into their bed just before the birds began their morning songs, holding her too tightly, sighing hard into her hair? Did he have other women? Is that why he hadn't yet made her his true wife?

Rachel's weeping became awkward and tumbling. It was the way she used to cry as a child, before the great emptiness of her parents' and Sleeps Sound's deaths left her stunned, without tears. It was the weeping of that child, that carefree child sheltered by love all around her. Why had she returned? Rachel saw her, standing by the Arkansas River in her mourning dress. She held out her hand, welcomed the Rachel LeMoyne who lived in the city of St. Louis with her brother and her husband who was not her husband. The little girl smiled though the glistening tears. Why was she smiling, Rachel wondered. Smiling, even as she mourned. Was it because this rupture, the one between her brother and Dare, might mend? Might she not be forced to choose between these two men she loved best in the world? Yes, she liked that. So did the younger Rachel, who began to fade from her memory, still smiling.

This was something to rejoice in. She was not alone. Her family had grown again. The mourning Irishman had joined her brother next to her heart. Rachel ached with need for the children that might come from the love she bore her husband, whose fine new form women loved on sight, as Atoka said. She had seen that herself, when she walked the streets on his arm. But he was still guarded from them and from her by his ghosts. Rachel was almost sure of that.

They were both proud men, her brother and husband. And a

little foolish, hurling their insults, standing on their high and mighty principles. But what men weren't foolish? She only had to help them love one another. A difficult thing, she admitted, but not an impossible one. Not for her. Not for them. They all had their courage to lead them.

The first step would be to find them. She wiped these new tears away as she had the ones of her childhood, with the back of her hands.

Back to work, Dare decided, after his feet had pounded around the streets of St. Louis, avoiding the docks and the shanty girls calling down to the fine English gentleman he wasn't. Atoka had him pegged correctly there. He had enjoyed their calls and sighs, like a callow idiot. Why? Because Atoka's little nunlike sister was pulling him toward loving a woman again? And he was afraid of that, much more afraid of that than a walk to Oregon. He'd rather flirt with women he cared nothing for than make an honest woman of the one who'd given everything to him.

There were no lack of priests in this city. Though French, they were Catholic. It was he who had yet to bring one, make them holy in matrimony.

Instead he slept as another brother beside her, carefully avoiding even a shot of whiskey after work, for fear it would throw his control over as he breathed her wildwood scent, watched the moonlight dance along her bare arms and loose sleeping braids. And he teased and courted her, as awkward as he was about it. Because they were paper-wed at least, and had had such a wretched start together. Because she was innocent as well as formidable. Because she'd feel free to toss him out if he displeased her, that was her way. It was not his way. For him marriage was a death pact.

And he wanted no more to do with death, as strong as its pull remained.

Maybe he could catch hold of Mr. Chambers's attention before he went home to his fine house on the hill. Maybe they could talk about how the *Dispatch* chose to tell the story of the killing of the missionaries.

Why hadn't such warfare erupted in St. Louis? This was a city full of foreigners and clashing cultures—a confederacy of foreigners, as far as Dare could see from his little time here. They made him dizzy, all the languages spoken on street corners. Even Rachel and Atoka had been brought up in a different country—Indian Territory, though Dare didn't understand what that was. It was hard enough understanding these city people day to day. But if Rachel and her brother could do it, he could. He must show his new Choctaw kin that they hadn't made a mistake in pulling him out from under that oak and up the mighty Mississippi. They would all jump off this blasted city at the edge of American civilization. Then things would be better, in the west. Different than the west of Ireland, where the bones of his ancestors called for his return, sometimes, in dreams. His own dead had not visited him since his opium-addled second wedding night. Were they angry that he was alive and waking with beauty he didn't deserve in his arms?

He'd not betrayed that beauty. He was ashamed enough for the venial sins flirting with the shanty girls were. He'd not taken up with whores, as Atoka had claimed, not even when Mr. Chambers bought him one for a whole night. That had been a mistake, a terrible mistake, promising to keep the nephew, Floyd Dorris, company of an evening. Dare didn't know about the whorehouse, the already-paid-for night until he was in the midst of it, praying for a way out that would not cost him his job.

He'd found it when the most beautiful of them, a woman whose hair was spun gold, claimed him as her own. She had not worked any wiles on him, but had sat with him in her silk dressing gown that dazzled his weary eyes with its painted peacocks. And she'd listened to his story, to his worries. Like the best confessor priest, Dare realized now, asking God to forgive him for the comparison.

Why had she listened, not laughing at him, not berating him for his resistance to her considerable charms? Because she was

Irish too, though she called herself Emily Southampton. She was a mask-wearer too, like himself. Hers was the mask of a fallen woman widow of an earl. She'd known somehow that he too was masked, though she was an Ulsterwoman, far from Connacht.

But she'd made a joke when the night was ending, a joke that would some day cost him dearly, Dare feared. When Chambers and Dorris demanded to know details of their liaison, Emily Southampton went dewy about the eyes and called him, Dare Swimmer, the fixer, the best man she'd ever known. He became suddenly the greatest lover of the world around. She'd even made a great show of begging him to return to her. His boss had laughed, winning some kind of bet he'd had with his nephew. About his quiet nature meaning he was a virgin, and seeking to have it verified by a hired whore. Bevin's chaste husband, and Rachel LeMoyne's celibate one, would have been just as amusing to them, he supposed. More jokes. Dare was sick to death of being made the object of rich men's jokes.

His countrywoman had turned this one around. But at what cost? He had to watch the spectacle of Mr. Chambers telling his nephew here was yet another area where he could use Dare Swimmer's instruction. There was no mistaking the intense hatred behind Floyd Dorris's playful bow to his uncle. Then to him, on the arm of the most beautiful whore of Winslow House.

Dare had returned to his wife's arms early that morning, pursued by those eyes that called him usurper, and the eyes of another whore, the one on Dorris's arm: haunted, bruised by more than what had left purple spots at her throat and arm and perhaps places he could not see. Mary, Queen of Heaven, but he was sick to death of them all.

Back to the task at hand, he chided himself, banishing even the image that replaced that of the battered whore, the sweet image of Rachel pulling Mrs. Casey's oat bread from the oven. So different from her corn cakes. She had learned to fashion loaves in their landlady's way to please him. Was he fattened enough for her, yet, he wondered. He was stronger, he knew that, and no longer indifferent, despairing, waiting for death. He wanted to tell her that, to thank her, to release her from her obligations to a dying man. Yet the thought of her wanting to be released was beginning to terrify him. For aye, it would be so easy to love her, if he could find the courage in himself for it.

He must somehow get Atoka his job back. Chambers would help. His publisher needed to be more careful about the words he chose. The overlanders depended on native and Mixed Blood guides. It wouldn't be responsible to encourage massive firings of men like Atoka, who knew the land and the animals. Men who could talk to the tribes holding the American desert that the emigrants have to cross to get to Oregon. There. There was his argument, he decided. Now, to spin it into fine English words to convince his master.

"Mr. Swimmer! How fortunate!" Speak of the very devil, Dare thought as he found his for-the-gentry smile. He wiped his hands on the oiled rag as the publisher continued. "Gentlemen, this is the man I've been telling you about. The man who is not content to be the best mechanic our ancient and ill-used press has ever encountered, but who now guards the place as well."

Dare watched the crop of silk top-hatted men smile indulgently. All but for one, a young one with small eyes. The nephew. Floyd Dorris, who Dare had taken pains to avoid since the night at Winslow House. The talk that the damned poppinjay was feeling his inheritance threatened by his uncle's new worker was fueling further hatred. And Dorris was already into his cups, and maybe something else besides, something making his eyes pupilless and glossy. Dare despaired. Not a good time to argue editorial stance with this family. Mr. Chambers put his hand on Dare's shoulder. "What are you doing back so soon? Your guard duty doesn't start for two hours yet!"

"Yes, sir. But I was concerned about the flywheel."

"You oiled it before you left."

"I wanted to make sure it was catching well again."

"Do you hear him, gentleman? Floyd, why are you not nearly as interested in my prize worker's ability with my machinery as you are with his prowess with women? And you should see the devotion he inspires among his spirited horses and serv— oh I beg your pardon, kinfolk. You might learn a few things in Dare Swimmer's company for a day."

Dare smiled. "I doubt that, sir."

"Just my point! And the source of my dilemma, my boy! Do you hear this yeoman, gentleman? Good stock, and some breeding I wouldn't wonder, though he enjoys being mysterious about his heritage!"

"I don't enjoy it, sir."

"Well," his employer smiled indulgently, "have a look and listen to that flywheel. Then come out to supper with us."

"That's most kind of you, except . . ."

"Except?"

"I'm hardly fit for company such as—"

"Nonsense! This is America, son. Where money, not title or clothes, make the man. I insist. I so enjoy our discussions. We've yet to talk about today's edition."

"That I would very much like to do."

This was just the opening he was looking for. Why did he feel so unwell? He was hungry, that's all. Rachel had not fed him, they'd not even had Mrs. Casey's tea before her brother barged in with his condemnations. He would show them he was worthy of their company. He would use this opportunity to get the editorial stance eased from condemnation of all Indians. Perhaps that would help Atoka to get his job back.

When Dare joined the company, he saw the real answer to his sour stomach. It dwelled in the hollow, drugged sparks from Floyd Dorris's eyes. He too, was scheming.

Baked potatoes, his *praties,* wrapped in old editions of Dare's newspaper warmed Rachel's middle as she walked. He would never think of her as a real wife if she didn't do better feeding him. And she wanted him to think of her that way. She wanted it more each day. She could not blame it on Atoka and his berry magic, or her own longing for a child at her breast. She loved her hard-working, wounded Irish husband. He was still in mourning, but he would not dwell there always, would he? It grew colder. It was never this cold in Mississippi, or Oklahoma. Rachel was drawn to the brick buildings, holding in their heat from the day's sun. Would Dare be warm enough, walking home after his guard duty? She thought of her husband's coat, hanging on the back of the chair as he kissed her. If only her love could shed his layers like clothes from his new, strong body.

Suddenly, she felt a rough grip on her arm. She was pulled into an alley. Three men held her against the warm bricks.

"Where you going, pretty gal?" one asked.

"Supper," she made her voice say.

"A fancy whore, one who does it in the back rooms of the restaurants!" the one with the dangling mustache decided. "Well, we're hungry. We're real hungry."

"Already got an appointment?" asked another.

"Don't do no off-the-street business?" the third man, with the scar that disfigured his chin, said.

"I don't do any such business," she told them.

"Oh? Hear that? This here's a pure lady of leisure out alone after dark!"

Rachel's blood iced. Had she made a mistake coming out alone? She'd thought only of Dare's missed supper. She hadn't asked Mrs. Casey if she should have gone out. She'd acted as she would have in her own town.

Another man approached. "She doesn't look like a whore to me, gentlemen. Let her talk." He had watery eyes and a high silk top hat, the kind the trappers cursed about when they saw them on the streets of St. Louis, because they were not made from the beaver. Her mouth made no sound. The first man gripped her jaw, turned her face toward him. "One of them high-yellow, proud mulatto gals, that's what we got," he decided.

Rachel searched for Water Eyes. He was her only hope. She heard his voice again, behind the other men, sounding lazy and indifferent. "Best be sure she doesn't have some planter's son's protection. That cost me a few broken ribs once."

"Naw, couldn't be. The planters, they set up their whores with fancy homes and chaperones."

The first three men eyed her closely, stubbled faces reeking, still trying to solve the puzzle of an unwilling female out after dark. They were playing with her now, Rachel decided, like a cat with its prey between its paws. Giving her time, and space. Enough space to get past them? "You going to your lover?"

"My husband. I'm bringing my husband his supper. He's a hard-working man, with two jobs. And very strong. Please allow me to pass."

"And who'd marry you, nigra?"

"Indian, she's a fucking Indian, that's what! I hear it in her speech!"

Rachel saw the light of the street lamppost making shadows. She heard other men's voices there, in the distance. The same kind of men as the ones who held her? Was the world after dark full of this kind of men? She tried to calm her panicked thoughts. Get to them, the others. Find your voice. Call to them.

The one who'd first caught her descended. "You think you're one of us, because some missionary learned you our talk, girl?"

"Cost the missionaries out west their scalps, teaching Indians. Is that what you want, little Cherokee gal? Our scalps?"

"They's always ready to turn back to savage, even the ones wear such pretty white woman's clothes." He tugged at her skirt, the one with the small woven roses that Dare had called her garden in winter.

"Dare!" she found her voice in her husband's name, before the leader slapped her silent.

Her call began an argument to erupt among the men under the lamppost. One of her torturers grabbed her wrist, twisted.

"Oh, now that will cost you, little savage."

She met his small eyes' stare. "I think my husband will kill you if you do me any harm."

They laughed, as one. "Still got yourself a husband?"

"Yes. He guards a newspaper. And owns a fine pistol."

"How very intriguing." Water Eyes was back. "And his name,

little one?" Though she did not like the look of him, he spoke kindly.

"Dare. Dare Swimmer."

"Ah." His hand slipped inside his coat. "Mrs. Swimmer. Delighted to make your acquaintance."

Rachel saw a glint of steel.

twelve

Time slowed as in a nightmare. The voice of Mr. Chambers sounded hollow in Dare's ears. Laughing at him. For interfering in a mere altercation between a gentleman and a whore. Dare raised his pistol, knowing his bad eyes for distance would sight Rachel dead as easily as one of her attackers. So he pointed at the night sky. Fired.

In the shot's ringing aftermath, he screamed the high wail of his ancestors in battle. He charged, knowing the rich whoresons he'd been entertaining a moment before would not follow him into the fray. He needed only their long night shadows, to give the appearance of it, to drive the pack away. It worked. All but one scattered down the alley.

That one knocked Rachel down. Knowing Dare's bluff, knowing that he had no army behind him. But not knowing the nature of his firearm. Rachel tried to scramble out from his reach. He pinned her by her hair, coming out of its neat bonds. Black hair, more densely black than his own, Dare thought, and as beautiful as a raven's wing. Pinned her by that hair, then straddled her. His knife descended. Mother of God. Again. Metal through muscle, scraping bone. Dare couldn't drive the sounds from his head, though he yelled loud enough to bring down the very stars.

When finally in range he aimed the firearm, found the English words. "Stop or I'll kill you."

Small, mad eyes met his. Dorris. Floyd Dorris, his boss's nephew, who'd left the dinner early. Dare felt vomit rise up his aching throat. Dorris laughed, raising the knife again. Rachel's arms rose to protect her middle. Dare widened his stance. Fired. Dorris stared at his crimson arm, before his face twisted in rage. He lifted the knife. Dare fired again. Again. One shot entered his neck, another clipped his shoulder, bolting him backward, off Rachel. Finally stilled.

Dare went to his knees beside this woman he'd thought was the one indestructible force on God's earth, trying to find her in the swarming clothes, the splattering of red.

"Rachel. Oh God, Rachel," he whispered.

Her face eased at the sound of his voice.

"Dare? Is it truly you?"

"Aye, lass."

Her hand rose miraculously and took hold of his powder-burned one.

"The potatoes," she said.

"Potatoes?"

How was she ranting about potatoes just as his wife had done as she lay dying?

"Your supper." Her voice was edged with annoyance, as if she'd heard his panicked thought. "The knife went through the potatoes first. It is not so bad. Help me up. Let's go home."

She leaned her slashed arm along his as she sat. "Oh. Oh, my," she breathed as she stared down at her clothes. Still, her hand found his face as her soft eyes filled with, what? Sympathy? He lifted her into his arms. She weighed barely anything at all, his Choctaw wife. Why had she seemed so formidable?

The whistle of the magistrate sounded, and approaching foot-falls, searching for a murderer.

Dare held something to her lips. It burned her throat, but, past that, warmed her. Then Rachel felt Mrs. Casey wrap her arms and breasts and middle with her gentle woman's hands. Cluck-ing soothing sounds, like her mother's when Sleeps Sound would cry. Was she crying? Rachel wasn't sure, she'd never heard such sounds coming out of her. She tried to apologize for them, but that brought on more soft clucking, scolding. The air was misty with the smell of lye soap and linen.

Later Atoka sat beside her, speaking in hushed, calm tones to her husband. Offering him a horse, his best horse, Raven Mocker. Why? Were they friends again? Had they settled their latest differences? Rachel wanted to ask them this, but she was so tired. Atoka looked pained by the sight of her, by the questions in her eyes. But he faced both with courage. She grasped out to-ward him, tried to make her eyes speak.

Atoka held her hand between his, nodding. Yes. He under-stood. They'd always understood each other, even from different sides of the world. "*Yalabusha?* I did not tell it to you in the right way, there on the trail, about what happened to the ones who were our parents."

She nodded.

"Only the child, the girl who slept so well bundled beside our mother's heart, only she died of the sickness. In our mother's grief for that small one, down at the river . . ."

Tears from her brave brother's eyes, then, strangling his throat from the story. Rachel tried to squeeze his hand. *Yes. Go on.*

"A soldier came, found our mother alone. He desecrated her ritual, her grief, her body. A soldier—"

"Yellow Hair."

He looked startled. "Yes. That one, who watched her, greedy, from the first moments of our journey to the New Nation. Our father killed this man. But other soldiers came, called him murderer. The white people will call your husband that if we stay here. The soldiers . . . sister, the soldiers killed them both, the ones who gave us life."

"You saw," she whispered.

"Yes. We'd left to gather the rattle I'd made for that small one, to put beside her in the earth. When he heard the screams, the one who was our father told me to stay hidden. But I did not. I came upon this place that burns inside my head still, a place where that bleeding woman holds her husband in her arms. They would have killed me too, but one of the soldiers listened to her, as she was dying, begging for my life. Sometimes, in the night, I am still angry that she did this.

"My heart was sick. I did not want to live, except for you. It is that way now. Rachel, we must move you to a new place. Find your strength. Please. Make yourself well. For me. For this man who now has Raven Mocker as his own. We are both too full of death."

Mrs. Casey appeared over his shoulder. Atoka pressed his face into the waistband of their landlady's apron. More Irish clucking as her brother wept. Then words. "Some color back in her face. Go, *macushla*. Pack your things now. Let me tend her a last little while, poor dove."

Mrs. Casey's hands disappeared. Another man helped her brother and husband lift her. A man who looked like Atoka, only older, like an uncle or elder brother. This man spoke in French, and was as gentle with her as her men. "She reminds me of my mother," he said. Then he disappeared, too. If he had ever really been there.

Then time got a little longer, between her deep sleeping. "Where did Mrs. Casey go?" Rachel managed to ask Dare, sitting in their landlady's usual place beside the bed. No, not bed. Box. Rough, straw mattress, sweetened with cedar. He smoothed the hair off her forehead.

"She hasn't gone, love. We have. We've started for Oregon, what do you think of that?"

"Too cold yet."

"Aye, well, we're not far as yet. Carondelet, a little French town on the river."

"I smell the river."

"Good. That's good. That means you're getting well." Yes. He'd said that when she'd asked him to braid her hair with his nimble fingers. Signs of her getting well. Her poor, worried husband was desperate for signs. "Atoka's flourishing with the local folks," he chatted on now.

"Another man was here."

"Aye, his friend. Baptiste. A trapper, a wilderness guide, a man of some influence in these parts. He helped us find this place, move you here. Now what else would he do after Atoka tamed three of his wildest horses, I'd like to know? He got too good a look at you, wife, I'm thinking. He's a woman's man, that one Baptiste, so I'd better keep a careful eye on you. What is this look from you now, Rachel LeMoyne? Do you think it's a story I'm telling?"

"Aye," she whispered. "Blarney."

"It's my only hold on you, wife."

"What is?"

"This mirror-cracked way you do not see yourself as the Queen of the May and the Choctaw besides!"

Rachel lost herself in the sound of his dancing voice, knowing it hid his fear, but enjoying it, along with his broad palm skimming her cheek.

"So, here we are, safe. I fix what needs fixing for the folks around, when your brother helps me talk with them. So you see we're in fine—"

"Dare, why did we leave St. Louis?"

He stared at his hands. "The authorities were following Mrs. Casey to her sister's laundry, where she'd had us stashed."

"Stashed?" Rachel smiled. "Good of her. The old busybody."

"*Oke,* my queen," he conceded ruefully. He looked so tired that the effort of smiling seemed to hurt his face.

"Dare. What is this place?"

"An abandoned homestead."

"Abandoned?"

"Aye. By death. But not by a warm stove, to help you feel better. And not by ghosts, to be sure. 'Would you not be in dread of going into a haunted place?' folks asked me, in that quaint blend of French and Indian that your brother and his friend Baptiste seem to understand. 'In dread is it?' says I, 'What would we be in dread of, with all our own dead thick as bees around us?' "

"Oh, Dare. You will make us more peculiar than we already are."

"Do you think that possible?"

Rachel thought of Water Eyes. Raising his knife again and again. "Is that man dead, Dare?"

"Not yet. But they're saying he will not last the winter."

Would Water Eyes join their ghosts then, Rachel wondered.

"Are you warm enough?" Dare asked.

"What if I tell them why you had to shoot him?"

"It wouldn't matter, Rachel. Because he is nephew of Mr. Chambers. Chambers is powerful. They have turned it into what it was not, my seeking his nephew's place at the newspaper."

"I'm so sorry, husband."

"Ah, whist. Hush, now."

"I only wanted to bring supper."

"And my potatoes saved you, just as you said, blunting the worst of the—of the—" He swiped his eyes with the back of his hand impatiently, "as your corn saved my people. It was only proper, wasn't it?"

She smiled. "And I wanted to hasten the peace between you and my brother."

"Aye. You've done that."

"Have I?"

"If you'll just get well. Please, Rachel."

"How badly am I injured?"

He looked at the dirt floor.

"If Mrs. Casey cannot come any more, will you help me?"

"Of course, love."

"Only you. Not Atoka."

"Why?"

"If the cuts are deep, and he thinks they will keep me from having, caring for—for children . . . I don't want him to be disappointed in me. Not until I have the strength to face it."

"Rachel, how could he ever—"

"You don't understand. We are the last of our family, Atoka and I. We are of the clan of the eagle, which comes down through the women. Atoka badgered me about marrying because he will raise my children in the ways of the Choctaw. That is his duty, and our way. I gave him hope for those children when I made you my husband, though I told him our circumstances, truly I did, Dare!"

"And what were our circumstances?" he asked her quietly.

"That you needed passage from your country. That you are in the black and still honoring your wife."

He sighed. A hard sigh, a man's sigh, that broke her heart. "Ach, Rachel," he whispered.

"Still, he hopes, you see? And if . . . Dare, if I cannot—"

"Rachel LeMoyne," he summoned her sweetly. "You're fussing *galore.*"

"What is this word?"

"What word? *Galore?* It means enough. Plenty. Yes, plenty enough fussing. You'll not be wanting to take on that reputation, would you now? Of a woman who troubles for no good reason?"

"But—"

"For it's sure as the rain I am that your wee *babs* will love you the way God and life has made you, just as Atoka and I do."

She loved the way he weaved his words, and wanted to draw more of them out of him, even if they were more of his wild imaginings, his blarney. "Do you have the Irish magic that knows this, husband?"

"I have more than that."

"Oh? What?"

"The . . . Well, if, that is to say I have the—the means by which . . ."

"What?"

He blushed deeply, her change-color husband, and did not answer further. She'd done the opposite of her intent. Was she being too brazen in her hunger for this man, and not a modest Christian woman? She took his hand. "Promise me, Darragh Ronan. We are friends and may make and keep promises between us, might we not?"

"Aye," he said in a gruff voice. "We are *anam cara*. Soul friends."

"Promise, then, *anam cara*. Only you changing the bandages."

"Well," he pondered, "I'll trade something in return."

"What?"

"I want to haul in a priest. I want us married properly."

"But I have already married you."

"I know. But I need to marry you in return now, you see? In my own religion. Now."

Rachel felt a cold stone seize her heart. "Now? Because I am dying?"

"No, love. Because I want to live."

"Oh? That is a good thing, I think."

"I hope to be worthy of you, Rachel LeMoyne. And your children, if your brother will kindly be allowing me look in on them now and again. Sleep now."

"No. Not yet."

He frowned. "I'll sing you to sleep if you don't behave."

"Yes. Do. Do sing for me, husband."

He pulled his hand through his hair. Hair full of dark waves like the Atlantic's at midnight. How beautiful her Irish husband was, with the hunger no longer taking him down. He began a sad and tender melody in his own language. Of course. He'd been a musical man, dancing in Mr. Combs's drawings with his high-stepping wife. His voice was as deep and clear as a stream in spring. Sung, his language's strange sounds were more beautiful, flowing. The music he made with it changed to the whipping sound of the sea against stone, then to a gentle mist rising above his homeland on Loch Allen. Was it a spell song? Yes. He sought to put her to sleep with it, like one of his children on a soft Irish night filled with stars and ghosts. Now they were the ghosts, his children, his shy wife, hovering there, at his shoulder. Listening to his words, his music. Did he sing the song longing for them?

He drew up her covers with the last notes.

"Translate," she urged.

"It will suffer, in translation."

"Do your best," she insisted.

"Close your eyes first."

She heard his callused fingers scrape through his many days' growth of beard. Thinking. Then he spoke in a halting soft whisper. "I thought, my love, you were / As the sun or the moon on a fountain, / And I thought after that . . . ach, Rachel, I cannot bend it into the English."

"Try again," she urged.

His head sank lower between his shoulders. "I cannot," he whispered.

Was it was a love song, she wondered. "Dare?" she had to ask him. "Do you sing your song for me?"

He lifted his head, smiled. "And is there anyone else in this room, Rachel LeMoyne?"

"You do not see them?"

"Who?" He touched her shoulder. His fear pierced through his fingertips. *"Dia Muire agus Padraig,* Rachel, who?"

She laughed, though it hurt her middle, then made her cough, which made his gray eyes wild with worry. "Listen to me, Darragh Ronan," she whispered, once she'd caught her breath again. "You've made me as full of questions as yourself. Come. Lie beside me. I'm cold, and you look destroyed in your weariness and . . . and my badgering."

When he did, she stroked his hair, still wondering if he'd sung, in that clear dark voice, to her.

* * *

Her husband kept his word, caring for her wounds as gently as Mrs. Casey did. Her brother brought the man Baptiste again, flesh and blood, and very handsome. "He's a bridge person, like you, Rachel," Atoka explained, "educated by Governor Clark, and Baptists and Jesuits."

She stared at his trapper buckskins, the braid woven into his long hair, his bear claw amulet. "Did you disappoint the missionaries too?" she asked him.

He laughed. "*Mais oui,* little one. I have disappointed a great many people. That is of little consequence, if one has true friends. You have those in this worried brother, in your very Catholic husband. You have one in me."

"Baptiste has found us a good price on a wagon, Rachel," Atoka said. "But I told him he must consult with you, that you make all such decisions. Rachel? Rachel, open your eyes, we need you to—"

"Let your sister sleep, Atoka," she heard Baptiste softly chastize her brother. "She can buy your wagon tomorrow."

She worried about the wagon, and her duties to fill it, and prepare their way to Oregon. Had she given Baptiste the money, or only dreamed placing it into those long hands? Then the deepest cut, one in her right breast became red and swollen and hot to the touch. All dreams burned away. She needed her brother, before the fever rattled her brain, she kept thinking, she needed to tell him to look after Dare should she die. They would stay alive, her men, if they had each other to look after. But Atoka did not come. Where was he?

Rachel had to endure her husband's suffering eyes. He loved her, then? This is what she wanted, his love. But now she realized its cost, and why he resisted so long, with even those echoes of his laughing eyes dancing away from their intimacy. Still, their friendship, their kinship with Atoka deepened. She wanted to tell him she finally understood this time that he needed to grieve, but her throat was swollen and she could barely swallow the trickles of liquid he offered.

Then Atoka came back, with Baptiste and a man with a wide black hat and doleful eyes. Why was he here? A priest. She did not want him. They had always disapproved, then cast her out, those Christians. She wanted to die a Choctaw peace chief, with only her men beside her.

Marriage, the priest said. Marriage. Yes, she remembered. Why her husband had turned away from her in the night. He did not think they were married enough. There, yes, she understood the priest's French, she was a translator's daughter. Wasn't this what Dare had asked of her? Marriage in his religion?

But she couldn't say the words, not even with Dare helping her. So she nodded to the questions, which made them argue among themselves, the priest and her men, with Baptiste in the middle, translating. They swam in a sea of babble. She wouldn't have this foolishness, not when she was dying. She deserved better. She pulled herself up on her elbows and yelled them all to silence. There. That felt good. She summoned her knowledge of French, found the words, and told the priest to finish his ceremony and get out. He did, as humbly as one of her students on one of those rare occasions she'd raise her voice.

Baptiste smiled. His teeth gleaming, his breath brandy, and dried mint leaf. "Your sister is better, I think," he said. Then he and Atoka took the priest out in the swirling snow.

Dare put a metal band on her finger. She closed her eyes. "Foolish men," she muttered.

"Aye, miss," he agreed.

"You can hold yourself to your death do us part, Darragh Ronan," she whispered, scraping his face with her long, almost bone picker's fingernail, "but you still must leave if I put your belongings out, excepting washday."

"I'll honor your religion, wife, as you've honored mine," he agreed, kissing her cheek.

"And shave, before you kiss me again."

He smiled. Did the smiles mean she was getting better? She felt better.

It was her men who looked thoroughly pummeled, she realized when Atoka returned, joining Dare in feeling her cool forehead, then laughing together as if she'd told a good story.

The Oregon Trail

1848

thirteen

Along the North Platte River
Spring, 1848

"Are you poor, Mrs. Gilmartin?"

"Poor? No."

"Mama says that's why you and yours are traveling so light. You only have two oxen hauling your wagon. Well, they are the prettiest in the whole of the train, I think. You're educated, ain't you, Ma'am?"

"Somewhat. I was a teacher."

"A teacher? Do tell! Do you have books?"

"Too many, my brother says."

"Ones with stories in them?"

"Full of stories."

Jessica Lowell reminded Rachel of a butterfly with her questions, her flitting movements around her own slower, deliberate ones. She enjoyed the girl's company, and the help preparing the evening meal. Rachel liked hearing her own new name, too, the one Dare had chosen to keep them hidden from the authorities of St. Louis.

It was his mother's birth name, Gilmartin. It had a solid sound and a wonderful story about a warrior saint who gave his coat away to a stranger who proved to be Jesus himself. Hadn't the English artist Mr. Combs said that Dare was generous like this man, this Saint Martin? Why were they hunting her husband? Atoka said shooting a rich white man, even in her defense, was why. She should understand these things better than she did, but to her the world of St. Louis was out of balance. She liked the smaller world of the wagon train better.

"Well, a teacher with books—imagine!" Jessica said. "The women will welcome you on the train for certain sure now, even if you come out of the wild folk of Carondelet town!"

"Why is this, Jessica?"

"I expect if you'd do us some teaching, when you're feeling better of course, you're just what we need!"

"Need?"

"Yes, ma'am. To keep the little ones from scattering about, or falling under wagon wheels. To have us all take some learning from you and your books. Would you mind teaching us, Mrs. Gilmartin?"

Rachel smiled. "I wouldn't mind at all."

"Well, that's all right then! Not many of us been to a regular school, not us from our part of Iowa, I can tell you that. We get along, in one way or another, with our parents getting us to cipher and read some out of the Bible. But it's been so hardscrabble since Mama and Papa themselves first come out. We never had us a school or schoolmaster, something our mamas have dearly wished for us. Imagine us finding one here, on our way farther into the wilderness still! That will be your link to us, Miss Rachel, on account of you and your men didn't come like the rest of us did, with relatives and neighbors. That'll keep you from being a peculiar people, you see? Though us Lowells ain't ones to talk! Even with us traveling with the Hydes, who had the farm next to ours in Iowa. Still, Papa's tree wagon makes us pretty peculiar, don't it?"

Rachel stirred the pot of soup, hoping the vegetables were

soft enough for Dare's taste. "I think it's a wonderful idea, starting a fruit tree farm in Oregon," she assured her young guest. "And your father's wagon brightens my husband's eyes. He loves all manner of trees."

"It was real good of him and your brother to help that wagon's oxen to ford the Big Blue. Now wasn't that a sight?"

"It was, indeed."

Rachel thought of watching Atoka, Mr. Lowell, and the Lowells' only son, sixteen-year-old Alfred in the water with the beasts, yanking. Behind the six-oxen team, two of the family's five daughters plugged the drain hole in the floor of the wagon. They then tied empty water barrels to the open wagon's side to help it float. Inside the wagon, the grafted seedlings of apple, cherry, plum, and pear trees shook to their foot-and-a-half to three-foot heights. Dare, white-knuckled, drove the wagon, singing out his silver Irish phrases to the oxen. As the water got higher, Rachel heard more of the names of his saints being invoked, but not a word about his lack of swimming ability. How she wished she were stronger, and could find a quiet calm bend in a creek to teach him. Well, summer was coming.

The Lowell daughters ranged in age from Jessica's fourteen years to Hannah's thirteen, sweet-faced, sickly Rose's ten, Callie's nine, and the doted-on Lucinda who they called Lulie's five. They were all industrious workers around mealtimes. Even little Rose, who Rachel had seen tending the fire and stacking the family's metal plates and forks for dinner. How she missed the company of women, sharing tasks and talk and secrets. Well, perhaps her teaching would gain her an entrance into these trail women's world. Would they truly trust her with their children? She was not the missionaries "dusky angel" here, but a stranger, and a sickly one.

Rachel was not doing nearly so well as the Lowell women at meals. The supper hour was still her worst time, after the long day's walk across the plains. "The sea of grass," Dare had called it, teasing her about insisting he had to cross two oceans to win her love.

Behind his laughing eyes, she knew her husband was worried about her slowly returning health. It was affecting his own, as she'd noticed the dark circles back under his shift-color eyes. Dare and Atoka were usually still out hunting with the men or settling the horses and oxen when this time of her greatest weakness struck. Rachel was glad of it. It would take even more of her precious energy to try to hide it from them. She sipped at the sassafras tonic as she worked over the fire.

Jessica fingered Rachel's collection of scrubbed camas roots. "Can you make yeast bread, Mrs. Gilmartin?" the butterfly girl asked, suddenly uneasy.

"Yes."

"There! That proves you ain't savages, for all the scrounging about you do under the grass. Indians don't know how to make yeast bread or wear proper clothes, Mama says, and they're reeling drunk most of the time."

"Is that right?"

"Oh, yes. Mama's plumb haunted by Indian stories since we left Iowa. Well, look," she whispered, lifting the flap of her bonnet to reveal her short light hair. "She went and clipped Hannah and Rose and me on account our very first day in St. Louis, a gang of them redskins making like they were sharpening their knives to scalp us on the spot!"

Rachel shook her head. "I'm sure they were teasing. Not a kind joke, but a joke, because they resented your fear."

"You think so?"

"Yes. That is how I see it," Rachel said in quiet affirmation, the way she would speak at council if she were still a peace chief of her people.

"Ain't you afeared of Indians, Mrs. Gilmartin?"

"No."

The girl backed away. "Maybe that's why you still got all that glorious hair—you ain't afeared, and they're all cowards and would run away from such as you!"

Rachel tried to mask her displeasure. Not toward Jessica, but toward the girl's mother, for filling her with her own fears. She wondered what state Mrs. Lowell would be in if she knew what

Rachel knew after her excursions for roots—that a growing party of Pawnee had been shadowing the train since it had entered their country.

"Your hair color's like midnight, ain't it?" the girl babbled now, perhaps uncomfortable in Rachel's silence. "You're Portuguese, Mr. Spikenard says, as they're dark folk. But Nanny Berry says you're French, on account of your brother's name is French, and they are dark, too, and you joined our train out of that Cannuck town. That wild-looking Frenchman guide asked so polite for all of you about joining up, telling Papa some Kentuck yarns, and spinning some clever ones in good German for the Reich family as well—none of us ever saw the like of him! That's what you are, ain't you and your brother, Mrs. Gilmartin? French?"

"Yes, we're French," Rachel said quietly, thanking the painter who married that grandmother for not making her a liar. "And my husband is from Ireland, across the great Atlantic Ocean, where people live in a green mist and are very pale. He would become burnt and sick in the sun without his fine hat."

"Do tell!" As Jessica Lowell giggled out her relief, Rachel thought of Atoka's beautiful long hair, shorn, as if he was in mourning, as if she had died under Water Eyes' long knife in a St. Louis alley. Would it have been better for her men if she had? She had burned all of Atoka's beautiful hair carefully, as she burned her husband's hair leavings, to keep them out of the hands of their enemies. It was not a Christian thing to do, but it felt right to follow the ways of her people here in the middle of the Anglos. And she was not feeling very much like a Christian lately.

The burdens of the day's fifteen miles closer to Oregon, along with her strung-taut answers to the girl's questions, finally stopped Rachel's action altogether. She sat by the fire and leaned her head on her hand.

Jessica approached, touched a long strand of hair that had loosened from its white woman bonds and combs. "Nanny Berry, she says your from-Ireland-man married you to get himself some children who would tan in the sun. You waiting on a baby? Is that why you're sickly, ma'am?"

"No. I—lost a child."

That was more of the story they'd agreed on telling, to keep the trail to them cold. But it made Rachel cold to speak it, though Atoka said to think of Sleeps Sound when asked the cause of her weakness, as her husband would think of his dead babies in Ireland. They had enough lost children among them to make the words true. Still, Rachel did not feel worthy of the sympathy in the young girl's eyes. She, who was both ship captain and priest wed, but still a virgin bride. "Now, that's right sad," Jessica whispered. "I am sorry for your loss, ma'am."

"Thank you."

"Did it mess with your innards, so's you can't have no more?"

Rachel thought of Water Eyes' knife, her scars. "I hope that will not be the case."

"Well. Mustn't be grieving your way plumb into anemia about it, either way. That's what mama would say, though truth to tell she was plenty sad when we lost Parker and Tim to their fevers."

"Parker and Tim?"

"Little brothers. Parker three years old, and Tim, barely one. Buried in St. Louis. They was pretty babies. Didn't live long enough to keep poor Alfred company 'mongst all us girls." Jessica ventured closer. "Aw, now, don't do that, Miss Rachel! Don't you be takin' up our burden, too, ma'am! That won't do neither you or any new baby you get started any good at all."

Rachel nodded, wiping her eyes with the back of her hand. But the tears continued to flow. She had been foolish enough to envy the Lowells' fine young son and five bright daughters. She had not seen the space where the missing children were. And she had resented Celinda Lowell's distrust of Indians, a distrust that had shorn her three elder daughters of their hair. Its root was fear, not something evil.

"Soup smells good." Jessica pulled her out of her thoughts. "You're a wonder at finding tasty roots, though Mama worries, saying you shouldn't stray so far from the train."

"Does she?"

"I'll finish that for you, if'n you'd care to have a lie-down. Mama said to be of help, because you're feeling poorly."

"That was very good of her."

"Not all that good. She wanted to know the cause, and I was supposed to be all crafty-like finding out. Do you mind that I asked flat out?"

"No. I prefer flat out."

"Oh, me too. Seems to me half the troubles of the world would be ended if folks would just talk plain. There, pot's going good. You lie down there and I'll keep it from burning any. Maybe your men found some game to meaten it up, too, give you strength. Your brother sets the best rabbit snares, everybody says so. And he always shares. And even taught our Callie to shoot straight with her slingshot and . . . Mrs. Gilmartin, you just got to hush me up!"

Rachel realized she had begun to nod. "I'm sorry, Jessica."

"No need being sorry, ma'am! Go on and lay your whole self down now, that's the way. Mama sent me over so's you could rest. Only you don't order about, like she does, so I forget and just keep you company like some grand lady. It's a failing."

"Not at all. You're good company."

"And you're already like my mama gets when she's got a baby at the breast, ma'am, all soft and gentle. You're going to be a right fine mama again, don't fret on it." She frowned, showing a hint of the crease of worry that was embedded between her mother's eyes, making Celinda Lowell more fierce looking than she was, perhaps, Rachel thought.

"Jessica?"

"Ma'am?"

"I liked when you called me 'Miss Rachel.' It's what my children called me at school."

"Well, we will too, then, you leave that to me. I'll gather them up each day and bring them over and . . . oh, look at you!" she chided suddenly, pulling Rachel's falling shawl from her shoulders. She shook it out and tucked it around her like a blanket. "Now take your rest before your men come trampin' in for the night."

Rachel closed her eyes. That was why Dare hadn't yet become her true husband, wasn't it? Because he was waiting for her strength to return. To carry their first child. Rachel loved his soft kisses, and his protective hold and the way they fit nightly in the bed of their wagon, so much more sparsely packed than the others. She imagined them entwining, picking up each other's scent the way her parents once did.

Atoka watched for signs that Dare had made her his true wife, she knew, there, from his respectful distance, sleeping outside their small wagon. But she still wore two braids, pinned up around the back of her head. Atoka slept under the open sky except on raining nights, when he grew a tent off the side. They were all getting used to their close quarters and the rigors of the trail.

The wagons were organized, like the military that drove them from their homeland, into platoons and companies. Even Atoka took his duties within the system in stride. Her men were thriving in their camp life, with their horses and hunting, and Dare's skill when all manner of their neighbors' implements broke. She would catch up. Soon. And perhaps when Atoka was on guard duty, and she and Dare were alone in the wagon for a few hours of the night, then her husband would make her his true wife.

Rachel woke under a hail of stars. Jessica Lowell was gone, replaced by Dare and Atoka slouched against their saddles, eating rabbit.

Dare grinned. " 'Evening, Rachel."

"Put the bones in the pot."

"Yes'm."

She shook her head at the sound of his voice mimicking the speech of their American neighbors on the train. Gone was his St. Louis voice, stiff and formal. His Irish one had returned, mostly, though he peppered it with expressions from the states and an occasional Swiss exclamation from Mr. Bodmer. It all disguised him further, but this time with his true self. "You won't live healthy on meat alone," Rachel chided both her men. "I found some camas root. Eat my soup."

Her brother frowned. Nothing could mar his handsomeness, certainly not his blue-black hair cropped closer than any white man's in their camp, or his current displeasure. "No need to plague us for spoiling your dreams. Feed her," he commanded Dare. "Gibson Rice is tuning up his fiddle."

Atoka stalked off in search of the music. Her husband brought her a steaming bowl. "Don't mind him. He wanted to make a present of one of his rabbits to a certain regular dance partner of his."

"Eveline Walker?"

"Aye." He tilted his head. "Now, the rabbits agree with your frown's disapproval of the match, it seems, wife. This has been the first day his snares came up empty. Or the rabbits finally have your crafty brother figured, maybe."

"From whom did the meat come?"

"They have to start figuring my cunning ways now, I'm thinking. Eat."

She did, enjoying her husband beside her and strengthened by her rest. Soon, the drone of a prayer meeting group began its nightly competition with Gibson Rice's lively fiddle and the stomping feet of the dancers. Their train was split asunder between the devout and those courting the devil's ways through his favorite instrument. Atoka sided with the dancers. Her husband had kept his distance from both. But Rachel knew from his tapping feet which faction held sway.

"Do you miss your religion, Dare?" she asked him quietly.

He considered before answering. "I miss the Mass and ceremony, I suppose, and the priests and nuns, who helped us and shared all they could in the hunger. But I have my religion, Rachel, here inside me, as you have yours."

"Truly? How splendid. I'm not as sure as you are. There were so many hard choices."

"Choices?"

"Between being a Christian and remaining part of my own people and the way they see the world. The missionaries said we had no religion, only superstitions. But there was more. More than what the missionaries called faint longings of moral sense. My parents were both Choctaw and Christian, but I had them guiding me such a short time, and then the missionaries took over my education. I tried to be a good Christian, I truly did, Dare!"

"You're the best Christian I know, love."

"I am?"

"I don't mean churchgoing proper, I mean . . . well, putting up with Atoka and me. I mean how patient you've been in your recovering, and how gentle you talk with the children. That's what Christ and his saints taught us about living when he whittled all the laws down to two, is it not? Love God, love your neighbor, the hard thing being that everybody, even the bloody English and your land-grabbing Americans, are our neighbors."

Rachel reached out to his face then. She wanted to remember the moment by the feel of him. His eyes let go of a measure of their worry with the touch of her fingers, making him look younger even than his twenty-five years. She breathed in the scent of her stew and the other campfires and the long grass beyond the trail. She felt his stubble of beard, but it did not scratch her as he pressed her hand closer, then kissed into her palm.

"Atoka would like your philosophy on this, I think," she whispered, almost breathless.

He raised his head, smiling. "Oh?"

"Our father told him that no Indian group of his knowledge considered its own religion complete and final. That a chant or a ritual or story learned from a trading partner or enemy was like adding a new weapon to a quiver."

"Just so, aye!" Dare agreed. "Our Saint Patrick was first a proud man, like your missionaries, when he came to us. But didn't he get the same idea, that he didn't have to vanquish the old ones . . . the tree spirits and immortals and heroes in order to fit his Christ and the one God in our lives?

"Listen, darlin'," he said suddenly, "they don't know anything of us here on the train. Don't know you got yourself in trouble with your missionary folk for marrying a heathen Irishman. If you're wanting to join the holy"—he stopped himself before he said "rollers." "I mean, would you like me to bring you over to the prayer meeting?" he asked more quietly.

"No." She smiled, listening to Gibson Rice sliding into a reel. "I lean more—"

"What's this now? Toward the fiddle, are you?"

"Aye, husband," she said shyly.

"Why, Rachel LeMoyne, do you dance, then?"

"Oh, no! It was forbidden at school."

"So your brother told me."

"He did? Why would he tell you that?"

"Oh, there's plenty he's told me. Instruction. To make me a decent husband to you. Kept me sane when you were fevered, I think, with his instructions."

A spark flew up from their fire as Rachel poked it with her green stick. "How did you stand his arrogance? You do not have to prove yourself. You were already a decent husband to another wife, and so much more!"

His laughing eyes sobered. "And how do you know that, Rachel?"

"From Mr. Combs's pictures. They speak of it."

"Do they?"

"Would you like to see the pictures, Dare?" she asked quietly, not knowing why. He reached over, kissed her forehead. "No," he breathed, but allowed her to see the pain that seared hot and swift, through his eyes, before he managed a smile. "I thank you for the compliment. But your brother does well in his husband instruction, I'm thinking. And it helps him feel useful. And I enjoy the knowledge of you he gives me within, so let's keep the secret between us, shall we?"

She touched her forehead where his lips had grazed. "Another secret?"

"Aye, Mrs. Gilmartin. Can you bear this one?"

She nodded, looking at her lap, trying to lose herself in the music as she felt her husband's eyes linger on her. Was he hungry for her, or wishing her the other wife?

"Did you like the music back then, at the mission?" he asked.

"There was no music at the mission. Except for hymns, which is barely music."

She felt a little wicked for causing Dare's snort of laughter. "Ach, but you're a harsh woman, wife," he claimed, though he looked at her as if he did not believe his own words. And both look and words made her feel warm, deep in her secret places.

"Did you listen to your brother dancing to the Choctaw music, outside the windows of your Presbyterian school?"

"He told you that."

"Aye, and did it make the prospect even more alluring?"

"Well, yes."

"Shall I teach you a few steps, now that you're a grown woman, able to make up her own mind about what makes you a Christian? So we can keep them guessing about the respected new schoolteacher of the train who not only married a papist Irishman but might join the to-hell-in-a-handbasket faction now and then?"

"Why, Dare! Did you talk to Jessica Lowell about my trade of teaching services?"

"Listened mostly, to that one and her chatter. Aye, I'm now mindful of my learned wife's position here. As if I don't have enough keeping me on my toes around you, Rachel LeMoyne."

Rachel felt that pleasant rush at her cheeks that this man could produce with his words, his touch, the look of him. Even as he was now, a little afraid, his fear igniting the scent of fragrant buttonbrush down under his leather and horse smells about him. Of what was he afraid? He took her hand and raised her from the ground, listening to the tune in the distance. "Nothing much to it at all. Walking to music, will you put that in your mind?"

She nodded.

"Now, I place you on my right, and you're only to follow my strides, finding the music, letting it go through you, come out your feet. Feel it?"

"Yes."

The tune ended. Rachel lost her courage and tried to pull away, but her husband did not release her. "Let's wait for the next," he suggested, a little breathless, as if he'd been dancing already. More buttonwood. He rested his chin in her hair. So close in the ringing silence. His face went lower and she felt his deep, male-scented breathing. His nose nudged a comb. Playfully, like his teasing. Rachel felt the pleasure of it to her toes. He stepped back with a small cough as the music began a new tune, with a different kind of sound. "Now, this one's got a skittering step, like this. He held her hands and brought her along as he slid sideways. Rachel stumbled, falling against him.

As his graceful wife never would.

Rachel could not look at him, but held his hands more tightly, frowning in her determination.

Dare's laugh startled her. "I'm not your schoolmaster, but your lover, Rachel LeMoyne." He pulled her close. "And so grateful for this excuse to hold you in my arms."

He was not thinking of the other, then? Her grip on his hands eased. She followed his movements, her head beside his racing heart. "There. Much better," he encouraged her. "Have your feet listen for, not all the curlicues of melody, but the beating under it, the rhythm."

"Drums."

"Yes, exactly, like drumbeats, guiding your feet."

"No, not like drumbeats. Drums. I hear drums."

The fiddle stopped playing. The drums continued.

The trailmaster called the men to arms.

fourteen

Dare reached for his pistol.

"I need to come," Rachel said quietly. "Where's Atoka? Dare, I need to find my brother."

He held out his hand. She took it. "Together," he promised. "We'll find him together."

Mr. Walker, who the men had elected trail boss captain, had two pistols in his trousers as well as a musket. He was not good at caring for his weapons. Atoka suspected that the finger he claimed a Mexican soldier blew off was really the result of a loading error. Rachel wanted to keep her distance from him, fully armed. But he approached them.

"Gilmartin, put this woman in your wagon, there's Pawnee coming out of the west."

"And a larger party to the north," Rachel said quietly. "And scouts posted at the other directions around our circle, sir."

"What in hell—"

"My wife isn't knowing much about hell, Captain Walker,"

Dare claimed, with that singular, cold smile he'd used to trick the English into believing he was being friendly. "But she knows Indians. She's a translator's daughter, and was a mission schoolteacher."

The man eyed her coldly. "Maybe she should have stayed there, teaching the heathens some Christian manners."

"Maybe," Dare replied evenly. "But she did not. She's part of us now, and willing to be of service."

The men's worry eased, she thought, by her husband's words, perhaps by her presence. She looked over Gibson Rice's lanky shoulder. There. At last. Atoka. Smiling, giving her the quiet nod of his approval. But Walker turned on her. She did not back up, but her grip on Dare's hand tightened. "And do you see through the black night as well, woman, to know their number?"

"No. But I've noticed them following us since we reached the Platte. They have been watching long enough to know we're not a war party because of the women and children among us."

"And what do we know of them, Mrs. Gilmartin? Like if they're responsible for the whereabouts of my missing cow?"

"Bet they stole it," Hiram Hyde claimed, before his mother's arm appeared out of their wagon and hushed him with a swat.

The other women had herded their children into wagons. Rachel had no children. Would that be enough of a reason for the men to consider her part of their company?

"If there's so many, what's to keep them from slaughtering us, and doing worse to the wives and children?" Mr. Lowell, the nurseryman, asked Rachel. His wife was not the only one afraid of Indians.

"I don't believe they're looking to make war, sir," she said quietly. "If they wanted to do us harm, they've had ample opportunity."

The trail captain's eyes narrowed. "And what do they want now, Mrs. Gilmartin? With their drums, and hovering over that hill?"

"I don't know, sir. Why don't we ask them?"

The men looked at each other. Atoka stepped out of his quiet place in their midst. "My sister and I will do it," he said.

"You're not leaving me out," Dare protested, keeping his grip on Rachel's hand.

Mr. Walker eyed them. "Who are you people? Do you talk Pawnee?"

"No," Atoka admitted. "But our father taught us signs that the people of the plains use when trading. He learned them from the Kiowa, good sign talkers."

"Signs?"

"Yes. Don't they use them in Texas, sir?"

"Boy, we don't *talk* to Indians this brazen in Texas. We shoot them."

Atoka bristled. Dare touched his arm, linking the three of them. That cold smile flashed again, showing his white teeth. "Well, we're not in Texas here, Mr. Walker. And we're trespassing on these folks' land. Seems to me a little courtesy's in order."

Dare's musical voice was now picking up the soft drawled expressions of the Southern-bred ones among them. And her husband was not the only salamander. After the short spit of flame, her headstrong brother transformed into a calm, abiding force. The wonder of it.

More of the men nodded, though one muttered, "Damned French."

"They'll talk to anyone," agreed another.

"Do more than talk. Them two's daddy did more than talk, I'll warrant."

"Well, they're one of us on this train," the fiddler Gibson Rice maintained. "I say let's let them have a go at the talk. More of us might be alive to turn brown come summer."

"Maybe we could offer presents?" Rachel suggested. "There's still half a loaf of the bread Jessica brought over from—"

"Rachel Gilmartin!" Amity Hyde, the Lowell family's neighbor in Iowa, called from her wagon. Her face appeared now, along with the strong arm that had swatted her son. "The idea of it! You don't have enough to spare." She slipped down from the wagon's confines. "Here's a whole loaf, and some coffee, in my best basket. Do they like baskets, you suppose?"

"They'd have to like this one, Mrs. Hyde. Thank you."

Mrs. Hyde faced Dare and Atoka. "Don't you let them touch a hair on her head," she warned them.

"No, ma'am," her men replied, touching the brims of their hats. The small woman nodded, satisfied, and climbed back into the wagon.

Rachel addressed the men. "Can any of you spare some tobacco?"

Walker bristled. "Tobacco? Why—"

"Our father found it a universal sign of respect among Indian peoples, sir," Atoka said. "We won't need much, an offering."

Gibson Rice pulled out a hank from his trousers and handed it to Atoka. "Here. I smoke too much anyway." Rachel gave the sack of coffee to her husband. "There. We're ready. If you'll lay down your arms, gentlemen?"

Walker's exploding objection was halted by her hand. "They're watching," she reminded them. "And I don't want my family martyred because of a slip of the finger." She hadn't meant it as a personal insult to the trail captain, but Rachel could tell from Atoka's wince that she'd stumbled in her diplomacy before talking to a single Indian. She'd made an enemy of the train's leader, the man by which the others allowed themselves to be guided. In the same way the Choctaw elected their war and peace chiefs. But Rachel stood firm. She was about to face an unknown. She would not put her family in the known danger of an accidental firing.

"Keep all guns within reach," Walker finally grumbled.

The three faced west. Rachel felt the Pawnee warriors' lively curiosity begin to dominate their wariness as they watched the scene at camp. Six were in plain sight on the grassy hill. There were many more than those allowing themselves to be seen. Their leader sat on a horse with a fine-tooled Spanish saddle.

Uncle Bridges's letters had warned that the Pawnee were more dangerous since their numbers' recent reduction by half from the white man's sickness. Rachel sensed the Indians' pride, tension, and mistrust. But she also felt the strength and protection of her men, like angels at her side as they approached the party of six on the hill.

At closer range Rachel noticed still, spare, rangy forms. They wore their hair shaved close to the scalp except for a middle strip. All were smallpox marked.

"Do you two really know these peoples' sign language?" Dare whispered.

"We'll find out," her brother said.

Rachel giggled out her nervousness.

"Stop that!" Atoka barked. "How should we start?"

" 'Friend.' Let's show Dare 'friend.' "

He watched carefully as Rachel and Atoka held their right hands in front of their necks, with palm out and second and third fingers pointing up. They raised their hands up the side of their faces. Dare followed exactly.

When they reached a distance of six feet from the line of Pawnee, they stopped, made the sign again. Then Rachel introduced her brother and he her as his sister. Together they slid index fingers across their foreheads from left to right in imitation of the broad-brimmed hat of a non-Indian, and presented Dare. No response. They tried 'friend' again.

A man with a seashell dangling from his pierced ear came forward. "You sign-talk like a Kiowa, sky-eyed *Métis* brother, brave little sister," he said, then held out his hand to Dare. "How do?" he asked cordially. "You from the wagon train lost the cow?"

He directed them to look over their ridge. A boy of about Jessica's age held the missing Walker cow by a braided buffalo hair halter. The animal scratched her head impatiently against the boy's shoulder.

Rachel smiled. "Yes. We're the train."

"She is suffering. No calf. Needs to be milked. We don't know how. Don't drink cow milk, makes us sick." He cocked his head in Dare's direction. "Turns us white maybe, like him?"

Atoka snorted. "Is that what did it, brother?" he asked.

Dare smiled with one side of his mouth. "I will confess a great fondness for cream," he admitted.

The shelled Pawnee translated their conversation to the others. All laughed, flooding the silent night with their mirth. Their leader then signaled. The boy came forward, handed the cow's halter to Rachel.

"Would you be wanting some coffee?" Dare asked the boy and his six elders. Rachel and Atoka held out their other gifts.

The translator explained in Pawnee to a man on the horse with the Spanish saddle. He was of middle years with legs as long as Dare's. He listened, then spoke quietly in the hushed silence. The shell man nodded, then turned to them, "Our chief likes your music," the translator said. "Our drums try to follow it."

"Dancing's just started. Would you join us?" Atoka offered.

The chief smiled slowly, understanding the meaning behind the welcoming sweep of her brother's hand, Rachel suspected. They had trade seashells, after all, here miles from any ocean. These people understood more forms of language than the white people huddled in their wagons below, Rachel suspected.

"Shall we bring our drums?" the translator asked.

Dare grinned. "Please do. My wife is just learning the steps. The drums will be a great help."

The party of Pawnee circled Gibson Rice's campfire warily. Rachel thought the lean fiddler's shaking fingers would fall off before they'd strike up a tune. When Atoka asked for "Yankee Doodle," Gibson looked from him, to the Pawnee, and back to her brother. Gibson raised the instrument to his shoulder. The bow seemed to remember what to do.

The Pawnee musicians smiled at the sounds he made. They began to punctuate the melody with their drums. That made the tune take on an even more American sound, Rachel thought. Barton slipped into "Sweet Betsy from Pike" next. Unfazed, the drummers softened their accompaniment. That encouraged some of the train's women to drift close beside Rachel, though they would not allow their men to pull them into the music circle.

Dare liked the combination of fiddle and drums so much that he handed Rachel his coat and began dancing like he did in Mr.

Combs's pictures. He was that man again, Rachel realized, his chest as broad his legs as strong in their leaping. The Pawnee delighted in his movements to "Cripple Creek." Atoka brought on his flute, and Harold Underdown his jaw harp. They joined the work of Gibson Rice's clever fingers. The night air rang out with "Redwing" and "Boatman Dance" and "Forked Deer." Two of the Pawnee observed carefully at first. Then they flanked Dare as their drummers beat out challenges to leap higher. Gibson's fiddle set the challenge higher still. Dare met them all, to the cheers of all. Sparks from the fire flew. He unbuttoned Mr. Combs's fine woven vest once his linen shirt began to cling to his form. Then the vest came into her arms as he let his shirt billow out, joining his dance.

The English artist's bright arcs of red and blue had tried mightily to capture this movement, Rachel realized. But, as fine as the colored drawings were, they had failed. The force of the leaping, beautiful dance made her heart pound with excitement and wonder. Amity Hyde leaned into Rachel's side. *"That's* what you're married to?" she asked. "The Good Lord should make him carry his own babies!"

Rachel blushed. Her heart pounded harder. They were not yet married to each other, she and her powerful husband, but she wanted for all the world to be. Wanted so deeply her mind chanted a prayer to the beat of the Pawnee drums, an ancient prayer of women that her missionary teachers had charged her to forget if she valued her soul:

> Oh you who dwell in the skies,
> Who love the rain—
> Oh you who dwell within the skies!
> Make it be that he will find all other women
> unattractive.
> Let him think of me,
> When the sun disappears in the west.

After the tune was over, the two Pawnee dancers collapsed, their effort expired. Dare laughed while other Indians began pulling on his long legs and talking heatedly among themselves. The translator turned to Rachel and Atoka. "They want to know this man's magic," he said. "How can he dance on broken bones that then turn firm again?"

"That's an illusion, a trick of the eye, is all," Dare tried to explain. "Here, I'll show you," he offered, pulling his two defeated challengers to their feet. One wanted no part of the lesson, but the second's curiosity overcame his fear. And his efforts were rewarded with Dare's compliment that he'd fit in at an Irish wedding or wake like a member of his clan.

Soon, the party of Pawnee warriors shook hands all around with men, women, and the few children peeking out from behind their mothers' skirts. Finally, their guests disappeared into the darkness. The Swiss merchant Mr. Bodmer opened his gold pocket watch. "Midnight," he proclaimed softly.

The music continued, more quietly, with waltzes that didn't need the pounding drums behind them. Atoka approached Dare. Rachel couldn't hear the words between them but guessed that she was the subject from the way her brother pointed toward her with his chin, then the nod of assent from her husband.

Dare looked displeased as he approached. He took the vest she held out first, thrusting it on with the vestiges of that displeasure. What had she done wrong?

"I'm sorry, Rachel, to be losing track of the hour in that way," he said.

"We were all lost in the beauty of your dancing," she offered quietly, along with his coat. "What kind of dances were they?"

"Purely pagan. Conjuring-summer-in jigs that the priest would have had me whipped for dancing in my country," he admitted as if he were that priest, whipping himself with the words. What a strange man her husband was, Rachel thought. But his mood changed again as he put on his coat more slowly than he had his vest, then kissed her forehead. "Her brother looks after my wife better than I do. Come. To bed with you now."

Atoka continued to listen to the music, standing beside Eveline Walker from Texas, the captain's yellow-haired daughter. He was enjoying his new prestige among the train's people, as he'd enjoyed ordering her husband about on the subject of her welfare, Rachel thought with irritation. But Atoka was not choosing well in this woman who was almost as proud as her missing-finger father. Rachel sighed. She would not worry unless she heard his flute in the night, she decided, raising her hand to his farewell.

As they reached their wagon, Dare did not hoist Rachel inside. She expected that further humiliation from one of these two men who sometimes treated her as their child. The look in Dare's eyes changed as he watched her, as he listened to the night sounds, his eyes sparking with them as well as their surroundings.

"Will you dance one dance with me here, shy wife?" he asked softly.

Shy. Did he see her as shy, not a child, then? "Mrs. Hyde would advise against it," Rachel said. "She thinks me too fragile for your wild dancing."

"Oh? And what do you think?"

"I was proud to be linked to you, in any way." She took his outstretched hands. But he did not dance. He kissed her, not at her forehead this time, but behind her ear. The soft kiss had all his power behind it. He was not her protector, her other brother, now. She thought of her chant.

"What dance lesson is this?" she asked.

He blinked. "A waltz," he said. "Waltzing's . . . well, waltzing's like this you see . . ." His head bowed, the tumble of glossy black curls obscuring his eyes. "Christ in His heaven, Mrs. Gilmartin, you look so well, so brave and beautiful to me this evening."

He was seeing her whole, at last. What had changed his sight? Was it the chant? Or their meeting with the Pawnee? It didn't matter. It was true, and right. "I feel what you see," she tried to encourage him. Atoka's flute music, beautiful and lonely, sifted on the night air with the last of the banked fires' smoke. Not for Eveline Walker, brother, she prayed into the smoke. Play for me. For me and this man so close that I see the silver spark of desire in his eyes.

"Your brother has guard duty, does he not?"

"*Oke.*"

"The Pawnee are going home to their wives and children?"

"I think so, yes."

"And Captain Walker will be milking his cow all night instead of looking for Indians to shoot?"

"That I doubt. But I hope his daughter is busy milking."

"Rachel, do you think we might—"

She kissed him for an answer, though she'd never kissed a man before, and had only what he'd done for her as example. It did not have his grace, her kiss, but he seemed to enjoy it immensely all the same, for he took her waist during it, and lifted her off her feet. He looked bewildered after, as he breathed into her hair, making her scalp tingle in a way that felt both carnal and sacred. She wondered again if she had done this to him, witched him into this hunger. She should tell him. She was an honorable woman. But would an honorable woman have sung the chant to begin with? His hands loosed her braids of their white woman's bonds as his kisses went deep inside her mouth, eating her. Urgent, like a fevered, starving man, were her husband's kisses. Then he tore his mouth from hers. His voice was panting and frayed.

"Where are you in your cycle?"

"My cycle?"

"When was your last flow?"

"Flow?"

He kissed her forehead, the sweat on his chin gliding his night whiskers sleek against her skin. "Bleeding, Rachel. Your monthly bleeding. I'm sorry, I don't know your words for it. I use words my mother used, in my country."

"Your mother," Rachel remembered, "the midwife."

"Aye. Do you understand what—"

"It ended two days ago. My flow."

"Good. That's good."

Counting. He was counting there, inside his head. She felt cold. "Should I have gone away? Will you send me away, to live with the women when I bleed?"

"No, love. It's a good time, a safe time for us to—" He looked at his feet, suddenly awkward. "That is, if you do not mind."

"I think I will never mind anything you think is good. Dare, what will I be safe from?"

"Conceiving. Us starting a baby."

"But I want children, husband."

"Aye, well. I want their mother strong, and happy in them, and without burdens too hard to bear."

"I want children," she whispered again.

"But not now, while you're still recovering. And we're all facing much harder traveling months—"

"Now. Before death takes us all, I want children," she maintained, her voice shaking.

He sighed hard. Rachel felt tears threatening. He did not love her then, this man. He wanted her in his bed, but did not want her for the mother of new children. *"Costasach, costasach,"* he grumbled out the Irish word as he shook his head, making her wonder if it was a curse. Rachel bit her lip hard against the sound. Dare took her waist suddenly, swept her onto the seat of the wagon, and climbed up beside her. Then he took both her hands in his.

"Rachel, listen to me. I'm not as strong as you are. Or as brave. Please. I cannot bear the thought of losing you."

"So you will take another woman, as you did in St. Louis?"

"I never took another woman in St. Louis, *costasach,*" he said quietly, making the Irish word sound like a prayer now. This man confused her greatly.

"Will you stand in cold streams and send me out of your bed instead of being my true husband?"

"No. That's what I'm trying to tell you. My mother taught me the signs to watch for, feel for inside you. I was a good student. My"—he faltered, looking away, then quickly returned his eyes to hers. "My children were three years apart in their ages while others in the village came one upon the last. It was that way in our family for generations. Some chided us for this, and the priest scolded my mother for passing on her wicca ways, with interfering with God's plan. God gave us intelligence, she'd tell him. To

use. To help ourselves, men and women and children. And the
men of our family had lovely, blooming wives, bearing full-term
children. Wives who did not lose health and teeth and tempera-
ment to constant childbearing. I do not seek to break that family pattern, even with the formidable Queen of the Choctaw as
my bride, for I'm fearing you less than those women haunting
me, Rachel LeMoyne."

"Your grandmothers," she said.

"Aye, just so. My grandmothers. All as stubborn as you are."

In the silence between them, Rachel listened to the end of
Atoka's song. In the ink black of the wide sky, wolves took up its
singing space. Dare's thumbs stroked their clasped hands to the
rhythm of the wolf's song as he waited. Rachel looked at the tips
of his boots.

"Nanny Berry says you want children who do not need to
wear hats in the sun, as you do."

"Nanny Berry does not know a thimble full of my wanting,"
he whispered. "Rachel, forgive me. Forgive all the time I did not
wish to be relieved of the burden of my loneliness for the others.
Tonight, might I make you my wife?"

"Aye. Yes. *Oke,*" she said.

He kissed her. She felt the heated breaths of his nostrils warming her cheek, then her neck as he found, pulled open her day
gown's ties so deftly she gasped.

"How did you know—"

"Rachel LeMoyne, I've been your husband, watching you at
your toilette since the captain's quarters of the blamed ship." He
casually pulled off his boots, let them drop to the ground. "A
man's got to have his mind working toward his eventual purpose,
if he's to keep out of the madhouse."

She giggled, which made him groan deep in the back of his
throat. She wanted to touch him there. She wanted to touch him
everywhere.

It did not stop, his stream of words, once they were inside the
wagon's confines and privacy. Once he freed her hair of its
leather ties and braids. "I could tell you about the star-shaped
mole you have here," he offered, kissing a spot beneath her

shoulder blade, "And the tiny tear that's started in the lace of the hem of your shift. Not this one, this creamy soft plain one, but the one with the blue ribbon woven into the eyelet."

Each of his words came slowly, deliberately, flooding her senses as he glided his fingers down bared skin. She resisted only as he reached her breasts.

"Rachel," he said quietly. "You are beautiful."

"Not here," she protested.

"Here, too, in your healing. Do you believe me?"

There are few things she wouldn't believe, from this man at this moment, she realized. That gave him much power. Did he deserve it?

"Tell me how you feel when I—"

His thumb sifted over a scar, then glided along a nipple, followed by his tongue. How was she to find the words for this? "Good?" he prompted.

"Oh, yes."

"And here? Let's see if—why, they're both quite eloquent!" He laughed out relief, joy. What did he mean? The way she felt swollen to bursting under his attention to her damaged body? The way her nipples went hard in knowing his wet pulls and kisses were coming? His soft laughter continued, a song in the night, as his hands and tongue continued their gentle, pulsing probe of her. She wanted to cry to the stars in her pleasure, but left her songs silent except for a small gasp when she felt something burst, leaving her languid and satisfied.

She reached up to his face. "Is it done, then?"

"Done?" he asked, his voice rough with desire.

"Am I your wife?"

"No, love, that was my finger, finding the part inside that tells me where you are in your cycle."

"It told me something else," she said, stroking his cheek.

Her change-color husband went red. In what? Anger? No. There was no anger in his soft, low voice. "Aye, Rachel. I'm glad of it. Your pleasure. And, I'll stop. I'll go, if that's all you have the strength for tonight—"

"No, please!" She took a firm grip at his shirt. "My strength returns with your words, husband, and those fingers. Does my body tell you the time is . . . safe?"

"It does."

She could do this thing, she decided then, wait for children, if she could have this man who asked it of her as her true husband. This man so different from the emaciated, death-dwelling one she'd married. She remembered being grateful he still had the warmth of life about him then. Now his strange Irish beauty hurt her eyes, even here in the darkness of the wagon that seemed barely able to contain his new form and wondrous grace. She felt the hardness of him glide along her inner thigh, and bucked at the intensity of feeling it produced. He entered slowly inside her, needing so much more room this time. Did she contain enough room? "Dare?" she whispered, biting her lip.

"A pinch only, love, then it will be much better, I promise."

There. She felt her blood flowing. His hands cleared the tangle of hair from her brow. She smiled. "Not even a pinch," she assured his anxious eyes. They lightened to the blue of the quilted pieces that patched the blanket they'd pinned up against the opening of the flaps of their small wagon.

"Rachel, m'darling," he whispered gruffly, tracing her hairline with kisses as he began to move inside her.

"Dare!" she gasped her astonishment at the new waves coursing through her.

"Good?"

"Oh, aye."

She felt his smile, there in the darkness. "Rachel, I never thought I could again feel. It has been such a long season without rain. Hold on, *costasach.*"

"What do you call me, husband?"

"Dear," he translated, "Beloved one."

She laughed her astonishment, and took his shoulders. She squeezed them with each thrust of his body into her. That's what the word meant. It was not a curse, but an endearment. Beloved. Soft moans of thanksgiving escaped from her mouth, for this new dance they did in the dark, beneath the pinpricks of stars shining through the canvas of the wagon.

fifteen

Dare still lay beside her, his arm about her waist, as Rachel smelled the dew of morning. She drifted back into contented drowsiness. True wife. A dream visited. She was at the tree ceremony of the Choctaw women, feeling her mother press the leaf of her oak seedling along her cheek. She opened her eyes. Not her mother, but her husband was above her, gliding the dewy blossom of the buttonberry along her cheek. Why was he doing that? More Irish madness, he told her—a wish for her health, her continued beauty. She was so different from his Irish wife. Did he truly find her beautiful, she wondered, as he pulled her close, apologizing for disturbing her sleep.

Rachel opened her eyes again. Coffee roasting. She sat up slowly, then fastened her clothes without waking Dare. She peered under the canvas flap and saw Atoka by the fire. The beans and bacon she'd set in the ashes of last night were now bubbling, along with the coffee. Their oxen team George and Victoria were already yoked and hitched. This taking on of all their morning duties was her brother's wedding gift, she realized and was deeply moved. Rachel wove a quick braid through her hair before she slipped out of the wagon. She rested her hand at her brother's shoulder.

He grunted. "Now they're wondering about him, too."

"Who's wondering?"

"This train. And the one behind us, which sent scouts up to us before dawn, sure they'd find everyone slaughtered after your wildman husband's midnight swirls with the savages."

"He was celebrating the coming summer. In the dances of his own country."

Atoka turned, smiled slyly. "And has he finally showed you some of them?"

Rachel shoved her brother's shoulder. "Eat."

He grunted again. "This food is not digestible without *tafula.* Make *tafula.*"

"What is it called, here in this place?"

"Johnnycakes," Atoka conceded with disgust. "As if the damned English speakers discovered corn as well as everything else they stole from us."

"Now you sound exactly like my husband." She grunted softly as she greased her iron skillet, glad that both husband and brother liked to eat. It was among her holds on her men.

"The two of you need sweetening this morning," Dare complained, tripping over the black boots he'd dropped off the side of the wagon before he'd bedded her.

"Shake them," Atoka warned. "Snake season."

If there was one thing that could knock her husband out of an early morning lethargy, it was the mention of snakes. The men of the company teased him with tales of those creatures he knew only from stories, since the Irish Saint Patrick had driven them from his island. Atoka did better than the taunting men: he schooled Dare on the snakes whose bite could kill. They had lost a childhood friend to a cottonmouth when the Arkansas flooded seven springs before. Atoka had taken his turn with the men in the desperate attempt to save him. Rachel's hand ached for days where the dying boy had clung to her.

The clear memory of it chilled her as she watched Dare knock his high boots against the wagon wheel. Empty. He grinned, banishing the cold from her heart. He smiled like their boy, Rachel decided, the one they would make together in Oregon. He cocked his head and it broadened, his smile, going lopsided. Had he seen her thought?

"Stir harder, I'm hungry," her brother complained, pulling her fond attention from her husband. Foolish man. Why should Atoka deny her the pleasure she took in the sight of Dare's taut, graceful beauty, the lingering scent of his desire? Their children would be her brother's to raise, too. Rachel went back to her corn cakes as her husband turned their horses toward the muddy water of the North Platte.

Rachel packed *oneheonotda* too, for they were heading into hill country. There was no English word for these cakes of corn and beans and bits of precooked meat, dried fruits and berries. The Americans preferred to pull at jerk meat and hardtack biscuits when they couldn't stop to eat. Dare called Rachel's concoction "pouch cakes," because she filled small pouches that hung on her men's suspenders as they spent parts of the day away from her. *Oneheonotda* was a good, sustaining food that a Seneca woman had taught her mother how to make. It did not provide the quick rush of energy that came by the other pouch, the one containing a handful of roasted coffee beans. Dare and Atoka would chew on a few of those at times other men chewed on tobacco. She was proud neither of her men used tobacco the way white men did—often, and without ceremony.

Rachel watched her own arms as she worked. They did not look different from the day before. But she was different. Married. Truly married. Did Dare feel different? Even though he'd had a wife before her? Something was new for him, too. He had not loved her, Rachel LeMoyne, his Choctaw wife, before. Did he feel like her, new and beautiful? Rachel missed her mother and sister, with whom she would have talked about these things. Would the women of the train know her newness, as Atoka did?

They knew something, Rachel thought, as the day went on.

But their signs were not sly and crafty, like her brother's, or a little clumsy, like Dare's at nooning. He'd almost trampled the box of pencils Harold Underdown had donated to her makeshift school to deposit a bouquet of wildflowers. Then he'd tried to speak twice, then ran his hand through his hair before trudging off to picket Raven Mocker. By this, perhaps, the women knew something was different between them.

Perhaps Dare was teased by the men that noontime, too. He returned, when the children were at the end of their spelling bee. It stabbed at Rachel a little, knowing what they had done the night before would not start one of their own. He removed his hat, Atoka's wedding gift, that she had adorned with a two-colored braid that looked like circles without end. "Mrs. Gilmartin," he greeted her softly when she looked up from the speller.

"Mr. Gilmartin," she replied, schoolmistress tone in her voice. "We thank you for the flowers that welcome our new school, don't we, children?"

At her nod they sang out their thanks together, startling him speechless. Again, speechless. Her brave, eloquent husband, afraid of nothing, except children. She thought they would send him back into the men's company, but he slipped behind her as she heard her new scholars' spelling recitations. He touched her back with his fingertips. This would not be permitted at her school at the mission. She would not be permitted to even have a husband. Could the children see Dare touching her? "That's correct," she told a tall girl who'd spelled "accomplishment."

"Yes," her husband agreed at her ear. "At long last. Accomplishment." Soft, intimate, like his night whispers. "What a bloody fool I was not to have—"

Rachel brought her book closer to her face as the next child in line approached. "Last night came at the fullness of time," she insisted. "Do not be disrespectful to your people, your beautiful ghosts."

She could feel his frown. "My ghosts pushed me into your arms, Mrs. Gilmartin. It was they growing impatient with me, I'm thinking."

"Truly?" she spoke her astonishment. Too loudly.

The face of the boy before her brightened. "Truly. T-r-u-l-y, truly," he proclaimed.

Rachel looked down at her Webster speller. "No, Peter, your word is— Oh, all right, correct. You may go to the end of your line."

Both teams cheered. The remaining spelling masters were evenly split, three to each. Jessica Lowell frowned. "What shall we do now, ma'am?" she asked. "That was supposed to break the tie."

"It was?" Rachel turned, eyed Dare, who gave her a truant-boy smile. She handed him a small mallet. "Here. Break up this chocolate into six pieces," she ordered. "Your punishment for distracting me, Mr. Gilmartin."

He grinned. "With pleasure," he proclaimed, "once your scholars guide me in deciding the lines of demarcation."

The children gathered around him, drawn by the prize that Mr. Bodmer had donated from the precious supply that came from his native Switzerland. Dare asked for ideas on how to divide the treasure. He heard them all out. Patiently. He'd found another lesson within her reward for the best spellers, Rachel realized. With his questions, always his questions. They engaged the children better than recitations of mathematical principles.

As the smallest of the Lowell sisters, five-year-old Lulie, pondered, she rested her hand on Dare's shoulder. Pain swept through his eyes like a storm across the prairie. Two of his ghosts were daughters, with bright, trusting eyes like Lulie's. Rachel watched as he bore the pain of their memory. It moved on.

When Lulie Lowell proposed he use the joints of his longest finger to mark the block into thirds, then half each, Dare asked the children what they thought of that idea. All heads nodded.

Except for the respect they showed him as their elder, Rachel realized they were treating Dare as, not a master lording over them, but one of them, a seeker of knowledge.

He'd been that kind of father, then, one like her own, not like most white fathers she'd seen, who were distant with their offspring and wives? She felt her mother's warm approval of her choice as her husband squatted before Lulie to whom he offered the first piece of precious chocolate.

Perhaps they should make a girl first in Oregon, Rachel thought, finding the next lesson in her day-planning book. Atoka could teach her to play his flute.

When she looked up again, Dare was gone.

Atoka must learn that they'd decided to wait. He would be disappointed when she did not soon grow big with a child inside her. Rachel struggled with the prospect of telling him once she'd released the children to help their parents prepare for the rest of the day's hard travel.

She smelled Dare's iron and buttonbush scent, then felt the light touch of paper at her back.

"What are you about now, disrupter?" she demanded, looking down at the creamy, textured paper she recognized as another item from Mr. Bodmer's treasures.

Dare looked as shy as Hiram Hyde, who rarely spoke and had never been to any school before hers. "Assignment completed," he said, with uncharacteristic succinctness.

She stared down at the dense black writing with the dancing sweep. She recognized it immediately from his signature on their marriage certificate.

"What is this?" she asked quietly.

"Translation."

She glanced at the first few words, recognized them. "Of the song? The one you sang when I was sick?"

"Aye."

He turned, but she caught his sleeve. Held. "Come with me," she demanded, pulling him after her like a recalcitrant schoolboy. And he followed her like one, to a rocky spot. At its edge was a small grove of cottonwood. Planted by earlier travelers who were growing mad from the lack of trees. She sat on an outgrowth of rock, and pulled her husband down beside her.

"Rachel, we'll lose our place in the—"

"Hush!" she demanded.

He squirmed, then took a great interest in the soles of his boots, then in the slate and bloodroot colors of the stones at his feet. But she caught him casting glances at her as well, as she read, her chin and mouth resting on the curve of her hand:

> I thought, my love, you were
> As the sun or the moon on a fountain,
> And I thought after that you were snow,
> The cold snow on top of the mountain.
> Then I thought after that you were more
> Like God's lamp shining to find me,
> Or the bright star of knowledge before,
> Or the star of knowledge behind me.

She folded the paper carefully, then pressed it against the beating of her heart. "It was a love song you sang to me then, in the ruined place, the place of the spirits?" she whispered through her tears.

"Aye, not a dirge, so there's no need for wearing out my handkerchiefs with the force of your fountain, woman."

She clung to his hand, and the white cloth it offered, pressing both to her face. "Sing it again, Dare."

He snorted indignantly. "I'll do no such thing, else I'll be cast off the trail in lonely exile for cold-hearted seduction of the schoolmistress."

"Not cold. You were never cold, even when I smelled death about you."

Pain, there behind his laughing eyes. "Ach, Rachel—"

"Tell me of your own schooling, Dare."

He shrugged. "That makes a short story. Hedge schools, secret places—taught on the sly by a succession of poets and bards in rags, but who know the old stories as well as English and Latin and Greek. But the lord would get wind of them, and they'd be off or arrested for sedition. Then I was hand-picked for attending a national school. Ah, there was hope for me then, as a bridge between my people and their masters."

"Mr. Combs spoke of you that way, as a bridge."

"I was not that. The price was too high, Rachel. I did not last long at the national school. I would not begin each day reciting 'I thank the goodness and the grace, that on my birth has smiled, and made me in these Christian days, a happy English child.' Paugh, not content to murder my own language, they murdered their own as well!"

"Atoka would not say the words either."

"Did the missionaries have words like those?"

"Blessing our Great White Father in Washington."

"And did you?"

"Yes. I tried to see the world as they did."

"There is no shame in that, love. I came home to some scorn. But some rejoicing, too."

"From Bevin, rejoicing," she ventured.

"Aye." A ghostly smile appeared. "Relief that I was not homemade into an English lord in my scant months away, from that one. And a great leap into my arms. What could I do but marry her?"

"What, indeed?" she whispered.

His smile disappeared. "This is a sacred place you've led me to, Rachel LeMoyne," he said gruffly.

"Didn't you know by the trees? I thank you for your story and your scholarship, husband." She took in a shuddering breath. "If you will not sing, will you kiss me?" she asked shyly, making him laugh, before he took her head between his ink-stained hands and ravished her mouth until she thought he was behind her.

Her men did not hunt, but flanked their wagon on horses as she drove the ox team that day. There were three false sightings of Indians, and Mr. Spikenard almost shot Gibson Rice fetching buffalo chips for his fire. Finally, the Texan, Captain Walker, who'd avoided her family all day, rode up beside them at dusk.

"Well, Mrs. Gilmartin, seems I must consult with you on the

whereabouts of the Indians before the women will agree to camp for the night."

She met his eyes and spoke quietly. "I think the Pawnee have left us, sir."

"You do?"

"And I think we are leaving their country. In Mr. Standhope's guide, it says that in his crossing of 1843 he encountered Pawnee only until—"

"Standhope's guide? Well, you're a curious mix, schoolteacher."

Atoka pulled his horse closer. She maintained an even voice. "Do you think so, sir?"

"Of book-learning and heathen tale-telling, according to my girl Eveline, who's done some talking with your brother, here. You'll have a care to pass no papist or squaw beliefs onto this train's children, I trust."

Rachel looked down at her hands, callused from holding the reins.

Dare rode closer, and spoke before Atoka could clear the growl from his voice. "Have the folks placed you in charge of overseeing the children's schooling now, Mr. Walker?" he asked with his for-the-landlord smile.

"I was voted trailmaster only *after* that half-breed with French airs talked you onto this company, Irishman. You might not have been with us otherwise."

Had this man no respect, even for a fellow guide as rich with knowledge and travel as Atoka's friend Baptiste, Rachel wondered. Her husband leaned casually over his saddle.

"Oh? I thought it was one man to a vote in your glorious country, sir."

"Men of influence rise above the defective, even in the states."

"And women of accomplishment do as well, it seems, in its territories. It is a glorious nation indeed. I hope you will tender my wife's observation and opinion of the lack of Indian presence to whom it might give comfort."

The trailmaster scowled under her husband's barrage of words. "Fall back," he commanded. "Your wagon circles up last tonight. And eats dust come tomorrow. That is, if your sickly woman can keep it from straying behind, leaving you alone with your wilder red devil cousins."

Once Walker rode away, Dare let out a stream of Irish vindictive before he handed the reins of his horse to Atoka and climbed up into the wagon beside Rachel.

"We have made an enemy," Rachel said quietly as he took over the reins.

"He has made himself one."

"I'm putting my flute away," Atoka muttered, falling back.

"I will practice the whip tonight, husband," Rachel tried to assure Dare. "And so keep the oxen moving at a good pace tomorrow."

Dare frowned. "That you will not. I'll ask the Lowells if they can spare Alfred to drive tomorrow. And their neighbor woman Mrs. Hyde has a present of a new feather bed she's plucked from her geese for you. It will help you rest better as we travel into higher country."

"Why would she—"

"Because her boy Hiram is spelling his name in the dust for the first time in his fourteen years, and his mother is sure his stammer will leave him as well, thanks to your teaching. And you charmed those heathen savages to go back to their families and stop trailing us."

"But the Pawnee are not—" She caught his teasing grin, "and I didn't do *that* at all!"

"Folks believe what they want to believe, Rachel. Personally I think it was tasting Mrs. Hyde's miserable hard loaf of yeast bread convinced the Pawnee that we are not such good company."

"I miss them," Rachel said, her eyes scanning the distance, so empty of the wild Pawnee and their beautiful horses.

"So do I," Dare admitted. He cracked the bullwhip over George and Victoria's heads. "Come on, your majesties, almost done for the day!" he called out. He'd never once touched their oxen's backs with the whip, despite the fact they were named for enemy monarchs of both the Irish and Americans. Rachel sighed, happy for his warmth beside her.

She leaned her head on his shoulder as he tucked her hand in the crook of his arm. He exhaled a tattered breath before speaking again. "Rachel, was last night too hard on you?"

She laughed. "It that what has your fine brow knit with worry now, Darragh Ronan?" she demanded. "Last night was rich and beautiful, a time when I thought you were, how is it said? The sun or the snow on a fountain?"

"The moon on the fountain," he corrected, his chin nudging the top of her head.

"Will you be the snow on the mountain tonight, *cos . . . costasach?*" she asked shyly.

He grinned. "Aye, *madame,* if that's your wish."

Atoka left their camp in the night. He returned before dawn, leading a new wild horse, a mustang mare the color of gunmetal. He'd already tamed her well enough that Rachel's gentlest touch could clear some brambles from her mane.

"Oh, wait until Dare sees her!"

"Where is your husband?" Atoka asked.

"He's gone to water the oxen. What do you call her, Atoka?"

"*Hacha,* because I caught her at the fork of the river," Atoka announced quietly. "Do you like that name, sister?"

"*Hacha.* It suits her," Rachel agreed. "Does she ease your heart?"

"I will have more care to whom I speak my pride in my sister's teaching, I think. Eveline Walker turned my words against you. I did not think such a thing possible, even here, among these upside-down people." He looked away. "I was taking out my flute to . . . to keep it oiled and beautiful. I had only a few thoughts on Walker's daughter." Rachel saw a fleeting smile. "*Hacha,* this new horse. She is not for me, or my scarred heart. I train her for you, sister." He tied the horse to the back of the wagon.

"Me?"

"Yes. Bride gift." He sat casually by the fire, then stole a look at her. "You have been more fortunate than I, I think? Your braid is single. You are a bride now?"

"I have a true husband," she told her brother quietly.

He nodded. "You and your husband must do as I do—ride out from the trail, see more than dust at your feet now that we've been put at the end of the train by that miserable man. *Hacha* will be ready for you soon."

"Atoka," she called softly, fearing her courage would fail. "My husband has fears for my health over this long journey. We are taking care to avoid starting a child here."

Atoka was so silent Rachel had to confirm with her eyes that he was still sitting before their fire. "I wasn't sure the missionaries allowed you this woman's knowledge," he finally said.

"They did not. My husband knows the signs."

He shook his head. "Irish white people," he exclaimed softly. "Men know women's magic?"

"Not all the men. But he does."

"Well. I will keep him busy in the forbidden times, so he will be good to you, even then."

She bowed her head. "Thank you, Atoka. I thought you would be angry that a baby will not come right away."

"We have buried a with-child woman and two suckling children since we began following the Platte. Maybe the women here don't have the knowledge, or the men are too greedy for their own pleasure and for new hands to place behind their plows. It's a good thing, I think, what you and your husband have decided."

"Oh, Atoka." She touched his shoulder.

He leaned his face into her hand. "Stay well, sister."

Lulie Lowell's screaming call from the riverbank came before Rachel's lips had touched her brother's brow.

sixteen

Rachel didn't remember kilting up her skirts, but she must have, to have kept up with her brother's run. She tried to understand what she saw: Dare shoving the child, the same child to whom he'd offered the first piece of Mr. Bodmer's chocolate—Lulie, the Lowell family's youngest. Why was he doing that? It made Lulie fall, scream again, harder, but not in fear or indignation. How did she scream? In warning. Dare made a small, choked sound as his hat flew back, the strings catching at his throat. He'd cleared Lulie from its raised head-over-coils fury, but the snake still sprang. At his arm, below his rolled-up sleeve. Strong arm. Not slack from sickness and hunger. Muscled now. Would that save him?

Rachel heard Atoka's short prayer to the thunder spirit, then saw his knife fly. It sliced the gray and red body from its head. The head remained embedded in her husband's arm until her brother lifted it out. Dare blinked. "Good throw," he said.

"Thank you."

"Diamondback. Fanged. Viper. Poisonous, yes?"

"Good," her brother complimented his knowledge.

"Prairie dog stole Lulie's doll. Under the rock she reached, you see? Startled—" His stance buckled a little. "Where's Lulie, Rachel?"

"Safe."

"She's crying. Did I hurt her?"

"No. Lie down now, Dare, we'll help you."

The area of his arm around the diamondback's strike was purple and swelling. Pain battled with shock and confusion in his eyes. "Is there help?"

"Aye. Please. Lie down."

She and Atoka eased him to the ground. He had already gone from pale to deathly white. Rachel wound a ripped strip of her petticoat above his elbow and tied it tight. Atoka wiped his knife's blade on his pants as she felt the rapid pulse at her husband's wrist. Not too late, please, she prayed before gently turning Dare's head to her.

"Does it sting?" she asked.

"Aye," he gasped. What was stealing his breath away? Fear? Or the poison working already?

"Keep your eyes on mine," she urged. "Stay calm."

"Yes, miss." He smiled. How could he smile?

Atoka made the first cut. A small wince. He could feel, then. That was good.

Her brother cut again, then closed his mouth over the wound. Dare locked his eyes on hers.

"I'll make Lulie another doll. I used to for my own. Haven't forgotten. Their names. Rachel, I must tell you their names. So you can write them on Mr. Combs's pictures. You have such a hand on you."

Sentences. Rachel wanted to cry in hope. "Yes, I'll do that. Tell me their names."

"Our first was a boy, with hair of red flame like his mother's. Egan his name was, born on the fifteenth day of September, eighteen hundred and forty. Would you write that too, their birthdays?"

"Yes. Egan," she whispered. Her brother lifted his head, spat into the dirt. "Tell Atoka too. We will both remember."

She took Atoka's place, remembering what the men had done on the shore of the swollen Arkansas. Her husband's blood was flowing freely. She pressed her mouth over the wound, pulled. Warm. Rich. Heartblood. Was she pulling the poison too?

Dare shifted his focus to her brother. "He was shy, like Bevin, Egan was. But our Rachel could have helped him speak, as she does Hiram. Your sister's a wonder with the children, Atoka."

"I know," he said, shoving her shoulder. "Rachel," he demanded, "spit!"

She let the profusion of red into the earth. A woman's hand offered a tin of cold coffee. A gulp rinsed her mouth. She spat again. A ragged cloth, smelling of lavender, from another hand. They were all a blur. She could only see her brother, her husband, and the wound clearly.

Atoka, at the arm. Her husband's eyes, searching, losing focus. She leaned in close. "The next child, Dare. A little girl?"

"Aye, *costasach*. Ossnat, full of bright liveliness." He was pulling up vast stores of strength for each breath a sentence took. "Born on the sixteenth of April, eighteen forty-three. Drawing, always drawing her pictures. On the shore. At the loch."

"The artist," she encouraged him.

"She was. I brought misprinted pages. From the pressroom for her. Empty on the one side. Good likenesses she made. Rachel, I'm sick. I need to—"

He tried to sit as he heaved convulsively. Another sign of the poison working its purpose.

Atoka spit more blood in the dirt. "Keep him down!" he shouted.

Blurred men's strength assisted her. "There's nothing to come up love," Rachel soothed, loosening the buttons of Dare's trousers and yanking his shirt out of them. "You haven't yet eaten, remember?" Her fingers found skin, massaged gently. "Better?"

"Aye. Thank you."

She drew more blood, willing her own her spirit to enter

Dare's arm, praying, like her brother did, to the powerful thunder and lightning spirits as well as her Christian god, for the life of her husband.

Dare groaned softly.

She spat, wiped her mouth, then raked his damp hair from his forehead. His change-color eyes stared at the sky, became the sky, darkening now, swirling with storm clouds. Atoka continued sucking at the wound. "Dare. Tell me about the baby now," Rachel urged.

"Baby?"

"Yes, your baby, his birthday."

"Hers. Sheea. The tenth of January, eighteen forty-six. Sheea, my heart. I caught her. Imagine. Oh, Rachel, she barely saw April. Bevin followed. In the morning."

"Bevin, your wife. The dancer." She could even endure her own jealousy of his dead wife's place in his heart for the gift of his life.

He smiled. "Dancer, aye. Faith, but. That one mixed her legs well. While your back was turned. She. Could walk up your sleeve. Build a nest. In your ear. I put them in the coffin. Together. The one I made. With the hinged bottom. So others could. Use it as well. In the monster graves. Ah, they thanked me. My neighbors. Ingenious contrivance. Handy. I'm so damned . . ."

His eyes stilled on clouds lit from within by a fork of lightning. Atoka raised his head. Rachel began sucking again. She heard her brother tease Dare about being the diamondback's first and last Irishman. But he did not respond. She wanted him to keep talking, even though his words swelled her soul with sorrow for all his losses.

Finally, when she was spitting his blood she heard his ragged, rattled intake of breath. "I don't regret trying to be useful to you, Rachel." He reached his good hand in the air. She caught it, though a sob escaped with the touch of him. "Ach, now, none of that. All I wanted was. Someone to remember me. As I remember them. And to bury me decent. Look how much more I've gotten, will you? This is a rich place. Your America."

The arm's swelling had gotten worse, spread. No. It can't

have him, Rachel's mind screamed as her hands checked the pressure, then tied another strip of petticoat above the first.

"Rachel?" Dare called.

"Yes?"

"Into the west, *Tír na nóg*. They will not allow me in. They will laugh. Me with my name. Seal's child who cannot swim."

"I will teach you. In the next water we reach. I promise."

His sky eyes lost their focus, and bore only the reflection of the tumultuous sky. The rattle again. But no words out of him. "Stay with us, Dare," she whispered.

No answer.

"We know only our own customs for burial, not yours," she persisted, her voice hissing shrill at his ear. "Atoka and I will become bone-pickers if you die. We will hasten your way into becoming part of the earth again!"

His eyes sparked in the fear her words produced, making her regret them. But then the brows above them slanted in amusement as he pulled in a tortured breath.

"You're a desperate woman, Rachel LeMoyne," he accused, all the speech her silver-tongued husband had left.

Her brother raised his head from the wound, looking dizzy with his effort. Rachel took another turn at the swollen arm.

They continued as if he was not dying, his breaths growing more shallow, eyelids flickering. Rachel became absorbed in the ritual, in rubbing Dare's middle. Her talking became a soothing babble of the Irish phrases her husband and Blind Maeve had taught her. Even Atoka managed greeting him with a few saints. They worked for an hour's worth of minutes all tolled, Celinda Lowell told her later, ten of them after Dare had turned completely still. The whispers started, about pulling them away from their kinsman. Rachel didn't heed them. She barely noticed her bloodied clothes, or felt her raw, swollen lips.

"Will you stop while I have a few drops left, woman?" Brought her up from his arm for the last time. Was that her husband's voice, that splintered sound? She spat, then laughed and cried out together.

"Jesus, Mary, and Joseph, the sight of you both!" Dare admonished. "Bloodthirsty savages."

Rachel was grateful that the powerful prairie storm stopped the train's progress that day. She liked the crashing thunder much more than the thought of her almost bloodless husband tortured further by a bruising ride.

Once the men carried him into their wagon, Rachel prepared Dare for his recovery. She and Atoka lay him on the gift of her featherbed, cleaned and dressed him in his good shirt. Dare never woke, even when Rachel lifted his vest and the deeply creased papers fell from its inner pocket onto his chest. She saw that some of his splattered blood had dampened the edges. She opened the document carefully. She could not read the words written in aged, fading ink and sealed at the bottom with blue wax. What language were those words, she wondered.

Long bolts of lightning rent the clouds and sky. They touched the ground in this place that was so little ground, so much sky. Rain and hail descended in sheeting, windswept waves. All of the train huddled under tents or their canvas wagon covers waterproofed with linseed oil.

Atoka looked down on her sleeping husband, smiling. "They wanted him, the thunder sprits." He glanced at the wagon cover being pelted with hail and wracked with wind. "We stole him back. They're angry now."

Another deafening crash.

"I'd best brew some sassafras . . . for the one who is not here," Rachel whispered carefully, hiding her even-breathing husband from the thunder gods with her words.

Her brother smiled. "I'll make a fire."

As the storm raged, Rachel allowed Atoka to pass smoking sage over the three of them, over the strange papers that Dare had held against his heart, to cleanse them all from the death of the snake, and the abduction of its prey back into the land of the living. Her brother looked tired after his ceremony.

"Enough," he breathed out, handing her the clay pot of steeped tea. "I am only learning to be a holy man, and I'm without guidance here in this sea of people out of balance. You two must stay well and without trouble for a little while."

Rachel smiled as the steam rose between them. "I am stronger than I look," she reminded him. "And this one who is not here will only need to sleep and make new blood. I will watch first. Take your own rest."

He nodded.

The lantern made shadows dance across her brother's face, allowing her to imagine his hair grown out again, and decorated with symbols of honor in the healing arts. Shells and beads and rattles would be part of his walk, too, if they were in their own country, the place of the Mound Builders. As a child, Rachel had loved the way the medicine men smelled and sounded when they walked, and the fierce-gentle look about their eyes. Her brother's eyes had it now.

Once dried, the diamondback's ringed black-and-white tail would go into Atoka's medicine bag. And if its spirit forgave her brother, he would gain much toward his own wisdom. Rachel believed this, she realized, and for the first time since she was a child of the missionaries, she did not feel ashamed for believing it.

"*Yalabusha*, Gathers Stories," Atoka called her out of her fond dream of him, "the three of us—we are all related now."

The flaps closed. He was gone, leaving her heart singing. He had tasted her husband's blood, along with the snake's magic. They were brothers.

Rachel placed the blue sealed document in the oilcloth pouch that held her precious things—marriage papers, Uncle Bridges's letters, Mr. Combs's drawings of Dare and his Irish family. She added Bevin and her children's names and birthdays. And the year of their deaths, all the same: 1847.

The thunder grew more distant. The rain fell hard. Dare woke.

"Moving?" he asked her.

"No, camped. Thirsty?"

"Oh, aye."

She lifted his head and offered him spoonfuls of the steeped tea. Rachel watched him swallow, hoping the liquid would stay down and help start his healing. He smiled contentedly.

"Sweet," he said, pleasing her so much she had to wipe a tear from the corner of her eye.

"Sassafras. It will thicken your blood."

"What little you've left me. Where are my clothes?"

"Waiting. For when you're better."

"My vest?"

She handed it to him, watched him feel along its heft with his good hand. Yes, she'd seen him do that before. His eyes panicked. "My papers. Rachel, where are my papers?"

"Safe. In oilcloth. I put them with my things."

"Ah." His breathing eased. "That's good, then. Thank you."

His eyelids sank again, too heavy. "Dare?" she called softly. "What are the papers?"

He smiled. "Land grant. Very old."

"And its language?"

"Latin. Making me King of Connacht. And so proof to you of my pedigree, Queen of the Choctaw."

"I see."

"For when we return. Someday. Might we, Rachel?"

"You never can tell," she whispered, watching him drift back to sleep.

The rain fell harder. A good, clean sound, now without the anger of the thunder. Finally, it lessened. Then the wrens and sparrows announced the storm over.

Lulie edged toward their camp, with the cigar box under her arm, and gripping her sister Jessica's hand. Rachel had spotted them, but went on kneading oat bread by the fire. They slipped past her, their feet sucking through the mud. They lifted the canvas of the wagon still smelling of the sage of Atoka's ceremony.

"See? Miss Rachel's taking good care of Mr. Gilmartin, Lulie," Jessica soothed in a quiet whisper. "Why he looks snug as a bug, don't he?"

Smiling, Rachel stole a sideways glance. Lulie appeared unconvinced. "Never seen that man still."

"For pity's sake, he's sleeping!"

"Never this still! You sure they ain't killed him?"

"Pa explained it, told us not to listen to the others! Said the treatment Miss Rachel and her brother gave was first-rate snakebite cure, better'n dosing him with any concoction, on account there ain't anything going can antidote the double-pronged bite of a viper."

"He told me," the little girl said, still sounding unconvinced.

Rachel wiped her hands on her apron to alert them, before she rose and approached the sisters. Her schoolteacher's frown of displeasure was firmly in place. "Come inside," she issued an invitation that was closer to a command.

She knelt beside her husband on the new featherbed. The sight of him made it impossible to maintain her own false face. She called his name softly. He opened his eyes. "Still raining?" he whispered.

"All done."

"Smells lovely. Fresh."

"Yes."

"Dark?"

"Yes, it's dark."

"I must see to—"

She kissed his forehead. "You've done your day's work, Mr. Gilmartin. You had a good sleep. And now visitors. Look."

As the sisters entered into the lantern's light he smiled, startling them. Jessica stayed behind Lulie, who made their offering. "Mama sends her whole scrap box, Mr. Gilmartin. Did you really say you want to make me another Anabelle, sir?"

"Anabelle?"

"My doll. The one the prairie dog stole away? Was it your wish to make her again?"

"And who told you that?"

"Why, Miss Rachel did, sir."

"Well." He glanced above their heads at her. "As Miss Rachel wears her honor like a crown, I must have expressed such a desire." He pulled himself up on the elbow of his good arm. "Let's see what you have there, ladies."

Jessica opened the box. Rachel recognized patches of calico and gingham checks, brighter versions of the same patterns on Celinda Lowell and her children's clothing and quilts. Here and there were remnants of silk and creamy lace.

"Miss Rachel?" she heard a soft call.

Jessica reached for the lantern. "That'd be Alfred."

"Alfred?"

Lulie nodded. "Alfred's givin' us some of his best whittled sticks for Anabelle's skel'ton," she informed them. Jessica took hold of the sleeve of Dare's nightshirt and whispered at his ear. "Make her for Alfred too, Mr. Gilmartin, on account of he's as bad as Lulie at believing you to be a haunt of yourself unless you start working with your hands again."

"Haunt?"

"You know. Ghost."

"Now, I don't believe a ghost would be nearly the trouble on my kin as I've been."

"Oh, they can be plenty pesky, sir. Don't you have them in Ireland?"

He glanced at Rachel. "We have them."

"Well, here they fly about breaking things mostly, not fixing them, as you do, or making new Anabelles, either, I'm sure. So if you'd be so kind to take the cloth and baubles and Alfred's bones, when you're feeling your strength again?"

"Miss Rachel. Look," Lulie called, lifting the canvas flaps back. Jessica raised the lantern higher. Outside stood Alfred Lowell and his offering of whittled wood sticks. Behind him his middle sisters, Hannah, Rose, and Callie, each presented Rachel with a small potted fruit tree. Beyond them, a silent delegation of a dozen of the train's party held a broken harness, yoke, Betty lamps, a leaking tar bucket, and frayed whip handles.

Rachel brought Dare's head into her lap so he could see them all. "Alfred isn't the only one who has doubts about your mortal nature," she said.

Lulie frowned. "My doll first!" she demanded.

Jessica began to scold, but was hushed by the music of Dare's soft laughter. "Aye, then. I'd best be about the new Miss Anabelle," he said. "Then all the rest besides."

seventeen

"One day more," she insisted.

"Ach, Rachel, Atoka says he feels the buffalo just over the next hill from where he was scouting. You wouldn't want me to miss my first sight of—"

She locked in the last stitch. "My brother did not hunt buffalo in the swamps of the Mississippi, no matter what tales he weaves or expertise he claims." She pitched the mended vest at her husband.

"But he knows horses! And he says Sassafras and *Hacha* fairly smell a herd."

Rachel tried to look away from the beauty of his long arms going through the sleeves. Fingers, buttoning. The boyish excitement in his eyes. Distraction. She needed it, or she would cry, or worse, start begging him to stay beside her one more day. She sat on the tailgate, stacking the spellers she'd use with the children at nooning. "Where there are buffalo there are Indians," she tried, in her firm voice.

"Rachel, is this you I'm hearing? We've had no trouble with the Indians, especially with you and Atoka to talk—"

"We are in the land of the Sioux! Different people, without a history of friendship and trading with Americans. Many nations of the Sioux live off the trail here, my uncle and the guidebook say. Some are angry at hide hunters who destroy the buffalo as the trappers destroyed the beaver."

He touched her hand. No, it wasn't fair, this touching, this soft, from-the-night-before voice. "But we're not profit hunting, just seeking passage across their land."

"This trail has already split herds in two, changing buffalo migration patterns, my uncle says."

"But we're not the kind who—"

"And do you think they will stop and ask what kind of white man you are?"

Her husband stopped his barrage, stared at her until she met his eyes. His adamant face gentled. Did he pity her? She did not want his pity. "Maybe they will ask. And I will tell them who we are. Be easing yourself from worry, wife." He flashed those white teeth. "I am much better with people than with snakes, am I not, then?"

Rachel looked at her trembling hands clutching the spellers. She was being foolish, she knew, but that knowledge did not allow her to stop. She could not keep him close to her forever. He kissed her cheek.

"Will you have pity on a man gone all black-and-blue from the tumble of the wagon?"

She tried to hide her smile. "You, who have had my new featherbed for your lying-in?"

"You share that very bed in the dark of the night, wife. Without complaint that I have heard." He leaned closer. "And have I not given you proof enough of my recovery there?" he asked at her ear, making her very warm. He swiped her ear with his nose. Leaving her without words or breath. "No?" he asked softly, not understanding her silence. Or perhaps understanding it too well. "Shall I work now, in plain sight of our good neighbors, toward that purpose?"

He pulled her onto his lap, there, on the wagon's tailgate.

"Dare."

"Aye?"

"It is—"

"A lovely dawning, I agree, *costasach*," he murmured, nudging at her braid, unlacing the stays of her corset to the sound of the first birds' song. Skillfully, without undoing the hooks of her loose-fitting bodice, without the knowledge of the outside world. Their world, the wagon train, came alive and busy all around while he was touching the curve of her responding breast, tracing her backbone's path.

"All right, then!" she fairly shouted. "If your hands can find only mischief, you'd best be off looking for more gainful employment with the hunting party today."

He sighed hard before tracing her hairline fondly. "It's time, *costasach*. Every wee lass has her poppet now, the boys their slingshots mended, and their parents have repairs to their wagon wheels and bake-alls and damned hair-curling irons."

Rachel mimicked the coquettish lilt of Penelope Kenyon holding her curling iron in supplication. "And where would either form or function be on this excursion into the wilderness without your skilled hands, Mr. Gilmartin?" she asked, then crossed her eyes in agitation.

He folded his arms. The frayed ends of the cotton gauze still wrapped around his wound did a small dance in the summer breeze. "Hmmm. I am not the only salamander in this family," he claimed sternly.

Rachel's fury dissolved. "Oh, Dare, do you think me terrible to imitate—?"

"Terrible," he agreed, his eyes merry, before he kissed her cheek. "And a scold besides. But I like your hair the way God made it, so don't you be burning that raven's wing beauty with the curling irons."

She would never have thought of such things as the nature of her hair compared to the other woman, Rachel realized, before him. Now she did, because she sought to keep this husband other women coveted. Was it because he was generous and skilled and handsome in their eyes? Could they guess the things he did in the night, and sometimes even in the daylight? Could they guess them from the way Rachel looked at him?

She should not be having such thoughts. The women had their own men. And her family had earned its respect on the journey. They had earned their value—Atoka with his skill with calming animals as they forded the rivers, Dare with his mending hands. Many of the train consulted Rachel on all manner of ailments, and the roots and cures she kept in her medicine box. They sent their children to her prairie schoolroom.

But as her family's position on the train grew more esteemed, the trailmaster's eyes grew brighter in their determination to slip them up. Walker watched them carefully when the train stopped at the trading forts. Rachel stayed in the wagon as much as she could in those times. No one seemed to notice, they were so caught up in their own business of supply and trade. But Walker noticed Rachel's efforts to make her family disappear, she felt sure. In St. Louis Dare had shot that man in the way that Atoka had killed the snake. Was Water Eyes dead? If he wasn't, if he was what she feared, looking for them—would their friends on the train understand, now that they knew her men better? Could she trust the Iowans who loved trees, the merchant with his wagonload of wonders, the gentle fiddler? Could she trust any of them?

Rachel saw her brother lead *Hacha* and Raven Mocker from their pickets. Both were saddled. A look passed between her men before they mounted the horses. Triumph. Perhaps Atoka had even won a bet that Dare would be out from under her care today for the hunt. "Keep your hat on," she admonished her husband in a gruff whisper. "And stay close by my brother."

Dare leaned over the saddle. "Aye, miss," he promised, and turned Raven Mocker toward Atoka's lead.

When they came in, Mr. Spikenard's mules were laden with the skinned and quartered meat. And Mr. Spikenard was loaded with stories. Rachel's brother and husband had combined their skills to claim one kill. Gibson Rice had shown himself to be as proficient with his musket as his fiddle. He'd brought down a buffalo that Hiram Hyde and his father had separated from the herd. "But we could not have gotten near those beasts without your brother and Dare leading us, and sign-talking with the Sioux, Miss Rachel! It was most . . . e-e-exhilarating!" a flush-faced Hiram claimed.

Rachel smiled past her fear of the Sioux. "My. Can you spell that word, Hiram?" she asked.

He did, without stammering, earning a glance of admiration from both his mother and Jessica Lowell.

Atoka dropped a shaggy buffalo skin at Rachel's feet as the men left to divide the meat among the families. "Here. Soak it in water overnight," he instructed. "Bright Dancer will be along after she finishes her own work. To show you how to scrape and clean it."

"Bright—?"

"Bright Dancer. *Anpaytoo Wachiwi.*" He smiled. "Try out the name."

Rachel worked the sounds through her voice. Her brother nodded his approval. "The band of Sioux had a good day, too," he said. "Bright Dancer will bring her mix of brains, liver, and soapweed. Then you'll soften the skin and fur by pulling it through a hole in the buffalo's shoulder bone. This woman is very sorry I have such an ignorant sister, who cannot make me a fine robe without her help. She likes me, I think."

He grinned at her astonishment. Dare grunted, pulled the saddle off his horse as his weary voice admonished Rachel.

"You told *me*, but you didn't tell your brother who to stay close to. Bright Dancer is already married. To their holy man."

"But has a little sister," Atoka claimed before Rachel's frown set, "who I will meet when I visit their camp."

Dare sighed hard. "Where's my featherbed?"

Atoka shoved his shoulder. "Featherbeds! After eating the heart of our kill with me? Your husband's blood is still thin," he complained to Rachel.

She took both men by their sleeves. "No featherbeds for either of you until you wash."

"Wash?"

"Yes. That's my gift to you, mighty hunters. My young scholars and I found a swimming hole. And I have not forgotten my promise, husband. You will learn some swimming tonight in this place."

Her husband's foot dragging had nothing to do with his weariness, Rachel surmised, as she led him toward the moonlit pond by the cottonwood grove. "I will not hold you responsible for any request I may have made in my delirium and now barely remem—"

"You remember it well, Darragh Ronan! What else lays claim to the terror that grips you now?"

"Me? Terror? Of water?"

"Of what, then?"

"Water moccasins. Very poisonous, Atoka says. There could be a great nest of them waiting for us to—"

"In Texas maybe, or Arkansas or Louisiana. Not this far north. Take off your boots."

"Rachel, Mr. Underdown says we're all not as floatable as . . . as—"

"Redskins? Indians? Children of the Forest?"

"Well, aye. He's been the wide world over, you see, and he says there's a kind of folks whose poor blighted nature it is to be sinking like a stone in water."

"You're not one of them. Pants."

"And are you Cassandra of old to know—"

"That an Irishman so full of hot air is bound to float nicely? It takes no prognosticator for that, my precious bane!"

"Well, now, you don't have to be lording your learning over me to be making a—" She stepped out of her own day dress to see his nervous smile go lopsided.

" 'Faith, Rachel, you look like a bare-armed angel out of

God's own heaven in that shift. I'd keenly desire to be taking you down in the tall grass and—"

"Get into this water!" He'd done it. He'd driven her to her worst schoolmarm voice.

"Yes'm," he said, her anger blunting his tongue silent. He took her outstretched hand.

She did not stop walking until the water reached her middle.

"A—and now?" he asked, unable to hide his teeth's chatter.

"Now, we dance," she told him quietly.

"Dance?"

"You do remember how to dance, Mr. Gilmartin?"

"Aye, miss."

"Then, I think we should dance."

"But—"

"Hold onto me. I will warm you up, at least. And at most— Ah, then, that's better. We don't need a fiddler, do we, husband? You're feeling the rhythm of the waves now."

"There are no waves," he protested gruffly.

"The ones we make, I mean. Along with our own music."

He remained stubbornly silent but came closer, and found her waist. They began a slow waltz, though back at camp, Gibson Rice was playing a reel. The moonlight cast silver glints on the sleek surface of Dare's hair. He'd barely noticed she'd enticed him deeper into the water, Rachel was sure of it, until he frowned.

"Badgering Choctaw wicca woman," he complained. But he continued swirling her about in the water. "The very idea!" He counterfeited both the expression and prim voice of his prime "holy roller," Mrs. Richards, "Bathing with a man."

"At least my husband is the man," Rachel tried to affect the same tone, "thanks to God for the well-being of my soul. And we are not bathing, we are preparing to swim. Lie back."

"Rachel—"

"Float first. Take a breath and lie back."

"But what if—"

"I won't let you sink, snake-fighter. Lie back."

He had to do it then, she'd put his manhood at stake. Once he realized she could balance him easily with her hand at the small of his back, Rachel felt him relax. "Breathe," she urged, and he did, rising higher in the water, until she could see his shirt bubble up around him, then settle, showing the lines of his chest. He was not a hairy man, her husband. His lean, dancer's strength was suited to the water. She would show him how well suited. She released her hold on his back. He stiffened slightly, then took another breath. "Rachel," he said like an awed child. "It's holding me."

"Aye, husband. Do you think any part of nature is immune to your charms?"

The night was warm enough to let the air dry them as they lay beneath the cottonwood tree. Bats sifted over the water, feeding on the insects drawn to the spot. Rachel rested in the crook of her husband's arm.

"You are a natural swimmer, dark one," she whispered Blind Maeve's name for him.

"No. But I will learn, with you teaching me."

He kissed their clasped hands. Rachel saw the deep desire in his eyes. "I think the water has done a fine job improving your disposition," she said, running her finger down his lean, handsome face. She climbed atop him. He was so easy to straddle without hoops and petticoats between them.

"Rachel," he breathed those ragged breaths of his desire that she loved evoking, "I must stay without. So it must be different between us tonight. You approach your time."

"Do I? How do I tell?"

He sat up higher, and ran the back of his fingers softly down her spine. "Well, did you have a little hitch in one side or another as you do your long day's walk?"

"I did! Just yesterday!"

"That's a sign. And have your breasts felt a bit more tender?"

"For a few days."

"There. Another. And inside, if you'll feel that place I showed you. I think you will find it softer, open."

"I like it better when you feel there."

"Aye," he laughed softly, shaking his head, "as do I, sweet wife."

"Do you mind my ignorance, Dare?"

"When you are so generous about my own in the water this night? Not hardly. And I am honored by your trust."

"I am very strong now. Do you still think it a good thing we wait?"

"I think that's your ripeness wondering on this question, Mrs. Gilmartin," he said softly. "Yes, I still think it a good thing. Even more than before you were almost left a widow by my ignorance of snakes."

"That was not ignorance, it was sacrifice!"

"Whist, it was my slowness."

"Slowness? Lulie would not have survived that snake! If you had not been so fast—"

"And I would have died without you and Atoka. Your knowing how to bleed me dry of the poison." He took their clasped hands, kissed deeply into them. "Rachel, I'm in your debt many times over. I have not even gotten close to procuring the bride price your brother waits for, I know. But please don't ask this as payment."

"My brother wants no more bride price, Dare. Not after . . ." Rachel searched for a circumspect way to call it to his mind, but not draw the attention of the one looking for them. "Not after he gave Raven Mocker into your keeping."

Her husband smiled softly, understanding. "Ach, Rachel," was all he said for a long time. "But your brother would be as pleased as you to enlarge your clan."

"He understands. He understands better than I do, Dare."

"Does he now?"

She nodded, trying not to cry. Was this another sign of her ripeness, feeling close to tears?

"I love you, Queen of the Choctaw," he promised with his voice, his lips, his hands calling forth joy from her secret places.

eighteen

"She is a little girl!" Atoka said in disgust. "Not yet menstruating. And her father wanted four horses for her besides. No woman is worth four of *my* horses!"

As her brother stomped off, Rachel shook her head, then went on scraping the buffalo hide with the fine stone knife Bright Dancer had traded for two of her hair combs. Dare approached, pulling his hand through his dark curls.

"Sounds like your brother's luck with women is holding steady."

"He's lonely, I think."

"He's desperate. And it's showing. He'll surely end up with a terrible stubborn scold, like I did."

She did not look up from her work.

"If he's lucky," he finished. She could feel his smile even before he sipped at the strong morning coffee. "You've made a fine job of it, Rachel," he said as she got off her knees, struggling to maintain her steadiness on legs gone stiff in her concentrated efforts.

He stood, moving closer as she checked the tautness of each tie. She wished him away. Rachel had awakened herself long before dawn, hoping to finish her task before either of her men saw her in this state. But the buffalo skin was so large. And, fine job or not, she was so clumsy and slow at the new task. The missionaries had not allowed her to learn how to prepare skins, even of small animals. Not Christian woman's work. Atoka was right to be ashamed of her.

"I'll strap that great beast's coat on the side of the wagon, so the children will see their nooning teacher is a woman of many talents."

Rachel tried to wipe the hair back from her face, but succeeded only in tangling the knife in it. Then a dry wind pulled more hair from its leather thong. Her husband caught her wrist before she tore any strands. He separated them from the knife, a gentle contrast to her exasperation. It worked its way into her being, though those long, ministering hands, his quiet voice.

"Do you think we can fit all of your scholars under the robe if we get caught in a snow drift in the mountains?" he asked.

"You'll conjure some way of making it large enough to accommodate," Rachel claimed.

"Like St. Bridgid and her nuns did?"

"Is that another story? Tell me that one, Dare!"

He folded his arms. "For a price, maybe. Do you think we might have a swimming lesson?"

Rachel smiled slowly. "I'm glad I don't have to drag you into the water these days, son of the seal people."

He smiled slyly. "Well, having buffalo stench about us both helps as well," he admitted.

Rachel caught no sign of her newly heartbroken brother that day. She wondered if she would ever hear his flute again. Dare missed his noon meal to scout for Atoka. He drew harsh words from the trail captain upon returning. After her schooling, Dare saddled *Hacha* for Rachel. He asked Hiram Hyde to drive their wagon. "We'll find him, Rachel," he assured her. "We'll find Atoka together." But by that time the worry was creeping into his own voice.

They'd hardly left the dust of the train before he called her horse to a halt and took her reins.

"Off," he demanded.

"But Dare, *Hacha* minds me well now. Atoka and I have been working with him to—"

"Off," he insisted.

She slid down from the saddle. He grunted, dismounted himself, and reset her stirrups. That was it. He didn't want her riding sidesaddle, as she'd done since remaking herself female again in St. Louis. "Straddle that horse, woman," he commanded. "As your father taught you to ride. We're out of their proper Christian sights, and I'll have you safely mounted."

Rachel tugged his fine hat's wide brim lower over his eyes. "Oh, that you've done, Mr. Gilmartin," she assured him, then watched her change-color husband look away and redden to the roots of his hair. Why couldn't she be more modest, she wondered. He shook his head, smiling. Had he forgiven her, then, for causing his abashed state? Yes, she thought so as he gave her backside a playful push.

Rachel climbed on *Hacha*'s silver-streaked back, with the sheer joy she'd once had riding beside her father as a child. Still, she adjusted the billow of her skirts so even her ankles were covered.

Now, on this brief sojourn into Dare and Atoka's wide-open world, Rachel was glad not to be worried about leaving a suckling child, or bouncing a child within her. Rachel wished all the women on the train could see the world around them like this, unfettered by the weight of their wagons, their worry about the survival of their children, their things. This was a community too, this place, ever changing. She was free to help her husband look for her wild, lonely brother. She wanted to thank Dare for this. She looked to him, searching for the words. He smiled.

"We'll find him," he assured her.

Hacha soon took the lead, smelling her own kind, maybe—wild horses. And where there were horses, her brother would be. The rolling grasses and luxuriant wildflowers that marked the way for the train had flattened out. Then they'd passed the carved-out places her uncle had described in the Valley of the North Platte—Court House Rock, Chimney Rock, and Scott's Bluff. Sky had invaded horizon in that country, making Rachel feel she was floated off the earth itself. Now she was again grounded by this broken, hilly belt of land with its rocky bluffs appearing along the streams.

She raised her hand to her eyes as she gazed to the west.

"Dare—"

"Do you see him?" her husband asked, the edge to his voice expressing his frustration over his own eyes' weakness for distance sighting. Rachel would buy him spectacles from Mr. Bodmer's store of them when she'd tatted enough yardage of the trimming he'd admired on Dare's hat. They would trade trimming for eyeglasses with fine steel rims. Would Dare wear them, or be too proud, like the trailmaster? Rachel hoped Dare did not share any traits with Mr. Walker. She hoped he would choose from Mr. Bodmer's lenses. They would help him see as well as she and Atoka did.

"Rachel? Is he there?" Dare called her back to their task.

"No. But . . . Are they clouds?"

Her husband stared hard. "Not moving clouds," he finally decided. "They go gray, don't they?"

"Yes! I think perhaps the whites are the peaks of mountains, Dare, the ones my uncle says are so high the snow on them never melts."

"Are we at the backbone of America, then? Are they the Rocky Mountains?"

They stared for a long time, Rachel describing the details she knew were more formless to his eyes. While her mind pondered the immensity, his hand covered hers.

"I don't understand how we're ever to cross them," Dare finally said.

"Others have. We will."

"Well, Fort Laramie first. We're getting almightly ragged. And the Lowells will need help repairing their wagons, if we're to get those trees to Oregon."

Rachel shivered involuntarily. Again, the location people on the train longed for—a place to post their mail, rest their teams, buy supplies, hear news of the outside world, was making her heartsick. But her dread of this large fort, the one the United States Army was in the process of taking over, was the worst. Neither the nature of the land and sky nor the Indian nations compared as the source of her fear.

She had managed to hide it somewhat as they'd entered the confines of Fort Levenworth and Fort Kearney. She'd busied herself with her sewing and tatting the two-color circles, and sent her men out for the few things they needed. She'd do the same at Laramie. But she worried about Dare's convivial, cordial nature drawing too much attention to them. She worried Atoka might allow himself to be pulled into games of chance with rough men. At the other forts Rachel had scanned notices and newspapers from the states quickly, voraciously. Would St. Louis police come to bring her husband back to stand trial for the death of that rich man, Water Eyes? Would Miss Wakefield's displeasure drive her to send the federals for him? Only in the forts did Rachel dream of Dare hanging on the gallows of Sligo. Only in the forts, not in the glorious spaces of this wild, beautiful land.

They were going to a land like Dare's, like Rachel's own in her barely remembered time. She tried to calm herself with that knowledge. It would be a land where her uncle and his wife waited for their family to flourish again, where Dare and Atoka would harvest the fields, where the Lowells would break juicy apples and pears and plums from their trees grown tall and healthy in Oregon soil. Rachel would lift her children and Atoka's children into their branches.

But first she had to help her brother find a wife, she decided as she finally spotted him in the distance, leading two new horses. Two, of course, to take the place of the Lakota sisters, one already married, one too young, this time. He always consoled himself with horses. But soon his horses would be eating them out of Dare's oats.

Her brother was bleary-eyed. These mustangs had cost him more than her *Hacha* had in their taming. But they still had the fire of wildness in their eyes, as *Hacha* did. There was not a horse her brother worked to bridle without the fire remaining. That was his gift. Even the men of the train marveled at it, no longer claiming these wild descendants of the Conquistadors could not be tamed without breaking their spirit.

"Hello, Rich in Horses," she greeted him.

Atoka looked from her to her husband. "Why do you look for me? I did not have duties."

Dare sighed. "No. But you've been tortured and scalped, fallen off cliffs, and drowned in canyons—in short, taken from us in as many ways as there are imaginations among our fellow travelers."

Atoka sniffed. "Not in so many ways then, I think. These farmers have not my new brother's head for conjuring."

"For your sister's sake, I wish you'd tell us before you—"

"My sister would know if I needed her. I think she wanted her first look at the Rocky Mountains, and lured you away with this excuse."

"Atoka!" Rachel yelled, incensed.

He raised his hand. "I have been taming these two females the day long, little sister. Make no further demands on me. A loan of your featherbed for my rest will be thanks enough."

He raised his flute to his lips and led the white and dun mares with a soothing call.

Soon they came upon the hunting party of Gibson Rice, Alfred Lowell, and Hiriam Hyde. They held up their hands in greeting.

"No luck, then?" Dare asked.

"Not luck of the likes of you folks!" Gibson observed.

"I'd give plenty to find horses like those, Atoka," Alfred Lowell said.

"Finding's just the start of it," Rachel's brother replied with a weary smile.

"Are we all in for night's camp now?" Dare asked the men.

"But for Captain Walker and Eveline," Gibson explained. "We were all following a flock of buzzards to see what was interesting them, until we split off from them. Walker spotted an eagle in the ugly birds' midst. Insisted he'd kill that eagle."

"B-bird of America, Miss Rachel! National symbol!" Hiriam sputtered his indignation.

Gibson nodded. "Well, the boys and me thought that right unpatriotic, but we couldn't convince Walker of it. He's still out there." The fiddler pointed to a grove of a few trees in the distance.

Rachel watched her brother gather reserves of strength. His sky eyes iced. "We'll see you at camp," he told the hunters.

"Now, Atoka," Gibson said uneasily, noting her brother's anger, "things are just calming down nice between you folks and the trail boss."

"This is not a sacred thing he does."

"Well, no. Didn't I just say so? But considering Mr. Walker's shooting ability, that eagle will suffer no great harm. Trail Boss will most likely straggle in with Eveline plucking a buzzard behind him, if he's that lucky."

A shot punctuated the dusk's stillness, followed by a mass of black wings rising from the tree limbs. Atoka threw the reins of his captive mustangs at Dare and bolted his mount toward the trees.

Hiram looked helpless. "M-M-Miss Rachel, should we—?"

"No. Come only if you hear three shots together from my husband's pistol. That will mean we need you."

"Yes, ma'am," they agreed, taking charge of the mustangs and turning their horses toward the train's circle of wagons.

Dare shook his head, despite his worried look. "Such a wee

girl, such a wondrous command of strapping men," he complimented her.

"My brother and I—Dare," Rachel explained, "we are of the Eagle clan. We hold the bird in great esteem."

"My obligation is clear too, then, Queen of the Choctaw," he said quietly.

Rachel was glad he had helped her sit her horse astride, for her brother had picked up more speed when they heard a second shot and Walker's cry of triumph.

When they dismounted, they saw signs that the trailmaster had left his horse and bolted through the dense underbrush around the trees. They followed. Atoka's Bowie knife was out of its scabbard. The rest of the scene took Rachel longer to understand.

Mr. Walker was not lording over a dead eagle, but on his knees, weeping over his apron-wrapped daughter. His rifle was still smoking where he'd discarded it a few steps away. His eyes seemed to hold neither focus nor attention as they looked from Atoka to Dare and Rachel.

"I took her for the bird. The eagle. I was sure I'd down it, and she was rustlin' about in here, see? I took her for the bird."

"Let my sister see to her, Mr. Walker," Atoka said quietly, in that voice that made Rachel believe he was indeed, growing in his holy man's wisdom. His knife's blade caught the slanting rays of the sun.

Rachel knelt at Walker's side. "Through the heart," he claimed. "Look. I shot her straight through the heart," he said in a way that made Rachel feel sympathy for this arrogant man.

"Please," she tried to make her voice as soothing as her brother's, "let us help."

He shrugged, his eyes glassy, and rose from his daughter's side. "Watch him," Rachel whispered to Dare.

Walker grabbed the rifle barrel and began smashing its end into a tree trunk. Rachel cast a quick look up. Her husband was standing quiet guard over another father in his grieving.

Rachel lifted Eveline Walker's arm and surveyed the damage

the bullet had done. "Shot through," she agreed with Walker's assessment, "but through the side of her breast. It has lodged in her arm."

"Can you see the ball?" Atoka asked.

"No. Give me your knife."

Rachel probed the wound with its tip until she hit metal. "Through the fleshy parts only, I think," she judged. "But very deep."

Atoka nodded. "And it took in other things . . . pieces of cloth from her clothes."

"Yes. I think we'd best make an opening, send it the other way. Flush it all out."

"*Oke,*" Atoka agreed.

"We'll start a fire," Dare offered putting himself and a stunned Walker to work.

As Atoka helped Rachel remove the downed woman's poke jacket, her eyelids flickered open.

"Get your hands off me, you filthy savages!" Eveline Walker demanded. "Daddy!"

Captain Walker turned slowly.

"Daddy!" she called again. "I'm shot!"

"I . . . know that," he said dully, not moving from his place by the fire.

"Well, do something! Kill them! Didn't I tell you that blue-eyed Indian was looking to get under my skirts? And now his stinking sister is helping him at me!"

"Hush up, Eveline. They're tryin' to help. And anybody might of shot you, rummaging around in them bushes like you was, scaring our birds off!"

"But, Daddy, I was looking for them roots like that smart-mouthed 'Breed woman's so good at—" she saw the hot metal of Atoka's fired knife and fainted into Rachel's arms.

Walker approached, Dare following. His red-rimmed eyes implored Rachel. "She's not dead?"

"No, sir. The wound shouldn't prove mortal, once the ball's out."

"You can do that?"

"She's seen worse over the years. She's patched up more of my lighthorsemen than you can count. Now. You're standing in my smart-mouthed 'Breed sister's light, Captain Walker," Atoka told him sternly.

"French," the big man said quietly. "We all know you're French folks, ma'am. Don't know what that girl was thinking in her delirium."

nineteen

Rachel felt her husband's anticipation, there beside her as they approached Fort Laramie. They were now eight hundred miles west of St. Louis. They would make preparations here to cross the backbone of America.

Indian tepees began to appear, pitched at a respectful distance off the trail. The fort was a crossroads of the western world of America, her uncle and the guidebooks said. Rachel recognized people of the Sioux nations, as well as Cheyenne, Blackfoot, Kiowa, Comanche, and *Métis* people. Many she didn't recognize. Many more than there had been at the other stations along the trail. The native people were dressed in everything from ribbon shirts to buckskins to blankets. Their heads were shaved and turbaned and feathered, braided and free-flowing. Some bore tattoos, some had bone or shell earrings. One cradle board device was pressing its baby's head as flat as his mother's. Would even her father be able to talk to all of these people, Rachel wondered.

How rich the Americas were in diverse cultures. These were their decimated remnants, she realized too, watching them through her brother's sad medicine man eyes.

Native women and children collected scattered goods, left by the immigrants. As the summer had worn on, Rachel noticed more and more of these items along the trail—heavy things like rockers and furniture and even a baby cradle, left to facilitate speed in face of the advancing winter. Trunks with iron straps were not hauled away, even by the scavengers. They were opened and gaping, like graves that the wolves had descended upon. The old, familiar fear that her parents' and Sleeps Sound's graves looked like these trunks filled her again. Then the new knowledge her brother had entrusted to her, of how their parents had died. Dare slipped his arm around her waist and pulled her closer to his warmth. Dare, who would be the father of her new family. Alive. And feeling her fear.

Word came down the train that they'd come on the first day of a trading fair held at the fort four times a year. By nightfall the place would be even more crowded—teeming with traders and trappers from a hundred miles around. The quadrangular form loomed larger, freezing Rachel's heart. Bastions hung at the diagonal corners. The large block house with its cannon eye peered out over the plains. Were the traders' tents and tepees out of that cannon's range, Rachel wondered, out of habit, wary of American soldiers.

Her husband's cheerful, lilting speech cut through her dark thoughts. "They say the army's about to be taking the place over from the American Fur Company, didn't you tell me that, Rachel? They'll have news here, surely—that Oregon has become part of the country, a territory? Out of the hands of the British forever, at least? Mr. Lowell says they were still arguing about it in your Congress, last he heard, as you first told me in St. Louis. Remember, *costasach?*"

"I remember," she said, her voice sounding hollow in her ears. Dare winced, then smiled more broadly.

"There must be a great pack of Irishmen in your Congress,

the way they argue everything out! Now, it is too far north to make Oregon open to slaves, isn't it? They wouldn't allow that, would they? I couldn't abide—"

Questions. Dare and his questions. How was he able to anticipate their stay here with such happy abandon? Has he become this other person Gilmartin in his mind, shedding his other names, his other selves like a snake shed its skins? Was that the gift of the copperhead that put its poison into his veins? Her social, gregarious husband—did he feel himself invincible now from the twin dogs pursuing them? Was the burden of their hiding now hers alone to bear? From her other side, Atoka began defending the Choctaw, some of whom owned black slaves. He said that slavery was only demeaning if the masters forgot their slaves were human.

It was all Rachel could do to remain upright between them.

Their words became meaningless as they entered beneath the blockhouse and its cannon. Inside the fort's walls, the air turned oppressively hot. Their world went suddenly, from the vastness of the open sky to a one hundred and fifty feet square, with houses built into all the walls, with doors and windows looking over the interior court. Overseeing them.

An important-looking man came out of the most important looking house and shook Captain Walker's hand. Rachel caught some of their talk about the trading fair, how things would settle down after the first day of "Saturnalia." The man apologized to the ladies beforehand for it with a sweep of his handsome hat. Her husband and brother ignored the official welcome. They continued to shoot their arguments on the morality and economics of slavery across her.

Then Rachel saw the men leaning against the stockade's wall. One pointed at her with a leering smile. The way the long-ago soldier had looked at her mother. She understood the look now. Hats. The men wore different hats from all the others. Tall, black hats.

"Rachel, tell your husband—" her brother's exasperated voice began, then halted, just as the wagon came to a stop. "Rachel?"

She dropped the reins into Atoka's hands. "I'm so cold," she whispered. "No, hot."

Her husband caught her before she slid off the wagon's seat. She heard his soft Irish curse as he lifted her with those broad arms, as she struggled against the blackness. Inside the wagon, she clung to his sleeve. "Don't go out," she pleaded, "Oh, Dare, the hats."

"Hats, love?"

"Tall, black. Silk. Water Eyes. Dorris. Pointing at me. They will kill you."

"Ach, Rachel."

She began to sob. Those fierce, freeing sobs of the child inside her.

Her brother looked in on them through the canvas opening, his face etched with worry.

"What have you done?" he demanded of her husband.

She tried to rise, but Dare rocked her, making soothing sounds. "I'm better, Atoka," she managed to say. "Keep driving."

"Aye. Doing nicely, keep going." He kissed her forehead. "Rachel. Listen to me now. They are the style of the day, those hats."

"*Oke.* Of course. Made of silk. Why the trappers can't sell their beaver pelts. Forgive me."

Another curse, then he held her closer. "It's not . . . anything else making you touchy? We weren't off, at the time we've loved each other? You couldn't be—?"

"No. My flow started this morning," she said, wishing she could keep the sadness from her voice for his sake.

"Aye, then, it might be that, and the heat, only. But you must be telling me your fears, love," he urged softly. "Don't let them eat at you."

"I have bad dreams at the forts," she admitted quietly.

"We should be heeding them, *costasach.*"

"Should we?"

"Of course. The Irish deem dreams sacred things, even if you Choctaw regard them as foolish."

"Oh, dreams are sacred to the Choctaw too!"

"There. Would you be telling me I married a foolish woman, then? That does nothing to increase my prestige on this train."

She smiled, which seemed to please him an inordinate amount.

Both her husband and brother tried to coax her from the confines of the wagon, with their new stores of coffee, sugar, and tea, preserves and pickles, a box of candles. But she didn't venture out into the dusty square.

Even the children, exploring in delight, could not lure her out on their holiday from her schoolroom. She retreated to a corner of the wagon with her books, her uncle's letters, her mending and tatting, the yards of tatting left before her husband could have his spectacles. Her shuttle, her hook wove and flew, but so did her thoughts. When would Dare finish helping the Lowells make their wagons stronger without extra weight? Was he leaving Atoka alone as he pitched in to help others? Would her brother fall in with bad company?

Jessica and her mother visited. They did not try to coax her outside, but sipped tea and ate currant cake as if it were the most natural thing in the world to be doing under her tent canopy in the sultry heat.

"I quite understand your reluctance, Rachel," Mrs. Lowell confided. "I hear things will get even wilder when the sun goes down and the men start their rampaging folly. But this is the most well stocked fort so far, don't you think? Even without this Rendezvous of theirs?"

"I wouldn't know, ma'am," Rachel whispered.

"Not that the quantity and variety has helped bring down the prices, as it might in the states!" Celinda Lowell went on cheerfully. "All quite too distracting, the stores, with their high prices. So many goods, so much pretty calico. In shades you favor too, just the blue that would match your man's eyes when he's working on one of those cloudless days, didn't you think, Jessica?"

"Which calico was that, Mama?"

"The bolt with the tiny yellow flowers on it, you remember!

That dreadful Mr. Grimes tried hard to get me to make a dress from it for Callie. Callie favors green, Rachel. But I told him to hold it for me, once I saw Dare Gilmartin's eyes on it."

She waited for a response, but Rachel was only confused by the turn the conversation was taking. "Look," the older woman demanded finally. "I am not going to skate around this any longer, Rachel. Your husband and yourself have done a great deal on our behalf, and Hiram Hyde got good American currency for the hides he had only because you scraped and prepared them fine as the Cheyenne squaw women your brother charmed over our way to help us. So we were wondering if you wouldn't mind us pooling our resources to purchase that bolt of cloth for you to—"

"You're very kind, Mrs. Lowell."

"No such thing. We're in your debt, and Lowells ain't debtors."

"I don't know—"

"If you'd like it? Of course you don't, not without seeing it! Why, you may just think us two the silliest women in the world if you don't take to it."

"I'm sure it's lovely."

"Rachel, if you'll come out with us this afternoon to get a gander at it . . . between me and Jessie here, if you're a trifle unsteady."

"I-I've yet to finish my mending."

"With that coarse thread your men brought you? They're solid lost in understanding the details of your list. There are spools of much finer quality and, oh, my dear, a collection of needles—"

"I cannot. I'm sorry."

"We are worried about you, Miss Rachel." Jessica finally entered their conversation in her simple, straightforward manner.

Rachel lifted her eyes to the mother and daughter. There, at last, the true purpose of their visit. Their worry. Mrs. Lowell looked apologetic, but Jessica was relieved, Rachel thought. She wished she could tell them her fears.

A peculiar anger took over in the awkward silence between

them. Why weren't these people more worried about themselves, instead of trying to find out the reason for hers? Why wasn't Mr. Lowell having more of a care with his wife, still worn from the loss of her little boys? Now she was looking to take on Rachel's burden when her own pregnancy looked due to bear its fruit in the dead of winter. Rachel swallowed down the anger, and recognized her envy of this bellied woman and her beautiful children.

"I'm sorry," she whispered, "I wish . . ."

"What do you wish, Miss Rachel?" Jessica implored before a rifle shot announced a new set of traders and their whiskey arriving at the fort. Rachel pressed shaking fingers to her mouth. "I wish I could feel safe," she whispered.

The next morning, after Dare had already left her side, summoned by Mr. Bodmer to have a look at his stopped watch, she heard her brother's call. From outside the wagon. Her name. When she did not respond, Atoka climbed into the wagon, smelling of whiskey and smoke and the sage of ceremony. His eyes were red-rimmed from lack of sleep. Dare had not been able to keep him from the Saturnalia, then?

"I need you," her brother said.

"Another horse?" she asked, thinking she could finish the coarse thread on his new animal's feedbag and have an excuse to send her men back for the finer kind Mrs. Lowell mentioned.

"No." He lifted the cover of the wagon. Outside stood a woman dressed in the filthiest rags Rachel had ever seen. Catching Rachel's surprised shock, the woman's eyes scanned her own hands, bruised, bare feet, hands again, in rapid succession. Brambles decorated chopped-off hair so dirty Rachel couldn't tell its color.

"She's had a hard time," her brother said. He went to the woman's side. "She needs to get out of here. I said we'd take her with us to Oregon."

"You—?"

"This is my sister Rachel," he spoke gently to the woman. "*Yalabusha,* the tadpole, who taught even her fearful husband to swim. She loves the water, but my sister is feeling a little shy here at the fort. Maybe you could show her where the river is?" He looked up. "A new river, Rachel—cool and clear, not muddy like the Platte. The Laramie River."

Rachel doubted this woman had visited the Laramie or any other for some time herself. Why was her brother saying these things in the tender voice of a dove? Why did he give away one of her Choctaw names to this stranger?

"Atoka—"

"Please, Rachel. Come outside. It's early. No one about. After last night's revels, almost all of them are drunk or exhausted. No one will be about for hours yet."

"I-I'm coming," she said, as quietly as he was talking, as if not to awake a sleeping baby. What was her brother up to this time? It didn't matter. His eyes spoke true. This woman needed her. Rachel gathered her extra dress, two petticoats, a shift, and some fresh linens, wrapped them around her brush and dwindling cake of the last of her perfumed soap. She took her brother's outstretched hand and climbed down from the wagon.

He put her hand into the damaged woman's slowly, carefully, as if in a ceremony.

Rachel didn't realize her own fears of coming outside the wagon had disappeared until she felt the woman's trust. Cooking fires hadn't yet started. Rachel breathed deeply of the morning air. It smelled of sagebrush.

The woman was taller than she, was her brother's height. She moved like a graceful willow, even in her deadened black state. As Atoka brushed and tended his horses downstream, Rachel tended the silent woman.

She pressed the linen cloth gently around the woman's burns, one under her eye, another along her neck. Brand burns, deliberately made, as were the slashes on her arms. Someone had done this to her. Her eyes were dull, complacent. Had she given up hope? No, those who'd given up all hope in this fierce country were dead. Then Rachel discovered a possible reason the woman's heart still beat—a small bulge beneath her waistline.

She wanted to weep. "My brother spoke the truth, I like to swim," she whispered instead. "Will you come into this water with me?" The woman didn't answer. She watched as Rachel stepped out of all her clothes but her shift. Still in her rags, Atoka's woman followed.

The water was cold. Her eyes grew fierce, as if Rachel had tricked her with the request. "Come," she coaxed, "it's not so bad once your shoulders are under." Silent Woman followed, and even plunged her head under the cool water, following Rachel's example. Her eyes eased with relief.

Heartened, Rachel began to peel off the scraps of cloth and skins.

"There. I won't worry so much about hurting you now. With the layers leaving, I can see where your skin is tender," she breathed out, taking up her precious soap and cloth from the rock. This was a white woman, Rachel finally realized, as the filth began to dislodge under her gentle rubbing around wounds. She was almost as white as Dare.

She stopped Rachel suddenly, taking her arm. Rachel looked down at herself. Her shift had slipped off her shoulder, revealing the work of Water Eyes, including what the woman stared at, the deepest scar snaking up Rachel's left breast. Silent Woman traced it, her finger hovering over its still raw red disfigurement. Rachel pulled in a deep breath. "Yes, well, I suppose it's only fair I tell you," she chatted, as if the woman had spoken the question that dwelt in her eyes—how?

"A man did this . . . and this, back east," she said, indicating her other scars, "until my husband shot him," she finished in a hushed voice.

The woman's eyes steadied on hers, and Rachel felt comfort from them. "So, you see, there are good men in my family. You are in a good place with us."

On shore, Rachel dropped her extra shift over Silent Woman's head and wrapped her shoulders in one of her petticoats. Then she sat behind her new companion, the stranger who had just heard her family's deepest secret. She felt a great peace descend like her own mother's love as she began the woman's grooming at the ends of her shoulder-shorn hair.

twenty

"You won this woman in a card game?"

"Well, no. I lost her."

"Atoka, I am in no mood—"

"She was the loser's prize, Rachel."

"What?"

"Hush with your yelping, don't wake her!" he reminded in a furious whisper. But his face softened as he looked down at the sleeping woman, her head resting in Rachel's lap. "No one wants her in this place. They fear her father. He paid a high ransom for her return from the Cheyenne, who stole her off the Santa Fe Trail, down south. But she'd been with the Cheyenne three years. Had a family with them, until her husband died."

Her brother sighed hard, then continued. "Her father saw the child growing inside her. He cursed anyone who tried to help her. The men who found her this way—battered and burned and abandoned by this father, all three of them died—one of a blood infection, one in a drunk fall off the stockade, one in a brawl. That was enough for the notion of the curse to stick. No one wants her, she's had to scrounge in their waste to survive. Some soldiers connived this way to be rid of her without having blood on their hands. What else could I do but lose the game?"

"You purposefully—?"

"The soldiers might have sobered, changed their minds. Maybe they'd start taking her silence as permission and pass her around. She was down to me or that pig Deems Miller, who they say has killed two women already. Of course I've got a bad reputation myself now, thanks to Eveline Walker, but the soldiers were still glad to foster her off on someone."

Rachel considered his words. And she knew from Dare that Walker's daughter had delighted in telling everyone who would listen at the fort that Atoka was a spurned suitor who had shot her in his wild grief. He was only still breathing because of her father's generosity, she claimed. Walker himself knew differently, of course, as did the three hunters who heard her father's shots that day, all fired while her brother was still mounted and racing to save his eagle brother. Atoka's innocence was strongly suspected by the rest of the train, too, which caused Eveline Walker the greatest indignation. So she'd carried her story to people at the fort.

Atoka had bore it all with silent good grace. And now he'd entered the world of these rough men for this stranger's sake. Rachel could only wonder at it. "You did a great deal more than lose a game, brother. Did she agree to come with us?"

"She hasn't spoken to me, or anyone. But she nodded when the priest asked her."

"Priest? What did the priest ask her?"

"You know how it goes . . . love, honor, cherish—"

"You married?"

"Well, if I didn't, your righteous Irish husband would accuse me of buying a slave. And my Christian sister would not allow a woman other than my wife to keep me warm over the mountains ahead. I am outnumbered. And the priest was so drunk he signed the paper without asking for a fee, so she didn't cost anything beyond the loss of the game, you see? You need the company of a sister, Rachel. And this woman needs us."

"She had deep hurting."

"*Oke.* But we know of these things, our family. We will help her."

"She's white."

"Yes." He frowned. "If she accepts me, I will have to raise up her children as well as yours. It's their way. Do you mind that?"

"Do you mind that your first child will be Cheyenne?"

He frowned. Rachel read in it that she was foolish to even ask such a question. Then his eyes softened to those of a boy who'd found a treasure under a stone. "When will this child come out?" he asked.

"When winter starts, I think. About the time Mrs. Lowell is due to have hers."

"That's why this woman lives, maybe. For the child. Admirable child. We must find a name that reflects this. But we must help the child's mother to live for herself, too, after."

Rachel smiled, proud that her brother for all his impulsive volatility, was such a good man. "Tell Dare how our family is expanding. And my dress does not fit your wife. I'll make her another, with room for her child space to grow. Buy the blue calico with yellow flowers on it from Mr. Grimes. Mrs. Lowell will show you which it is at the dry goods store."

"That was supposed to be for you! Lowell's woman said—"

Rachel's eyes narrowed. "So, you were in on that ploy?" She shook her head. "Well, what you have done got me out of the wagon with much greater speed, if that was your intent, brother. Go on. The colors of the cloth will suit your wife better than me."

He grinned wide, then turned.

"And I need a cake of lavender soap," she remembered. "No, two cakes."

"Sweet-smelling women," he grumbled, then frowned over the sleeping form of his wife. "Her hair is the color of honey," he observed of its drying strands. "Strange."

"So is the sky the color of your eyes. I love that slice of our artist grandfather in you, even so. You will get used to your woman's honey hair. Go," Rachel admonished again.

"Two badgering women all the way to Oregon. I must have been drunk."

"The whiskey stench was on your clothes, not your mouth, you great fraud. And I smelled the sage of ceremony. Did you free yourself from her father's curse?"

His scowl deepened. "No," he said. "I do not fear her father. I freed her in my ceremony. Now I need to find an animal guide, I think, to help me understand this woman I married."

Rachel bowed her head. *"Oke,"* she agreed with the wisdom he spoke alongside his arrogant teasing.

Atoka returned with Dare and a dozen of the train's children leading their family's horses. Would the woman recognize the animals and children as a sign that no one was going to hurt her here? The mustangs were beribboned, braided, and painted. Their finery almost matched the still-wild fire in their eyes. Rachel fastened the last hook of her dress over her new sister's wider girth as they approached.

Silent Woman's grasp was cold.

Rachel smiled. "Here comes my husband, Dare. And my brother, your husband, whose name is Atoka, in case he has not yet introduced himself."

"Aaaa." Rachel wondered how long she had been a silent woman. Then, softly, slowly: "Aaatoka should not play at cards."

Rachel felt tears sting the corners of her eyes. "Perhaps that was his last game."

Atoka was clean, even under his fingernails, and wore their father's wedding shirt and a red woven sash about his waist. Looped to it was a large deerskin pouch. Dare and the children stayed with the animals while he came forward. He gently brought the woman to her feet, looking sheepish and bewildered. "I went up to the hills, looking for an animal," he told Rachel while casting sidelong glances at his new wife. "This is who I found. Like this. Without life. I have puzzled and prayed, but I don't know what it means."

He offered the buffalo skin parfleche sack, hesitated, then grimaced and held it out again. Behind him, Dare was stifling a smile.

What had her brother found? Rachel hoped his bride would take the gift. She said a small prayer that the Cheyenne people had helped her understand the sacredness of all the animals. Her brother's intentions had been honorable, no matter what he found. Silent Woman took his offering.

The flaps of the tied parfleche fell aside to reveal a dead porcupine. Atoka's bride's eyes lit with . . . what was it? Delight? She knelt beside her bundle with a joyfilled gasp, then began pulling the sharp quills with adept fingers, admiring them, pulling more.

Rachel smiled. "I think you have won a quillworker, brother," she said.

The woman lifted her head as if called. Slowly, she brought the heel of her hand to her chest and nodded.

Atoka knelt beside her. "Quillworker. Has my sister discovered your name?"

She bowed her head.

"You are a fortunate man," Rachel proclaimed. "Your wife will honor you and your children with her skill."

Atoka smiled, satisfied. "This is a good day," he said, gently wrapping the animal back inside its parfleche, and helping Quillworker rise.

Her gown only reached his tall bride's ankles as she stood beside her same-size husband. Its waist rode high over her expanding middle. She must make the new blue gown's hem longer. And she must sew a line of tatting along the sleeves. And find her a wide-brimmed hat like Dare's; no, a bonnet with a wide brim and scarf or ribbon, to protect her healing skin. Rachel sought to keep her thoughts busy, to keep the tears from spilling from her eyes. Her men already thought she cried all the time.

Quillworker allowed her hand to remain in her new husband's as he brought her to his mustangs.

"Do you ride?" he asked her.

She nodded.

"Choose one," he told her.

Rachel felt Dare behind her. He took an easy hold at her hip. "I suppose marriages have succeeded with worse beginnings," he conceded.

"I can think of one."

"Are we a success, then, Rachel LeMoyne?" he teased at her ear. "Before we're married even fifty years?"

"Fifty?" She felt a girlish giggle bubble up her throat. Her husband was good at coaxing those sounds out of her. "Will it take as long as that to determine it?"

"Longer, I'm thinking."

"Longer?"

"Oh, aye, as you'll have the strength to divide our blankets and fling my poor belongings out the door well into the next century."

Laughter filled Rachel as she leaned into her husband's chest. They watched her new sister choose the white mustang named Sky-Reaching from among Atoka's horses. The Lowell children gathered around, showing off their handiwork on her braided mane. A small smile eased the crushing burden of pain from the widow bride's scarred face.

Dare held Rachel closer. "She is a different person now," he maintained, "one her father will never know, does not deserve to know. Just as I am Dare Gilmartin now, you understand? Only himself, the fixer, husband to the schoolmarm on Walker's wagon train bound for Oregon. Not anyone men with silk hats would have interest in."

Rachel nodded, glad he couldn't see the lingering doubt she knew was still part of her expression.

"Safe," she whispered.

"Aye, safe from any pursuing those other people, at any rate." His eyes lightened in their mirth. "Not safe from these fierce American mountains and deserts and any Indians who dare to remain uncharmed by your polite peace offerings, mind you."

"I'll remember."

"Good. Wouldn't do to have you too fearless."

"Dare, we need to go on. Soon."

"Have you dreamed this, Rachel?"

"I—" she began, but her thought was interrupted by Hiram Hyde's run to them. He stopped before Rachel and Dare, pulling off his felt hat and grinding its rim in his fisted hand as he struggled to speak.

Dare lay his hand gently on the boy's shoulder. "Catch your breath. We're listening."

Hiram hit his hat against his leg, then took a deep breath. "Ccc-could you come?" he asked. "Help?"

By the time Rachel and Dare reached the train, the argument between Captain Walker and Jake Lowell, with Hiram Hyde's family in the middle, was attracting an audience and gaining more.

"Don't be a damned fool, man! That load is going to kill your oxen and strand your family in the wilderness."

"Your saying it will not make it so."

"Hyde, talk sense into him!"

"We've been neighbors of the Lowells since they were wed— almost twenty years past, Captain. Always made their living off the apple, cherry, plum, and pear. Wouldn't leave them seedlings behind any more'n they'd leave one of their brood."

"Well, they're not holding this train up anymore. And we leave in three days." Captain Walker's pronouncement was final, Rachel knew.

"We'll travel on alone, then. Dare Gilmartin has checked our repairs. Pronounced them sound. We'll leave tomorrow."

Walker shook in his agitation. "Do you know what dangers that would be opening up for you? Why, when the Indians see a lone wagon—"

Jacob cast Celinda a look. Rachel saw it ask for confirmation. They'd talked this over, this decision they were about to make public.

"Yes, we understand. So do the Hydes."

Rachel touched Hiram's shoulder. He left her side and joined his bespeckled sister Ora beside their parents.

Mr. Hyde removed his worn hat, then ran his hand through his hair, reminding Rachel of the same gesture when Dare did it, except that Mr. Hyde's hair was thick with silver. "We worked this out together, us folks from our Iowa," he began. "My missus and two young ones are in agreement on it, Captain. You're the expert on chances and all. All I know is the Lowells, they're the first and only folks who didn't see us as lazy squatters on their land. They gave us a chance them years back, to hold our heads high again, when we were in terrible debt. Well, we worked it off. Now, this here fruit business is our last chance as I figure it, partnering off with our young friends here, helping them out with the trees. We'll stick with them, sir."

Rachel admired that look between the neighbors of such different means and generations, and all the fears overcome to achieve it. She wanted to learn more from these families who had already offered her own so many kindnesses. She squeezed Dare's arm. "Let's ask to join them," she whispered. "They're going now. We must go, too, now that Atoka has what he came here for, his wife."

He grinned, glancing back as her brother and the wedding party approached. "Mother of Life. Atoka isn't the only one with surprises today," he said.

twenty-one

All the predictions made before they left Fort Laramie seemed to be coming true, Rachel thought, as she woke to the sounds of Celinda Lowell trying to coax the lame ox to his feet. The animal's cry pained her ears.

"Stand aside, what you're doing ain't a mercy," her husband told her through the darkness. Then, the crack of his rifle's shot. Quillworker's arm tensed, pulled Rachel against her so hard it drove the breath from her lungs.

She cried out a Cheyenne word that ended in a sob.

"It's Jeanie," Rachel gasped, "the Lowells' ox, sister. Shot to release her from her misery."

Quillworker's grip eased, though the trembling started in her hands and rode through her body. Rachel sat, took the woman into her arms as her sobbing grew louder. The back flaps of the wagon parted. Dare appeared, his eyes alarmed, his face smelling of shaving soap.

She nodded, still rocking Quillworker as her brother joined her husband.

"The lowing of the poor creature the night long," Dare said quietly, "it invaded all our dreams, did it not, Atoka?" He shoved her brother closer. Close enough to touch his wife's trembling arm.

"It did, Quillworker," Atoka whispered.

She lifted her head from Rachel's arms and met her husband's eyes. Rachel smiled, releasing her to his care. "I'll bring some coffee," she said.

Dare put out his hand, helping Rachel from the wagon.

Rachel heard the soft croon of a lullaby Atoka had sung to her after their parents' death on the trail to Oklahoma. She watched her husband wipe the shaving soap from his face, pull his suspenders up over his shoulders. He wrapped the rims of his spectacles around his ears. She smiled, remembering his delight in her gift, grateful to the Swiss merchant who accepted her tatting in trade before they'd spit off from Walker's train, though she was still seven yards short of their agreed amount. Her husband, whom she thought even more handsome when he wore them, stood, entranced as a child before sunsets now.

"The coffee can wait," he warned her away from the pot. "Where does it hurt?"

"Hurt? I'm not—"

"Rachel, would you be caught in your lie?"

He touched her side exactly where her sister-in-law had taken hold. She winced. "Sore only. A little sore. There, see? Better. All I needed was your touch."

He snorted his displeasure, like Atoka's horses, but his fingers at her side remained gentle, soothing.

"She was afraid, Dare. She didn't mean—"

"Ach, but she's a powerful woman, love. Your brother should be seeing to her. You do not have ribs to spare her nightmares."

"Let me warm you coffee," she urged.

He shook his head. "I'd best help with the grave digging for poor Jeanie." He lifted his hat over those beautiful, bespeckled eyes, and left their camp.

Jeanie's yokemate had died the day before, poisoned by something she ate. They were the lead team, so the Lowells had only their swing and wheel teams remaining.

The stony Sweetwater River trail had never seemed more desolate as Rachel joined the families silently gathering around the tree wagon in the predawn light.

"They served us well, did Emma and Jeanie," Mr. Lowell admitted by way of obituary.

"They have given us their very last steps," his wife added softly.

Gibson Rice began a short, mournful Scottish air on his fiddle, lending a grace to their gathering. Rachel was grateful again that the shy bachelor had asked the Hydes if they could use an extra hand, thereby casting his lot with their small, broken-off party. His bravery honored him. Rachel had tried to compliment him, but he'd only laughed. He'd told her his decision was purely selfish, that Dare's dancing feet coaxed out fine notes from his fiddle. And he was in service to his instrument, so he must follow them. Rachel thought the notes he played now, while they were all still, were equally fine, even holy.

As the tune was still resounding in the silence, Bartholomew Hyde put his worn hat back on his head. "Face it, Jake. The four oxen left can't do it," he said.

Jake Lowell cast a pained look to his Iowa neighbor. "But, Barth, the load's lighter. Almost a hundred trees have died already."

Jessica wound her arm around her mother's thickening waist. Alfred hit his hat against his leg as two of his younger sisters sniffed. All futile gestures in this still, poisoned place, Rachel thought.

"Maybe we should listen to the trees," Dare offered quietly. So quietly Rachel thought she was the only person close enough to hear him. But they were all listening, even to the air for help.

"What do you mean, son?" Mr. Hyde asked.

Rachel touched her husband's arm. Dare stared at her through his new lenses. He looked at Quillworker in her habitual place behind her, then at Atoka. Wanting something of them all. Permission. Sacrifice. Rachel smiled, nodding. Her husband knew about sacrifice, from all those he'd made for his first family, for his Irish clan. Whatever it was, she wanted to hear it, to help him achieve it, for the good of all. Quillworker did not meet Dare's look, but she touched Rachel's back with the callused tips of her hardworking fingers.

But Atoka scowled. "My horses do not pull wagons, Irishman."

"I'm not asking for that."

"*Oke.* Then I will listen to what you ask."

Dare faced the circle, studied the men, women, and children of their train. Rachel watched his lips move silently before he spoke. Was he praying to his Irish god for guidance, she wondered. "We're heading for the South Pass over the Rockies," he began. "We've lost many of the wee trees. This wagon is now too heavy for the lesser weight. We might abandon it to the trail, I'm thinking."

"I'm not leaving the trees!" Jacob Lowell maintained. Young Alfred and his women stood stoutly by him. Lulie stepped out of her family's united stance. She threw the doll Dare had made her at his feet.

He winced, picking up Miss Anabelle. It looked sad and abandoned as it dangled, the quills Atoka's wife had sewn onto the dress's hem clicking against his leg. Quillworker had carefully dyed Atoka's marriage gifts with the juice of berries and flowers, then sun-dried, then flattened her treasures with her teeth. Finally she'd sewn them on something belonging to every member of their newly formed community.

Dare rubbed his thumb over the *wihio,* a spider symbol his sister-in-law had sewn onto the right brace of his suspenders after seeing him dance. "I am not speaking in a clear way," he said.

"Try again," Rachel urged, squeezing her husband's arm gently in encouragement. His fingers closed over hers, pressed, before he spoke.

"Mr. Lowell. I'm saying maybe we should move your trees to our wagon, sir. It's lighter. But strong, I'll tell you that. We'll all manage better then, with three wagons among us. That's what I'm thinking."

Rachel watched him make an almost courtly bow, his tall graceful form a contrast to the gnarled forbidding place. They took a step back from the circle together.

Celinda Lowell approached Rachel. "But, your things."

Rachel smiled. "I gave most of my books away to the children on the big train before we broke off." She made her mind skip only lightly through her scholars' good-byes, like skimming stones tossed across water. "My men and I, we don't mind giving up a wagon in service to the trees. If you could spare the room for our foodstuffs," she glanced over to Atoka, "we can pack our tenting on my brother's horses."

The nods of assent wound their way around the circle. Then smiles of hope.

Everyone shook each other's hands in agreement with her husband's plan, even the children. Lulie approached Dare carefully. She kicked up a little of the trail's dust at her feet as she eyed her doll. "Arm might fall off, with you holding her like that," she reprimanded him.

He scowled. "Not any arm I fastened on, miss."

She reached out tentatively, then ran her fingers over Quillworker's gift to her doll. Dare crouched, offered Miss Anabelle back to her owner. Lulie took the doll slowly, then climbed on his knee and kissed his cheek.

"Well. I'm glad my wife makes me shave each morning."

She did no such thing, Rachel thought. He merely sensed her gladness as she felt his smooth face. She wanted to tell the child this, for she would think her a scold.

"And I'm only too happy to oblige her, of course," he declared, grinning at her scowl of displeasure. Was she a scold, then? Now he laughed aloud at her distress. This man knew her too well for such a new husband.

Rachel watched her brother cross his arms before his chest as Dare approached him. Why did Atoka make that challenging gesture? He was more broad shouldered than her husband. His stance accented that difference. Perhaps he still envied Dare's taller height? Men were such strange creatures. "Tie no pans on their backs," Atoka commanded. "My horses are not pack mules."

"No pans," Dare agreed. "Thank you, Atoka. The blessings of St. Brendan the Navigator be on you." He held out his hand, trying to break the lock at his brother-in-law's chest. Atoka only scowled.

Coming out from behind Rachel's shadow, his new wife gave Atoka's back a poke with her strong fingers, startling him enough to loosen his stance, then give Dare his hand. Rachel stifled a giggle as Quillworker retreated behind her again.

"Ruled by trees," Atoka said.

"Aye," Dare confirmed.

"Trees are living things, full of promise, like the children," Rachel reminded her brother, who would soon become a father to a child with no maternal relatives willing to raise him. Atoka cast a fleeting look at his wife's middle before he headed off. To give his horses the news, Rachel surmised. Quillworker drew her shawl tighter around her.

As hopeful as her poke and her brother's earlier morning lullaby were, her sister-in-law had spoken only to Rachel since the day she and her brother married. She had never been alone with him before their short time in the wagon that morning. At night she'd slept only beside Rachel, sometimes clinging to her when the spark of a fire flared or at the screech of an owl in the night. The men camped out under the stars nearby. Sometimes Atoka would sense his wife's lingering fears, and play his flute, Rachel knew.

"I wanted to give you a sister," he'd told her the day before. "Have I done wrong, *Yalabusha?*"

"No. Quillworker belongs with us," she'd said. "And I am fortunate in both my generous and patient men."

Amity Hyde, Celinda Lowell, and their female children approached Rachel as she decided on what to leave by the side of the trail. Cautiously, as they were learning to do around Atoka's skittish wife. Alerted, Quillworker reached for Rachel. Her hand. It felt cold with fear.

"We can fill our own pots and pans higher with food, and all take our meals together, how would that be?" Celinda Lowell offered. "Starting now. With a hearty breakfast. Please. Will you join us?"

Ora Hyde cast a quick look in Alfred Lowell's direction before she pushed her spectacles up with her thumb and grinned. "There's just the seventeen of us now. A big family, is all."

As the men began the process of transforming the wagon to become the keeper of the trees, the women returned to their cooking. Until Quillworker patted Rachel's back.

"We will return," Rachel whispered, as her sister-in-law pulled her away from the women's company. In the shadow of their wagon, the tall woman slowed her long strides, then stopped. Her sister-in-law was a strong woman. Rachel still felt an ache where she'd held her in her panic, even after Dare's ministrations and though she'd given her corset ties a looser hold on her ribs. "Quillworker," Rachel said, breathless. "Are we too many for you to—?"

"No," she said quietly, firmly, looking at her hands. Struggling, it seemed, to bring forth more words. "Rachel. Is that the name your mother gave you?"

"Yes."

"Lissa is the name my mother gave me. Perhaps it would make us . . . less peculiar? Now. Here. Among the women, to use it?"

Rachel smiled. "It's a pretty name. And goes well with my brother's name, LeMoyne, which is yours now, too. Together they are graceful, like you."

"I'm not." But the way she tossed her head in denial had a playful quality. It reminded Rachel of the same gesture in Sky-

Reaching. She wished her brother had seen it. Then realized he had. He turned away quickly, going back to his work. But not too quickly, Rachel hoped, for his wife to see the pleasure in his eyes.

"Are you ready to return to the others, Lissa?" Rachel tried the name, loud enough for Atoka to hear.

She nodded.

"Lissa LeMoyne. Yes, a good name," she decided, before she introduced her sister-in-law to the women and children with the names her mother and new husband had given her.

When they came together again around the breakfast fire, Mr. Lowell left his family and approached Rachel. He pulled off his hat.

"Before we take this first meal together, I need to say something to this woman," he announced.

Rachel felt her breathing tighten with worry. The small ache around her ribs returned. Were the Lowells and Hydes angry that Lissa didn't speak, or that she would do work almost connected to Rachel? That would change, Rachel was sure of it. If they would give Atoka's wife the time and patience her men were bestowing. The Iowa nurseryman cleared his throat twice, then looked at his wife, who gave him an encouraging glance.

"My missus and me," he began with a bow to Mrs. Lowell that made her roll her eyes. "We were with the others at first, Miss Rachel, ah . . . Mrs. Gilmartin. Thinking you folks wild, worried about you telling papist or heathen stories to the children, along with their ciphering and letters. Well, now we're right glad for your tolerance of our ignorance. You and your folks here have been sent by God to us, that's the way we have it figured."

Barth Hyde skittered a look at his wife now. Why didn't the women speak for themselves, Rachel wondered, when they had such shy men? This was peace-making. And women made good peace chiefs. "It is my belief that God lives in all of us, sir," Rachel said.

"Is it? Well, that's a fine belief. Sounds downright Christian to me, too." He cleared his throat twice. What was the man up to now, Rachel wondered. She was hungry for breakfast, not words. "Does . . . Mrs. Gilmartin, does this uncle of yours believe that too?"

"My brother and I have not seen him in many years, sir. But that is how I remember him, laughing, welcoming all onto his porch."

"Porch." Celinda Lowell sighed, her own speech finally loosened. "A house with a porch. Seems like a dream after all this time, don't it?"

"It does indeed," Rachel agreed, grateful for the tin plate of buckwheat cakes Mrs. Hyde placed before her.

But Mr. Lowell got back to what Rachel began to surmise was the business at hand, so she left the fork in her lap. "How much land did you say this uncle of yours has, Mrs. Gilmartin?"

"Two thousand acres. Only one hundred of them cleared. But rich, river bottomland."

"Sizable."

Rachel smiled, inhaling her steaming breakfast. "Beyond my Irish husband's considerable powers of imagination."

"Aye," Dare conceded, "a farm that size, with no tenants? Only in America." He took a large bite of Amity Hyde's buckwheat cakes, which seemed to please her even more than it did him.

Atoka sipped at his coffee, his eyes hooded. Mr. Lowell turned to Rachel again. "My trees, they'll need to be heeled into good soil if they stand a chance in Oregon. You know we're hardworking folks, Mrs. Gilmartin, Mr. LeMoyne. Do you think, if Barth and Hiram, if Gibson the fiddler and my boy and I promised to help him open up more acres, your uncle might consider allowing us a place?"

"I can't see him turning away any good neighbor," Rachel ventured. "I think you'd all be welcome."

Atoka grinned, a flashing, unexpected reaction to all around the campfire, Rachel surmised. "My sister will see to it that you are welcome," he said. "She could charm the shingles off Uncle Bridges's cabin as a child. And she's worse still, now."

"Atoka. I don't remember that at all," Rachel protested.

"Then it's a good thing you still have elders, little sister," he informed her tartly. He feasted on the small smile from his wife that his words produced, though he shoved his pan at her and said, "Biscuits."

The gray outlines Rachel and Dare had first spotted had turned into timbered foothills, then grassy mountain slopes. The dark conifer forests and cool August nights told their small party they were reaching the timberline. It was not the arduous struggle Rachel imagined crossing the Rockies to be. Within the ranges were forests opening onto stream-fed lakes ringed in forests of pine, spruce, and aspen. The men found game. And a friendly Shoshone hunting party that admired Atoka's horses, even after he refused to trade any. The Shoshone were the first of the native people they encountered delighted not to be offered whiskey. Rachel found them as temperance-minded as the strictest Presbyterian, decrying strong drink as a stealer of souls. The women traded and watched the children of both races play together. Rachel saw a longing in Lissa's eyes as she watched the Shoshone women and children, and wondered if she was having thoughts of leaving her brother and the train and becoming Quillworker again. Rachel wouldn't blame her if she did, but worried about her brother's heart.

The day she stopped worrying was the day he and Dare had joined her expedition to find some white pine bark or wild sarsaparilla to make a tonic for Rose's coughs. They led Atoka's horses over another summit after a climb that was gradual, even easy. Atoka played his flute as they walked.

"Imagine," Dare proclaimed, "now all the rivers run to the Pacific." He lifted Lulie Lowell to his shoulder. The little girl held up her doll in the same way to her own shoulder.

"Why is that?" Callie asked, taking Dare's free hand as she

caught up beside them. Rachel felt a small pang of jealousy walking behind her husband and the children who she strongly suspected adored him.

"Because we've just crossed the mighty backbone of North America. We are in Oregon Territory." He turned. "Isn't that right, Miss Rachel?" he asked her.

"My husband is a good student."

Lulie looked so perfect on his shoulder that her eyes hurt.

"Will we see it soon, then, Miss Rachel?" Rose asked, "The Willamette Valley?"

"Oh, no. The place where my uncle and his wife have their farm is in the western part of the territory, not far from the great Pacific. We have still to travel through the eastern and middle sections. Mr. Standhope in his guide describes great diversity of climate, topography, rivers, rainfall, and timber, and soil types in these sections."

Atoka finished his tune and slowed his leading steps. "My sister doesn't need those heavy books of hers. She remembers everything in them," he maintained, lifting Rose Lowell to Red Cedar's back. Hannah reached for her sickly sister, but Ora Hyde held her back. "She's safe, Hannah."

"But the horse has no saddle."

"Look how he steadies her back. And Mr. Dare's right there as well."

"But, Ora, Atoka LeMoyne ain't like Miss Rachel and Mr. Dare," she insisted in a furious whisper. "He's wild! He up and shot Eveline Walker when she wouldn't have him! And his new wife won't even—"

"He didn't do any such thing!" Hiram Hyde proclaimed, stopping their procession.

The Lowell sisters cast frightened looks to Rachel. She glanced at her brother, who remained silent, watching, as Hiram stood to his full height.

Ora Hyde approached her brother. "Now, Hiram," she said in her steadying voice, "we all understand that Mr. LeMoyne was out hunting that day and didn't mean to—"

"Atoka wasn't out hunting. And he had no feelings for Eveline Walker once she quit working her wiles on him to get what she needed to badmouth Miss Rachel, we all know that!"

Rachel cast a worried look at Dare, whose eyes urged patience. Hiram continued.

"And that he's a crack shot, Atoka is! If he'd of been in a mind to shoot Eveline on account of that badmouthing of his sister, he wouldn't have made such a poor job of it." He scanned the adults in their small party with scrutiny. "Now, I don't know what these folks agreed upon to help old man Walker save face about what he done to his own kin, but I didn't make no agreement with anybody! Me and Alfred and Gibson Rice were the ones out hunting that day that Atoka LeMoyne came in with his new white and dun mares. We heard all the shots while Atoka was still fuming over that damned fool Walker taking aim at an eagle! In our plain sight, he was, so none of them shots were from his rifle. You all hear? None of them! And that's all I got to say on it!"

He whacked his collection of wildflowers into Hannah Lowell's arms and stomped down the ridge toward the wagons.

"Mercy," Hannah breathed. "Our Hiram didn't stammer once, did he, Miss Rachel?"

"No, Hannah, he did not."

Atoka grinned. Rose patted the hand that rested over hers. "More, please?" she asked him.

He led on toward a grove of white pine. His wife left her habitual place behind Rachel and walked at his side.

Rachel smiled. "It is very good of Rose to help my brother show his new wife he will be a good father. See how she watches."

The girls walked closer to Rachel. Jessica spoke. "Why doesn't she talk, Miss Rachel? Did her father really cut out her tongue?"

"No. She talks a little. To me."

"Used to be she was all in your shadow. She's better now. Maybe Atoka can kiss her soon. He wants to kiss her, don't he?"

"Jessie!" Hannah reprimanded.

"Miss Rachel likes straight out talk, she told me so, didn't you, ma'am?"

"Yes, Jessica. My brother would like Lissa the Quillworker for his true wife. I think our Hiram has done him a great service. Listen. Atoka plays his flute to court, to show her she has chosen a tender man."

"Chosen? Back at Fort Laramie, Mrs. Barton, she said he drank too much whiskey and the filthy gamblers tricked him into—"

"My brother is not so easily tricked. And he does not drink whiskey at all. Atoka knew what he was doing."

"I think he knows what he's doing now, too, ma'am," Ora Hyde said, as they watched Atoka help Rose down from the horse and into his wife's grasp. The little girl coughed a small, dry cough. Both he and Lissa's hands went instinctively to her back, rubbed. But the hands lingered, entwined. And they held, even after the little girl had ducked under their grasp to tell her sisters of her ride on Red Cedar.

Rachel watched her brother relinquish his horse to Dare, then lean over to say something softly at his wife's ear. Lissa raised startled, frightened eyes to Rachel. They might belong with other men, those eyes. They did not belong with her brother. Rachel tried to make her eyes tell these things to the wounded woman. Her sister-in-law turned slowly, faced Atoka, then walked over the ridge at his side.

"There. He'll kiss her now," Jessica said with confidence.

"He'll ask her first, if he remembers my advice," Rachel said.

Ora Hyde raised her brows so high her spectacles slipped down her nose. "Truly? Should we wait for a man who asks, Miss Rachel?"

"Oh, yes. That kind of man is worth the wait."

"Tell your brother that, Jessica Lowell!" she said, grinning widely.

"And," Hannah ventured, "maybe you should tell Hiram the same from me? If he ever takes such a notion into his head, I mean."

twenty-two

Rachel worked half the night on the letter. She felt the sweet company of the wolves' songs, and bathed in the light of one of the Atoka and Dare's gift candles.

She addressed a man she barely remembered, but felt she knew well from his own beautiful, loyal missives. It was the least she could do for her mother's brother, this man who kept the hope of family alive for so many unanswered years. Finally, she sealed her letter with the brass stamp and cranberry scented wax Amity Hyde had brought all the way from Wyndom, Connecticut, from her grandmother's trousseau that dated from the time when the United States were colonies.

In the letter Rachel told Uncle Bridges the story of the pineapple imprint on the waxed seal, how it meant welcome to the ancestors of her friend. She thanked him for his welcome, for his guidance across the plains and mountains and deserts. Then she told him of the trees they carried, and of their need for new soil, along with those needs of the people who loved them.

Enough people to start a village, she wrote, if he and his wife were willing.

When she blew out the candle she realized that the moonless night was alive with stars. Rachel lay down under those stars, beside Dare. He only woke enough to murmur "Warm?" at her ear and pull her in against his chest. She loved having such a husband, who was not disturbed by her late-night pen scratching, and kind to her, even in his sleep. And he'd been so tolerant in the days that Lissa had clung to her. Had her brother learned from her husband's patient nature? Rachel thought so. For now he had earned a wife warming him at night.

At Fort Hall the next day, the postmaster raised his brows at a letter going west instead of east. That was all. No questions about from where they had come, or who they were. Rachel felt men's eyes on her skirts as she left the post office. Was it a mistake, sending her letter off? More eyes. Perhaps it was the men's hunger, then, and not suspicion? She tried to temper the easy sway of her hips she'd developed walking the trail. Was it not safe, the sway, in the way going out after dark had not been safe in St. Louis?

She was still not used to what her presence did out here where so many men had come without women. Some, even as she rode or walked beside her men, looked ready to devour her with greedy eyes, and to destroy Dare in their envy. Some pierced her heart with their rudderless longing. They would not be so tired and desperate if they had brought their women along, Rachel thought. They would appear handsome and purposeful, like her husband and brother, like Jake Lowell and Mr. Hyde. And Gibson Rice, who had no woman, but often kept them company, playing his fiddle to help them keep up their chore pace.

Even Rachel was not exotic enough to draw much attention once word spread about the tree farm in the wagon. The inhabitants of Fort Hall made them into a joke, laughing at their small party and its burden. But some faces, even those of the most hardened soldiers, grew wistful at the sight of the Lowells's sprightly seedlings, here in this remote station that bordered a sagebrush desert. How long had it been since any of them had seen a tree?

As she and Lissa dribbled water into the roots of the seedlings, Rachel heard the three kick back on their roughhewn bench. Their own men were busy waterproofing the new tree wagon as tightly as the old one had been. These three were not engaged in such industrious activity. The space beneath their feet continued to mount with the shavings of their knives' whittling as they spoke.

"Two bits says them trees go before the whitewater past Fort Boise."

"Four says in the first crossing of the Snake."

"Aw, go on. Wind'll kill them, 'fore they reach the Snake," the third claimed. He put a dollar on it.

The whittlers began to wonder how big a game of chance they could get going among the fort's inhabitants and visitors.

Lissa stopped watering. She raised her head. A slow smile spread across her face as her hand fisted at her hip. The smile reminded Rachel of Dare's for-the-landlord one. Both her husband and new sister had the charm of this face weaving. This trickster charm had protected them, allowed them to live another day. "We'll tell you where to send our cut, boys," she shouted toward the men.

Rachel stared at Atoka's wife. A full sentence? And not to her, but to strangers? Men? Rachel didn't remember hearing that tone of voice—low and smoky—from her sister-in-law before, either.

The bench thumped forward. The three men seemed as surprised as Rachel that Lissa had addressed them. The whittling stopped. They tried looking everywhere but at her expanding middle. "We . . . meant no disrespect, ladies," the first man claimed.

Lissa's stance did not waver. "That's good. We welcome your respect. And will be glad to welcome half the pot as well, if you're honorable men. Being the odds will be so long in favor of our failure. Being we're doing all the work upon which your idle speculation is based."

"Yes, miss, uh, missus," the youngest, a man-child of about twenty stammered, removing his hat.

"We are Mrs. LeMoyne and Mrs. Gilmartin," Lissa presented them both, smiling again. "That will be, care of the Lowell Orchard in the Willamette Valley of Oregon. Shall we write it down for you?"

"Uh . . . yes, if you please."

Another hat got pulled down over a chewed-off ear. "If it wouldn't cause you too much trouble, ma'am."

Lissa turned. "Rachel, would you mind?"

"Why, no."

"No?" Chewed Ear looked puzzled. "Does that mean she won't do it, Mis Le . . . le?"

"LeMoyne. On the contrary, sir. It means my sweet sister-in-law is agreeable toward our proposal. She fetches her paper and writing implements even now. Rachel?" Rachel woke herself from the wonder of her sister-in-law's stream of words to rush into the Lowell wagon for what was needed. And Amity Hyde's sealing wax to make the document look more official. She returned to Lissa overseeing the three men, now her partners. They were feeding the last of the seedlings their precious water allotment. And Lissa was still in command of the conversation's flow. "Our Rachel has a very fine, clear hand, gentlemen. And was a most respected teacher back east. She has been gracious enough to share her knowledge with the children of our train as well, imagine that?"

The last hat got whisked off a balding head as Rachel completed her task with a firm press of the brass pineapple.

"We are most pleased to make your acquaintance, ladies," its owner declared. "And wish you every success in your family's endeavor. My money's on you both, to the tune of . . . of fifty dollars!"

Man-child looked skeptical. "Burdock, you ain't seen fifty dollars in your sorry life."

"I'll have it in the pot before them trees bear their first fruit, on my honor."

"Well . . . well, I'll have sixty!" said Chewed Ear. "There! I'm declared for the opinion of you grand ladies getting these here trees to the Willamette Valley, safe!"

Rachel and Lissa excused themselves from the men's company while they were still besting each other's wagers.

That's what Lissa needed, then, to help find herself again? A challenge? Atoka will be pleased, Rachel decided, when I tell him this story of his wife and the whittlers.

She nourished herself with remembrance of the story two weeks later, when Atoka and Dare's fingers sifted the dry earth that bordered their third deadly lake.

"Even the Irish could coax nothing from the soil of this place," Dare said, his voice's tone echoing the harsh wonder of his words.

"Soil?" Jake Lowell contended, "Your imagination works too hard, friend. This is dust."

It was dust. Alkali dust. And it sifted into everything, even the lines around her husband's eyes that were the gift from the laughing in his other life. No one, not even Dare, laughed now. To do so would be to let the dust in to strangle already sore, dry throats. So Rachel kept Lissa's story in her heart as Amity Hyde tore her family tablecloth into masks for them to wear through the storm.

Huddled inside the Lowell wagon, Rachel read to the children from her uncle's recollections of the strange formations he'd seen on this part of the trail. But her throat protested. So she and the children made a game of guessing what kind of faces they were making behind their tatted linen finery. Only one word and a shake or nod of the head was required in response. They advanced in their game from "delight" and "trepidation" to "suspicion" and "despair."

"Surprise?" Rachel tried to conjecture Rose Lowell's turn.

The little girl shook her head vehemently, then pointed beyond her. She choked up some dust which had worked it way into her throat, even through the weave. Rachel offered water. She felt a nervous hand tap her shoulder as she patted Rose's back.

"I'll see to her, Miss Rachel," Jessica offered. "You'd best find out if that fellow's dead or alive."

"Fellow? What fellow?"

"Look. Just past that lava pillar. Wait till the wind clears . . . see him?"

Rachel realized that Rose Lowell had not been playing the game. She'd been pointing to the crumpled form. Her shock was real. A man was laying facedown, half buried in the sand.

Rachel lifted her mask up over her nose before she jumped off the slow-moving wagon and waved down the first horseman riding beside it. It was Dare, his fine hat coated gray, his mask just beneath it, who hoisted her smoothly onto the saddle with him. He followed the directions she spoke at his ear and soon they dismounted beside the downed man.

As Dare turned the lean form over, Rachel found the pounding pulse in his wrist.

"Alive," she whispered.

"An Mhaighdean Mhuire," Dare's Irish robbed his breath along with the blowing dust. *"Costasach,"* he then summoned her with an endearment. "Tell me I am not gone mad. Tell me who this is."

Beneath the dust was a fashionable blue frock coat, brocade vest, and strapped trousers. A paintbox was tucked under the man's arm. Beside it, half-buried, a canvas with a wash of sienna and amber. Rachel finally focused on his face, with its painful-looking bruise over the left eye. "Mr. Combs. It's Mr. Combs."

She heard Dare exhale, unburdened by the fear of losing his mind. Lying in his arms was the English artist who had sketched Dare and his other family, the man they had left in the twin gallows jail in Sligo.

"Let's get him to a more sheltered spot," Rachel urged her husband, who was still staring, stunned, at this being of his past in Ireland. He nodded, handing her the paintbox before dragging their burden into the shadow of the lava pillar.

Rachel shook the Englishman's shoulder slightly. He stirred. Dare dribbled water into his mouth in the same way she and Lissa had watered the trees. Mr. Combs swallowed, then opened eyes that soon went wide with fear. Rachel nudged her husband to pull down his tablecloth linen mask.

"*Inis sceal, cumbreag, no biamuish,*" he demanded, while doing so.

"*Dosaire!*" the downed man shot back at him, before a spasm of coughing brought the sand from his throat. Rachel pounded his back and helped him to sit up higher. The battered Englishman's eyes softened. He reached long, trembling fingers to her own mask, and pulled it down. Then he sighed hard. "It's a great mystery to me why you still tolerate this barbarian's company, Miss LeMoyne."

"I'm Dare's wife now, Mr. Combs. Mrs. . . . . Gilmartin?" she said carefully.

"Ah. Of course. Congratulations on your nuptials. I heard about that part of your adventure from a delightful American ship's captain, once I'd convinced him I was not one of a long line of clerics and constabularies out for your necks."

"You followed us?"

"Well, not without being pushed in your general westerly direction."

"Are you hurt?" Dare entered their conversation gruffly.

The Englishman frowned in both pain and irritation, Rachel thought. "Not as badly as was hoped by my attacker. I imagine the completion of my demise would have been accomplished by this blasted storm of sand. It already wrecked my view of that stunning formation I was attempting to capture on—where is my canvas, my paintbox?"

Rachel laughed. "We have them too, Mr. Combs."

"Excellent woman!"

Dare growled. "What are you doing here?"

"Finding you, ungrateful wretch. I became somewhat distracted by the beauty of a landscape as wild as the west of Ireland."

"Mr. Combs," Rachel gently summoned. "Where is your party?"

"I . . . well, I was abandoned by my companions."

Dare snorted now. "Abandoned, was it?"

The artist touched his forehead gingerly and winced. "We were ill-suited, if the truth be known, all the way from our starting point of St. Louis."

"St. Louis?" Rachel whispered.

Dare let out a stream of Irish.

Mr. Combs suffered her husband's barrage until it was spent. Then he smiled. "Is that part of your greeting, Dare . . . Gilmartin, is it? After that initial Celt invitation to tell a story, compare a lie, or get out? I'm afraid my meager command of Irish does not accommodate this addendum."

"You joined them," Dare accused. "The damned mercenaries sent out from St. Louis. Hunting us."

"Dare!" Rachel chastised.

"How did you ever find enough sense to marry this woman?" the artist asked, "and bury your twin selves back at Devil's Gate besides?"

Rachel touched his forehead.

He laughed, which again twisted his mouth in pain. "Ah, yes. This matching couple's passing was a great tragedy, sworn to by every member of the wagon train headed by Captain Walker, have you heard of him? Overbearing man, not fully fingered. He confirmed the story, though to do so appeared to pain him slightly."

"What in hell are you—?" Dare began.

"Whist, husband!" Rachel chastised again. "Listen."

The artist grinned when Dare complied. "My companions— never cohorts, as your wife has already realized, included two slick silk-hatted agents of a certain publisher in St. Louis. They've been behind the suspects, fort to fort, checking on names, mail sent out, habits of the wayfarers. Thought they had them at Fort Laramie, traveling with this Captain Walker's train. Yet Walker's train moved on while they were on a drunk during a trading fair. We followed, and soon discovered a wagon abandoned. When we caught up with Walker's train we were told that it was, indeed, that very couple's wagon. A diamondback viper got the man, and good riddance, for he was a mean cuss. His lady was shortly after run over by a wagon wheel she'd slipped behind. All mourned that loss, saying his sweet wife didn't act so much like the murderess, but more like a schoolmistress. Now these hired killers, overjoyed that nature and clumsiness had accomplished their grim duty, well, they grabbed a few items from inconsolable children on the train, to wit: a schoolbook from the Choctaw Academy in Oklahoma and a queer child's whirling toy, that looked for the life of me like a flyweel section of a printing press. Well, as they have their evidence of the notorious couple's identity and demise, they are presently on their way back to St. Louis to collect their fee without firing a shot."

"You're a damned liar," Dare muttered.

"I beg your—"

"I fixed something for every mother's son and daughter on that train. They didn't good riddance me."

"At least you received an exciting end," Rachel complained. "I couldn't get out of the way of my own feet."

"Blinded by your tears of grief over my release from this mortal coil, m'darling. Do you like that better, now?"

"No," Rachel maintained. "I'd rather have been hit by a bolt of that astounding forked lightning."

Dare's scowl deepened. "I'm sure Combs can arrange a storm into the story once he removes a few stitches from his patchwork of balderdash."

Mr. Combs sat higher, and gave Rachel a courtly half bow. "For you, Mrs. Gilmartin, anything," he promised.

Dare snorted.

The artist's eyes went troubled. "Dare, Rachel," he called. "There was one in our party who remained unconvinced."

"Who?"

"Floyd Dorris."

Rachel felt spirited to a place of darkness. She felt her husband's hand cover hers.

"He lives, then?" Dare whispered.

The Englishman shook his head. "I have more than once wished your aim was better, since he and his devilish fast horse joined us in his recovery. Once his uncle's hired men left, Dorris was furious. But grateful that I agreed to stay with him on the trail. I tried to use that to my . . . to our advantage. But it was no use expecting anything decent, even loyalty, from him. He doubled back to the Walker train. Seduced the trailmaster's daughter before getting another version of events out of her. One I couldn't dissuade him from believing. His mind is poisoned. The very air about him is poisoned. I'm sorry I could not do better at—"

Dare pressed the big heel of his hand into the man's shoulder. "No need for sorrying," he said.

"Well, neither his money nor his whiskey will get him more hired guns for awhile, I suspect."

"He asked your help in his pursuit of us, did he, then," Rachel asked quietly, her fingers hovering around his injury, "and that's how you were hurt?"

"Demanded help would be closer to the truth." The Englishman's laugh was as hollow as the hollow place. "I couldn't reason with him. Or convince him I was an artist, in their company purely by serendipity. He's not stupid. And he's a man possessed. I wish I'd had the strength, the firmness of mind to . . . to . . . "

Rachel touched the Englishman's suffering face. "Now, sir," she tried to soothe him. "I am glad neither my husband nor you has this man's blood on his hands. We must continue to stay out of his reach, and leave him to God."

"I'm afraid that might become difficult."

Rachel felt her husband's cracked dry lips press her forehead. "You were right," he whispered. "At the forts. You were right not to send mail to your uncle, and to stay out of the way of those high-hats."

"When are you going to listen to your women, Darragh Ronan?" the Englishman chided as he took Rachel's arm and tried out his unsteady legs. "Think of all you'd have missed if you went against this little one's wishes and let them string you up in Sligo?"

Dare frowned. "And why didn't they string you up in my stead?"

"The best my family could do was plead my temporary loss

of sanity. It rid me of my job and made me *persona non grata* at the *Times* and in my own country. Is that good enough for you?"

"Not if it sent you here to plague me."

"Dare," Rachel chided impatiently, "give Mr. Combs more water, then let's welcome him on our journey."

Rachel watched her brother's splendid form turn in the light of their communal campfire. When had his voice gone so measured, so rounded and patient, she wondered. Was this her impulsive, hotheaded Atoka, explaining their plight to the circle? He only toward the end became his old self—the eagle clan man who would brook no fault-finding of her.

"My sister is a good Christian woman. She did not lie. She does not lie. We have French blood flowing in our veins, but we are also Choctaw. When her husband, who is one of you, shot another of his own in her defense, I think it was the right action in a desperate time. We do not see Dare Gilmartin as a criminal, the way he is seen in St. Louis, and his own country, and by this rich man who seeks the death of my family. We will separate from your company on our horses and free you all from—"

"We ain't voted you free, Atoka," Gibson Rice drawled, standing. "We ain't voted to free ourselves of you, either."

Atoka stared at the fiddler. "Voted?"

"Sure. Don't the Choctaw vote?"

"We voted before your ancestors wrote down your Magna Carta."

The fiddler sighed. "I don't know much about my ancestors, truth to tell. But I was neighbors with the Cherokee of North Georgia growin' up. Don't everybody get to say his piece before you Choctaw folks come to any decision, too?"

"Yes. But we thought—"

"Shouldn't think, till you've listened to what the rest of us have to say. That's democratic. That's American. That's . . ." He looked around, suddenly looking stunned at the full attention of the group. Rachel thought she saw his fingers twitch for the company of his fiddle. "That's ahhh . . . the way I see it," he finally finished.

"Hear, hear!" Mr. Combs shouted, and to Rachel's amazement his peculiar affirmation was taken up by every mother's child of their party.

Atoka passed his hand before his eyes. "I should have let my sister speak. She knows you all better. She is a great peace chief who brought our corn to the starving in Ireland. I thought I was protecting her. That you would hate us now. Our animals are already packed."

"Well, unpack them, son," Mr. Hyde proclaimed. "And sit down while we try to convince you to stay amongst us."

twenty-three

The trees began to die. Rachel found puddles of precious water in evaporating pools. She and Lissa boiled it before feeding the seedlings. Still, the five hundred and ninety saplings that had survived their Rocky Mountain crossing dwindled to four hundred and twenty. Jake Lowell counted their casualties the way his wife counted graves along the trail.

The hot wind swirled about the train and around the strange formations of lava rock. Lulie cradled her forlorn potted cherry tree. She emptied a portion of her own day's ration of water into its soil.

Finally, Rachel saw Atoka riding Red Cedar hard toward the wagon, harder than he should have with their water supplies so low.

"The Snake!" he called, triumphant.

Dare winced, there beside her, as he halted the open tree wagon. Rachel hugged her husband's arm. "The river, not the animal," she assured him.

"Oh, of course," he said, smiling. "Didn't I know that?"

Though the sight of its rushing and spray gave them all hope, their water supply had to wait to be replenished until they passed the Snake's deep canyons and rapids.

When they found a place to traverse the river, it was so dangerous that the men chained all the wagons together. The Hyde wagon led. In the middle wagon, Celinda Lowell kept a worried glance on her eldest two and a white-knuckled grasp on her smallest daughter. Rachel had the reins of the third, the tree wagon.

Lissa joined Jessica and Hannah Lowell to check that the drain holes Alfred had made in the new tree wagon's floor were plugged and secure. Dare and Atoka removed the wheels and tied the empty water barrels to the wagon's side.

Dare smiled his lopsided grin at Rachel and Mr. Combs from where he'd mounted Raven Mocker. She felt their joint happiness in Mr. Combs's decision to join them. He added strength to their family and the tree wagon, though both her men still watched the artist warily. They tested him too, with newcomer challenges Atoka remembered from their lives as Choctaw—making him carry large bundles, and fetch water in a leaking bucket, losing him when on hunts. Men must have had tests like that in Ireland, Dare took to them so. Or perhaps having finally passed Atoka's challenges as brother-in-law, he was ready to make Mr. Combs suffer his own indignities. The Englishman bore it all with good grace and pungent humor. And under her brother and husband's scowls, Rachel knew they were glad for Mr. Combs's help and company.

Dare and Atoka were ready to lead George and Victoria across the swirling water. Feeling a chill of fear, Rachel reminded herself how well Dare had taken to his swimming lessons, as if he was born to the water.

The crossing progressed steadily until her potted cherry tree slipped from Lulie's lap, there in the middle wagon. She leaned over for it and tumbled out of her mother's reach. She splashed into the river's mighty flow. Rachel thought Celinda Lowell's scream would haunt her until the day she died. That was why she snatched for the little girl speeding by, why she held on to something that pulsed with life—a wrist? The current carried her off the seat, tethered only to Mr. Combs's strong, artist's grip at her ankle. Then she felt something else, the leather strap, being tied, then tightening until she thought her foot would come off. Finally, she stopped feeling the foot at all.

She kept watching her grip on Lulie, hoping it was strong enough, hoping the river and her efforts would not break the small bones of her arm. The youngest Lowell was crying. Not for herself. For the cherry seedling floating downstream. Rachel could hear her crying, dimly, while her own head went under the water.

She saw something wondrous under the bubbling water, the powerful whithers of Raven Mocker. And Dare's boots, firmly in the stirrups. Then his calm voice. Her Dare, always calm at times like these.

"I've got her, love. Let go. Take Mr. Combs's hand. There, before you. Please, Rachel."

She did, earning a snort of approval from both her husband and his horse.

Dare made it to the shore first, with his small burden cradled snug before him on the saddle. The wagons followed, grounded at last. Once dismounted, he tested the strength of Lulie's arm. Rachel heard him softly reprimand the child for reaching for the broken-potted cherry tree that the river had miraculously thrust upon its bank not ten feet from them.

But Lulie cried harder, pointing to it with shaking, swollen fingers. Dare sighed hard, then retrieved her treasure. He swooped both tree and girl into his powerful, millwright's arms and relinquished them to Celinda Lowell.

It was her turn to feel Irish eyes mounting with dark anger, Rachel realized, as he fixed his gaze on where she lay, still tethered to Mr. Combs on the riverbank. He shook the Englishman's hand. Then he knelt at her feet, surveying the damage the river and the leather ties had done.

"So fast," the artist said, his cold hand rubbing Rachel's shoulder. She only realized she was shivering when Atoka brought blankets. He wrapped one around her as Gibson Rice did the same for Mr. Combs. "Dare," her accomplice implored, "it all happened so fast. I would have, I thought to try . . . except I cannot swim, you see?"

"Oh, please don't apologize, sir," Rachel said. "And as for the swimming, Dare could not swim himself, before I taught him. I shall be glad to—"

"You'll do nothing of the kind," Dare growled out, looking up from her foot to her clinging, soaked clothes. "I'll be teaching him, if he cares to learn."

The artist laughed. "Now why do I feel that under your tutelage, I'll either swim like a fish or drown trying?"

"Because that's exactly your choice, Englishman," Dare told him, "and you'll only have those choices by way of your efforts on behalf of my foolish wife."

"Come on, then, Mr. Combs, Atoka." Gibson Rice showed the way, laughing. "Let these two have it out. Mis' Hyde's got some coffee on to celebrate the crossing and Lulie's deliverance. It'll warm us."

The Englishman stood with Barton's help, then stumbled against him.

"Oh, I beg your pardon," he beseeched.

"That's all right, Mr. Combs. You're welcome to my arm, sir, after what you done for our ladies."

"My name is William," he told the fiddler as they walked to the fire together.

"Well, that's a right fine name. They call you Will where you come from?"

"Why, no. Might it suit me here in America, do you think?"

Dare frowned at Atoka. "My mother fed that man for a good seven years of his blasted artistic excursions! Never told me his Christian name."

"And he never signed it to his pictures," Rachel remembered.

Atoka grinned. "Did you ever ask it?" he asked her husband.

"No. Why would I do that?"

Atoka snorted now. "I'll get you both some coffee," he offered, abandoning Rachel to her husband's wrath.

Dare's eyes glinted as he gently released her from the knots Mr. Combs and the river had fastened around her ankle. She tried combing her fingers through his hair to relieve his worry, but he shook her off.

"Ach, Rachel, you don't think."

"It would have taken too much time. Thinking."

"Aye," he agreed begrudgingly as he gently lifted her already swelling foot out of her lace-up shoe. "Can you move your toes?"

She did, making him smile at last.

Their remaining trees began to revive along with Rachel's ankle. While recuperating, she finished letting the seams out of Lissa's blue dress. The strain of their long days walking began to show on the faces of both their uncomplaining pregnant women. At the higher elevations the nights became cold. They finally entered the pine forests of the Blue Mountains on the twenty-fourth of September.

William Combs, already in high esteem after the river crossing, proved his worth to the train and its children daily, in less dramatic ways. He sketched them all, making their clothes more brightly colored than they were now, and their faces less careworn, Rachel thought, though she did not give him anything but compliments. His sketches and Gibson's nightly playing of "Chester" and "Free America," and "Saro Jane" kept all their spirits higher than their circumstances should have permitted.

William Combs and her husband argued about everything except the Englishman's talent. She didn't understand this gruff tenderness between men. And why Dare and Atoka and now Gibson Rice hovered about the man like angel guardians, carefully hiding their watchfulness. But Mr. Combs knew it. And he was still out of his element enough to be thankful for their efforts, she thought. He said nothing, but once presented Dare with a charcoal sketch of Rachel sleeping on his shoulder in the campfire light, with "a belated wedding present" his only explanation.

The whole train appreciated its beauty. Dare would not let it leave his hands so they had to gather around him for a look. Later he rose from their family circle and disappeared into the back of the Lowell wagon, where their few remaining belongings were stored. Rachel did not follow, but she imagined him tucking the sketch into his part of their light load, adding it to the things she'd saved for him in her oilskin pouch—William Combs's pictures of his Irish family, with the names and dates she'd carefully inscribed, and the papers that made him the King of Connacht.

When Dare returned to the circle his eyes were red and swollen. He did not dance that night, though Atoka coaxed him with a sprightly flute variation of Gibson Rice's tune for "The Eighth of January." Dare watched the children dance. Pensively, Rachel thought. And with something new added to his sad eyes. Yearning. Despite his gruff welcome, and his earned place among the men and their whole party, William Combs was a reminder of Dare's home. And all his losses.

The mountains became more rugged and difficult to travel. After being able to see vast distances for so long, they were now hemmed in by the evergreens towering overhead, blocking sight of the trail. Rachel felt more bothered by this than the women.

It was getting colder.

"My trees need a new home soon," Jake Lowell said one night as the survivors, now replenished by their ample water supply, began their first bright display of fall foliage, a miracle among the evergreens.

"We all need a home," his wife remarked, rubbing her fist into the small of her back. Rose put her own fingers there and kneaded. "When will the baby come, Mama?" she asked.

"Around Christmas."

"The same time I will become a father," Atoka said, glancing at Lissa to see her reaction to his public claim to her coming child.

She smiled and went back to her quillwork pattern—a bright rainbow design on Lulie's twirling skirt, celebrating the river's return of her. Atoka's wife had many sides, Rachel thought, like a gem, being repolished now, as she recovered from her mourning. Her brother liked this shy, beautiful side, now thanking him for his claim with her almost secret smile.

The child inside her kept Quillworker alive during those desperate days after her father abandoned her and she had nothing but her wits to live on. She loved the child, Rachel was sure. Did that mean she, a white woman, had loved her Cheyenne husband? Rachel thought so. So, perhaps, she would grow to love her brother, a Choctaw with sky eyes.

Atoka had laughed his astonishment when Rachel told him the story of his wife and her claim to the whittlers' wager at Fort Hall. Was his heart making room for all the women who lived inside Lissa LeMoyne?

Mrs. Lowell smiled at Rachel's brother and his wife. "Won't our babies be good Christmas presents, Mrs. LeMoyne?"

"Lissa. I am Lissa," she said quietly. "Yes," she agreed, taking Rachel's hand. "For us all."

The children and their companionable bachelor artist and tunesmith smiled at the prospect of her words.

Mrs. Lowell leaned close to Rachel's ear, because of the men about. "Your turn is coming," she whispered. "And if not, I'm afraid you'll have to take our Lulie, after you and your man snatching her from Death's jaws twice. It will only be fair we foster her out to you."

Rachel nodded, laughing, though she felt tears welling. Not from where they might come, envy. They came from her awe of the transformation of Celinda Lowell, who was once so frightened of what Rachel's family might be—savages. Now she was speaking, even in jest, of leaving her bright Lulie in their care.

Though that fall night was tranquil, Rachel could not get over a new feeling—that something was wrong, in the very air around them. She began counting the children's heads as they nodded off to sleep under the buffalo robe, then were carried by fathers and big brothers to their places inside wagons or tents. When Amity Hyde asked Jessica to fetch some creek water, Rachel insisted on going too. She brought along Dare's five-shot pistol, which she hadn't touched since he'd taught her to use it as she was recovering in Carondelet. She left it in her apron pocket as she squatted by the creek side, listening above the water's sound. To a screech owl, the scurry along pine-needled ground, a wolf call. The moon was almost full in this month of the falling leaves. Among the whispering pine, the cold and the rustle of their fruit trees' leaves reminded her of the month.

They spoke something else, those leaves, something borne to her by the night air sifting through them. Cries of children, dying. No, the owls' cry, not the children, please God, Rachel prayed to the Creator. Children, ghosts of suffering, answered her prayer. It's done, they seemed to say, in a language Rachel didn't understand, but in good sign talking, too, beautifully sifting through their little fingers. As if her father had taught them, too. Watch, the fingers warned. Watch. For the anger left among the living.

When Rachel returned to camp, Atoka was alone at the campfire, with his rifle across his knees, reading Uncle Bridge's letters. He raised his head, stared into her soul.

"You feel them too," he said quietly. Not a question. A statement.

"Who are they, Atoka?" she whispered, kneeling beside him.

"The Cayuse, I think. This is their place, our uncle's letters say. And the ones who killed the missionaries, they are hiding out from the militia." He closed his eyes. "Nearby, I think."

She touched his arm. "Their children visited me," she whispered. "Warned me of the grief, the anger."

"Yes," he breathed. "I know it. I understand it."

He pulled her close under his arm's protection, as he had on the trail to Oklahoma.

twenty-four

Rachel felt them first, moving through the pine woods in the light of early morning. There were many warriors, mounted on good horses. Their spirits were wounded, perhaps maddened by a terrible grief. There were many more than needed to overwhelm and kill their small party. Was that what the great rushing sound brought? Death? Rachel felt curiously at peace, until she thought of her husband and brother.

Dare and Alfred Lowell were walking beside the lead team of the first wagon. Rachel kilted up her skirts. If they were to be the first to die, she wanted to die with them. She ran, hearing the rush of her heart's blood in her ears as the band of Cayuse emerged from the trees, blocking the train's way at about fifty yards. She heard a soft, musical grunt from Gibson Rice, as he put one hand into the mane of Sky Reaching and the other on William Combs's shoulder.

Everyone, even the birds of this dark forest it seemed, froze as the two peoples looked at each other. As she sped by, Rachel saw Jake Lowell stretch behind him and into his wagon, where Celinda had his rifle ready. His fingers closed around its barrel.

The leader of the painted Cayuse gave a signal.

They began a war cry.

Dare shoved Rachel behind him as his hand went for the revolver in his coat. He had never before carried a ready weapon against his heart, the place where children reached to find the maple sugar candy he'd bought at Fort Laramie. Dare had sensed this moment coming too, then?

He drew in a long, even breath. Alfred began a low, droning sound. Dare's yell was different. It matched the Cayuse war cry. His strange, ancient language filled the air and all of Rachel's senses with his rage for the losses of his life. It was like the cry she remembered pouring forth from him on that deadly night in St. Louis.

Rachel added to it. *"Chahta Hapia Hoke!"* The Choctaw battle cry. Her brother took it up. Close. Close behind them. She was so hoping Atoka and Lissa were farther back and might escape between the shafts of light, between the trees. So that Uncle Bridges's heart would not break beyond recovery.

Suddenly, everything stopped. Their ringing voices. The men's hands, frozen on their weapons, of both steel and wood. Rachel's fingers were numb where they held Dare's arm. The thought scattered across the top of her mind. Would the Cayuse desecrate them, after, his beautiful arms?

The mountain breeze whipped down the trail, sifted through the fruit tree saplings, scattering a shower of their bright red and yellow leaves in the shafts of sunlight. One rested on Hannah Lowell's head, another on her sister Lulie's shoulder. Even she, their party's youngest, most rascal member, did not move as the leaf danced there, then skittered to the ground.

The Cayuse warriors stared intently at the tree wagon, at the seedlings' show of bright autumn color. Stared, as if expecting the trees to wail, too.

But the trees were silent.

Their leader spoke. Gruff. A note of doubt.

Another man countered his words.

A third backed the leader, adding wonder, then something else—conviction.

As their argument continued, the leader looked at the women, the children. Lulie showed him her doll.

He muttered something in the back of his throat. He raised his hand, as some of the other peoples on the trail had done in a kind of universal greeting. But he quickly lowered it, directing retreat. The horsemen disappeared into the shafts of light between the trees.

Rachel's arm ached. She looked down to see that Alfred Lowell had been holding it the same way she was holding Dare's on her other side. The three of them, their company's vanguard, stared at the trail ahead, at the dust, the hoofprints of the vanished horses.

She could smell again. And she smelled pine, and sunlight, and promise.

"They *were* here, weren't they?" Alfred asked, as if he were waking from a dream.

"Aye," Dare answered.

"A-and they were going to attack, weren't they, Miss Rachel?"

"I believe so, yes."

"But they . . ."

"Changed their minds."

"Were you yelling in their language?"

They looked to each other, she and her man, and smiled. "No, in our own," Dare told the boy.

"It was a powerful curse, Miss Rachel!"

"It was our battle cry," Atoka explained, stepping forward. "My sister is a schoolteacher, and holy woman. She does not curse."

"Well, it turned them clean around!" Jake Lowell proclaimed, as if he didn't believe it yet.

Dare shook his head. "Your trees turned them around, I'm thinking. The sacredness of your trees."

Mr. Lowell put his hand on Dare's shoulder. "Our trees," he corrected. "They own us as much as we own them. And we are all family." He turned to Atoka.

"Mr. LeMoyne, I wonder if you could find us another trail through these mountains? Let's try to avoid those fellows, in case they decide to do battle with your sister or the trees. We'd hate to lose a particle measure of either, wouldn't we?"

Rachel found her husband in an even more dense part of the forest than where Atoka had led them to camp for the night. She heard his voice as companion to the jay. A soft companion, hushing the bird's shrill whistle as if he were bedding down their company's little ones with his fairy stories. But his words did not make stories. She knew that by their cadence, because she could not understand their sense.

He came into her view at last. He was on his knees, before a mighty pine. White people often knelt when they prayed. This was a sacred thing he was doing, then? She should not be here, Rachel decided. She knew where he was now, and would not worry. She would know where to find him. But her retreat was not as silent as her coming. Her feet found a dry branch of hemlock that cracked, startling his beautiful voice silent. The jay's softer song went off-key before he flew away.

Dare turned, squinted through the gathering darkness. He reached into his vest for his spectacles, pulled them on.

"Rachel?"

She rushed forward. "Yes, only me," she assured him.

He smiled. "You're a formidable 'only,' Queen of the Choctaw."

"I was your Celt wife this morning, going into battle beside you."

"Aye. And that composed equal parts of pain and pleasure in my heart, love."

He put out his workman's hands in that offering way she loved. She took them and they sat together beneath the sheltering tree. "What did I disturb?" she asked.

"My prayers."

"I thought so. Oh, Dare, I'm heartily sorry."

"Ah, whist, woman. You've come to make them true, maybe."

"True? What do you mean? What prayer was it?"

"A night prayer. A rest benediction." He looked at the carpet of pine needles under their feet. "One I . . . I have not done in a long time."

"How does it go?"

He ran his hand through his hair. "Ach, Rachel, you know I'm useless at the translations."

"I know no such thing."

When he wasn't forthcoming, she crossed her arms before her, and set her mouth in a thin line.

"The three-faced Brigid save me from that look!" he intoned.

"Your saints would love to hear it in English too, I think," Rachel maintained.

"Stubborn woman," he muttered, before his eyes lost themselves in the branches of the white pine, and through them, found the moon. Was he finding the words of his prayer in their common language there, Rachel wondered.

"Bless to me, O God, the moon that is above me," he began in halting English. "And the earth that is beneath me, and my wife and children, and myself, who have care of them. Bless to me the bed-companion of my love. Bless to me the handling of my hands. Bless Thou to me, O God, the fencing of my defense. And bless to me the angeling of my rest."

His eyes came down from the moon and settled softly on her face. "I would lie with you this night, Rachel LeMoyne," he whispered. "If it's your will as well."

She leaned her back against the pine's trunk. "Dare. The time . . ."

"I know the time. And my own foolishness in holding this holy possibility of a child between us . . . holding it away from you. It took a band of Cayuse to bring this about, my teacher, but I acknowledge this foolishness to you, to all the generations of my grandmothers and their ways with the white arts. We are in

Oregon Territory now. And your ripeness hurts my eyes with its beauty. Rachel, will you welcome me inside you during this time of conceiving?"

She could barely find her voice. "Yes."

"Yes?" he whispered, as if he expected another answer.

"Here," she demanded, though in a whisper.

"Here?"

"Now. Without any more of your questions."

Surprise, then delight entered his eyes. Green eyes since they'd entered this forest. She pulled off his spectacles, for there was nothing wrong with his close vision, and she wanted him closer than even his vision would allow.

He kissed her there against the tree, and loosened her bodice in that crafty way he must have perfected when he slept in a roomful of relatives. She liked it. As she liked his tongue mapping a line from her chin down her throat.

Full of her need for this man, she fumbled at his buttons and mounted him, draping them in her shawl. He did not mind it, she could tell by the way he was left without the power of his silver speech, except to call her name in delicious whispers at her ear.

No birds answered until they were done with their delighted duty and in a drowsy spoon. Then the night creatures, led by Dare's prayer-companion jay, trilled without mercy, chasing them from beneath the white pine tree and back to camp.

twenty-five

The horses grazed contentedly, easing Rachel's mind. Because the horses would sense if they were in real danger, or going off course, wouldn't they? The air was so white just beyond where she and Gibson Rice held their reins. Rachel could not see the three men approaching, but their voices carried clearly.

"We're lost, are we not, gentlemen?" William Combs said.

"Can't be lost," Atoka barked out. "Not with you and your precious compass along."

Rachel imagined Dare straightening his stance as he stood between her brother and Mr. Combs. "This does none of us any good," he said quietly. "Let's go back to the train, settle everyone in for the night. The misting is making it a hard thing to see the hand in front of us."

The Englishman's pocket watch, opening. "Teatime. Very civilized suggestion. But it is fog, not your 'misting.'"

"Beg pardon, Master." Dare made a mock bow. It was the first thing Rachel saw of them. The artist cringed, reminded of his world upside down, maybe, where her husband was a leader, and himself dependent on the hospitality of strangers. She frowned at Dare for driving this point home with his mock bow.

"Now look what you've done," her husband groused. "Put me out of grace with the Queen of the Choctaw."

The Englishman laughed. "Ah. You must sit for me in this temper, Miss LeMoyne. I've love to do a life-size portrait of you out of grace with your husband."

"You'll do no such thing," Dare stormed. "Will he, Rachel?" he asked so softly Atoka and Gibson Rice laughed.

Rachel touched her own face as they laughed. Was she as overpowering as that? Did it make her ugly? Dare pulled her close and planted a kiss on her mouth, there in front of their friends and her brother. It made her cheeks flame. She buried her face under his arm. She thought of his promise to love her as God made her, even if he didn't want portraits constantly reminding him of the possibilities of his vow. She decided in his favor. She would refuse. Their Englishman would not capture her likeness frowning in displeasure.

She started suddenly at a sound, and came up from her husband's embrace. She raised her hand to silence the men's mirth. Listened. The horses felt it too, on the wind. Rachel found her brother's eyes.

"One horseman," she whispered.

Atoka nodded. His eyes narrowed. "Easy gait. Searching."

"—For?" Dare asked them quietly.

"You."

The new voice traveled out of the fog, the misting. Deep. Amused. The lone horseman came through the white. Buckskins. Indian. And not Indian. White. And not white. Rachel remembered him, this bright light of their season in St. Louis. She smiled shyly as his beautiful dark eyes found hers.

". . . Or, rather, I'm looking for the ones who carry the dwelling place of the Great Spirit in a wagon. That would be this party you vanguard, yes?"

Dare grinned. "Baptiste. It's good to see you here."

"Needs A Priest," the horseman acknowledged curtly. "Did you need to bring Creator with you on your travels as well?"

Atoka laughed. "Is that what the Cayuse thought?"

"It's what saved you all, horse trainer," the trapper guide told her brother, "that and the two Choctaw bone-pickers and their white Choctaw kinsman, Screams Away His Enemies." He glared at Dare. "You have a great many names, From Ireland."

Baptiste took advantage of their stunned silence to slip off his horse soundlessly and approach Rachel. She caught the subtle scent of mint as he took her hand and kissed its knuckles delicately. "Bride of Very Catholic is keeping well, I trust?"

"Very well."

"Good!" he approved. "But if ever you put him out, I will come steal you, *d'accord?*"

"Oh, *mais non!*" She giggled.

Baptiste stopped Dare's advance with a backhanded whack at his chest, all without taking his for-women eyes from hers. "I will come for you without fail, *ma chère*. If your husband is so foolish as to give chase, I will shoot him and then fetch another priest for you to castigate!"

Now Rachel hid her eyes with her hands in the roar of laughter. She didn't understand why men found so much amusement in teasing her ways, whether bold or shy. But she liked the sound of their laughter.

"Who are these new ones?" she heard Baptiste demand while she was still hiding.

Her brother answered. "Gibson Rice, our fiddler."

"Right pleased to—" Gibson began, holding out a hand that Baptiste ignored.

"Can you play '*V*' *la L'bon Vent*'?" he demanded.

"I can, sir."

"And '*Marie-Madeleine*'?"

"That too."

"*Allons la Belle?*"

"Now, you've got me there."

Baptiste cracked a smile. "I will teach it to you, Tennessee."

"Be obliged, sir. But I'm from Georgia, the Dahlonega hills. Close."

"Pardon, Mr. Rice. And who is your partner, in a fine broadcloth coat?"

"Combs. English Artist," Dare said. "I lost him his job over there, across the Atlantic, so he's become a kinsman."

Will Combs eyes grew wide with wonder as he absently shook Baptiste's hand. Now why hadn't her husband once said that to him, instead of all the sparring? Rachel didn't understand men at all.

"Welcome to the New World, Mr. Combs," Baptiste said, his ever-changing speech now sounding as clipped as the Englishman's. Her father would have admired his ear for language, Rachel decided. "I trust your watercolor pots are holding up in this terrain which wrecks havoc on—"

"Baptiste, what are you doing here?" Atoka interrupted.

The man turned in a graceful arc to her brother. "Helping to steer you around this war that some Cayuse are having with the whites over years of damning them to hell, then wiping half their numbers out with measles."

Rachel felt the Cayuse leader's eyes watching Lulie again. "That was their madness," she said quietly, "the death of the little ones."

"Yes. Most of their children are gone from them."

Atoka spoke to Dare. "I told you there was a reason for the killing. Not an excuse. But a reason."

Baptiste nodded. "You might have become victims of this war. But you had your Spirit-dwelling trees protecting you. Even against the riches offered to kill you and your kin, Rachel LeMoyne."

"Riches?"

"From the one who followed you."

"Dorris. Water Eyes," Rachel breathed.

"Yes. He tapped into the rage of the Cayuse. Fueled it with his whiskey. But he tapped into something else. Floyd Dorris never had the measles. He has it now. He is dying."

Dare stepped forward. "Can you take me to him?"

"I can, but—"

Rachel took her husband's arm. "No. Don't go near him. Don't leave us," she whispered.

"I have already survived the measles. I will not get sick. I must see this to the end." He smiled, touched her brow. "I'll find my way home, Rachel. Camp. Wait here."

Behind him, Baptiste nodded, looking so like her father that Rachel had to release the black sleeve of her husband's coat.

Dare returned with Baptiste as Rachel was lifting the loaf she'd made from the last of their oats from the fire.

"He died listening to the Cayuse stories of Screams Away His Enemies protecting the dwelling place of the Great Spirit," Baptiste explained to the gathering homesteaders.

Rachel stroked her husband's white sleeves. "Where is your coat?" she asked.

Dare shrugged. "He was cold."

Rachel stared at him until he shifted his weight from one foot to the other, like a recalcitrant boy. "And you gave him your coat," she finally whispered, "like the warrior saint you're named for, Dare Gilmartin. That's how you answered all the hate."

"I left him to God, as you instructed, that's all," he insisted.

Baptiste stepped into the circle of families, his calm eyes sensing their worry. "We buried Dorris, then built a good sweat lodge and bathed." His eyes softened as he looked to Rachel. "You need fear him no longer, little one."

Rachel felt the betrayal of her knees. But her sage-scented husband took over their work and lifted her high in his arms. He cooed softly against her hair. "You'll keep me warmer than any coat, Rachel LeMoyne," he told her and she felt as pampered as one of her brother's horses.

Around the night's campfire, Rachel worked diligently at cutting the seams of Mr. Combs coat, now the second one he'd bestowed on her husband in his need. Celinda Lowell had given her some fine scraps of wool to refashion it to fit Dare, for he and the artist could no longer wear the same size. Baptiste sat with them, fitting in among their diverse company so well that Rachel wished his benefactor, the great American pathfinder William Clark, could see what became of the child who had so disappointed him.

"We have gained much along this way," Celinda Lowell declared for herself, without nudging her husband to speak.

"Thanks to your party's very loud war cries, madame," Baptiste maintained.

"And now you, sir, another charm."

"Yes. How have we come upon this good fortune?" Rachel asked.

He swooped over her again, knowing, delighting in the fact that his powerfully handsome presence unnerved her. "I am in the employ of a certain farmer whose wife prepares the best Salmon Englade in the Willamette Valley."

"Willamette Valley?" Rachel could barely speak.

"You know this man, yes? And the Nez Percé woman waits for her children to come home." He finally raised his eyes to the rest of them. "You, I take it, are those children?"

"And more," Dare grinned. "Seventeen in all."

"The tree farmers, I know. Your beautiful wife has a good hand on the paper, Ireland."

Rachel touched her throat. "Baptiste. The letter went through?"

"Went through? Was delivered. By the post rider here before you."

"You? Delivered my letter? Uncle Bridges—"

"Is well, and waiting. And remembers your brother would rather train horses than set a straight course through the wilderness, even with Bridges's instructions leading you. So he hired me to intercept, and bring you home. Paid me well, too." His laughing eyes turned crafty. "But this money was not enough to delay my journey south to the new gold fields of California. It is not money but the great love I bear your wife brings me to guide you

home, and that's the truth of it, Ireland. I am hopelessly senti-
mental when it comes to women!"

"Home?" Rachel could hardly believe the word. "Baptiste,
you are bringing us home?"

His eyes misted with tenderness and this teasing scoundrel of
the wild again reminded Rachel of their father in his prime.
"Mais oui. It is like your home, Little Bird Woman. It is rich and
beautiful and being grabbed up fast. You do well to bring others
willing to work this land. The way is ahead. I will show you."

After a peaceful sleep in the cool and fragrant air, the morning
mist lifted from the valley below as they stood on the bluff. The
sight robbed Rachel of her breath. Below lay a rushing river cutting through the dense green pine.

"The Columbia," Baptiste told them. "I first saw it when I
was wrapped around my mother's back. But I remember, and
still love them both. We will make flatboats there on shore to
carry your wagons. Then the river carries us all to Fort Victoria.
From there we travel to the Willamette River Valley, your kinsman's settlement of Milwaukie."

"By Christmas?" Rachel asked him. "We have two babies
coming at Christmas."

"Oh, long before Christmas, Rachel LeMoyne. By then I'm
on for California. My heart is so wounded by your rejection I will
need to make a great fortune, to support a number of wives to
take your place."

"You have been guiding Mormons too long, maybe," Atoka
said.

"Maybe, Horse Trainer. Maybe I will need as many as
Brigham Young himself to make up for the loss of your formidable sister."

The Willamette Valley

Oregon Territory

1849

epilogue

Willamette Valley, Oregon
Harvest, 1849

"A good twenty more, Mama!" Alfred announced, crashing into the Dutch door while still holding Ora Hyde's hand.

"And a post rider, coming clear from Fort Hall, who saw, said he believed, and has a big bulging package for you and Lissa, Rachel!" Ora continued.

"All coming up the hill from Mr. Combs's place," Alfred finished.

Rachel bolted from under the heavy rug in her lap.

"Rachel, sit down!" Celinda Lowell chastised, before addressing the women and girls. "Let's put the water on. They'll be looking for gallons of cider, no doubt, but they'll have to make do with tea and a few currant cakes."

She glared at her son. "Why is that man so good at pointing all in this direction? As if he and Gibson Rice didn't have a plot of trees of their own that might abate curiosity!"

"He says 'artists need time for quiet contemplation, and we farm folks are better suited to deal with the endless rabble.' "

"Oh, does he, that pompous—" Celinda raised her arm toward the form of a firstborn that now towered over her height. He only grinned.

"Well, don't kill the messengers, Mama," Alfred countered, looking at Rachel. "That's what she's doing, isn't she, teacher?"

Rachel smiled, earning another frown from his mother.

"Why I was so on fire to have you and your sisters all book-learned scholars sometimes escapes me," she said, exasperated, but without any real rancor.

Celinda Lowell was a fraud. She was as fond of the fiddler and the Englishman as they all were. Rachel thought of Mr. Combs's recent portrait of the Lowell family, complete with little Oregon, born on Christmas Eve. It captured them, from delicate Rose, whose eyes were looking less sunken here in Oregon, to capricious Lulie, fun-loving Hannah and Callie, and Jessie, as sociable as her brother Alfred was shy. Celinda's determined beauty, her daughters' new-grown manes of hair, and her husband's pride in them all were shining there, too, like the bright blue eyes of Oregon in his mother's lap. Dare said Christmas Eve was a lucky day and would give the baby the ability to understand the speech of animals.

Oregon was napping on a mat in her aunt's pantry, beside Blue Star, who was also Elizabeth LeMoyne, named for both her grandmothers, and also Atoka's favorite quilled pattern of her mother's making. Atoka had beamed like a star when Rachel had presented him with Lissa's baby, his daughter in all ways but one. When Rachel last checked them, Blue Star had a sleepy arm cast over Oregon's shoulder.

"Why do we feed all these visiting people, ma'am?" Ora Hyde asked, peeved, bringing Rachel back into her present in her aunt's bustling kitchen.

Celinda Lowell stopped her activity as if poor Ora had blasphemed in church. "Because they'll be customers," she explained. "By next season this rich soil will give us plums, pears, and cherries, and apples that will weigh a pound each. And the next will give us new seedlings for the folks who want to start their own orchards."

"We're Johnny Appleseed!" Callie and Hannah proclaimed, making their mother smile.

"Well, our guests will be, as our fruit grows all over Oregon. Which is why we need to show them hospitality this year. Rachel!" she bellowed suddenly. "Mind your stitches."

Celinda Lowell was beginning to remind Rachel of her missionary school teachers. She looked over the rag rug she was trying to finish for the front hall of her uncle's big, welcoming cabin. The room's fine planked wood was suffering under the wear of the overcrowded household and now the swarm of curious far-and-wide neighbors looking for the sign of the appearance of the first cultivated apple grown in Oregon. Rachel loved Uncle Bridges's serene wife, Lark Riding, who had welcomed them all as fully as he did, despite the clamor they'd brought to the quiet homestead. She wanted her gift to be beautiful as well as useful. But the winding stitches had gone mad, looping like a drunken sailor along the bright pattern.

What was wrong with her? She'd been an excellent seamstress since a child at the mission school. She'd made a mess of the quillwork shirt Lissa was guiding her through too. That was for the baby, hers and Dare's, who was coming soon. Perhaps it was the heat turning her into another. A person who lived in her dreams, who was not useful at all. She didn't even realize she was crying until the tears fell off her nose and onto the rug in her lap.

Lissa was there suddenly, taking hold of her hands, then rummaging in her deep pockets for a beautiful, lace-edged handkerchief her brother had bought her to celebrate Blue Star's birth. "Blow," she commanded, "and put that thing away." Rachel rested her head against the lean woman's side, taking refuge from the swirling activity around them. Would she ever be lean again? Would she ever leap on one of her brother's horses? She sniffed.

"Good Lord, will you blow?"

"But it's so pretty."

"So are you. Blow." She smoothed Rachel's hair back from her forehead. "Then tell me why you're crying."

"My fingers are swollen," Rachel confided. "And I can't keep the stitches straight, or my mind on where I am and it's so crowded and hot and there are so many people everywhere!"

Lissa threw back her head and laughed. "Is that all? Let's get out then. Why don't we—"

But her words were stopped by a whimper in the pantry, quickly followed by Lissa's bodice spotting with milk. Annoyed, she pressed her forearm against the flow. But Rachel thought it wondrous, the way her body responded to Blue Star's needs. Would her own breasts work, after the damage done to them? "Lissa, you'll help me, when it's time? I'm so ignorant."

"You? Ignorant? After seeing Celinda and me through our confinements?"

"I mean, with the feeding."

"Feeding? You see how I still spout like a spring! You'll be able to feed triplets!" She looked down at Rachel's breasts and her voice became more quiet. "On one side if need be, I promise," she soothed.

Her baby's fretful sounds turned into a wail. "Oh, Rachel, you need to get outside. And I have to see to my own, and everybody else is busy waiting on strangers because of those damned trees!" Her eyes scanned the roomful of women. "Where's Dare?"

Feet tramped up the wide porch steps as if she'd summoned them. She looked out the small window, smiled. "Crafty Irish haunt." She grinned at Rachel. "Wipe your eyes! Pinch your cheeks!" she advised. "He's so worried about you as it is." She slipped through the doorway to tend her daughter.

Rachel turned, with only time to stuff the handkerchief into her pocket before her husband was before her, scented with his hard work among the trees. He placed his burden of wildflowers gently in her dwindling lap. His spectacles reflected the light from the window.

"Babies cared for?" he asked her softly.

"Lissa's in there."

Blue Star's wailing abruptly stopped.

"Good. And your brother's got tour duty with today's latest

company." He tucked a tiny yellow bird's-foot in the middle of her long braid. "Shall we sneak away from them all, then?"

She gave a quick glance at her unfinished work, then held out her hands. *"Oke."*

Lissa popped her head out of the baby room with two blankets she gave to Dare. "Keep her out until we get rid of the guests," she advised.

When he helped her from the rocker, Rachel felt a strange hardness take over her middle. Dare cocked his head. She blinked twice, and thought his eyes changed color between the blinks. Or were they picking up the hues of the green and blue blankets he'd flung over his shoulder?

"Rachel?" He held her hands tighter.

She wanted to go outside with him so badly, the need much worse than the dissolving pain's claim. "It's very hot, isn't it?"

"Oh, aye." His face eased. "Shall I show you to a cool place, then?"

They walked to the shade of a willow that hung over the bend in the creek the children used as a swimming hole. Why were none of them here, Rachel wondered.

"Bribed them clear," he explained, as if she'd asked. "With promises, as we're all mighty low on cash until these trees bear more fruit."

Rachel smiled. "The cash will come. Sometimes I can't quite believe we're really here, Dare. That it isn't a dream."

"It is a dream for me, wife. A dream of Ireland at its most green and glorious, this place you've driven me to, with people who treat me as one of their own."

"And now we're bearing fruit together, the trees and I," Rachel proclaimed, feeling her serenity returning with the cooler air around the water.

"You're looking mighty ripe to me, miss," he said quietly, like in the days of his courtship, "and never more beautiful."

The hardness came again as he was watching her. And something else. A grinding pain between her legs. No, not now. Not if he loved her so deeply like this, just the way God made her, with their child inside. Suddenly she wanted to stay misshapen forever. It passed, the deep pain, leaving her hot, tired, and afraid. She held out her hand. "Let's swim."

He took it, pleased. At the bank of the creek he helped her out of her full linen apron and day gown and tied high petticoats. While he was undressing she slipped out of even her shift before plunging in, the way she used to as a child in Nanih Waiya. He laughed and followed, as naked as she.

It was better in the cool water. The feelings came, but it was so much easier to ignore them as she let the water make her feel light and graceful and that girl again. A girl with her Irish seal prince swimming rings around her like he was born to the water. Diving, disappearing, tickling the small of her back gently in the water's depths. She had never felt so happy in her life, she realized suddenly. *Remember,* all their dead said at once.

When they surfaced together, Dare swam to her side.

"Rachel."

"Yes?"

"You look different."

"Do I?"

"Cold? Your lips are blue."

"Are they?"

"Enough with your questions. It must be that Irish rascal inside you driving you to such deviltry. Best come ashore now."

"No. Not yet."

And she dove as deep as the pain, and stayed under the water's depths until it was over. When her head came up, he was more desperate. "Listen, *costasach*. The women will be after me if you look worn out from this. Mrs. Lowell will whack me with that big pan of hers, surely. There, now. Come. There's my love, my sweet girl."

He'd coaxed her into the shallows with his blarney, as if she were Raven Mocker or Sassafras, Rachel realized. Where he could stand his ground and use his landed strength to hold her. She turned, determined to dive into the middle again. His grasp remained firm. She splashed him, and fought, until the hardness came again, and robbed her strength.

His hands probed her childspace. "Rachel, what is this? Look at me! Are you laboring?"

"I'm swimming, if you'll get your hands off—oh!" She couldn't speak through this one. She leaned on him, pressing her forehead into his shoulder. It was the strongest, leaving her limp and whimpering and ashamed.

But he lifted her, cradled her there in his strong arms, as the current of sweet clear water flowed around them.

"I'm sorry," she whispered.

He kissed her forehead fervently. "Not sorry, splendid. You're splendid, Queen of the Choctaw."

"Please. Let's stay, Dare. In the water. It's so much better."

"As long as you'd like."

"Am I heavy?"

"Light as a branch of apple blossom."

"The blossoms are gone. The fruit here."

"*Oke,*" he whispered against her wet hair.

She rested her head against his chest, enjoying the feel of his gleaming, protective body supporting hers. Another pain came, lasting forever, tearing her apart. She ground down her cry.

"Lord, is it as soon as that?" he asked. To whom? Not her. He was not even looking at her as he moved into shallow water, where her knees could plant themselves, where she could better do what he kept telling her to do: breathe when the pain came. She lifted her hands from his forearms, saw the welt of her fingers' imprints there. Laughed. "How did you survive your other children's comings?" she asked.

"Oh, it's the easy part's mine," he said like his calm, jovial self. A constant, a comfort in this new place the creekside had become, a place full of dense, overwhelming pain. "Rest now," he advised softly. She leaned against him, closed her eyelids against the steady beat of his heart.

They were shoved open again by the pain. From nowhere, this time. Not like the others, not climbing in intensity, but peaked, then peaking higher. Cold, it was suddenly too cold. Her lips were trembling. Dying. She was dying. Where had Dare gone? Why had he left her alone? She screamed his name.

"Rachel," he called softly. "Open your eyes love, I'm here."

She didn't deserve him. She had to tell him that, now that she was dying. "Dare. On the trail. On the night of the Pawnee. I sang you a love chant. While you were dancing. I witched you Dare, into wanting me. Into becoming my true husband."

"What?"

"And before that. On the Mississippi. Atoka fed you berries, remember? That was the same. To make you desire me. Forgive us, Dare. Please. Before I die—"

"Rachel LeMoyne, what is this nonsense? I have desired you since first I laid eyes on you."

The pain eased, allowing her to see him clearly. "You . . . have?"

"Aye, even when I thought you from *Tír na nóg,* come to take me to heaven. I still think that's what you're about. So no more talk of it, or of dying. That's not our business here, and haven't we both done with that for now? It's life we're about here, if you'll kindly bring it forth." He rested his big, fixer's palm on her knee as his voice softened. "Ach, my wife, *costasach,* my beautiful Rachel, the baby is coming, so close now, I promise."

She was lying on one fine blue blanket, and covered by another, the green one. A curtain of deeper green was all around them. The willow. Under the willow. He helped her to sit up, her back against the trunk. His pants were on now, and his one-piece unbuttoned, and sleeves pushed up over his strong, beautiful arms. His shirt lay between her legs. Waiting.

"For the baby?" she asked.

"Aye, love."

"The women—"

"No time to fetch them, I'm thinking. Will I do?"

"You caught your daughter, Sheea. Your heart."

"Aye, Rachel. I'll do right by you, I promise."

"I know."

The baby was coming, then. That's what this was all about,

not death. Life. He'd proclaimed it in his melodious, calm voice. Only the streaks of tears gave him away. But they gave her patience. She touched his face. "Husband," she whispered. "All will be well."

He nodded, but kept on weeping. "Warm?" he asked.

"Aye. I will fight the next one. Watch. I will not let it have me."

"Good."

But when it came she had no choice about what to do. She felt the small of her back grind into the tree's trunk as she pushed with a might she didn't think she had. It was better, much better than the other ones. She wanted to tell her worried husband that. So when the urge left her, she grabbed his shoulder and took his head between her hands, bringing his mouth to hers. She kissed him deeply, then delighted in his astonishment, then in the return of his own passion. It lasted as the urge came again. She pushed him down to her feet then, as guttural sounds ground up from her throat.

She didn't want her child to come into the world hearing the strange sounds she was making.

"Sing," she gasped out, peering down at Dare, kneeling between her legs.

"What?"

"Sing this baby out."

"Oh, for the love of God, Rachel—"

"Sing!"

So he sang, a broken, sweet song of welcome to the child whose wet, gleaming head eased out, was turning in his hands. Shoulders next. One, then the other.

> Thou art my joy,
> My delight and my care
> Fair and playful
> On my shoulder
> As I go blithely
> About the homestead
> with my treasure
> My magnificent child.

Rachel pushed to the music, to the longing prayer in her husband's voice. She heard the song in their common language, English, though Dare swore for the rest of his life that he was in no mood to sing a translation of the song his wicca woman mother had once sung to him.

The rest, all the rest slipped out, feeling that word in his song: magnificent. Silence. Then a cry. A soft cry, Rachel thought, as she struggled up higher on her elbows. Of a boy, asking his father, his da, to sing another verse.

afterword

Rachel LeMoyne had its genesis in a footnote in the sad history of An Gorta Mor, the Great Hunger of Ireland, 1845–1850.

Among all the donations from various parts of the world there is one that is singularly appreciated. It comes from a small tribe of Native American Indians, the Choctaw tribe from central western United States. These noble-minded people, sometimes called savages by those who wantonly released death and destruction among them, raised money from their meager resources to help the starving in this country. This is indeed the most touching of all the acts of generosity that our condition has inspired among the nations.
——March 13, 1847, diary entry of Gerald Keegan,
    schoolteacher of County Sligo, Ireland,
    and victim of the Famine

Only sixteen years from a Trail of Tears–like banishment from their homeland in Mississippi to the Oklahoma Indian Territory, the Choctaw people had drawn up a constitution, some of which is still part of the Oklahoma state constitution. They ruled themselves by council and had established prosperous trading towns along trails to Texas and California. They were already schooling their children by way of Native American teachers—graduates of their own and missionary schools like Rachel's. They often sold the surplus of corn crops to their neighbors and travelers.

Learning of the plight of kindred spirits half the world away, the Choctaw wanted to help. While the "hungry fiend" was loose in Ireland, *The London Times* gleefully reported that the hand of God had struck the "pagan" Irish and "soon a Celt will be as rare on the banks of the Liffey as a red man on the banks of the Hudson." Meanwhile, the Choctaw people quietly gave, by one account, close to half of Queen Victoria's personal donation toward the relief of her starving subjects. Huge metal tanks for boiling American-sent corn meal still stand on present-day Irish farms.

In May of 1995, a thousand people tramped across western Ireland to mark the anniversary of the Great Irish Famine and warn of the hunger still facing the world today. Among their number was a member of the Choctaw nation. I like to think of him as a spiritual descendant of my fictional Rachel LeMoyne.

Elizabeth LeMoyne's leading of the women in their farewell ceremony to the trees that begins this book is a Choctaw Removal story handed down through the generations.

Chief Cobb's words are his own, spoken to a United States federal agent in charge of emigration.

The United States government removed the Choctaw people to Oklahoma (a Choctaw word meaning "land of the red people") over the three years of 1831–33. The first party experienced the worst snowstorms in the history of the southern Mississippi Valley. Without enough provisions, equipment, or blankets, many died. Hundreds more starved. When the cost was deemed too high by the government, the army was put in charge of the next year's division. This was Rachel's journey. Peter LeMoyne's worry about provisions was well-founded. With both food rations and the number of wagons reduced by the army to economize, even the elderly and infirm had to walk. Army captain William Armstrong said: "Fortunately, they are a people who will walk to the last, or I do not know how we could go on." Many didn't go on, when this second party became infected with cholera, which in my novel took the life of Rachel's sister Sleeps Sound. The third wave of the removal was easier than the first two, but by the time the Choctaw had reached Oklahoma, at least twenty-five hundred of them had died.

Dare's education by way of "Hedge School" was a common one for Irish Catholics in the early part of the nineteenth century. These meetings of scholars were held outdoors, taught by itinerant schoolteachers in the Irish language, though English, Latin, and even Greek were media of their classical and Irish legend and lore instruction. The flavor of these schools is wonderfully portrayed in the plays of Brian Friel, especially *Translations*.

Dare also attended a national school, which the British introduced in 1831. Much like the Presbyterian mission school of Rachel's childhood, at these schools children were punished for speaking their native tongue. English was the language of the classroom, just as it was the language of business, administration, and the dominant culture.

The Mississippi steamboat era was in full swing in Rachel's time. These vessels' accommodations reflected the American economic class structure. In order to travel cheaply, Rachel's disguise was imperative, as there was what Timothy Flint in his 1831 *The History and Geography of the Mississippi Valley* describes as "a separate establishment for the ladies," for deck passengers (largely men who had floated their goods down the Mississippi in flatboats and were returning to their upriver traps), and for servants. Rachel, Dare, and Atoka's lodgings were much rougher than the carpeted, rich woods of staterooms. The only thing egalitarian was the view, which Flint describes this way: "varied and verdant scenery shifts. . . . The trees, green islands, the houses on the shore, everything has an appearance, as by enchantment, of moving past you."

The Irish, like the Choctaw people, shared an intense love of place. For poor farmers like Dare, who had been working to improve the yield of their families' tiny plots of land for centuries, the rich land of Oregon's Willamette Valley, with its climate of mild wet winters, was a potent reminder of home. Most emigrants of the Famine years were not as lucky as he was to reach such a place—they were too poor to afford passage west and became stuck in the slums of eastern cities. Infamous NINA laws (No Irish Need Apply) were in force there and even in midwestern cities like St. Louis. The Irish, like the Indians and slaves, were deemed by many to be "unfit for liberty." Rachel's walk alone after dark proved disastrous because, although wives and daughters were relatively safe in town (but not if their own fathers, brothers, or husbands proved violent men, of course), prostitutes and nonwhite women were often physically attacked.

There are many fine firsthand accounts of the pioneers who took the trail west to Oregon in the 1840s and '50s, and more coming to light as western attics and cellars are emptied. Why did they come? For many reasons: to escape poverty, to practice ambition, to seek adventure, or to alleviate just plain restlessness. Most sought a better life for themselves and their families. They took great risks. Many who had not learned to swim the way Indian children had, still guided their animals over countless crossings of western rivers. Some, like Captain Walker, who couldn't wait to fight Indians, shot themselves or loved ones.

Many were convinced by the nationwide propaganda slogan of the age: Manifest Destiny, that the "great experiment of liberty and self-government" should stretch from the Atlantic to the Pacific's shores. To the Indians who believed themselves to be the custodians of the West, what the doctrine meant was that there was dwindling hope of saving their lands or cultures. Rachel and Atoka's uncle saw the Americans coming, so determined to find himself land as far from them as he could get without being underwater. Ironically, with the word out of the rich farmland of Oregon Territory and the gold discoveries in California, these most western lands proved themselves the first to be settled by our expanding nation.

The Lowell family in *Rachel LeMoyne* is based on Henderson and Elizabeth Luelling and their eight children, who left their fruit farm in Salem, Iowa, with one of their three prairie schooner wagons holding seven hundred baby fruit trees. They produced the first grafted fruit in the Oregon Territory. In the Blue Mountains, they were charged by a group of Cayuse warriors, who halted at the sight of the tree wagon. A missionary later told them that they were left unharmed because the warriors believed the Great Spirit lived among the trees and was therefore protecting the family who carried them along. Elizabeth's ninth child really was named "Oregon," and was born soon after they arrived. Once the family's young trees had borne their first fruit, people visited the Luelling orchard from great distances to treat themselves to the rare sight of a juicy apple.

The story of Atoka finding a wife and Rachel's care for the misused Lissa LeMoyne I based on details from accounts of Indian captures and ransoms during the long struggle for North America. I hope it also honors a story I've been telling children for years—"Strong Wind and Changing Moon." It's a Native American version of Cinderella.

Finally, the wilderness guide Baptiste, who pops up now and then in the story is a historical character who I used fictitiously.

He shares my last name and was a cousin—Jean Baptiste Charbonneau. His mother was the Shoshone woman Sacagawea.

As a baby who his mother named Pomp ("First Born" in Shoshone), Jean Baptiste Charbonneau was, like her, an unpaid member of the Lewis and Clark Corps of Discovery. The expedition of 1804–06 was commissioned by President Thomas Jefferson to chart its way to the Pacific for the infant United States, which had just purchased the Louisiana Territory from Napoleon. I have been to Monticello to request back pay on my relatives' behalf. The docent was not amused.

Sacagawea's son was a Mixed Blood, like Rachel and Atoka. Captain, later Governor Clark called him "my dancing boy" and sponsored his early education by Catholic priests and Baptist missionaries. As a young man he was further educated and traveled to Europe with explorer and naturalist Prince Paul of Wurttemberg. Baptiste Charbonneau spoke English, French, German, and Spanish, as well as a number of Native American languages.

At the time of *Rachel LeMoyne* he was forty-three years old and back in the American West. He'd scouted for wagon trains, rode with frontiersmen Kit Carson and Jim Bridger, and guided the Mormon Battalion (an auxiliary force to strengthen the U.S. Army in the Mexican War) to California in 1846. John C. Frémont was said to have favored Baptiste Charbonneau's mint juleps and boiled buffalo tongue.

While in California, military Governor Colonel R. B. Mason appointed Baptiste Charbonneau the alcalde at San Luis Rey, the largest of California's missions. That made him mayor, justice of the peace, and magistrate. His proudest achievement at this post? He established an Indian school. Contemporaries described him as a man of principles, honor, integrity, and honesty. But he resigned after much white dissatisfaction with him for "treating the Indians too fairly." I think I would have liked my cousin as much as Rachel does.

Selected
Bibliography

Bierhorst, John, ed. *The Sacred Path*. New York: Quill Press, 1984.

Breathnach, Michael. *A Basic History of Ireland*. Dublin, Ireland: Educational Company of Ireland, 1971.

Carmichael, Alexander. *Carmina Gadelica, Hymns & Incantations*. Hudson, N.Y.: Lindisfarne Press, 1994.

Catlin, George. *Letters and Notes on the North American Indians*. Edited by Michael M. Mooney. New York: Gramercy Books, 1975.

Cavendish, Marshall. *A Multicultural Portrait of the Move West*. New York: Petra Press, 1994.

Coleman, Michael C. *Presbyterian Missionary Attitudes Toward American Indians, 1837–1893*. Jackson, Mississippi: University Press of Mississippi, 1985.

Delaney, Mary Murray. *Of Irish Ways*. Minneapolis, Minn.: Dillon Press, 1973.

DeRosier, Arthur H., Jr. *The Removal of the Choctaw Indians*. Knoxville, Tenn.: University of Tennessee Press, 1970.

Durant, John and Alice. *Pictoral History of American Ships, On High Seas and Inland Waterways*. New York: Castle Books, 1953.

Erickson, Paul. *Daily Life in a Covered Wagon*. Washington, D.C.: The Preservation Press, National Trust for Historic Preservation, 1994.

Ewen, William H. *Days of the Steamboats*. Mystic, Conn.: Mystic Seaport Museum, 1988.

Farnham, Thomas J. *An 1839 Wagon Train Journal, Travels in the Great Western Prairies, the Anahuac and Rocky Mountains, and in the Oregon Territory.* New York: Greeley & McElrath, Tribune Buildings, 1843. (Copyright © 1983 by Northwest Interpretive Association.)

Focloir. *English/Irish, Irish/English Dictionary.* Ireland: The Talbot Press, 1976.

Foreman, Grant. *The Five Civilized Tribes.* Tulsa, Okla.: University of Oklahoma Press, 1934.

Foster, Harris. *The Look of the Old West.* New York: Viking Press, 1955.

Gallagher, Thomas. *Paddy's Lament, Ireland 1846–1847, Prelude to Hatred.* Orlando, Fla.: Harcourt Brace Jovanovich, 1982.

Hastings, Lansford W. *The Emigrants' Guide to Oregon and California.* Bedford, Mass.: Applewood Books; originally published in 1845.

Keegan, Gerald. *Famine Diary, Journey to a New World.* Dublin, Ireland: Wolfhound Press, 1991; first published 1895.

Lepthien, Emilie U. *The Choctaw.* Chicago: The Children's Press, 1987.

Milner, Clyde A. II, Carol A. O'Connor, Martha A. Sandweiss, eds. *The Oxford History of the American West.* New York: The Oxford University Press, 1994.

Morgan, Ted. *A Shovel of Stars, The Making of the American West 1800 to the Present.* New York: Simon & Schuster, 1995.

Nardo, Don. *The Irish Potato Famine.* San Diego, Calif.: Lucent Books, 1990.

Niethammer, Carolyn. *Daughters of the Earth, The Lives and Legends of American Indian Women.* New York: Macmillan Publishing Company, 1977.

O'Rourke, Canon John. *The Great Irish Famine.* Dublin, Ireland: Veritas Publications, 1989; first published 1874.

Platt, Rutherford. *A Pocket Guide to Trees.* New York: Washington Square Press, 1960.

Rathbone, Perry T., ed. *Westward the Way, The Character and Development of the Louisiana Territory as Seen by Artists and Writers of the Nineteenth Century.* St. Louis, Mo.: City Art Museum of St. Louis, 1954.

Riley, Glenda. *Women and Indians on the Frontier, 1825–1915.* Albuquerque, New Mexico: University of New Mexico Press, 1984.

Stratton, Joanna L. *Pioneer Women, Voices from the Kansas Frontier.* New York: Simon & Schuster, 1981.

Waldman, Carl. *Atlas of the North American Indian.* New York: Facts on File, 1985.

Wells, Samuel J., and Roseanna Tubby, eds. *After Removal, The Choctaw in Mississippi.* Jackson, Miss.: University Press of Mississippi, 1986.

Wing, Stephen. *Daily Journal 1852–1860.* Edited by Phyllis Gernes. Garden Valley, Calif.: Phyllis Gernes, 1982.

Wood, Forrest G. *The Arrogance of Faith, Christianity and Race in America from the Colonial Era to the Twentieth Century.* New York: Alfred A. Knopf, 1990.

Woodham-Smith, Cecil. *The Great Hunger, Ireland 1845–1849.* New York: Penguin Books, 1991 (first published 1962).